Keeper of the Cuckoo

Alexis McGill

Published in 2009 by YouWriteOn.com

Copyright © Text Alexis McGill

First Edition

The author asserts the moral right under the Copyright, Designs and Patent Act 1988 to be identified as the author of this work.

All rights reserved. No part of this publication may be reproduced, stored in a retrieval system, or transmitted, in any form or by any means without the prior written consent of the author, nor be otherwise circulated in any form of binding or cover other than that in which it is published and without a similar condition being imposed on the subsequent purchaser.

Published by YouWriteOn.com

*To
Annie Reader
My kindred spirit
who never fails to catch me*

Acknowledgements

*Thank you to my dear husband, Jim,
and our four beautiful children
for their endless patience and love*

*To my parents, Jill and Glyn,
for believing*

*To
Kim Thomas,
Sandra Scheffler and Lesley Closs,
heartfelt gratitude for your help and support*

Part I

Iain

As me and my companions were setting off a snare,
'Twas then we spied the gamekeeper, for him we did not care,
For we can wrestle and fight, my boys and jump out anywhere,
Oh, 'tis my delight on a shining night in the season of the year.

The Lincolnshire Poacher - Anon

Prologue

1909

Iain Macdonald met the Hart brothers in Harrowmead Wood, down in the dip among the beeches where the badgers' sett nestled between the roots. The two boys played a game with bows and arrows made of supple branches and pieces of string. A secret innocence echoed through the trees, the happy call of children's voices. The air smelt of warm earth and falling autumn leaves, and the dappled early sunlight threw shadows deeper than they could have dreamed.

Iain towered over them, immense in height, superior in strength. He almost turned away. They weren't doing any harm. But his mood was disturbed; the meeting with his new employer had unsettled him, stirring up the muddied waters of his past.

John Denham's hand had trembled slightly, holding the letter from Bruce Sinclair, the Laird of Glenleven.

"Bruce tells me you are a superb gamekeeper," Mr Denham said. He was embarrassed, unable to hold Iain's gaze. "I am delighted to have you here, you're very welcome and I hope you'll be happy. Bruce is a good friend you know that. I want you to understand you're not here as a favour to him. I've been without a keeper for almost a year. I need someone reliable, hard working, and I believe you are that man. I have a few ideas for the estate. We could discuss them – soon. Things have been let go."

Iain craned his neck in an effort to see the curled writing on the page, so similar to his own. "You have had a difficult time," Denham continued. "All that is behind you now. You can start afresh." If the laird had written about the murder charge, Iain wondered what else he had shared with Denham. As if hearing his thoughts Denham said, "You look like him," and bravely met Iain's eyes, forcing a smile of reassurance. Denham was obviously at pains to convey it was all right; Iain's legitimacy was not an issue here. He shouldn't feel ashamed.

But Iain did feel ashamed. It burned in his chest like fire. The word 'bastard' had been bandied about his entire life, usually when they thought he wasn't listening. He could not wait to escape the oppression of Denham's hot study.

He marched through the woods, distracted, absorbed by their conversation, trying to brush off the past that clung to him, like a tick sucking blood from his veins. He was keeper of Harrowmead now. He could take immediate possession, no leeway, no question – his woods, his estate, his job. He would assert his new found authority. Finnigan would have done it, that's what the keeper did. This was his new life, a new start. Everything had to get better for him now.

When he saw the two boys flitting between the trees he checked himself.

Freddy Hart was a robust thirteen year old, Tom a year younger, two boys engrossed in their game. Iain's first thought was that he would allow them to play. When they turned their bright carefree eyes towards him, liberty mocked him in their fading smiles. There was something in their careless abandon that he resented.

Before he could prevent it, his voice cut the air alerting the boys to this stranger – to his strangeness. "You're trespassing." He held a gun, dully shining metal, a black puppy at his heel, floppy limbed with giant feet.

Freddy wasn't frightened. "No we're not." Absolute certainty was bred into his bones. "We've always come here. We own North Farm. Our land borders these woods. We've come here all our lives."

"We fish in the stream too," Tom said.

"Well that's called poaching and it's against the law."

"Who are you to say what we can do? The squire is our father's friend and we've always come here," Freddy persisted, chin jutting.

Turn away, Iain thought, leave it. He didn't like this boy instinctively. He was cocky, he belonged. Iain hated that more than the lad's cheek. "Well I'm here now, laddie, and I am the law which means what I say goes. I'd better not see your skinny wee arses in this wood again. Do you hear me?"

The boys exchanged a glance. The keeper had eroded their rock solid confidence, casting doubt on their absolute right. Bullied into temporary submission, they scarpered on sturdy legs. At a safe distance they paused to shout obscenities, which bounced off Iain like stones on an iced pond.

The shame burned deeper in Iain's heart. He turned away, stamping up the incline. He had behaved no better than Finnigan, who was long dead and whose tyranny should have died with him. He hated himself. This wasn't how he wanted to be, a loud-mouthed bully, frightening kids who couldn't defend themselves.

He had been moulded by his upbringing, a childhood without parents, and a youth at the hands of Finnigan, the keeper of Glenleven. His desire to change did not match his ability to do so.

Later, in conversation, Mr Denham explained he understood Iain's eagerness. He was, after all, only doing his job, but as a special dispensation Mr Hart's sons, Freddy and Tom, would be allowed to play in the woods if they wished. No harm done, easily rectified.

But harm had been done - a fire had been lit. Untended it burned bright and strong. Iain wished he had walked away, and it would always be too late now.

Chapter One

1914

Iain paused at the threshold of the bar. Although he had decided to veto the pub for at least a week, finding an excuse to return after a mere two days had been easy. He lowered his head to avoid the blackened beam above the door. Faces turned expectantly, conversation severed, a momentary hiccup, their evening interrupted and then recognition, a cough and the hum of voices continued. His Scottish accent alone served to alienate him, his acceptance was borne of necessity.

The atmosphere was thick and smoky, heavy with duplicity, and the smell of hops and tang of spirits. There were a couple of calls of welcome, an age-old obligation to humour the keeper. His apparent popularity was a double-edged sword, endured by many for the various favours he could bestow upon them.

He had not intended buying a drink, but now he was here he could almost feel the liquid gold at the back of his throat. "A pint," he told the barman who obliged with a genial smile.

He took a long draught of the amber beer, it slipped down easier than water. Before he finished swallowing Jasper Potter clapped him hard on his back, the beer spilling down the glass.

"Macdonald, how's it going?"

"Aye, good enough, Jasper."

"Have you come for a quiet drink? I heard you say not two days ago you weren't coming here any more." Jasper laughed, beckoning the barman to refill his empty jar.

Iain meant it at the time. His eye was still tender, the black fading to purple and yellow, from the fight two nights previously. His only consolation, and it wasn't much of one, was Tim Goddard and his mate had come off worse.

He lit a cigarette and offered one to Jasper who shook his head, taking a pipe from his waistcoat pocket. "No, son, got this here, thanks."

"I've got a few ditches need clearing." Iain scanned the room for a likely candidate. He spied Noah Brown, young, strong, biddable, he would do.

"I would oblige," Jasper offered, "but I'm busy this time of year with Mr Yeates." Jasper laboured for the local builder, in season he was a regular beater.

Iain dragged on the cigarette, narrowing his eyes to the smoke curling from his mouth. "Excuse me, Jasper, I think I've found my man."

He was already stepping across the bar room when he noticed, too late, Noah was keeping company with the Hart brothers from North Farm.

He couldn't turn away now so he pulled up a chair placing his glass on the table, carefully, soberly. Freddy and Tom exchanged a glance, the usual one, loaded and secretive. They only wished to indicate he was the unwanted outsider – go home, we belong, you don't. If it affected him, he hid it well behind his cigarette smoke, rubbing his upper lip with the tip of his thumb. Noah glanced nervously between his friends and the keeper.

"I have a wee bit of work, Noah," Iain stated, pausing to inhale the smoke, "if you want it."

Freddy glared at Iain, undisguised contempt in the dark eyes glittering in the lamplight. Iain returned the look adding a sardonic smirk to prove anything Freddy expressed, facially or verbally, meant nothing. Tom, less impertinent, kept his eyes down and his thoughts to himself.

Noah's fair complexion coloured and he laughed, relieved that this was the keeper's interest in him. "Yeah, thanks very much, Mr Macdonald."

"There's a long ditch I need clearing. Be at my place by eight and if you have a like-minded pal bring him too." It went without saying - not the Hart boys.

"I'll be there, Mr Macdonald, thanks very much. Let me get you a drink." Freddy rolled his eyes at Noah's over-zealous civility.

Iain picked up his glass, magnanimous now, authority asserted, proving there was no loyalty amongst friends when it came to money and work. "No bother, Noah, I've got one." He stood up and the bar room shrunk. "Just be there on time."

He sauntered towards the bar and was waylaid by Mr Price of Tump Farm. He pumped Iain's hand as if he were his long lost son. Iain sat down and they engaged in animated conversation, punctuated by great guffaws of amusement from Mr Price.

* * * *

Two pheasants flew across Iain's path chortling loudly, wings flapping wildly to escape. He raised his gun to his shoulder. Two shots rang out clear in the spring air reverberating through the stillness. The sudden commotion silenced, their heavy bodies falling into the undergrowth. Iain whistled for his black dog, Delilah, but she was already crashing through the brush. She retrieved them one at a time, laying them with great care at his feet. He patted her in appreciation and her fringed tail wagged.

The chill day held the promise of spring, the faintest green fuzz visible on the hawthorn, the trees not quite so forward in their display. The gun hung under his arm, dull and metallic, such a natural part of him, an extension of his limb. From the shadow of a beech tree a fat grey-mauve pigeon puffed out its chest and called to its mate who echoed it.

He followed the woodland path, carrying the brace of pheasant, old stock from the previous year. He checked the snares he had set, they had trapped a couple of rabbits and a stoat. The rabbits and birds would go to the house for the table. He whistled to Delilah who had been sidetracked by a mole and was snuffling in the earth.

The sun eased through the clouds. His heavy tread did not disturb the deep brown leaf mould. He came to a clearing where a copious carpet of delicate yellow primroses spread at his feet, weak rays of sun trickling through the thin canopy. A young girl stooped to pick the flowers, a wicker basket close by. She artfully tweaked the fragile stems adding to the posy of pale blooms in one hand. He leaned back on an oak tree. Children from the village rarely ventured here, into the woods proper. They were scared, of the stories, of getting lost, of him. It made him feel like a legend, mythology, whispered about in the schoolyard. It disturbed him but he could not alter it.

Her chestnut hair shone like a polished nut, curling over the long knitted cardigan she wore, held with a clasp at the nape of her neck. In profile she was pale, lips a pout of concentration. Iain was like that sometimes, in his own world, his own thoughts, another life, another home, five hundred miles away.

Delilah, who had lost interest in the mole, crashed through the bramble. The girl raised her head and seeing Iain she leaped upright. Startled, the blood rushed to her face, hand to her chest, dropping most of the primroses. It was comical, reminding him of a giant cat watching a small mouse at play, and he laughed.

"Oh, God help me," she gasped.

"Sorry if I scared you."

She drew herself up to her full five feet, her composure quick to return. "No," she said, "you didn't scare me, not in the least. I don't like all that skulking about."

She wasn't a child, he realised that now. Her eyes were shrewd, older than her years. They had witnessed more than the smooth youthful face betrayed.

"Where are you going?" he asked.

Her eyes narrowed with suspicion, mulling over her answer before speaking. "Up to the house. I work in the kitchen and my sister Joanna's above stairs."

"I've not seen you before, you're new."

"We've been here ten days."

He remembered Cook saying something a week ago. He hadn't been listening, hung over, an aching head taking precedence. "Oh, not local then?" This made a change, everyone here, born and bred, proud of never having travelled further than market. Anyone born in the next county was suspicious, from "o'er yonder".

"We're from Brackenheath on the coast. We were working in Bournemouth. A proper town house, not out in the back of beyond like this." She stopped herself, aware of the gun held with easy familiarity, and the accent, so foreign to southern ears. "You're not local yourself. Do you work here?"

He raised his battered hat, an old gentlemanly custom he had stolen as his own. His black hair fell across his brow. "I do," he said. "The name is Iain Macdonald." He waited for her to reply with her own name, she was staring, mouth gaping so he prompted her. "And you are?"

"Nell Blake."

"Nell?" Little Nell died, he thought immediately. He hated that part of the story. He didn't want her named after someone dead, she was young and alive. Her name did not match what he saw, what he thought he saw. "That's part of a name not what you were christened."

"Everyone calls me Nell it's short for Helena."

"Helena," he rolled the name off his tongue making it sound somehow exotic. It satisfied him. By telling him her full name she had revealed some secret part of herself, a name probably only her mother and father knew and even then never spoke. He peered into her basket at a clutch of small, speckled eggs.

"Peewit eggs," she said, gathering the fallen primroses, "at least I think they are. Cook says the Denhams always have them in season, for breakfast."

"Lapwing eggs," he teased.

She blanched. "Crikey, are you sure?" If he had frightened her previously, she had quickly forgotten her fear and wanted reassurance now.

"Don't worry, lapwings, peewits, same bird with two different names." Like you, he thought. "You've got the right ones."

She shrugged, thin shoulders under the knitted wool. "I didn't like to tell her I'd never seen a peewit – lapwing egg before. She was so busy shouting out her orders and I thought if I didn't get something right soon..." What she thought was left unsaid, blue eyes widened to indicate severe death or something similar.

"Making your life hell is she?"

"A little bit."

"She's all right really."

She blew air through her lips to express her doubt. He was staring at her and she caught him. She pulled a face that turned into a smile, radiant, lighting her up. It was a new experience for him - this young girl, making fun and at ease, not the usual reaction. He knew where he was with the brazen flirt, or the embarrassed, shy maid or the fearful lass, out of her depth, too scared to even meet his eye. He fooled himself that he knew what a woman wanted by the way she looked at him, or didn't. But not this one. It was as if she saw him as he really was, past the tough façade that shielded him.

"I have to go," she said.

"See you after, Helena." He pulled a Woodbine from its packet. He waited until she had walked through the trees, gently swinging her basket, diminutive and child like, confident. She did not look over her shoulder not even once. She was already in her own world, where he had found her, unreachable, beyond him somehow.

* * * *

Noah arrived promptly with Jack Potter, Jasper's eldest. Iain set them to work, clearing a long run of ditch by the house. It was necessary to check their progress at regular intervals. They were stripped to the waist, sweating with exertion. Iain was silent in his inspection and they kept their heads down, increasing their efforts under his scrutiny. Reassured, he went up to the big house, Delilah at his heels. He had bought her in his first week down south from a gypsy at the town market. She was a faithful ally, a steady companion.

Harrowmead was a substantial square Georgian house of mellow stone. It had an awkward Victorian brick extension tacked on to it. A sprawling wisteria, yet to leaf, crawled over the building and had gone some way to marrying the two together. His path took him under the horse chestnut tree at the edge of the gravelled drive, opposite which was the back door leading into the kitchen, wedged open with a rusty iron. He clicked his fingers at Delilah who sank onto her haunches by the three stone steps. He took off his hat and placed his gun inside the porch.

Cook huffed over her pastry. Her solid floury hands grasping the sturdy marble rolling pin with the same grip she would use on a struggling hen's neck. She was a heavy woman, dark hair frizzing under her cap. Formidable. Iain had heard Mrs Denham use the word to describe her. Gentle, fluffy Mrs Denham was intimidated by Cook's manner and her brisk no-nonsense Lancashire vowels. Choosing the weekly menus was a stressful affair under her gimlet eye. Mrs Denham rarely came to the kitchen. It was very much Cook's domain.

Her name was Bertha Jackson, unusually she only answered to Cook; she had worked hard for the title and was most particular about its use.

She smiled at Iain. She had a soft spot for this reserved Scotsman, despite the talk of his fighting, drinking and women, well one woman in particular.

"Tea, Iain?" she asked. He laid the game on the marble slab by the window. The kitchen was fragrant with food. Aromas drifted like ghosts, fried butter, crushed herbs, yeast, echoes of past dishes and overlying them all, something like carbolic soap.

"Aye." He sat down at the vast oak table resting his battered hat on the chair next to him. Iain and Cook were mutually bound, set apart from their contemporaries because they did not belong. They might as well have come from Siberia. If Cook were more acceptable than Iain, it was only because she was a woman and worked inside the big house with its order and gentile routine. Her authority was no greater than his but she had age and experience on her side. Besides which, everyone knew she had come south with her late husband twenty years ago. What did they know of

Iain? Nothing beyond rumours, and there were always rumours in a place as rural and small as this.

Besides this connection, and the obvious appeal of feeding his stomach, he liked her honesty and in a brusque, tight-lipped way, she mothered him. She cared, and for no other reason he could see apart from liking him for who he was.

"Nell," Cook called. She appeared wiping her hands on her apron. He noticed she blushed when she saw him. He was almost disappointed by her reaction. "Make us some tea, love. This is Iain the keeper."

"Aye we already met. I gave her a scare in the woods, eh, Helena?" he teased.

She hid her blushes by filling the kettle. She arranged the cups on the table and said, "You didn't scare me. Not in the least."

Cook laughed at her, seeing amusement glint in his green cat eyes. "Don't take on, Nell. He's teasing you. Iain, behave yourself."

He smiled, watching the ribbons of steam rising from the rose painted china teacups, too dainty for calloused male hands.

"Who blacked your eye?" Cook asked. Nell raised her eyebrows in interest.

"Tim Goddard. Encouraging those tinkers again. I had an inkling it was him, then he dared bring one of them into the pub to flaunt it under my nose." His anger was rising merely at the thought. Regular poachers were bad enough. When travelling folk were added to the melee, increasing his workload, he needed eyes in his backside.

"What does Goddard have to do? What does he gain?" Cook asked.

"He's their eyes and ears. He lets them camp in his field, tries to keep tabs on me so he can tell them when the woods are clear, then he gets half of whatever they take without even dirtying his hands." He gulped the tea too quickly in temper, burning his throat.

"It's a bad business when a man can't turn his back for thieves and poachers." She abandoned her assault on the pastry to drink her tea, subsiding on a chair, a habitual groan out of her mouth before she could prevent it.

"Aye, well he'll think twice before taking me for an idiot again," he said. Nell was listening intently, Cook noticed her hovering and tutted.

"Where's that sister of yours?" he asked.

Nell took a moment to answer, not realising he was addressing her. "Oh," she replied after a pause, "she's a housemaid. She doesn't come to the kitchen much. We had to take what work we could get."

He pushed his chair back, balancing it on two back legs. "Why's that? Two bad girls who had to leave in a hurry?"

She disliked his tone. "What are you implying?" Her voice was sharp. "The man of the house was a no good freebooter. He gambled and lost any money he had made, took his poor wife and children down with him. The staff were dismissed and the house closed down. I didn't work the kitchen then."

Cook gave her a withering look. She blushed again and disappeared into the scullery, banging pots noisily. He felt slightly ashamed. He should have bitten his lip instead of embarrassing her, raising Cook's annoyance.

He said, "Right one you got there."

Cook frowned and blew on her tea. "I thought she was the quiet one, looks as if I got her measure wrong. You should see the sister, a right saucy little madam. Not kin either despite what they call each other. Never seen two girls less alike, in looks anyway, maybe not in manners. Both are sharp as vinegar."

"Airs and graces. Perhaps she's homesick," he said. He knew all about homesickness. He wondered if Cook did too. He had never asked her and probably never would.

"You still see Polly?"

He pressed his lips together and letting his chair fall forward he leaned his chin on the steeple of his two hands. "Do the gossips never cease? Is there no privacy to be found in this damn place?" he spoke softly.

She laughed. "People talk, Iain, you'd do well to remember it. A place as small as this? Folk have nothing else to do except tattle behind their hands, twitching their curtains. Polly's married. You'll bring grief on your head."

"If her husband is stupid enough to leave her night after night for his preaching and prayer meetings, well." He shrugged, mystified. "I'm not taking anything she's not willing to give freely."

Polly Took was a slatternly woman who took liberties with her poor, skinny, self-righteous husband. Took was not a bad man, a religious zealot, naïve and self-absorbed. Quite ironic that he had married a pretty maid with the morality of an alley cat. He was blind to Polly's faults unable to see past her pretty face and voluptuous body. Iain did not care to see further than that either. What did he care for her integrity? It was of no use to him.

The scullery had grown suspiciously quiet and he caught Cook's eye, gesturing with his head towards the scullery door.

"Stop your eavesdropping, Miss," she bellowed, even surprising Iain with her loudness. There was a bang from Nell's direction but she did not reply. No doubt she had caught the general drift of the conversation.

He drained his cup. "Thanks. I've got Noah and Jack working the ditch by the driveway. It should stop flooding every time it rains."

"There are birds to hang in the cellar, Nell, if you don't mind," Cook called, then to Iain, "I suppose they'll need an occasional prod to keep them working hard."

He nodded. Nell pushed past him in the doorway, putting her hands on her hips and glaring at the dead game petulantly. "I've never dealt with dead animals before," she huffed. "I hope I'm not expected to skin and pluck them."

Cook frowned at her. "I can't believe Mrs Denham sometimes. She has no idea about running a house. Employing a housemaid in the kitchen! When the time comes I shall give you a tutorial on skinning and plucking, then you'll be an expert won't you? Meantime they can hang for a bit, so get them out of my kitchen."

Nell opened her mouth to protest. Thinking better of it, she picked up the offending creatures at arm's length and proceeded to take them to the cellar.

Chapter Two

The hedgerows were thick with leaf and the burgeoning blossom of the blackthorn, the grassy banks strewn with bluebells and white campion. Iain, astride the roan gelding Mischief, trotted along the chalky road. In the distance the carrier jolted its long-suffering passengers to market.

On his rare trips to town he took any horse available. Mischief was his favourite. In its youth the gelding might have lived up to his name, now he was quieter, steady under Iain's firm hand.

Iain enjoyed this freedom, something denied in the past. He had always loved the horses, back in Scotland, at Glenleven, creeping to the stables most evenings. The groom would allow him to exercise the stabled horses, lead them out to the meadow, or brush their coats until they gleamed and were ready for the comfort of a blanket. He had often wished to work in the stables instead of with the keeper. The only consolation was working with his gun. Horses apart, he loved his gun. The first time he had held it, cold and heavy, he could barely lift it to his shoulder. Now he felt unbalanced walking without its reassuring weight. It hung on his arm, importance, accountability and power rolled into one, waiting to unleash its explosive latent force.

He caught up with the carrier easily. Henry George raised his hat. Betsy Yeates and Jasper Potter bid him good day. Mr Brown, at the helm, nodded amiably. Iain wished them all a good morning and with the tap of his feet Mischief sped away in front of them. He lifted himself out of the saddle, the wind pleasantly cool in his face, the thud of the hooves leaving a cloud of dust behind him.

Town was bustling and Mischief picked his way down Fisher Street between the people, carts and wagons. The odd car made slow progress between the traffic and a couple of motorbikes, engines sharp and buzzing like angry hornets, zig-zagged impatiently through the crowd. Iain was mystified by the appeal of these motor driven vehicles. The noise was abhorrent, drilling through his head, and the smell was acrid, black fumes that closed his nostrils.

He stabled Mischief at the rear of The Red Lion. His first port of call was the gunsmith to stock up on machine oil, metal shot, cartridge cases; he had a list that he took from his pocket to refer to. Mr Mason, the Smith, scuttled around the shop assembling the order, running up and down his stepladder to reach the inaccessible shelves overhead. While he weighed, wrapped and fussed, Iain inspected the display of rifles and shotguns. He picked one up, stroked the barrel, the shine of the stock smooth under his fingers. He held it up to his shoulder, squinted down its length, the trigger melding to his finger. Regretfully he returned it to the rack.

"Good one, isn't it?" Mr Mason said, completing the order.

"Aye," he said and sighed, "a couple of nice ones here."

Although his interest in the new guns never waned, there was little hope of a sale being made. "Perhaps next season Mr Denham might add one or two to his collection," Mr Mason said. They nodded in unison, without confidence.

He lifted up the weighty bag. "Thanks, see you in a month or so."

Mr Mason touched his brow in deference. "Good day, sir."

The bell above the door jangled as Iain stepped out into the warm air.

He placed an order at the fusty, dust heavy seed merchants, to be delivered to Harrowmead the following day. He made up his own mixture, having little faith in the branded pheasant meals. No self-respecting keeper bought in ready-mixed. There was a secret to it, knowledge passed on from keeper to lad.

At the Corn Exchange business was brisk. He did not linger, wandering through the many market stalls instead. All manner of produce was sold here; eggs, butter, cheese, dressed chickens, fruit and vegetables.

There were ribbons of every colour and bolts of material on display, an ironmonger's stall with nails sold by the pound and gypsies selling posies of flowers and woodland crafts. The sheep and cattle were penned on the far side of the square, the fast-tongued auctioneer selling them one lot at a time. Farmers gathered to bid, sell and gossip. Beyond that, at the Poultry Cross, wooden cages were stacked, crammed with birds clucking indignantly.

At the Red Lion he stopped at the crowded bar for a pint before his journey home. The carrier would not return until late afternoon and the road was quiet. In the distance a lone traveller trekked at speed holding a sizable box. He recognised the primrose picker from some distance and drew his horse alongside her, slowing to a sedate walk.

Nell squinted up at him, the sun blinding. "Can I help you?"

"No. Can I help you, Helena?"

"Well, Mr Macdonald, I didn't see it was you, good day." She did not slow her pace. Lowering her head, the brim of her straw hat shaded her face.

"Do you want a ride?"

She guffawed at the suggestion. "No, thank you. I don't ride."

"You only have to sit, I'll do all the work," he said in encouragement.

She shook her head firmly, picking up speed. "No, thank you, Mr Macdonald."

"My name's Iain."

"As you say."

"I can tie the box to my saddle, it'll save you carrying it." He reined Mischief to a halt and dismounted. He was struck again by how small she was.

He followed her since she kept her pace brisk. "It's not heavy. Look." She stopped, raising an unsteady knee to balance the box while she lifted the lid.

It was a hat adorned with bird plumage, ash blonde feathers with chocolate spots, interspersed with snowy white. She wrinkled up her nose and laughed. "Isn't it hideous," she said with heartfelt passion.

His laugh was false. "It's a barn owl."

"It's Mrs Denham's new hat."

He smiled at that. "I meant the feathers are from an owl. They look better on the bird."

"I told Joanna I would pick it up for her since it's my day off and I was going to town anyway."

"When I was a lad..." he stopped himself. He thought he sounded like his father, except he had no father, not really. She put the lid back on the box and looked at him, waiting, so he had to continue. "When I was a lad I tamed a barn owl."

She was speaking, asking questions he didn't hear. The sun beat down and the heat was making him feel sick. He did not want to tell her about the owl. It was an unhappy story. It would bring misery into the desperate heat of this summer day.

He did not answer any of her questions and she did not hear the crack in his voice when he spoke. "Ride back with me."

She bit her lower lip, toying with the idea. He detected her unspoken fear and her acceptance surprised him. "Oh, all right then. How do I get on? It's a heck of a long way up," she said. He linked his two hands and gingerly she placed her foot in them. He slung her into the saddle with ease and she squealed quietly, like a stunned mouse. Her skirt was unsuitable for riding. Unable to sit astride, and without a side-saddle, she clung to the mane in an effort to maintain her dignity. "Perhaps this isn't a good idea." She was shaking now, almost shivering.

"Hold on a second, you'll be fine." He tied the hatbox to the saddle and jumped effortlessly up behind her. He held the reins loosely in one hand and put the other comfortably on her waist, as though it belonged there. She did not wriggle or protest at his familiarity, it was as if she had not noticed. Mischief broke into a trot and her waist constricted under his hand as she dragged the scream back into her mouth.

"All right?" He lifted his boot under her feet so she could rest them there.

"Yes," a puff of breath, barely a word. He took advantage of her unease to pull her tightly to him, narrow shoulder bones sharp on his chest. They could see over the hedgerows, a different perspective on a familiar world. He felt her slowly relax as she began to anticipate the steady rhythmic lurch of the horse's hooves. She leaned back on him, found her voice again. "Tell me about the owl then."

"I found it." A slow start. He couldn't tell her the half of it, perhaps the beginning. Yes, it started well. "On my fourteenth, birthday under a rowan tree, I found a wee ball of fluff with a murderous beak and great, black eyes." He could not tell her how he had hidden it from Finnigan, installing it in an empty store shed at the back of the keeper's bothy.

"What did you feed it on?"

"I trapped small animals and birds. Trained it to come to my hand when I whistled." Finnigan discovered the owl and laughed, that slow sardonic laugh Iain loathed. Surprisingly he had allowed him to keep it, ignoring its presence, even when it perched boldly on Iain's arm.

"Did you wear a glove? I saw trained hawks once, flying in the New Forest."

"An owl's much the same. I found an old leather gauntlet in one of the sheds. I attached jesses to its feet, you know, like leather thongs and it flew for me." Great circular flights over his head, a ghost of a bird, silent as the grave. He could feel the back draft of its wings on his cheeks. He lifted his face now, in remembrance, in anticipation and he scrunched up his eyes to the burning sun. "If you spin a piece of raw meat on a line it brings the bird down."

"How wonderful," she said, "to take a wild creature in hand like that."

"Aye," his chest tightened with emotion. He could hardly bear to talk about it.

"What happened to it?"

Her question was innocent enough although he could not tell her. "I kept it for six months. Then it flew away."

"Oh, what a shame," she said, and he tightened his grip on her waist, deep in thought.

The shame was that it hadn't flown away at all. He should have freed it. His pride had been the owl's doom no wonder pride was sinful. The memory of that evening was sharp, the sights, sounds and smell. A still autumn evening before the savage rains and winter winds had ripped the leaves away and the trees glowed orange, red and every shade of brown, the damp smell of soil and ripe fungi.

Iain was exercising his owl in the meadow where they raised the game birds. The coops were empty, the pheasants long since taken to the woods. In the dying light the ethereal owl flew on noiseless wings, delightful proficiency. Alighting in a mighty oak, it squinted down at him, glowing, liquid orbs. At that moment it was a wild bird surveying him, as if he were a pleasant diversion from the coming night. He put the bloody lure between gauntleted fingers, his whistle, shrill and piercing. The magnificent bird floated down to his outstretched hand, no longer wild but tamed. He held the owl at arms length, the powerful beak tearing the flesh.

Suddenly an explosion, apparently from nowhere, blasted his ears, ripping away the silence, the fleeting happiness and pride. The whole glade rippled with it. For a moment he didn't breathe, a dreadful seeping numbness deep inside. Feathers, blood and tissue spat wetly in his face. The owl was thrown into the air, a ball of feather and gristle. Particles of shredded bird clung to him, the remainder a shattered heap upon the grass. At first he couldn't move, transfixed, the gauntlet withheld but empty. His fingers still gripped the bird's meal while his heart hammered against his ribcage, the dreadful buzz of silence, like deep water in his ears. Slowly, he turned his head, seeing him - Finnigan - on the edge of the copse, shotgun raised to his shoulder, laughing. Iain was paralysed. Finnigan lowered the gun and chuckling he strutted away.

Now, another noise, Iain's voice, screaming madness and despair. He dropped the gauntlet and ran, mad energy spurring him across the meadow, hitting Finnigan square in the back with the full weight of his body. Finnigan did not fall, he staggered and dropped his gun. He leered, a possessed fiend, heavy jowled, dark with wrath. Iain was momentarily disarmed by the expression. An image of the bloodied bird renewed his determination. With a bellow he charged the keeper like a bull. He was as tall as Finnigan even at fourteen, not the scrap of a boy who had arrived at Glenleven four years previously. He was lean and sinewy, powered by youth. Iain's head engaged with the keeper's paunch. Grunting Finnigan fell back. Abruptly, without pause, he was back on his feet. Inhuman, Iain thought, unfeeling. He grabbed Iain's throat, pinning him with a sickening thump against the large oak where not so long ago the owl had settled. Iain's attempt to ease Finnigan's stranglehold was futile, his feet were out of contact with the ground, scrabbling off the tree bark. He gasped and choked as Finnigan's heavy palm pressed his Adam's apple.

Finnigan's face was very close, bloodshot eyes starting out of his head, spittle spraying from his slack mouth. "If you ever lift your hand to me again, I will kill you. I'm waiting, you bastard. Do I make myself clear?" His mouth puffed whisky fumes into Iain's smarting eyes. He released the boy who dropped to his knees, coughing, gagging, supporting his weight with outstretched arms.

Darkness had settled on the meadow before he was able to sit up and steady his breathing, rubbing his sore neck. Finnigan had departed, no doubt to the tavern or back to his whisky bottle at the keeper's bothy.

Shakily Iain found his feet. His throat hurt and he could hardly swallow. Finnigan was a hulk of man, not so much in height, but breadth and brute strength. Iain had seen him suffocate a deer with one hand.

Iain carried the fragmented bird to the edge of the meadow, dug a hole, carefully placing the remnants in the bottom and covered them with the black, peaty earth, a ritual and duty. He knelt over the grave in the gathering darkness. Desolation smothered him like a shroud, covering his bent head.

He arranged a makeshift bed in the woodshed and slept there for several chilly nights thereafter. When he saw Finnigan the following day it wasn't mentioned. In fact they never spoke of it again.

Nell jolted against him in the saddle, tearing him sharply back to the present. He pushed the vision away, closed his eyes to the autumn, and opened them to the hot summer day. Suddenly her proximity was unbearable. He wanted to be alone. He had to suffer her presence. His sadness was deep and oppressive. He wished he had never chanced upon her with that bloody awful hat.

Their conversation had faltered, he made no attempt to revive it and neither did she. They rode the remainder of their journey in a strange silence.

When they arrived at Harrowmead he helped her down and reunited her with Mrs Denham's unpopular hat.

She smiled, unsure of him. "Thank you, Mr Macdonald."

"You're welcome. I hope it wasn't too uncomfortable for you."

"No, I was only scared at first. It was rather pleasant once I got used to it." She blushed, merely for confessing to her fear and took the hatbox from him.

"By the by," he called after her in an effort to shake away the shadows of that distant autumn and make light of it all, "I hate the hat too."

She giggled, passing Mr Denham who appeared in the stable yard. He was a portly man, a good deal older than his wife. He had married late and the youngest of his four children was only six years old.

Iain handed Mischief over to the care of Paul, the stable lad.

"Sir." He raised his smart hat. He always dressed well for a visit to town.

"Mr Macdonald, how are you?"

"Very well, back from market." He wielded the heavy leather bag. "The pheasant should be quaking."

Mr Denham laughed. "I'll walk with you."

They fell into step, Iain slowing to the older, shorter man's pace. Mr Denham loved these woods. They were always here to escape to. Never the same, with the changes of the weather, the seasons, the light - altering images, the smells, the rustling leaves, quaking branches, the call of the birds and the deep quiet that frightened them away. He had run wild in them as a child, when he had been small and lithe, capable of flight and fancy. Full of savages and dragons, they were as magical now as they had been then. It was easy to let the imagination race away. Shadows of light and dark mottled the leaf mould as they walked.

Iain left his purchases at Keeper's House and they strolled to where the trees opened up into a flat green meadow bordered by the woodland. Large piles of branches and twigs were heaped for the young broods of pheasant to shelter from carrion and hawks. The chicks were susceptible to the wet and the grass here was cut short to protect them.

"Haven't lost too many," Iain said as the little birds scampered under the woodpile.

"Got a brood hen sitting?" Mr Denham asked noticing the nearby hencoop.

"Aye, two clutches of partridge eggs for hatching. Mr Hart saved some from the mower."

"Freddy or Tom?" Mr Denham knew full well he meant Mr Hart Senior. Iain's face tightened, his black brows knitting together.

"Beg your pardon, sir, I meant the older Mr Hart."

Mr Denham refrained from laughing. They discussed pheasant numbers and fox and rabbit movements while patrolling a length of the stream, keeping an eye open for perch and trout.

"No more trouble with poachers of late?" Mr Denham enquired.

Iain shook his head. "There was a net across the river last week. Left it a couple of nights, camped out a bit. Nobody turned up so I took it down, nothing else. Some travellers camping east of the old pond, moved them on sharpish."

Mr Denham chuckled. He had never doubted Iain's ability when he had arrived at Harrowmead aged nineteen and the intervening five years had proved him more than capable. "I bet you did." There was a pause in conversation as they crossed the stream and Iain showed him a new fence, keeping out the sheep. "I've not fished for a long while," he reflected. "I used to fish a lot when I was younger. Sinclair used to come here for weekends and holidays. I don't think I've got the patience any more, time goes too quickly."

Bruce Sinclair, Laird of Glenleven, here with Mr Denham, two young men idling their summer away until they returned to university. Iain lifted his face up to the sun. Being idle was something too unfamiliar for him to contemplate.

Chapter Three

The Cuckoo Fair was held for two days in the last week of May. A welcome annual diversion over-running the village green, and up and down the high street. An excuse, if one were needed, to shirk, sink a few pints, escape the wife and steal a kiss from a maid; wooing and estrangement. There were fair rides, shooting galleries, palm readers, coconut shies and purveyors touting their wares from stalls or baskets.

A May Queen was selected from the troupe of adolescent village girls, dressed for the occasion in white. A float carried her through the village pulled by cart horses adorned in burnished brasses and polished leather. Children skipped around the maypole, spinning patterns with lengths of coloured ribbon. Morris Men danced, bells jingling, waving sticks or white handkerchiefs. Pagan rituals transformed into twee village traditions, all acceptably Christian now the dark undertones from the past had long been lost and forgotten. On the Common there was horse racing, a chance for a flutter, for a man to lose a week's wage and get a fire iron over the head from his wife.

Iain would dutifully allow an hour out of one day to saunter through the stalls stopping for a word here, a joke there. Caps were doffed, heads bobbed in courteous recognition of his importance in their narrow world. He noted those who eyed him with malice, whispered behind their hands, the shifty ones, unable to meet his gaze, scurrying away hoping to avoid detection. He missed very little. His eyes were as sharp as the hawk's that preyed hungrily on his pheasant chicks.

When times were tough these people would come, cap in hand, desperate for casual labour to see them through the hungry weeks until spring. Beating during the shoot, wood cutting, digging ditches, clearing weed from the river, many tasks that kept them fed. With his permission they gleaned much needed wood from the forest floor, their children gathered nuts and sloes to sell. It guaranteed his status as a man of considerable authority. It wasn't his title that mattered, his gun or the land under his control. The basic truth was they needed him more than he would ever need them and that was the gamekeeper's power. Living with their resentment was part of the fabric of his life.

Polly Took was buying cakes from a seller's basket and hoping her prattling neighbours would notice how easily money left her purse. She wasn't the sort to do her own baking, she had a girl come in from the village each morning.

Iain was careful to survey the crowd before approaching her. She was smartly dressed, though he was blind to the fashionable cut, the nipped in waist. He only saw the colour, cream and pale green, because it suited her and the hat, fancy with dyed feathers, he could hardly miss. No doubt the hat was new, she was quick to spend her pious husband's earnings, her hair pinned under it was the colour of honey. She turned around, a warm open smile already fixed before she even knew who it was. In her local husky voice she said, "Mr Macdonald, what an age since I've seen you." Had he not been in her bed only the night before?

Warm with the memory he grinned, keeping a respectable distance between them. He lifted his tweed cap. He looked smart, freshly shaven with a dark green jacket. "Mrs Took." He pushed his hair back with his hand, replacing his cap. "What are you wasting Mr Took's money on today?"

"Fancies, mere fancies." She opened the paper bag in her hand. The miniature biscuit she pushed into his mouth was over sweet and chewy. His tongue warmed the tip of her finger, he darted a glance left and right. No one observed them. She brushed a crumb from his lip and put it to her own mouth raising her eyebrows.

He laughed at her, she was shameless. He was very glad not to be in her poor husband's shoes. If he had not noticed her clothes, he noticed her skin, remembered it salty and damp. "It will do us no favours to be seen," he said quietly. "See you after."

She flashed a smile not in the least thwarted and sashayed away from him, stopping before she was out of sight to share a joke with young Jack Potter, no doubt thinking to rouse Iain. It didn't, he was content. She could never affect him as she might hope, her role in his life was pleasant but functional. He didn't know how to feel any deeper for her.

Old Mr Baker, bent from rheumatism, clutched Iain's arm, his hand crooked and claw-like. "Sir, been wondering about paying you a visit," he wheezed. Iain had to stoop to catch his words. "I need some good reeds to patch the roof. Thought to send my boy down to your reed bed. Would that be all right with you, son?"

"By all means, Mr Baker. Send him early to my place and I'll show him what he may take for nothing." He would reap the benefit of this charity at a later date, Mr Baker understood this and nodded his head happily. Iain knew whom he could rely on to repay a debt in kind. Mr Baker had a strong son with four big lads of his own, it was always advantageous to have free manpower on tap.

"Thank you very much, Mr Macdonald. I'm sure he'll bring one of his boys with him too if that's suitable?"

"Very good. How old are his brood now?"

"Eldest is twenty, getting wed next month to little Nancy Brewer." Mr Baker showed his broken teeth in what could have been a smile.

"Good match," Iain said, glad to be single and unencumbered by a wife, especially Nancy Brewer, a terrier chewing a wasp.

He bade the old man good day eager to move on. He was always short on time. He spotted Nell in the company of his least favourite pair, the Hart brothers. He wanted to walk away but he had already ignored the instinct although he knew how such a confrontation would go. He addressed her, nodding his head in a little bow. "Good morning, Helena." Her name dropped off his tongue like syrup.

Freddy and Tom turned suspicious eyes on him. She echoed Iain's gesture with her head. "Mr Macdonald."

A girl stepped forward to separate herself from the group, to be noticed. And he did notice. The wind caught her thin home sewn summer dress and it clung to her form, outlining an ample bosom and the generous curve of her hip. Her fair hair was smooth, tied with ribbon, and her golden brown eyes appraised him with undisguised interest. She held a rifle from the shooting gallery.

He had been unaware of offering his hand and yet there it was firmly grasped in hers as she shook it like a man. "I'm Joanna." She was one of the brazen flirts and more than that.

Freddy glowered, his dark eyes glinting like polished jet. Iain ignored him. "You're Helena's sister, no doubt, the one who doesn't work in the kitchen."

"That's me and if Nell's silly enough to lower herself to kitchen maid, it's not my fault," she said.

Joanna received a poke in the ribs. "I had no choice," Nell said. "One of us had to, and it wasn't going be her royal highness was it?"

Joanna laughed. "I'm no skivvy."

Three words, and in those three words, she summed everything up for Iain. He didn't like her. "Where did you learn to be so high and mighty?" he asked.

Freddy and Tom were aghast at the insult aimed at their new friend. Joanna wasn't offended - she had thicker skin. "Listen to you," she said. "You look like someone who thinks himself rather grand." It was the right moment to discourage her, but he wanted to cut her down to size. Over confident, he pinned her with his stare, waiting for her inevitable loss of composure. Instead she took it as a challenge and held his gaze, folding her arms defensively across her chest, rifle clutched in one hand.

Nell looked between the two of them and rolled her eyes as if she had seen these flirtations a thousand times and found it tiresome beyond belief. Freddy's anger flashed into his mouth. "Why don't you bugger off, Macdonald."

Iain had failed to flurry Joanna and glared at Freddy. Impudent bastard, he thought. "I should hold your tongue if I were you. They're free to pass the time of day as they please. Entertaining the village idiot can't be all that appealing, even out of pity." He ignored Freddy's balled fists and furious expression and said to Joanna, "You shooting with that or holding it for show?"

She swallowed the hook and aimed at the targets in the shooting gallery, the gun unsteady at her shoulder. She pulled the trigger and hit wide of the mark. Behind her Freddy and Tom jeered at her marksmanship. Iain gave a snort of derision.

She stuck out her hip, placing her hand on it. "Well Mister, why don't you show me how an expert does it?"

He glanced at Nell, she was stroking Delilah, knelt at his feet. She briefly looked up and smiled. Her eyes held the sky. She had removed herself from the banter, the carry on, to her other place, somewhere she retreated, a place he would have liked to follow her to. She was cut from a different cloth, silk, soothing and cool compared to her sister's coarse wool, warm but scratchy.

He shook his head saying to Joanna, "You have attention enough from this sorry pair, so I'll bid you good day and perhaps see you again when you're not in such poor company." Then to Nell, "See you after, Helena." She stood up and one hand remained on Delilah's satiny head. She was preoccupied, he could not even speculate on what she might be thinking as she looked at him.

He had not gone four yards when Joanna pulled on him, both arms linked in his. He kept walking without looking at her. "You're not done with me?" he said.

"Most certainly not," she cried.

Glancing back he saw Freddy encompassing Nell in his arms, an excuse to help her shoot straight at the rifle range. Sneaky sod. "Your sister got the short straw for kitchen maid then?" he said.

She giggled. "Poor Nell. She's such a martyr. We wanted a position in the same house like before and this was the only post we could find. I've taken a step down the ladder too, I'm not that proud. I was a ladies maid in Bournemouth, not a housemaid. It's quite a blow I can tell you. As soon as ladies maid comes vacant I'll apply. Clearing ashes and polishing isn't for me thank you very much."

"Perhaps Helena shall apply and get the position over you." He wanted to pop her self-made bubble of importance.

She snorted at the idea. "Nell? She wouldn't do that, not to me. She loves me, she would always put me first."

"Who do you put first?"

"Stop teasing me, Mr Macdonald," she said laughing, squeezing his arm with her hand. "You're being bad to me on purpose." She was pushing one large breast against his arm and it was all that prevented him from brushing her away, that and now something else, curiosity, what did she want with him? He thought she was looking for more than someone to go walking with. She was one of those young lasses willing to give away something for nothing. Not that he wanted something, not from her.

"You and Helena, sisters eh? You sure you didn't fall off a different tree?" he repeated Cook's opinion.

"You're bright, Mr Macdonald." Her tone implied she was unimpressed by his acuteness. "We're not true sisters, my mother took Nell in when she was two. We lived next door to each other and her mother died after a horse kicked her. My mother had lost three other children and only had me. When we were ten my father died. We were born in the same month, me and Nell, like twins." The most mismatched twins he had ever seen but he held his tongue and she continued. "Mother had a stroke three years after Father died so we went into service at a place in Bournemouth. We were there four years." She was aggrieved, a frown creasing her brow. "You think me careless of Nell, I'm not, she means everything to me."

"I don't think anything."

"It's sisterly banter, we tease each other. Nell is the best of us, I suppose." She looked down hearted, though he knew she was merely playing a card, the repentant sister.

"Where's your mother now?" he asked.

"She lives with my Aunt Cath, two doors down from where we were brought up. She can't talk, can only walk a few steps. She doesn't seem to know herself or anyone else, it's really sad," she said.

"Sorry to hear it."

"And why would a man from Scotland live this far south, then? What are your secrets?"

"I have none." He lied easily. Jasper blocked their path, raising his hat.

"Morning, Mr Macdonald. Miss," to Joanna. "Good information," tapping the side of his nose, "travellers, passing through, camping on one of Hart's fields."

Iain was surprised. "Does Mr Hart know? It's not like him to be so lax."

"He does know, indeed, young Freddy gave them the nod before Mr Hart could say otherwise. They're saying they've come for the fair and probably they have. They're the bad lot that caused a riot in Ringwood. Best check, keep an eye," Jasper said in a low voice.

"Thanks, if you're in the Hound later I'll get you a pint."

Iain absently browsed the shepherds' crooks and walking sticks on the next stall.

Joanna's grip on his arm remained firm and possessive. He pulled out a fine stick with a fancy swirling horn handle. He had no use for such a thing although he admired the work in it. "What would that be for?" she asked as he studied another.

"Beating nosey women who ask too many questions," he said dryly.

She tittered, a high, sharp sound. "You're not telling me your secrets then?"

He pushed the stick back into the bucket. "I told you I have none, came here on a whim."

"I don't believe you're the type of man who would act on a mere whim."

"I might tell you one day." A lie. He would never tell her, never tell anyone, dark as death, locked inside him where it must moulder and decay.

She was disappointed, the wind was chilly and she pulled in closer to his arm.

"I have to be on my way," he said turning towards, obliging her to release him.

Her mouth made a little O of disappointment. "Won't you bet on the horse racing?"

"I'm not a betting sort of man."

"Oh, yes, a Scotsman, short arms, long pockets."

He held out his long arms. "Possibly, but not in this case." His gaze lingered on her cleavage, white as alabaster and pimpled with goose flesh. He let his arms drop and clicked his fingers. Delilah skulked out from under one of the palm reader's caravans.

A white awning had been erected beside it and in flourishing letters it promised all opportunities and expectations would be revealed. "Come and have your fortune read before you go," she said.

"I have no time for soothsayers and if I were you I wouldn't waste your pennies on them. They're all no good pilferers and scoundrels, out to rob you blind and then some."

"It's a lark that's all. Have you no room in your life for a bit of fun?" She threw him a seductive look through her eyelashes, pushing her chest forward, rocking on her feet as a child might, and all to no effect. He was immune, she was a disease he had caught before. He could sneeze without catching influenza.

"Aye, that'll be right. See you Joanna." He whistled to Delilah who appeared, a black shadow, at his heel.

He walked back through Harrowmead woods to check on Jasper's information, stopping to collect his gun on the way. On the cusp of summer, the sycamores were in full leaf, ash trees in bud, the horse chestnut adorned with glorious spikes of cream and pink. Under his large boots the carpet of azure bluebells bent and broke, the air sweet with their cloying scent.

There was a camp, as Jasper had said, right on the boundary of the wood in the fields belonging to North Farm. A herd of brown and white ponies cropped the grass. Two tents had been erected, alongside a motley group of caravans with ornate paintwork and curving roofs. A crowd grouped at the fire, a billy-can hanging over it and several rabbits skewered on a long stick. Four scruffy, dirt encrusted children played tag nearby. A goat bleated from its tether. Slinking between the caravans was a dog of uncertain origin.

The adjacent Harrowmead fences were broken, the wood freshly splintered and pale, obvious gaps, fuel for their fire. Iain's temper mounted, red and furious, as he watched the camp. Mr Hart would hear about this. First he had to vent his fury before he exploded with it, give them a chance to run. He covered the ground quickly and they only saw him when a couple of yards separated them. His gun was loaded, slung under his arm, Delilah at heel.

"You got permission to be here?" he asked.

There were five men crouched by the fire and three women, two toothless hags, one more comely plaiting a string bag. The men, poor specimens as far as he could see, bared brown teeth in uncertain smiles. One spat a wad of tobacco into the fire as if giving his opinion of the intrusion.

"Yeah," a voluntary spokesman stood up, burlier than Iain first surmised. "We got permission from the farmer. What's the problem?"

He peered over his shoulder. "The fence is the problem."

The man craned his neck. "What's the problem with it?"

"It's been broken, vandalised."

"And? What's your point?"

Stay calm, Iain thought. "I presume you broke it."

There was a chorus of protest. "No – not us – we never – no proof – you call the law then – if you think you got a leg to stand on – we never."

"You'll be off this place by tonight, the lot of you, do you hear?" he raised his voice.

"We got permission," the man said stepping forward, determined.

Iain lunged, grasped his shirt at the throat, pulling the man towards him. He spoke slowly as if to an idiot. "I will be speaking to the farmer. If you are not off this land by tonight, I will be back and you will be very, very sorry to see me. Do you understand?"

He struggled to free himself. "You can't threaten us." The other men scrabbled to their feet moving towards Iain uncertainly. He propelled his captive backwards with force into the middle of the group.

"You've not seen the last of me." Iain waved his gun in their faces, no harm in pointing out the obvious, testing their courage. He stormed away towards North Farm across the fields with profanities being hurled at his retreating back.

He was surprised to find Mr Hart in on the day of the fair. Despite Iain's expression, Mr Hart received him with good humour. Iain cut straight to the point. "What's with the campsite in your field?"

"Ah." Mr Hart put his hands up, a gesture of helpless surrender. "I told Freddy this would come back on us. He told them they could stop there when I was at the fair. He's a silly boy. I was angry I can tell you. You know it's not my way, Iain."

He knew Mr Hart to be a judicious man. This reeked of Freddy's ineptitude, more than that it was petty and vindictive. Freddy knew allowing the tinkers in that field was like putting a dog before a juicy steak, they could hardly help themselves. He had hoped they would break Iain's fences and steal his game and filch the wood and cause mayhem and destruction.

"You should have turned them off, Mr Hart," he said, struggling to keep his voice level.

"I know but I didn't want to make Freddy appear foolish. He will run this place one day. I thought he could make the decision for himself and if it turned bad he could deal with the consequences." He shrugged, feeling foolish himself now.

"Oh, he will deal with the consequences I assure you. He will hear me, that's for sure. I know he's your son and I mean no disrespect to you, sir, but do you not think he might have done this to rile me just a bit?"

"I must admit the idea hadn't entered my head, I can't think he's that small-minded. Have they done any damage?"

"Of course, fences have been broken although they've denied it. They are to be gone by tonight, Mr Hart, tonight."

He nodded. "I shall go and speak to them." Mr Hart was a strong wiry man, of no great stature, and no match for the five Iain had recently encountered.

"I'll come with you," Iain said, "and I'll speak to Freddy before nightfall and he can make sure they keep their word."

Chapter Four

Iain watched them from under the cover of the horse chestnut tree. Being invisible was easy for him. He had been taught how to stalk wild deer, alert to every alteration. On the barren Scottish hills the only cover had been the weather-hardened heather, possessive of its delicate frayed pink bellflowers, barely reaching a man's knees.

Freddy and Nell held hands, their fingers entwined, talking, heads down. He had worked fast. What persuasive charms he must have employed to absorb her with such speed, bind her in intimacy and promises. Their familiarity and Nell's easy submission to Freddy's practiced game was loathsome to Iain. Did she think herself special?

A short way behind them Joanna held Tom's arm, much as she had clasped Iain's earlier. She flirted, stroking his arm with her free hand, giggling, looking through her eyelashes, turning from him, blushing. Her only charm was her transparency and predictable moves. With no allure, she laid it all out like a trader at market setting up his stall. She had wrapped her body like a gift, showing enough to entice, but not to give away the surprise, which was really no surprise at all.

The four of them spoke at the back door. Joanna, surprising Iain, was clearly relieved to be home and left Tom like a gooseberry on the doorstep. Nell and Freddy found their leave taking harder. Joanna reappeared at the door to drag Nell in, bored with them. The couple grudgingly released hands. Joanna closed the back door swiftly and the brothers laughed together walking back down the stony drive.

Iain stepped out in front of them, receiving a pleasing instant response.

"What do you want?" Freddy said.

"A word with the simpleton who let travellers camp on their farm," he replied, his height granting dominance the two brothers lacked.

Freddy's expression clouded, pondering his reaction, then he squared up to Iain. "What the hell has it got to do with you?"

He smiled, Freddy was easily riled. "They've broken my fences for firewood, no doubt raided my stock. Your father has given them notice to leave and you have to make sure they do it. Understand?"

Tom, dubious and careful, replied, "Father told them? Did they agree to go?"

"Aye, they did. You have to see them on their way and if you're too chicken to do it, maybe I'll have to help you out." His words baited Freddy as he intended.

Freddy flushed with anger. "I can handle it, so piss off and mind your own business."

"I have told your father you'll get my assistance should you require it."

Freddy stepped forward. Iain put his hands out in a placatory gesture. "I'm not here for a fight." He realised he would fight if Freddy wanted to and now, suddenly, he was ready for a fight.

Tom grabbed Freddy's arm. "Don't," he said steadily. Iain backed off, no he wouldn't fight, no fighting, what was he thinking? He had no argument with the Hart boys.

"I'm glad to see you're not all so hot-headed, Tom. I'll be up to check on things later, you understand. I don't want any more trouble from anyone." The words were building in his head and he couldn't bite them back, though he knew they were heavy with threat. "If you want trouble Freddy Hart, you can have it in double measure with me."

Freddy pushed past him, making enough contact for Iain to have to step backwards to keep his footing. He watched them leave, lighting a Woodbine. As he waited the sky blushed a deep rose pink. He had time to go home for a bite to eat before nightfall.

The woodland marked only half the total land within the boundaries of Harrowmead and Keeper's House was built in the middle of the estate, on the edge of the wood.

The front aspect faced the trees where the oak and beech grew in magnificent companionship. The rear over-looked the rich meadowland, the river running broad and shallow, bouncing over the shale towards the woods. It was nothing fancy, an honest building of brick, its walls crossed with beams, and dark weathered thatch on the roof. The two tall chimneys ensured a good draw on the fires. The rooms at the front were brighter in winter than in summer when the thick tree canopies blotted out the sun.

Inside, the range had long since gone cold. He located the lamp and lit it in deep shadow. Immediately the room took on the welcome of home, his home, he would never take it for granted, this simple necessity. He hung his gun on the beam crossing the kitchen, as thick as a man's body and black.

He did not keep a particularly tidy house. Shelves of books occupied the alcoves and various piles of papers, pamphlets and magazines littered the floor and table. He read anything. As a child he had wanted answers to his questions. There was nobody to ask. He discovered books held answers, not usually the right answers, not to his own questions, but other answers to different questions, ones he hadn't even thought to ask. All books were special to him, except the Bible. He did not own one and its pages held no allure.

As a child, before Glenleven, before the keeper, he had been force fed a daily diet of religious texts. Failure to know the catechism resulted in harsh punishment from the nuns. Whilst the bite of the birch had not permanently scarred his skin, the marks inside him remained unhealed. He had not attended a church or read a religious article since he was ten. Finnigan had not been concerned with holy instruction, and spirituality came in a bottle.

Iain could not be troubled with lighting the range so took bread and cheese from the pantry and washed it down with a bottle of brown ale. He was capable in the kitchen and could manage to throw a rabbit in a pot with a few potatoes, except Cook did it so much better. He relied on her for dinner when he could.

He fed Delilah in the back yard, leaning on the doorjamb. He had a smoke while watching the sun sink, a shimmering golden orb. Bats flitted around the back door, tiny and darting, gobbling up all the biting insects with gusto. He took pleasure in their aerial display as if they obliged him personally. There could be delight in such small things if one chose to see them.

He felt restive, rocking from one foot to the other, fingers drumming, each nerve fibre stretched to breaking. His mind raced, on edge, ready for trouble at North Farm. He was mentally prepared for it, Freddy had aggravated him, provoked a feeling of irrational annoyance. He had a fleeting image of Freddy bleeding profusely, a satisfactory thought. He must steady himself, not act foolishly. There was no need to make enemies, it was stupid to pull rank for the sake of it. He had to live with these people, work with them not against them. He wished he had more ale or, better still, whisky but he knew he had drunk the house drier than the Sahara. He envisaged a visit to the pub later. Ire spent, he could get steadily inebriated.

He set off with ammunition weighing down his pocket, gun loaded under his arm and Delilah alert. It was a moonless twilight.

He could easily see his way, a path he could have walked in his sleep. An owl hooted at some distance and creatures scuffled in the undergrowth. Delilah was not distracted, she knew her master's mood, they had been here before in this pensive state of limbo. The smooth bark of the silver birches shone in the gloom, peeling like onion skins, pale and ghostly. His tread was quiet, he moved with a precision that belied his size.

Their fire burned brightly through the trees, a guiding beacon. They had no intention of leaving tonight. If it surprised Iain to see Freddy and Tom talking with them he barely registered the fact. Their banter was merry, they were not discussing eviction, he knew it by instinct. Freddy watched Iain's approach. "What's the score?" he asked before Freddy could speak.

"They'll go in the morning." Freddy's smile was sure. What can you do now, Keeper? The travelling men laughed, one of them clapped Freddy on the back. Tom stood, a little more reserved, but supporting his brother nonetheless.

"In the morning," the burly man echoed, raising a bottle that, evidently, he had almost emptied.

Iain spoke low, none of them caught his rumbled words. "What's that?" Tom asked nervously from behind Freddy.

Iain lifted his face to the heat of the fire. "They will leave now." His voice was clear and weighty.

"First thing in the morning, Macdonald," Freddy countered.

"I spoke to your father and he agreed they go tonight." He was spoiling for a fight.

The burly man began to laugh, he could not believe the gall of this Scotsman. The others joined in, a flock of mimicking parrots. Iain, looking at the numbers he faced, wondered about going back to the village for extra muscle. The thought of the walk and raising support drained him. It would be so much easier to get on with it. He would only have to deal with a couple, probably, and the rest would turn tail and run. He needed a large stick for a start. He walked back into the wood. After a short search he cut a stout branch for a staff, which was heavy and thick at one end and felt good in his hand. He hid his gun out of sight and returned to the field.

Freddy and Tom were some way off in the distance strolling home, thinking they had won their argument. The field dwellers could not have been more astounded to see Iain had he been the King himself. They had resumed their evening around the fire and were caught completely off guard. Quick to see his advantage, Iain hit the burly man first around the back of the skull, a sharp thwack, wood on bone, he hit the earth heavily. The others scrabbled to their feet and Iain sent the staff, left, right, centre, bracing his body as contact was made, the strain of each hit traversing up his arm, echoing in the muscle. There were three on their backs, legs in the air like stranded beetles. Iain flung the last assailant off with ease, kicking him in the ribs, using only half his strength and taking into account the solidity of leather boot.

Delilah attacked at random, nipping heels, bottoms, ears and any protuberance soft enough to satisfy her sharp bruising teeth. Iain swung at the burly man again, though he was groaning now, his boot forcing a rushing gasp from a prone midriff. He was relieved when the last pair scrambled to their feet and ran.

He had not counted on the women folk who appeared at their caravan doors like a band of banshees. Delilah paused in her assault, astonished. Half a dozen set about Iain brandishing implements as varied as a frying pan and an old Turkish slipper. They weren't playing at it either, the slipper stung in sharp persistent slaps. The flat iron base of the pan cracked against his elbow, knee and the dome of his head, a near miss. Freeing his stick he warded them off with sharp sightless jabs. They squealed and swore as the stick thumped painfully. He hastily found his feet before the young comely girl from that afternoon jumped on his back squealing like a stuck pig. Try as he might he could not reach her with either his hands or stick. She was heavy with a stranglehold at his throat, his face turning purple, eyes tight in their sockets, while her knees dug into his ribs with her feet crossed around his midriff. She was like a possessed witch. The moment stretched slowly. He was unable to think, befuddled by pain and her amazing strength. He threw himself backwards onto the ground, squarely on top of her. The air rushed from her lungs and she lay gasping, a landed fish unable to breathe.

He was spent, he'd had enough. Freddy and Tom were running down the hill towards them. Iain shouted, "Now get out before I get my gun and shoot the whole bastard lot of you." And he was ready to, more than ready, he could imagine them, falling like dominoes, dead on a summer evening, drawing the flies. He took his leave, clicking his fingers at Delilah who relinquished her hold on one of the old hag's ankles to follow him.

He retrieved his gun and reclined on the limb of a tree to wait while his heartbeat slowed the rush of fury through his veins. They admitted defeat and made short work of packing up. Freddy and Tom squatted by the embers of the dying fire in deep discussion. As the last piebald pony left the field Iain showed himself and strolled across the field to join them as if it had been the easiest job in the world.

"Very bloody clever," Freddy said, keeping his eyes averted. "Mr Big Man."

Iain spat into the grey-red eye of the fire. It hissed and spat back. "You will learn, in time, a threat carries no weight unless you intend seeing it through. That is not big or clever, that is a fact - that is how it works. If there is no law, there is chaos. I do not deal in anarchy. You two best keep out of my way for a long time." He made a move to leave.

"Are you threatening me now?" Freddy could not resist a final jab.

He laughed low in the back of his throat. "Are you deaf or stupid?" He hunkered down level with Freddy. "If I make a threat, did I not say I would carry it through?"

"So are you?"

"What do you want me to say? That if you piss me off sometime in the near future I will give you a good hiding?"

"Yeah? Is that what you're saying?"

"Aye, it looks as if it is." He looked past Freddy to his brother. "Why do you hang around with this wee shite? Surely even blood can't be that thick."

Freddy stabbed a finger towards him. "You'd better watch yourself Jock. One of your threats might come back and bite you on the bum."

Iain stopped himself laughing in the boy's face, though he wanted to, if only to prove how ineffectual Freddy was. "What did I say about idle threats? Now you'll have to make your move and I'll be so ready for you when you do." He stood up. He took his time withdrawing a cigarette from his pocket and lighting it. He inhaled deeply and the smoke felt good in his lungs. "Sorry to abandon this pleasant party so soon. I'll leave you with your idle threats." He smiled and sauntered away into the night as if he had nothing in the world to fret about or worry him.

He walked away without hobbling, although a strained muscle in his leg burned and his back ached. A big lump was forming on the back of his head when he prodded with his fingers. He hated that his temper had run out of control. It was sometimes as if it were not his to command, a benevolent force of its own volition.

The pub had lost its appeal, he wanted sympathy. He knew where he could get that and a draught of whisky at the same time.

He peered in at the window to see whether Simon Took was home. Polly had drawn the curtains and he sneaked around the back and searched for a chink. She was alone in her parlour, sewing buttons on a pair of white gloves. He tapped quietly on the window. As she put her head on one side like a bird listening, he tapped again. Presently the back door opened an inch. "Is that you?" she asked the darkness.

"Is he home?"

She giggled. "No, he's back tomorrow. You'd best come in."

He lowered his head to walk through the door. Delilah settled in the hall.

"What happened to you?" She laughed at his dishevelled state.

"Got any whisky?" He went through to the bedroom and lay down on her bed, boots and all on her dainty white lace.

She arrived with a glass and gasped. "Boots, Iain, for pity's sake." She placed the glass on the bedside table, unlaced his boots and tugged them off one at a time, throwing them to the floor.

He raised his head from the cool pillow, swallowed the whisky in one. "Christ I'm all spent." And he was. He had an overwhelming longing to sleep, heavy as lead, mind, body and spirit.

"Let's see what Polly can do," he heard her say and he knew she was taking off her dress and unpeeling stockings from her dimpled white legs. He opened one eye, the better to see her undoing her corset.

Chapter Five

The gunroom was a windowless chamber off the boot room, hung with rifles and shotguns. Iain kept it locked, using one of many keys heavy on his chain. Sometimes he felt as if he were the keeper of a jail rather than of the game, with the weight of keys jangling at his hip, keys for gates, outhouses, store rooms and the main house.

He liked the gunroom. Captured within its walls was the cold smell of metal, the vapour of gun oil, an underlying pepperiness of gunpowder with the subtle aroma of wood. He sat on the only chair, comfortable buttoned leather, worn and scratched. He unrolled the velvet pouch that contained his miniature gunsmith tools. Time here passed unmarked, no day, no night, with only the gentle steady warmth of an oil lamp to light his work. It was off limits to the household, no one came here. It was exclusively his place at the big house, his arsenal.

He had finished repairing the locks on Mr Denham's gun and was clearing away his tools when he noticed someone in the doorway. He had been so engrossed in his task she might have been there for some time.

"Joanna," he said. "Thought you were above visiting us down here."

She grinned, ventured into the room, shutting the door behind her with a dull click. "I heard about you and the tinkers on North Farm."

He remained stern and uninterested. "That was last month, old news, surely."

"Yes, I suppose." She leaned back on the door, pushing out her chest, breathing more heavily than he thought necessary. "You're a hard man to pin down."

"Hope you don't want to pin me down." He enjoyed watching her face change colour as he regarded her. She giggled, girlish and high, walking closer so he had to look up at her. She was taller than he remembered.

"Well, there's a challenge," she said.

He slipped the tools into the velvet pouch, complacency his only defence. "I heard you and Tom were walking out together."

Joanna blew air through her teeth in annoyance. "We're not walking out. We're just walking. Can't a girl go out once in a while without everyone saying she's about to wed?"

"Only what I was told. None of my business."

She made a high squeak of disappointment in her throat. "Ooh, it could be, Iain, if you wanted." He didn't want it to be his business.

He stood up, immediately putting her at a disadvantage by his sheer size. "You're not allowed in here, miss. I should get back to work if I were you."

"You can't talk to me like that. I don't work for you. You're the same as me, another lackey for the Denhams."

He moved towards her and she stepped back towards the door. His eyes were as green as glass. "I'm nobody's lackey, lady."

Her hand groped for the doorknob, it reassured her. He could see the relief on her face. He wanted to laugh. He had intimidated her when moments before she had been acting like a wanton hussy.

"I'd better go," she said. As if to make amends she smiled and added, "Perhaps you'll think about what I said?"

"Which bit? The lackey bit or the walking out bit?"

Amusement lit her face. "You are such a tease."

He lifted his eyebrows. "I don't think so, lady, you're the one doing the taunting not me."

"Tom said you were magnificent," her voice was a dreamy sigh.

"Really?" The comment threw him, flattery getting the upper hand over sound judgment, lending encouragement she didn't need. "Tom Hart said that? I bet Freddy didn't."

She shook her head. "He said a few things. Not that. He's walking out with Nell you know."

Why did she think this might interest him? Why did it? "Really? No I didn't know. Thanks for the information."

"Information?"

"Knowledge is power, miss." He placed two cartridges in his gun, leaving it un-cocked, hanging over his arm. "How did you know I was here?"

"Your dog is flat out in the main hall as if she lives here, she doesn't keep your secrets very well."

"Secrets? I told you before, I don't have any."

She clicked her tongue. "Why haven't you got a girl?"

"Maybe I don't want one."

"A strapping man like you?" a gurgle of laughter, "I can't believe that." He thought it likely Nell had overheard his conversation with Cook about Polly and passed it on.

"Believe what suits you, I have to go." He pulled on his hat and tugged it down over his brow. He blew out the lamp and shooed her out of the door like a hen, locking it securely. His shrill whistle brought Delilah bounding down the backstairs.

"What are you doing?" Nell appeared in the doorway as Delilah barged past. Her glare was accusatory.

"Nothing," Joanna said as innocently as she could manage. He glanced between them.

"You don't ever come down here if you can help it." Then Nell raked Iain with her eyes. "Cook told me to make you tea." She jerked her head, giving him a welcome excuse to leave them. He and Cook listened to the two girls arguing in the corridor, their voices low and hissing.

"Do you cause trouble wherever you go?" Cook asked him.

He smiled broadly. "Nought to do with me. Women and their prattling, that's why I steer clear of the whole lot of them, present company accepted, of course."

Her expression told him she knew differently and she shook her head.

Leaving Cook to eavesdrop, Iain discovered Isaac Smith lurking in the wood waiting for him.

Isaac was a gypsy who lived in an old shepherd's hut on the far side of the Common, unfrequented by most villagers. He was a wily man who looked much older than his true years. He told everyone he was eighty. Wiry, lean and fit, his age was nearer fifty. It didn't matter, the history of his birth was lost in the sands of time, and he could weave whatever stories he wished. Story telling was his forte. He knew how to spin a tale, grip his audience until the last syllable, pick them up, shake them and throw them down. He had skin as brown and weathered as leather, his few teeth were stumps in baby pink gums. Folds of skin hid his eyes, except when widened in an expression of horror, an essential part of a grisly tale, when they could be seen as bright, dark and sharp. He was the oracle on many things, weather, flooding, fire and gossip.

They were good friends. Iain was suspicious of the travelling man, the loafer passing through, the vagabond and wandering Romany. These people could quite easily get up to no good then slip off to the next town with half his game. Isaac was different, a local gypsy, an invaluable source of information. More than that, they liked each other, an intangible, inexplicable connection, obvious from the moment they met. Iain valued their friendship highly. Isaac was welcome at his house and in turn he would visit Isaac, outside by the fire or on colder nights inside the shepherd's hut. His comforts were few, a one room cob hut and a roof patched with all manner of materials that might once have been wholly slate. His bed was a pallet and two wooden boxes for seating. The fireplace, a niche in the wall, had a tendency to smoke. It was all the ease he required.

Isaac's face creased into a smile. "I was wondering if you might have some traps? Not big ones, some right for catching rats. Horrible big rats been bothering me for some nights, can hear them crawling round, afraid they might come chewing at me ear one night."

"Aye, traps aplenty. Come on." In the wood the ditches brimmed shakily with peat-black water from a morning of heavy downpours. Every leaf dripped with an array of glittering drops. The gulleys gurgled with rushing water, the trees showering the earth as if it still rained.

Iain unlocked an aged lichen clothed shed near the house. In the weak light issuing through the open door Isaac could make out innumerable varieties of trap nailed to the walls. There was a jumble of implements on the floor. Iain rooted around in the shadow to locate what Isaac required.

The rooks cawed noisily in the trees, Isaac eyed them with suspicion. A crow fluttered down by his head. He stamped his foot at it, lifting his arms. The bird flew up only to land a few yards away.

"Ruddy crows," he muttered. They were bad luck, belonging to cults and the devil.

Iain looked up from his search. "I'll shoot it in a minute if it's still there. Drive me mad killing all the pheasant chicks. They're bigger now, danger's passing. Crows are worse than the hawks."

Isaac twitched nervously. "Bad sign, bad." The old man peered into the gloom, his eyes adjusting to the dark. "Good Gawd Almighty," he gasped, "what the hell is that?"

Iain followed Isaac's line of vision, up above his head. An enormous trap hung high, safely out of reach, it shone dully with lethal pointed teeth. "Och," he said, "a medieval monstrosity." He came forward, a trap in each hand. "These should do the trick."

Isaac sucked on stumpy teeth. "Very good, perfect for the job, perfect."

Iain locked the door behind him, his watch read well past noon. "Fancy a wee dram, Isaac?"

His face lit up. "Oh, aye, very good, wouldn't say no."

In the kitchen the range burned warm and welcoming. Iain hung up his gun, fetched glasses and a bottle of whisky.

"So?" Isaac ventured, taking his glass, "That medieval thing out in the shed, what's it for? Bears?" Laughter wheezed in his chest.

Iain shook his head, offered Isaac a Woodbine, taking one himself. "I should have got rid of it long since. It was here when I came, it's a mantrap."

Isaac screwed his face up. "It would make a mess of a man."

"Aye, it would. Rest easy they're not allowed now, against the law. Nobody uses them anymore."

Isaac had a glint in his eye. "Think if you could though." The idea blew through his imagination, stirring the dust. "I know a few folk I'd do away with."

Iain shifted uncomfortably in his seat. "Tell me something on the Hart lads."

Isaac swilled the spirit round the glass where it clung thickly. "Nothing you've not heard before. Mr Hart's a good sort of fellow, as you know. His wife don't keep as well as she did, nice woman mind. The boys have lived off the fat of the land. Too much freedom, do as they please. Never had the wolf at the door that lot. Wouldn't know about doing without. Freddy's first born, always got exactly what he wanted. He's a mischief-maker. That's the trouble with youth of today, all larking about."

"Used to getting what he wants, eh?" Iain liked the idea of denying him something.

"And what d'you think he wants most right now?"

"No idea. A good harvest."

Isaac chuckled and said, "You're so literal, son. You only ever got work on your mind?" He chuckled some more, spluttering on raw whisky. "Ah, no that'll be right, you and Polly. Not all work and no play, eh, son?"

"Does everyone know? Should I move on?" Isaac would know the extent of the gossip.

"There's talk, but no one speaks to Skinny-bones Took, anyhow, so wouldn't give it too much thought. If he can't see what's right under his beak, he deserves all he gets," Isaac said.

Iain wasn't sure Took deserved anything he got, or if Polly deserved Took. "So Freddy Hart?" he tried to get Isaac on track.

"You wan't to get at him personally?"

"Aye, that'd be good, wouldn't it?" Iain said.

"Well, the harvest wouldn't upset his apple cart."

"Wouldn't be interested in that anyway, affects the village and the family. I don't have a problem with his family. It's him, he's a cocky little sod. I heard he's courting, is that the way your mind's going?"

Isaac grinned, eyes beady over his glass. "Knew you'd come to it yourself."

Iain sighed and said, "Such small things to be bothering over. Easier to let it lie, can't be troubled with women."

"You taken the carrier to town of late?"

"No." Iain was slightly mortified by the idea, blowing cigarette smoke out of his nose. "I borrow one of Denham's horses if I must go."

"Oh yes, you're good with horses ain't you."

"Needs must. I can ride. I can handle any animal, pretty much."

"You got a gift," Isaac said with awe. "I know. I can see things. I can feel when folks are special and you got a gift with healing. Could turn it on people if you were of the mind."

"You talking your hocus pocus, Isaac? You know I don't hold with all that. I've no gift. And the only thing I can turn on people is a good, stout stick."

Laughter melted with the heat of the spirit that drained from their glasses and which Iain refilled.

"What about the carrier? You keep telling me half a story," Iain said.

"Took me four hours to go three miles last week," he grumbled. "Mr Brown was so drunk he fell off his perch, nobody noticed for a mile. Me and old man Potter had to go back and fetch him. Quicker to walk at the best of times, but mercy, it's never taken me four hours."

After Isaac departed, Iain checked on his young birds. In the distance, at the edge of the woodland two horses pulled the grass-cutter, heads dipping with the effort, eyes blinkered. In the neighbouring field two men and a woman twisted the hay into heaps with pronged forks, a wagon lurched over the uneven ground to collect them, three more labourers hunched in the back. Dust would dry their throats, lace their hair and coat their clothes, muscles would strain and ache in sleep that could never come a moment too soon. When harvest time encroached, the villagers would be recruited and the children kept from school. Even Iain had not been immune in previous years, with Mr Price from The Tump keen to exploit his speed with the scythe for the more awkward corners.

The piles of brushwood he had cut were still favoured by the young birds. Three of old man Baker's grandsons had dug and planted two large squares of corn in the middle of the field, providing shelter and, later, food to prevent the pheasants wandering too far too soon. From a distance the corn resembled water, green waves rippling in the breeze. Patches of yellow buttercups bordered each square, later there would be poppies and cornflowers.

He took aim and shot four loitering crows that Delilah rushed to retrieve. He tied them to the fence by their spindly, scaled legs as a deterrent to their friends and families. Like Isaac, he detested crows. His was not a superstitious hate, it was their thievery and destruction he loathed; nipping out lambs' eyes and robbing nests. Their brazen one-legged hop was like a dance of provocation. The raucous jay was a crow with a fancy coat but to Iain they were more acceptable than their black cousins. Unlike the crow there was a good market for their decorative feathers. Most things had some value; the crow had none.

Not many songbirds ventured into the woods proper. The drumming woodpecker's beak was a common sound and a robin regularly accompanied him on his rounds, hopping from branch to branch chirruping gaily.

Cook had requested pigeon for dinner and although he managed a good bag, it was late afternoon by the time he and Delilah arrived at the house.

"I'd given up on you. Should've brought them yesterday," she said oozing disapproval. "They've got chicken instead."

"Well, that'll please Mrs Denham, I'm sure," he replied, knowing menus were worked out the week before.

"Her opinion is of no importance, it's sloppy not sticking to the menus. Slack. I'll be blaming you if called to account. I need trout for tomorrow, think you can manage that?"

She was all bark and no bite, but he preferred her favour to her scolding. He sat down heavily, pulling out a cigarette.

"Don't smoke in here," she said, her sharp voice resonating as she clutched the pigeons and disappeared out of the door to the cellar, bottom wiggling with annoyance.

Nell stood by the marble slab, mashing potatoes. "What's wrong with her face today?" he asked.

"One of those days. Her chicken terrine didn't set and we both seasoned the soup, so I'm not very popular either."

"No tea for me then." The chair scraped as he got up. Isaac's conversation played back in his mind. He glanced at her. She had returned to mashing, her narrow back twitched with the vigorous action of her arm working the masher. The heavy skein of hair at the nape of her neck was escaping down her shoulders in long curling tendrils. He knew how it would feel resting in his palm, soft and dense. A memory stirred, his mother, tall and dark, a lock of hair twisted around his plump squat finger, tight enough to stop the blood. Nell stopped mashing and put the lid on the pan.

"What is it?" she asked turning round.

The words tumbled from his mouth unchecked. "Ever tickled trout?"

A moment of silence. What made her pause? Freddy's disapproval? Iain's company? The slow smile transformed her face into prettiness. "No," she said.

"If you've finished here," he glanced at his watch to check the time, "and the gorgon's happy to let you go, I could show you."

"Who's the gorgon?" Cook ambled through the door.

"You," he said and smiled. Nell's eyes widened with shock, waiting for Cook's response.

Cook disappointed her, sniffing huffily. "She can go if she's of the mind. Be back in time for serving," was her curt response.

Nell didn't dawdle, hanging her cap and apron by the door, rushing into the yard at Iain's side. She paused then. He could read her expression, she had forgotten about the gun, steel spitting serpent, and Delilah, a Hades hound panting at his feet.

"I don't bite," he said smiling. "I have Delilah to do that for me." And he licked his lips and laughed as if he might prefer eating to biting.

They walked in silence through the deep shade of the trees. She was here and he wasn't quite sure how it had happened or why he had wanted it. She answered his unasked question unprompted, reminding him of the real reason she was here - not because he had wanted it, but because Freddy wouldn't.

"Freddy's calling for me at seven, I forgot. I don't have the time on me." Her cheeks turned pink, her teeth clutched her lower lip.

He smiled invitingly, a wolf in sheep's clothing, indicating his wristwatch. "I have the time, we'll be back long before that," and so she would not question his integrity he added, "Trust me, Helena."

And she did. "Thank you."

He led her to the deepest part of the wood, unlocking gates to where the river pooled in great dark ponds. Below the bloated seed heads of spent irises, golden kingcups glowed on the bank. Delilah swayed from side to side deliberating whether to leap into the river. He raised his hand and she sank into the shadow of a Spanish chestnut, black against black.

He removed his jacket and draped it on a low branch, unbuttoned his shirtsleeves, rolling them to his elbows, indicating for her to do the same.

Pulling off his hat, he lay flat on his stomach, head hanging over the bank and beckoned to her. He stared for a few minutes into the shifting water, past his shimmering image and the water boatmen skating on splayed filament legs. Together they searched the glimmering reflections of the sky through the treetops. She did not flinch when he reached for her. He lowered their joined hands gently into the water, palm outwards. The water was an icy glove, numbing fingers and arms, stopping short of her rolled sleeve.

She could not feel the movement of his fingers on hers. She slowly became aware of the swaying blackness of a large fish by her hand, her fingertips stroking its slippery scales. The moment stretched magically, an infinite vacuum, their heads touching, eyes hypnotised by the undulating fish. She now caressed its belly of her own accord, the fish leaning into her, bewitched. The wood was silent save for the eternal whispering of the water as it jigged along the banks.

Suddenly he reached across her, his other hand darting into the pool. In a shower of sparkling water the fish, no longer black but shimmering pewter, was stranded on the bank, lurching drunkenly on the grass. The spell was broken. He jumped up and dispatched the trout with a quick blow to its silvery head. Her laughter was a tinkling chime, cut short by the thud of speedy death that made her wince.

He leaned back on a young birch, knees raised, arms resting on them. "We'll be lucky to get another that way."

She supported her weight on her hands, facing the river. "That was magical, you cast a spell."

No, he thought, you cast a spell. "It mistakes your fingers for the tickling of the reeds, no trickery, no magic." He knew she was disappointed. He should have spun her a tale, allowed her to believe. He didn't want her to. He didn't believe - why should she?

She hugged her knees to her chest, making her a neat little package. He thought how effortless it would be to hide her. He, who lowered his head for every doorway, stooped for beams and ceilings, made allowance for low growing branches, could never hide so easily. He wondered how it would feel to be so small.

Aware of his scrutiny she turned away from the river to look over her shoulder at him.

"Where do you come from?" she asked.

The question surprised him. "Glenleven, the heart of Scotland. Near Loch Leven."

"Like in the song," she said.

"No, that's Loch Lomond."

"Oh yes, so it is. Is it bonny though?"

"Aye, bonnier than Glasgow."

"Do your parents live there?"

"I haven't got any."

She studied him harder as if he had suddenly become more interesting. "Neither have I," she said almost to herself. "What happened to them?"

"My mother died when I was four. I only found out about that later." He stopped. He didn't know why he was telling her this. He didn't want to tell her anything and yet he felt compelled to continue. "She left me on the steps of a church in Glasgow." Did he really remember? Or had he been told? "I thought she would come back, it was cold and it went dark. A priest asked me into the church." If he narrowed his eyes he could almost see her. No one was that beautiful or perfect, nobody real – she had never been real.

"You must have been scared." She had been lucky, with Joanna's mother to care for her.

"I was." Not of that, but of everything that followed. Living a life he did not want to live, going where the homeless went, the unwanted. Always pain and fear, quite often he was unable to distinguish between the mental and the physical. "We'll have to go back to the house to get a wire to catch some more."

"What happened after the priest took you into the church?" She would not be sidetracked.

He fumbled with his cigarettes and lit one. "He took me to an orphanage, The Sacred Heart in Glasgow."

"You're a Catholic," she said.

"No. I was turned away from all that. I didn't find much godliness there."

"How old were you when you left?"

"Ten. I went to Glenleven as the keeper's lad."

"You should have been at school," she said.

"Aye, probably." He stood up hoping to end her curiosity.

"Did you like it there? At Glenleven?"

He offered his hand to assist her. When he spoke his voice was sharper than he intended, "Come on I have to get the wire." Her question remained unanswered. She grasped his hand firmly. He pulled her up so fast she stumbled against him.

"Don't you use a hook and a line like ordinary folk?" She was making fun.

His tension dissipated. "Not if I can help it." He ground the butt of his cigarette into the earth with his boot.

The path was narrow in parts and Iain walked ahead, the trout impaled by his finger through its gill. He took his time, pointing out nests, a badger sett, a squirrel bounding up the side of a beech tree. He had to keep her here as long as possible.

"Listen," she said pausing on the path, staring up into the trees.

"It's the cuckoo," he said stopping to wait for her.

"I've never heard a cuckoo. I've always lived by the sea."

"No, well you won't find a cuckoo on the beach, they like reed warblers' nests, down by the river." They continued walking.

"Don't they build their own nests?" she asked.

"No, they lay their eggs in other nests for some other bird to bring up."

"I don't know if that's clever or heartless," she said.

"A bit of both probably. Not so heartless though, the wee reed warbler is a good mother to her adopted bairn. She doesn't care that it's not really hers."

They listened to the insistent call of the cuckoo, two repetitive notes; expectation making it audible even in the brief pauses. "It's a pretty sound," she said.

"Later in the year it will fly away again."

"I think the warbler has it right. I think it must be a lonely life for the cuckoo. I suppose they don't know any different do they?"

He laughed at the idea. "You're giving them human emotions, Helena. It's nature. Birds don't get attached to their families, not even warblers. They bring up a new brood each summer."

"How do you know they don't get attached? They might meet up in the autumn for a warbler party, generations of warblers from the same family." What silliness, she smiled.

He laughed harder. "Aye, you never know. Here we are." The cuckoo's call was lost to them as he ushered her inside.

He did not have to entice her, she was eager. He hoped she would tell Freddy she had been inside his house. He hoped Freddy's head would fall off with rage. At least this is what he told himself, perhaps he did not care about Freddy any more. She peered into the parlour, put her head around the scullery door and admired the size of the kitchen, running her hand along the mellow wood of the table, knocking with small knuckles on the giant beam above the range.

He had never had a woman in his home before. Dainty and pale, flitting around like a woodland sprite that had flown through the door by mistake. He was absorbed by her enthusiasm and forgot why they had come to the house. Her presence had altered the place, it would be different now even when she wasn't here.

Finally she alighted in his armchair by the range, a resting white butterfly. A table by his chair held an oil lamp and papers were stacked beside it. She picked up a periodical from the top of the pile. She tucked her legs under her, a position he could never have managed, and peered at the page.

"You like reading," she said, flicking through the magazine.

"Aye, there are long dark evenings to fill."

"That's when you're not beating up the publican's customers," she said trying not to smile.

"Yes, well, so many people don't know their place," he said lightly.

"Like Freddy Hart."

They both laughed. "Aye, like Freddy Hart. You should reconsider who you allow to court you, Helena."

"That's my choice. He can be very attentive."

"You're easy pleased."

"You're very impertinent." They both laughed again. She was enchanting when she laughed. He felt at ease with her, as if he had known her forever and there was nothing he could say that would shock or disappoint her.

One of his half finished carvings lay on the table beside her, a hare in repose. She picked it up, turned it in her hand, smoothing the uneven surface. She turned frank blue eyes on him, which shook him from his thoughts and said, "Have you the wire or whatever it is?"

"No." He was leaning against the doorjamb.

"Are you going to get it?"

He nodded. "Yes, it's in the shed." He had no reason to have asked her into the house at all, she would know that now.

"Did you do this?" She held up the hare and he nodded. "It's very good, you know. I enjoy sketching, but I could never do this."

It meant something coming from her. From anyone else it would have been said to curry favour, a hollow compliment to ingratiate. From Nell it was honest. She thought it good, so she said so. Part of him was glad he had shared his past with her. He thought there was a connection somewhere, to do with the loss of parents probably, there was no other common ground. Somehow that was enough and he found it strangely comforting.

He smiled at her, wondering why he was doing this, bringing her here to incur Freddy's wrath. It made him feel petty. He left her in his chair and went to the shed to search for his wire. When he returned she was standing at the window looking at the trees. She followed him out of the door.

"Did you know your parents?" he asked.

"No. I don't remember Mother. She died when I was two and my father is a name on my birth certificate, I don't even know what became of him. You've not told me about your father."

"Oh, nothing to tell, similar story to your own really." More lies, sometimes it was hard to remember what was real and what wasn't.

"Two little orphans. Well," she said and smiled, looking him up and down, "not so very little."

"You are. How old were you when you forgot to grow?"

She gasped and then giggled, cuffing his arm. "I think you forgot to stop. Did someone stick your feet in the compost heap?" Their laughter echoed through the trees.

They went to a different part of the river, closer to the house. Sitting on the bank she watched him work the wire that was attached to a length of pole. He extended his arm, sliding the hoop across the shale on the river floor. Slowly he approached the idling fish, easing the hoop over its head. With a sharp tug it was on the bank thrashing wildly in a spray of water. A hangman's rope for fish.

He caught five trout and was content. He looked at his watch it was almost seven o'clock. He hoped by the time they returned Freddy would be stamping about, irritated beyond belief.

She saw him check the time. "Should we head back?"

"A bit late, sorry." He could not bring himself to say more, he felt guilty about misleading her. He threaded the fish on a line and led her on a brisk, quiet walk back to the house.

He was not disappointed. Freddy impatiently paced the back door step. His face was as black as a storm cloud when he saw Iain, a scowl to sour milk.

"Where the hell have you been?" he said to neither one nor the other.

Nell was astounded at his outburst and said nothing. Iain answered for her, rather pleased with himself now. "Fishing!" He held up the fat glistening trout, evidence of the truth.

Freddy stabbed a finger in Nell's direction. "Cook's after you for serving."

"Don't speak to me like that," she said. She stomped past him to the back door and held her hand out to Iain for the fish. He was unable to meet her eyes. "Thank you, Iain, for taking me fishing," then sharply at Freddy, "I enjoyed it." She slammed the door behind her.

Freddy marched up to Iain, pushing him in the chest with the pokey ends of his fingers. Iain stepped backwards laughing. "You got a touch of the green eyed demon?" he said.

"I'm warning you, Macdonald, you stay away from Nell." Freddy moved forward and pushed him again. Iain put his hands up, he was not in the mood for a fight. In a different frame of mind he might have been tempted to give the boy a slap, but his fishing trip had left him feeling serene. He turned away. He wouldn't allow Freddy to spoil it, easily brushing away the fact that the whole thing had been about Freddy's anger. "I'm warning you," Freddy repeated.

"More empty threats, what have I told you?" Iain threw over his shoulder. He almost expected Freddy to land on his back as he walked, but he did not. Delilah slunk by his side, ears flat to her skull. At the horse chestnut tree he stopped for a smoke. He watched Freddy return to the back door and beat on it with the flat of his hand. Cook sent him away with a sharp rebuke. Iain retreated into the darker shadow and Freddy passed without noticing him, kicking at the gravel in fury.

Chapter Six

Retribution, Iain knew it would come. He hadn't fooled himself into thinking that was the end of it. Freddy would keep the vendetta going for the rest of their lives. Iain would get jaded with such sport long before Freddy did. He was the mindless sort; repetition did not inevitably lead to boredom. So Iain waited, without even realising he was. Knowing, without knowing, that Freddy would have his petty revenge at some point.

He followed the well-worn rigmarole of his days. He checked the pheasants, pausing to watch a hawk being mobbed by four swallows. With one sideways swerve the hawk could have plucked one straight out of the sky with its mighty claws. Instead, it idly threatened them, tipping sideways and swiping ineffectually. The swallows ignored these feeble efforts, dipping and diving, backwards and forwards, baiting the mighty bird in a fascinating display.

A movement in the trees caught his eye. It was young Miles Denham, the squire's eldest boy, with two of his school friends. He had recently turned seventeen. He and his younger brother were home for the summer and already the boys were at a loose end. Miles had thought to impress his friends by seeking out some sport with the gamekeeper.

"Good morning, Mr Macdonald." Miles offered his soft white hand.

Iain shook it. "Morning, Mr Miles." He nodded at Miles's companions, a pair of gawky adolescents. Miles was a stout boy, perhaps a bit too stout this year, his hair the colour of ripe corn, a rosy blush highlighting his plump cheeks. His friends were sorry looking specimens, pale, thin and gangly, as if a lack of sunlight had stunted them.

"Wondered if you were very busy this morning?" Miles said in plummy tones. His friend's voices veered between squeaky croaks and lost in the cellar.

Iain smiled pleasantly. He could have done without this trio. He had fences to mend. He could not abide broken fences. "What did you have in mind?"

"Perhaps you could suggest something?"

Iain suppressed the temptation to roll his eyes. He was yet to meet an aristocrat who could make a decision, although their ilk ran the country with apparent success. It was amazing to him that they got out of bed in the morning, managed to choose between eggs or bacon for breakfast, or what colour shoes to wear and yet somehow they did, if only to ruin the keeper's day. He thought for a second. "How about rabbiting? With ferrets and nets." It was not really a question, he didn't have a day to waste by offering them options.

Miles and pals nodded, guffawing as only private school boys can, muttering words Iain did not bother to catch. He was already striding away towards his house to collect the necessary. The boys were eager sheep, straining to please, to say the right thing to him.

Iain kept four ferrets hutched in a lean-to at the back of the woodshed. They were smelly beasts, but very friendly. He was rather fond of them; they had endearing little personalities all their own. Some keepers kept a terrier for rabbiting. He preferred ferrets because they could manage the smallest holes without getting stuck. He had names for them. He kept that quiet, it was soft, akin to naming hens in a hen house.

Equipped with nets and ferrets he took them to a likely spot. Even with instruction he felt unable to leave them, they were hungry for reassurance and attention, like three small children. The smallest ferret gave one lad a nasty bite on the ball of his thumb. Iain hid his smirk at the extreme fuss this induced and sat with the aggressor. She was perfectly affable, squirming on his lap while he tickled her whiskers and lay on her back to ensure her long cream tummy got full consideration.

It was a beautiful sunny day and they did not get bored as quickly as Iain had anticipated. By four o'clock their bag was heavy and with much self-congratulation and backslapping they decided they had had enough. Pressing a coin into Iain's hand, a paltry sum compared to the effort he had put in, Miles suggested perhaps a bit of fishing tomorrow would be nice. Iain wondered if this were something they could accomplish on their own without him holding their hands. He tipped his hat and smiled and they would never know what he thought.

He went to the pub at opening time and was greeted by the usual faces. He sat at the bar with Noah Brown and his father, the previously drunken carrier driver.

"Good day?" the older Brown asked.

Iain sank half his pint before he answered, wiping his mouth with the back of his hand. "Ferreting for rabbits," he said.

Brown sighed. "All very well if you got nothing else to do."

He shook his head. "Aye, I wouldn't argue with that. Have you been falling off the wagon lately, Bert?"

Brown frowned in an effort to recall the event. "Me? No, not me," Brown said in puzzlement, rubbing his head. "Did I?" Iain snorted into his beer. "Who told you that?"

Iain shrugged in an effort to contain himself. "Can't recall now, pal, don't worry, if you can't remember, it didn't happen, eh?"

He was well into his fifth pint when the Hart brothers arrived with their friend Alan Stock. They huddled in the corner, heads drawn together, secrets and mischief mixing with their beer. Alan was sent to order the drinks. Iain wished him a good evening, made a point of it, giving Alan no option other than to return the greeting. The three of them were still engrossed when he left.

He would have visited Polly, except recently he had steered clear of her. He had no particular desire tonight, not for her anyway, it had never been about her. He had called time on Polly without even reaching a conscious decision to do so. He couldn't finish with her, there was nothing to break off, no promises or affection. It was best to end things before they went sour rather than after, tidier, no ill feelings that way. And he knew women often harboured ill feelings for no reason at all that he could see.

* * * *

Iain strolled home with an easier mind than he had a right to, while the Hart boys and Alan were hatching a plan. It was something Freddy had been dwelling on since Iain had taken Nell fishing. With hay making over they had a short spell of respite before harvesting began. This gave them the surplus time and energy to take action. Freddy was sick of waiting and had persuaded his brother and friend to help him teach Iain a lesson. It all seemed very effortless in the muggy warmth of the public house, with several pints of bitter in their stomachs and another round of drinks on the table.

At midnight they stumbled unsteadily up the road, arms draped over stooped shoulders singing Auld Lang Syne, in memory of the soon-to-be late Mr Macdonald. If killing Iain was not really an option, maiming him for life was very appealing.

Haphazard disguises barely covered their faces as they stumbled into the wood. Their aim to creep stealthily was thwarted by the uneven ground and the brambles snagging at their clothing. Tom disappeared into a ditch, climbing out sodden and muddy. Under the cover of the trees, with the screech of a night owl and the scuffling of they knew not what in the brush, they did not feel quite so self-assured.

"What the hell is the noise?" Tom whispered. They stopped stock still, listening. There was a mad scrabbling to their left then a deep silence before it started again. The owl hooted. They bolted scared witless, dodging trees and bushes. Freddy grabbed out mid-flight catching the end of Tom's jacket, a handful of Alan's sleeve.

"Right," he hissed, "get a bleeding hold of yourselves. We're in a flaming wood, it's full of animals. Now if we're doing this, we need to do it right." There were brave nods of agreement all round.

Their movements became furtive. They were big game hunters, soldiers trailing a savage to his death. And what if the savage should spot them? What if the big game had sharp eyes and a big gun? Tom began to giggle, the image of the three of them, a cartoon strip from a comic, blundering like dodos through the woods. The laughter bubbled from the depths of him and the more he tried to stop himself the worse it became. Like an infection Freddy caught it too, the laughter snorting out of his nose. Alan stood between them catching his breath, unable to see the cause for this unseemly hilarity.

"Would you two pack it in," he cried. "I might as well have posted an announcement in the newspaper." A fresh attack of laughter burst from the brothers. Propped against a tree, they were rendered helpless.

"That's it." Alan saw his chance to escape from what now seemed a ludicrous plan. "I'm going home. Give me a shout when you're feeling a bit steadier." He turned in his tracks. Freddy and Tom fell on him from behind, one on each shoulder, almost pushing him off his feet.

"Oh no you don't," Freddy said. "Brothers in arms, right? We're not letting some Jock get the better of us are we?"

Their hysteria was barely controlled, brimming very near the surface, frothing with the beer. They forged ahead.

* * * *

Iain was sitting by the range thinking of bed. The idea of wasting the day fishing in the company of three dunder-skulls was becoming less and less appealing. He needed more wood for the range if he didn't wanted it to burn out by morning. Delilah stretched, yawning with him. He wandered outside to the woodshed, Delilah rooted in the bushes doing her business.

He had six logs stacked in one arm when he heard something. Delilah appeared at his side, one ear pricked, the other flopping over, as was its custom. She had heard it too. He put a hand on her head to prevent her barking. An axe leaned against the woodshed wall. He reached for it, held it firm, palming the axe-head, his intention was to hurt not take life.

With the silent tread of the stalker he circled the trees to the front of the house. There it was again, the sound of feet, sticks breaking and, straining his ears, their breathing, heavy and drunken. For all the noise his midnight visitors made they might as well have knocked on his door and introduced themselves.

There were three of them and as they crept towards the front door Iain crashed through the undergrowth behind them. The axe handle hit Freddy in the middle of his chest, air rushing from his lungs. He landed in the soft leaf mould and Delilah attached herself to his leg. Left, right, left, Iain swung at the remaining pair. He caught one on the side of the jaw, a painful crack of bone, while the third ran, Delilah close behind him. Freddy scrabbled to his feet, his breath carrying no further than his throat. Iain brought the handle down across Freddy's arched back. He collapsed. Iain kicked out at the second man. Tom, who had run, doubled back, attacking Iain from behind. Caught unawares Iain staggered, colliding with a tree, the rough bark scraping his cheek. Delilah bit Tom's rump, an offering for her desperate fangs. Freddy pulled Alan to his feet with some difficulty, since he could barely catch air.

"Run." Freddy wrenched Tom off Iain. They barged through the undergrowth careless of direction. Delilah was desperate to pursue them but Iain whistled her back.

He swore at them as they escaped, an indecipherable rumble. He went into the house and bolted the door, the axe slipping from his grasp onto the hall floor. He knew his assailants, two of them at least and he could guess the third. A good night's work, he fetched the whisky bottle to celebrate and poured a tot into a glass. His head ached and his cheek was bleeding but he had come off lightly. Tomorrow he would enquire after the health of Freddy and Tom Hart.

* * * *

The full flush of summer was past, the crops bleached yellow in the fields, rich red berries forming on the hawthorn bushes. A heavy blackberry crop brought the village women and children out in droves with baskets and bowls, little mouths bruised with the telltale berry juice. With the evenings drawing in every available pair of hands were put to work in the fields. Groups of casual workers roamed from farm to farm, village to village, as the harvest was brought in. Poaching increased alongside Iain's vigilance. It was rare for passing visitors to accidentally wander into the woods, more often they were up to no good, intent on stealing game.

One late August morning, while the mist still hung between the trees, Mr Hart came to Iain's door.

"A quick word, Mr Macdonald, if you please." Mr Hart's expression was fixed and friendly.

"How are Tom and Freddy doing?" Iain asked. Their midnight visit had been a good six weeks previously.

Mr Hart's smile was strained. "Sorry about that, high spirits really."

"They need to be kept in check. I could have called the constable."

"I know, and I really appreciate it." His hard hands twisted his cap. "Freddy was quite bad after, Tom got off light, and I suppose you heard Alan Stock had a broken jaw."

"Aye, a shame that. It wasn't easy fending off three at once. Still, I've no argument with you, Mr Hart. What can I do for you?" He did not like watching the man squirm, all for the sake of his two stupid sons.

"We've got the thresher coming. It's been so hot, the pond we usually use for the water has dried up. I was wondering …"

Iain concluded for him, "Aye, use the river by all means. Who's your carter? Jack Middleton?"

"Yes that's right." Mr Hart's grin was borne of nerves and relief. He had been furious with his sons for raising the keeper's displeasure again. The threshing machine was powered by steam, a very thirsty creature. North Farm was at Iain's mercy and Mr Hart's gratitude was heartfelt.

"You're welcome. Think no more of it, no bad feelings. I'm sure Freddy's learned his lesson."

"From me and all," Mr Hart said. "Them and their larks, lands them in nothing but trouble. I've warned them, don't worry."

"Have you got your workers together?"

The great threshing machine did the rounds, performing its dusty work. Each farm was required to supply the water for the engine and a good strong gang of men recruited from the village.

"It's Derek Parsons machine. He'll be driving, I've got two of the Baker boys, me and my two and I'm hoping to get a couple more by this afternoon." A hectic few days lay ahead for North Farm and all the farms round about.

Later, Iain watched from the pooled shadow of the woods as Freddy and Tom sweated in the baking sun over the steaming thresher. Farm work was unappealing. He whistled to Delilah, laughing at the Hart boys' misfortune and strolled towards the cool, rushing river.

Chapter Seven

The Harvest Supper collided with the war in Europe. To many the supper took precedence, the pinnacle of the farming year. The news from abroad was confusing. What was it to them if an Archduke had been murdered in a city they couldn't even pronounce?

The schoolmistress had shown the village children Belgium, Austria, Russia and France, pointing with her stinging cane on the ancient pull-down map. The young men were full of it, eager and over-excited, many had joined up already and awaited news. Mrs Parry's two sons had pre-empted the call up and left for training camps. Others, displaying caution, were not so keen to volunteer. Whatever their feelings on the matter, it was the main topic of conversation.

Freddy and Tom Hart were flying on high spirits, the promise of great adventure on the tail of a good harvest. They had not enlisted although the words were on their lips, alongside tall tales they had heard from the continent. They made a noisy group in the company of Alan, Noah, Joanna and Nell.

The supper was held at Tump Farm, Mr Price's place. The enormous barn was decorated with paper lanterns and lamps, effusing it with a warm, hazy glow, already part of a rose-tinted memory. Huge beams swept up to the gothic arches in the vaulted ceiling more akin to prayer than agriculture. Great trestle tables sagged with pies, pasties, sliced hams, cheese, boiled eggs and bread, supplied by the partygoers. Another trestle table was weighed down with bottles, propped up underneath by barrels of ale and beer. An improvised bar, run by the publican, was arranged for when the contributions ran dry. All the villagers attended, young and old. On a raised platform the band consisted of the fiddle, bass viol, clarinet and squeezebox.

Bales of straw skirted a central dance floor with more bales edging the outer walls for improvised seating. Small wooden tables were dotted about for glasses and plates. Outside, great gilded bonfires wig-wammed, waiting to be lit when the night air chilled. The clear evening would later bring autumnal dew, a welcome coolness for the revellers who, by then, would be stoked with drink and hot from the dancing. The excitement and trepidation was tangible, a party not quite in full swing and with the anticipation that the best would follow.

Mr Price was reliable and honest with a good sense of humour. Iain did not always attend village events, it was because Mr Price was playing host that he decided to make the effort. He arrived to the dizzy tune of a merry folk jig, the dancers whirling around the dusty barn floor. The smell of dry earth and spilt beer was kept sweet by the air wafting through the open door.

He visited the bar and, with a full glass, was immediately caught in conversation with Mr Brown, Noah's father. Across the dance floor, Freddy's little group made a lot of noise. The boys were embarking on a drinking competition, sixpence for whoever could sink a pint the quickest. Nell had her back to them, her hand cupping her chin, watching the dancing. Joanna, taking more interest in the beer drinking, started a slow clap as Freddy, Tom, Noah and Alan put the glasses to their lips.

"Don't suppose Noah'll join up," Mr Brown said dismally to Iain. "Don't think I'll ever get rid of that one. Course, not to say they'd take him. Though not too much wrong with him physically..."

Iain watched over Mr Brown's shoulder as the quartet attempted to drain their glasses without swallowing. Freddy won, glassy eyed and cheering. Noah was still drinking when the other two had finished. Their jeering and backslapping was audible above the noise of the band and general chatter.

"I like to think when push comes to shove the lads would stick together," Mr Brown droned. Iain wasn't following, although some small part was trying. A hand pressed his shoulder, it was Isaac.

"How are things, Isaac?" He was glad to escape Mr Brown's drunken jabbering.

"Not bad, son. You were watching Freddy."

"Can't help drawing attention to themselves."

"Recovered from the beating though. You got him good that night, Iain. Broke two ribs, so I heard. Doctor says near punctured his lung. Black and blue, says Mr Hart." Isaac chortled merrily.

"I see Alan's recovered too."

"Been left with a clicky jaw. It's set straight enough. Lost a few teeth they say. Who ain't?" He grinned to prove the point.

"It did the trick," Iain said. "I've not seen any of them since that night."

"What can you do, Iain? You're doing your job, you don't ask to be set on during the night by a gaggle of yobs," he said shaking his head.

"Getting a drink, Isaac?" The old gypsy nodded in agreement and they returned to the bar. Later, sitting on the barn perimeter they were joined by their host Arthur Price, Matthew Yeates the builder, and his wife Betsy.

Betsy was worrying over their eldest two sons who had enlisted. The pair in question weren't worried, propping up the bar flirting with two village girls.

"If it's all going to be over by Christmas," she said, "I told them there's no rush. They're saying with the building going quiet this time of year they won't be missed."

"Aye, true enough," her husband said sucking on the stalk of his pipe.

"So you're not bothered about it then?" his wife asked.

"I don't mind if they're back in time for Christmas, wouldn't want them gone much longer mind. They're building in town come spring. Wanted to put in an estimate, see if I couldn't get the job."

"Where's that then?" Isaac asked, taking a cigarette from Iain.

"Along the London Road, building not one street, but two streets of terraced houses." Mr Yeates marvelled at the ambition.

"Some of them proper town houses too," Betsy Yeates said dreamily, "with a proper inside privy." Such a thing was more luxury than she dared hope for.

Isaac crinkled his nose in disgust. "Isn't right doing your business indoors. Isn't proper if you ask me."

"Not at all," Betsy said in reproof. "All the best new houses have indoor privies, don't they Mr Yeates?" addressing her husband.

"Water closets, Mrs Yeates, water closets. Indeed they do," he paused. "I don't see any advantages," another pause, "except a warmer bum."

"Mr Yeates," Betsy cried, shocked. Iain laughed into his beer.

"Would you be joining up now?" Mr Price asked him.

"Can't see there's any great hurry. If it's over by Christmas then it can't have been about much can it? If it's not – well who knows."

Isaac nodded in agreement. "No war's a good war. All them young ones thinking of the glory, they know nothing about the guts. War's full of guts." He always spoke with great authority, even about things he knew nothing of. Because he could imagine it he felt he knew.

Betsy Yeates said tearfully, "Oh, dear. Don't like the sound of that."

"Isaac, stop it with your tales," Mr Price said. "This is a modern age, we won't fight wars like we used to. Not like the Boer or the Crimea, things have moved on, Mrs Yeates. A modern army, that's what they'll have now."

Reassured, Mrs Yeates emptied her glass. Iain went to fetch another round of drinks. While he waited he received a little poke in his ribs with the end of a finger.

"Don't look round, Iain, Mr Took is across the way," Polly said. He stared at the empty glasses in front of him. "Not been calling of late. Are we all done?"

"Have you missed me?" he asked the empty air ahead of him.

Polly gave a sharp laugh. "Things have got complicated. Mr Took has opened a little chapel, you may have heard, in the school room every evening."

He had heard and been glad of a further excuse not to call. "No more travelling then?"

"Some, not so much. Have found myself to be in the family way too," she added.

He turned to look at her. She was immaculately turned out as always, with her almond eyes and an unusual pinkness rouged onto her cheeks. She smiled broadly and said in a louder voice, "Good evening, Mr Macdonald," then in a whisper, "don't look so alarmed it's not yours."

"How d'you know?"

"I know how far on I am and you've not called of late. Mr Took isn't as careful as you about how to prevent these things." She smiled again baring crowded teeth, he'd never noticed before. "I gathered you weren't coming again anyhow."

"What makes you say that?" He could pretend she was finishing with him rather than the other way about.

"You've never left it so long before. Found a sweetheart?"

He laughed. "No, Polly, not that."

"Shame." She placed her gloved hand on his for a second. "You're a closed book, you never let anyone in and if you don't you'll end up alone and lonely."

Barely a foot separated them and yet she was as distant as the moon. He would never touch her again, hear that throaty sigh or feel the drag of her thigh against his hips. He would never know her and he didn't want to. Deep in her eyes were flecks of dark brown, he had never noticed that either. There were probably many things he had never noticed. He returned his attention to the bar. "I've always been alone and lonely, Pol. I like it that way." They stood side by side not speaking while his glasses were filled. He stood with the tray, uncertainly. "Thank you Polly." There was nothing else to say, he could not think of anything else to say. She smiled at the barman dismissing Iain with the gesture and ordered her drinks.

He returned to his seat. Isaac came close to his ear and in a low voice said, "Mrs Took paying you a bit of attention, lad?"

He sighed, he imagined how many people had seen her touch his hand, although it did not matter, not now. Looking over Isaac's head he could see Polly sitting with her rook of a husband. She resembled an exotic bird beside him. "Aye," he said, "she was taking her leave."

Isaac nodded, he had understood the situation before Iain had said a word.

Iain was quiet for a while listening to the conversation, smoking. How easy he was to dismiss, he thought. How little she would miss him. How little he would miss her. Women were so much more direct. He would never have told her it was over, it was drifting naturally all by itself. He would not have visited her again. That was what he did. It had reached a natural conclusion. No melodramatic farewells, tears and tantrums. He unconsciously, perhaps, picked women who did not really need him.

"You dancing, Mr Macdonald?"

Joanna. Standing over him, hand on hip, her usual forthright self. Brazen enough to ask a man for a dance, her expression daring him to refuse her. The low cut dress pushed up her large bosom. Her curled hair frizzed at the edges where the tongs had been too hot, her cheeks glowing pink. She widened her golden eyes at him to hurry up his decision.

Isaac pushed at his arm to move him and Betsy said, "Go on, Mr Macdonald, join in the dancing."

He wouldn't give himself time to think. He stubbed out his cigarette, grabbed her hand and briskly led her into the crowd of revellers. He was an adequate dancer, his schoolmaster at The Sacred Heart had been a firm believer in the boys learning life skills and had considered dancing to be one of those. They had learned to waltz, polka and reel and the traditional Scottish dancing. The classes always caused much hilarity because, of course, one boy in each pair had to play the part of the girl. It was the only hour in the week given over to fun and not a boy in the class resented such a trivial pursuit, which was probably the reason his brain had absorbed the steps so readily.

The band, recovering from a fast folk tune, played a sedate waltz and he held Joanna round the waist, her left hand encased in his. She had not received an education at the hands of a liberated schoolmaster, hers had been a village school, strictly the three R's. She continuously trod on the front of his shoe.

He viewed the company over the top of her fair head as he danced. He did not need to concentrate on his feet like she did. Freddy attempted to engage Nell in conversation and although she listened, she was distant, that vacant faraway look on her face. Tom and Jack Potter arm-wrestled. Polly Took flirted with Noah Brown who, on the way to ask Nell for a dance, had been diverted by her. Old Mr Baker's son Lionel with his new wife, Nancy, helped themselves to food from the trestles. Iain wished he had drunk more, he felt very sober.

He glanced down at his partner, her bottom lip caught in concentration, her feet divorced from her brain, the sweep of eyelashes dark on her flushed cheek, no rouge there. He had a good view of bared cleavage and took advantage of her inattention. Her waist was soft and giving, he could not feel a corset beneath the seersucker. He pressed his hand into her back pushing her against him, she gasped in surprise and met his eyes.

"Stop counting," he said. "It doesn't matter."

Nerves vented in a flustered giggle. "Sorry, you're very good aren't you?"

"Aye," he muttered, "man of many talents." He could sum up his many talents in two words, guns and horses – it didn't sound like much.

Her thigh brushed his crotch, he wasn't sure if it were intentional but he was in the mood for games. "I imagine you are," a definite invitation in her tone.

He laughed pulling back a touch. "What are you after?"

Mock horror lit her face. "Nothing at all, Mr Macdonald. What are you offering?"

He could smell cider on her breath. "Are you drunk?"

"No!"

"What have you been drinking?"

"Lemonade," she said and laid her head on his shoulder, "or something very much like it."

"Who gave you that?"

"Tom and Freddy got the drinks," she said.

He wondered if Nell had been plied with the same stuff. Looking at her it seemed unlikely, unless alcohol made her sour. She was talking to Freddy, arms folded, her body bristling with irritation.

Iain was unsure now what it was about Joanna he disliked. He certainly enjoyed the feel of her body curving along the line of his. It had been a while since Polly. He ran his hand down her back feeling again for stays. As he thought, there were none. The only thing holding it all up and in was a camisole and the dress itself. He would undo it and her bosom would tumble out. He pulled her in tight against him. She jumped, trying to move back, except he did not allow it.

"Feeling shy now?" he asked.

Her cheeks burned red. "I think I need some air. Perhaps you're right, maybe it wasn't lemonade."

He took her arm to lead her out of the door. Freddy blocked their exit. "Going somewhere, Macdonald?"

Iain was disparaging. "Get out my way, Freddy, I can't be bothered with you tonight."

Tom arrived at Freddy's elbow, second in command. "You're not going anywhere with him, Joanna," he said. "You're with me, now come on."

"Who the hell are you to tell her who she can go anywhere with?" Iain raised his voice, a few faces turned in their direction.

"Don't start your crap. She's with us, come on Joanna." Freddy held out his hand to her.

She wavered uncertainly. Her face drained of colour. Clamping her hand over her mouth she ran outside, with Tom racing after her. Iain laughed. Freddy shot him a venomous glare and followed them. He shook his head, foolish girl, wasted on a glass of cider. He walked straight into Nell.

"What's going on?" she said. "Where is everybody?"

"Freddy and Tom are outside with Joanna who is puking up her cider."

She groaned. "Oh, I told her not to drink it. I got my own drink. Lemonade - my eye."

"Can the girl not tell the difference?"

"Oh, she acts as if she's a woman of the world. She's about as unworldly as it gets, follows crisis with drama. She's never happy with what she's got, always wanting something else. Now she's ruined the evening by being sick. I suppose I'll have to take her home." She was cross, folding her arms across her body, chestnut curls escaped their pins. He removed a pin hanging on a coiled tendril of hair. She took it from him and smiled, the alteration to her face was remarkable, crosspatch to exquisite.

She, who had curled up in his chair making it look so big, her small white hands running along the dark furniture in his house, the little things she appeared to take pleasure in. And he recalled the notion, what had he been thinking? To hide her and how easy it would be. He wanted to pick her up here and now - light and bony as a bird - and take her to his house and keep her there, safe, protected. How wonderful, he thought, how ridiculous. He had to force himself to turn his eyes away from her, she was blushing and he was making her feel awkward.

"I was sorry for what happened with Freddy and Tom, when they set about you," she said.

"They suffered more than me."

"If it makes you feel better Freddy did suffer. You dislocated his shoulder, cracked his ribs. The bruises were something awful."

"Aye, it does make me feel better."

She didn't speak, but stared at him with confusion in her expression, an emotional struggle to understand him.

"You'd better go see to Joanna," he managed to say hoarsely. He knew she was going to reach out before she had moved to do it and yet her touch still surprised him. His hand dwarfed hers and the cool clamp of her fingers sent a frisson through him. For a second they were somewhere else, alone, not two people, one person and there was peace, wonderful and ghastly at the same time because it wasn't real and he needed it to be. He pulled away as though she had burned him. He didn't wait for her puzzled reaction. He walked away, dry mouthed and lost, thrown off kilter by the touch of a hand.

He sat between Isaac Smith and Mr Price. He took a cigarette out of the packet and lit it, even the smoke grated in his throat although the eventual effect was calming. When he glanced up she had gone outside, presumably to find Joanna.

After a time, he went to the bar and ordered a double whisky. He knocked it back in one go and another for good measure to follow the first. He did not dance again. He drank steadily.

The band stopped playing. Isaac, in a corner of the barn, regaled his audience with a tale about a seafaring man who set sail for the West Indies. His true love swore she would wait for him to come back to her. Her promises of love and devotion helped him endure across the many miles. When he returned from sea, she had run off and married the squire's son. The sailor, burning with jealousy, obtained a mantrap and set it to maim his rival. Alas his true love fell into its mighty jaws and met a bloody end. The prolonged tale was punctuated with sinister silences and appropriate gasps of menace. Isaac was very drunk and embellished the story as he went, binding the listeners in his spell of words. He finished to a round of enthusiastic applause. Several more drinks appeared at his elbow.

Joanna's return to the party went unnoticed. Suddenly she was there much recovered from her nausea and leaning heavily on Tom listening to the story. Beside her Nell sat within the arc of Freddy's defensive arm. Isaac was busy diminishing his line of drinks when Freddy leaned forward. "Isaac," a soft, friendly tone, "where would you find a mantrap? Surely there's no such thing?"

His eyes twinkled, his voice slurred, "Oh aye, there is that, young Freddy." Leaning into his ear so Freddy could smell the stink of him he whispered, "The keeper has such a one in his shed." Freddy nodded and smiled, sitting back with Nell.

By the time Iain got up to leave the band had packed away. The party showed no signs of breaking up. The plaintive voice of Mrs Potter singing and Lionel Baker playing the spoons carried out of the big barn doors. He said goodnight to several villagers as he left. He held his drink well, but he was intoxicated nonetheless. The bonfires, which had flared so brightly earlier in the evening, smouldered hot and glowing. In their dying light, paired off couples took advantage of the dark.

He breathed in the fresh night air tainted with the smell of wood-smoke. The grass underfoot was wet with heavy autumn dew, windless and chilly, good hunting weather. From the corner of his eye he recognised Freddy spooning with a girl at the side of the barn.

Freddy leaned back on the wooden wall his hungry lips on Nell's mouth. His heavy kiss pushed her head back. Her small hands on his chest clutched a handful of shirt. Was she pulling him towards her or pushing him away? He clinched her waist with one hand, tight and possessive, the other roaming like an inquisitive terrier. A wave of revulsion swept over Iain, his gut twisting with jealousy. His reaction was automatic, undeniable, the only response to an impossible situation. He strode across to them. Nell abruptly pulled away from Freddy, her eyes widening with fright when she saw Iain's expression. Her hand flew to her throat to fasten the buttons there and she smoothed her skirt. Iain glared at her in disgust and grabbed Freddy by the lapels.

"Iain, stop," she cried, too late. His balled fist sprang towards Freddy's nose, one quick jab. Blood spurted out splattering Freddy's shirtfront, spraying Iain in the face. He released him and Freddy fell back clasping his hands over his face.

"M-my dose, h-he's broken my buddy dose," he gasped as blood squeezed between his rigid fingers. Iain marched away wondering why the hell he had done that. The immediacy of his jealousy was now the mere ghost of a thought and by tomorrow he would have forgotten it completely. The bonfire was hot on his retreating back.

Chapter Eight

The season began with the hollow sound of the huntsman's undulating horn. The foxhunters invaded Iain's woodland astride sweating horses with dilated vapour-snorting nostrils. The hounds bayed hysteria over the land, through the trees, a living fluid beast, dissecting, spreading and re-joining.

The morning the hunt passed across Harrowmead he patrolled the estate, the air redolent with fungi and decay. Branches dripped with the even falling rain. Stray brown leaves clung to the naked tree limbs, twisted in their infinite dance, black against the grey sky.

At his waist dangled his chain of keys. With steady patient hands he unlocked every gate, pushing them wide ready for the intruders and their minions. He thought it an imposition on his life, on his woods, on his work, unavoidable, unbearable. It was how things were. The master of the hounds had permission from the squire. And the squire loved it. His two sons and twelve year old daughter rode into the fray, shouting and swearing, over hedges and ditches, through woodland and meadow. Iain lowered his eyes and bit his tongue until they had passed.

Like a dog draws fleas the hunt drew spectators, ambling along on foot, eager to walk the hallowed woodland, only open to them on rare occasions. These interlopers took advantage. Each senseless act of destruction affronted him; broken fences, trodden down gulleys, mushroom rings trodden into the mould, branches wrenched from the trees, mistletoe pilfered from the highest branches. At the end of the day he followed the same path locking the gates, an unconscious mental list of offences forming in his head.

The noise and rush of horses and hounds panicked his birds, scattering them randomly throughout the wood. It could take up to a week for them to settle and flock together. The day before the hunt he was well tipped to block up the fox earths, he quietly considered this to be sacrilege and unfair sport. It was not a regular occurrence, but it left him feeling peevish and resentful. In Scotland there was no trespass law, even so they had never unlocked all the gates for a hunt to ride through the estate. He could not imagine Finnigan's face had he suggested such an outrage. With men like Finnigan such a law was superfluous.

With the gates hanging wide, Iain went home for breakfast. He expected the hunt after ten in the morning, nothing inconveniently early for the gentry. Delilah came to him with a stick and he threw it into the bushes. She dived into the dying bracken and vegetation her wagging tail, a visible marker.

In the dim solitude of his house he ate breakfast to the accompaniment of the hollow whirr and tick of the old granddaughter clock that he wound, by habit, once a week. When he first came here, in a moment of boredom, he had dismantled the clock mistakenly thinking its inner workings might resemble a gun. Old Mr Feeney had obliged by putting it back together. It was reliable and kept good time.

As he cleared away, a quiet tap on the door disturbed him. It was not quite nine o'clock. He thought it rather early for Mr Denham, and wondered if perhaps it was Isaac. He was surprised to find Joanna on the doorstep, arms folded to repel the chill, damp hair flat to her head.

He didn't speak, he didn't know what to say. She smiled at him. "I'm frozen, can I come in?"

He hesitated. He didn't want her to come in. Indecision, then resignation, he stood aside to allow entry. It was out of his hands, her coming and his acceptance of it. She hurried to the range, pulling over a small footstool to sit on, and surrendered her cold hands to the heat.

He watched her. "What do you want?"

She shrugged off her wet coat onto the floor, making herself at home, making it more difficult for him to evict her. "Mrs Denham wanted me to take the carrier into town to fetch a package from the chemist. I missed it didn't I, and I'm not walking in this. So I'll say they didn't have it in and I'm to go tomorrow."

"So you're passing time, are you?" he said. She was downcast and he didn't want to know the reason.

She stared into the fire. "I've wanted to come here many times," she said, her voice betraying her nerves.

"Well, I have to go out later, so you can't stay here," he said.

She frowned then. "Well aren't you helpful. I only want to sit a while." She suddenly turned a sunny smile on him. "It's a nice big house."

He shrugged. "I suppose so. Built for a family I should think."

"Did the old keeper have a family?"

"I don't know," irritation crept into his tone. "He was dead by the time I arrived, his wife too. I think there might be grown up children in the village."

Colour rose in her cheek. "You should have a family."

A stupid irrelevant comment, he wondered what she was thinking coming here, her real motivation. "I don't think so, it's not something I aspire to, thanks very much."

"You make it sound perfectly vile." She stood up, edging closer to him. "Did you hear about Nell and Freddy?"

"No." Her grey working dress was modestly buttoned to the neck, doing little to disguise her magnificent chest.

"They're getting married in eight weeks." There was no happiness in her voice or face; her opinion of the union was clear.

He took a deep breath. Nell was a fool to marry Freddy. But it was her life, her choice. It was none of his business. It meant nothing to him. "I hope they'll be very happy."

"I didn't think you'd be very impressed." She was disappointed by his reaction.

"She might have done better for herself," he said. Now he actually looked at her, saw her, really saw, he was distracted, mainly by the deep caramel colour of her eyes. She was attractive in her way. She licked her lips as if she had something on them, the tip of her tongue red against their pale pink. The action stirred him. He wanted the red and pink on his mouth. He gripped the tops of her arms, pulled her towards him and kissed her. She made a little startled sound, although he knew he hadn't frightened her. When he drew back she smiled at him.

"Why are you here?" he asked.

"I – I don't know." She was shaking slightly.

The news about Nell and Freddy was disappointing. He wanted Joanna to leave before they both did something regrettable. "Perhaps you'd better go." There was no harm in suggesting it. He settled in his armchair, legs outstretched, reaching into his pocket for cigarettes. He put one between dry lips where it hung unlit. She stood for a second, undecided, before sitting down on his lap.

"Don't make me go," she said, sickness threatening. He would turn her away and she could never come here again, or look at him again. She would feign indifference, stick her nose in the air as if she had never cared either way.

He took the cigarette out of his mouth, putting it on the table at his elbow. "You're not what you pretend to be, Joanna. You'll only wish you hadn't later." The pressure of her bottom in his lap was arousing. He placed his hands on her waist. There was still time to step back, tell her to clear out, offend her, her feelings were of no consequence.

She moved first, halted thoughts and doubts instantly by kissing him. He pressed his hand to the back of her head and his tongue was in her hot mouth. She wouldn't play shy now. He hadn't pushed her away, ordered her out the door. Bravado played its part, her hands catching on the roughness of his unshaven face, up into the black softness of his hair. His fingers fumbled with the covered dress buttons, bulging breasts caged by a corset. Her throat was smooth as silk to his lips, his fingers pulling at laces, until she spilled out, free. Deftly, the lumpy weave of the floor rug was under her back and he was above her, taking command and the speed of it all was robbing her of air.

He took a moment to look at her, exposed like some ripe earth bound goddess, her eyes drugged by fear and excitement, skin flushed with self-consciousness. He pushed up her skirt, pulling away the layers between them. Strong, competent fingers encountered limited resistance. He persisted until his hand slipped against her and she cried out, shocked by her own response. He was in control, she was powerless, she was liberated, unable to resist opening her legs in invitation. She gasped at the pain, sharp and burning, a pause, her eyes wide, nails digging into flesh before she slowly brought her hips up to meet his. She clung to him, torn and whole, fear and desire. For Iain there were no misgivings just intense, hot pleasure, no need to question his lust. She was young and ready for this, for him.

The second after the moment of carelessness, he cursed himself for not withdrawing, absorbed by the climax. He kept his full weight from crushing her, catching his breath. He rolled off. There was a token smear of her blood on him, her gift, unexpected, unwanted. Too late, he had taken it now, lending weight to that which was meaningless. He pulled his clothing together with one hand, lying on his back vacantly gazing at the broad crossbeam in the ceiling. He closed his eyes, replete, drained and numb. Drifting far away, not here, not now, somewhere else, pleasant and warm.

"Iain." Her voice brought him, too soon, back to the room.

He grunted a reply, putting an arm over his eyes. Always there was the reality, a room, a woman and, today, the fox hunt riding through. He heard the creak of the floorboards as she stood, pulling up her drawers, re-lacing her corset, fastening her dress. Her shoes scuffed on the floor. When he looked she was trying to straighten her hair in the reflection of the clock-face.

He got to his feet, fastened his belt and came up behind her. She froze at his touch, not like before. He pulled the loose strands of her hair into place, taking out pins, re-pinning. He turned her round, hands on her shoulders.

"You all right?" It was her first time and it had shaken her. He wanted to be kind, to reassure her. He gave a wry smile, rubbing her arms with passionless hands. Not an atom of him wanted her now, all spent in one ejaculation, he wouldn't care if he never saw her again.

She smiled too, unsure, but nodded. "Yes, yes."

"I have to go. You can stay if you must, I'll be back in about an hour." He hoped she would leave, reaching for his gun from the hooks on the mighty beam.

Her insides fluttered, her loins ached dully and something leaked from her. She was embarrassed. He wasn't, that was obvious. She wanted him to kiss her again, hold her.

"No, no," she said. "I think I'd perhaps better go into town after all. Wouldn't take long to walk would it? Looks brighter now."

He laughed, a few minutes ago they had been conjoined on the rug and now she discussed the weather, controlled and virtuous, passing the time of day.

He locked the door behind them, gun under his arm, battered hat on head. He whistled for Delilah who appeared from the back of the house.

"There's a track takes you onto the town road, much quicker." The path was narrow so she fell into step behind him. They did not talk, she didn't know what to say. Where was their common ground? What had she been thinking? He was content with the silence; she felt awkward. They had made love and it had altered her world beyond recognition and yet he acted so coolly towards her, as if it hadn't occurred. He didn't hold her hand or offer his arm. It was as if they had met by chance a few minutes before on the pathway through the woods.

She was dismayed to see his shirt collar was frayed, that worn old hat and his jacket cobbled and patched. He was a countryman, more interested in serviceable comfort than gentlemanly togs. She wondered who did his mending, neat as it was. She never imagined he did his own.

After an interval he stopped and pointed. "Keep following the left fork and you'll get to the road. There might be folk about today, the hunt's coming through," checking his watch, "anytime now."

She paused long enough to smile. He saw now she was upset about Nell marrying Freddy. By coming to him she had been seeking solace of sorts. "See you after," he said, hoping he wouldn't, knowing it was inevitable.

She gave a little high laugh that grated on him. "Yes, see you later." She strode away with purpose, her heart feeling as if it would explode in her chest at the enormity of what she had done.

Later on, alone that evening, Iain remembered Freddy and Nell. What powerful emotion made him gravitate towards her like a bee to nectar? He was surprised at himself. Push it away - denial was easy. Time would prove her to be a momentary fascination, a passing fancy, nothing more. Now he thought about it Joanna would provide the perfect diversion.

* * * *

It did not occur to Iain to seek Joanna out. Far from it, he was happy to let it lie. But it was no surprise to him when she called, ten days later on her Sunday off.

Iain did not attend church. He had no faith. Religion and belief were like a faded flower that had lost its colour and scent. It had been beaten, starved and frozen out by the Catholic sisters who raised him. Even so, some small part of him still clung on. He prayed, even at Glenleven, but eventually that stopped too. His final defence against Finnigan was God, so he would beg God every night and morning to return him to the orphanage. When a year passed, to the day, he stopped. No more prayers, no more hope. The final religious lesson – God helped those who helped themselves.

All the villagers in Harrowford went to the squat stone church in the middle of the village, hemmed in by a wall to keep in the dead. The exception - himself and Isaac Smith. It was often on a Sunday he would visit Isaac or vice versa for a 'wee dram'.

Not this Sunday. This Sunday Joanna arrived so early he had not even got out of bed. It was a rare event when Iain rose later than seven o'clock, but he had finished a bottle of whisky the previous night. He fell out of bed when he heard the knock, peering out of the window. He couldn't ignore her, though it was tempting. He lazily wrapped a sheet round himself and answered the door.

Her eyes opened wide seeing his state of undress. She had not expected this. She had been writing their names in overlapping hearts waiting for him to call and he hadn't. She was proud. She wouldn't visit him. She waited. She looked out for him coming to the house. Was he staying away on purpose? What would he think of her calling on him – again? What did she care what he thought? Her pride gave way and she ignored Nell's protestations. Now it was as if he had been waiting all this time for his lover to return, greeting her naked from his bed as if to save him the time and bother of undressing.

Her shocked expression made up his mind for him. She either wanted what he could offer or she didn't. He could only give her more of the same. He indicated with his head up the stairs. "First door on the right."

She swallowed her protest and climbed the stairs ahead of him. The large iron bed was tousled, still warm from his bare skin. How dare he! All cool and collected, callously taking her virginity and then not even having the grace to call at the house to walk out with her. What was she? Some dark dirty secret? He had used and debased her. She wouldn't stand for this, she would tell him exactly what she thought.

He followed her into the room, looking at her as if he could see through her, right into her very soul. She couldn't speak, silenced into submission, disarmed by his self-assurance, fascinated by his fingers unhooking her dress. His unwavering gaze made her feel naked already. The mattress sprung under her bottom as she sat down and he was kneeling at her feet, still wrapped in the sheet, removing her shoes, and then her stockings. Still she could not speak. Later she was not sure how he invited her into the comfort of his bed and yet he did. His hands were slow and steady, his mouth hot and careful. Sensations were like water, rinsing away her anger and irritation, irrelevancies washing away in the stream of his caress. She relaxed and melted into the heat of his skin. She almost hated him for it, except she wanted all this so very much.

Afterwards, laying together, sated, it was as if they couldn't bear to touch each other, not wrapped together, a tangle of limbs, like he had with Polly. They drifted in and out of sleep until the morning grew late and fell into the afternoon. Iain sat on the edge of the bed and dressed.

"I hate Harrowmead," Joanna said, her face pressed into the pillow.

He was miles away thinking about the challenges of the day, the jobs that waited. "What?" Incredulity in his voice, as if she had said she were from Mars.

"I hate all this countryside. I hate having to catch the carrier to town. I want to live in a big city." She rolled onto her back, stretching her arms above her head. "I want to live in a town house with a proper bathroom and an indoor privy. I want to go to the dance halls and shop in department stores. I don't belong out here."

It was a woman's dream, one so very different to his. "A lady's life, Joanna. You think you're for better things."

"Yes." She sat up, holding the sheet modestly to her chest. "Yes, that's it, I am, how perfectly right! I'm not going to be some farmer's wife like Nell," she screwed her face up in disgust, "I couldn't bear it," a heartfelt shudder of distaste.

Her hair tumbled round her shoulders, hugging her knees, breasts squashed, enhancing her deep cleavage. Her eyes were lit with her future.

"No," he said watching her, "I can see that. Well, perhaps you'll land yourself a nice army officer or a gentleman from town. You won't find one sitting round here though will you?"

She caught his gaze. "No, you're right." And she knew for all her romantic notions this man would never do for her. "I won't will I." She could afford to be generous, to be fond of him. She didn't love him, or care for him at all. She sidled over, her hands on his bare shoulder, resting her chin on them. "And what about you handsome keeper, what do you want?" Even if she didn't actually love him, her vanity demanded a reaction, jealousy, adoration, even disapproval.

He paused in his dressing, belt hanging undone, turning his head slightly to look into her eyes. She stared at him owlishly, unblinking, waiting to hear his most secret desires. A smile twisted his lips. "Bacon and egg," he said, laughing at her earnest expression. She pushed herself away from him.

"Oh, you men, not a dream or aspiration among you," she joked, secretly annoyed by his brevity. "Well I intend making something of my life. I won't be wasting my youth in the back of beyond. I want to experience everything." She opened her arms expansively, falling back on the bed.

He pulled on his shirt, stood by the window buttoning it. The rain hit the panes, drops running down the glass. A lone magpie jumped from tree to tree lifting its tail up and down in the air. One for sorrow, he thought superstitiously.

"I've got stuff to do," he said. "Get dressed and I might feed you before you go." He remembered, suddenly, a slap in the face - he didn't like her. She made him feel empty. A man would be melted down in the furnace of her arrogance. The body was pleasurable. What of the mind, spirit and soul? She would be bought with a diamond and an evening gown.

Left alone in his bed, Joanna realised she had probably said exactly what he wanted to hear. It was true she didn't want Harrowmead or Iain. He was commanding and exciting but he made her feel cornered. She would bend to his will because that was what he expected and she would not know how to alter him. He wasn't a man to be altered. She didn't want to be in Nell's position, in love with a man who wanted a woman to cook and clean and bear his children. Now it dawned on her it would be equally awful to be in love with a man who did not reciprocate her feelings.

* * * *

Downstairs Iain let Delilah out into the rain. The raindrops fell through the bare branches, water running down the front door onto the tiled floor. He had no aspirations for the life Joanna envisioned. He had known the city and had no wish to return there.

A runaway orphan, shivering in the grey wintry gloom of St George's Square in the centre of Glasgow city. Lonely, hungry and miserable, he had sheltered in doorways, begging for a penny from well-dressed audiences leaving the concert halls and theatres. The city's bright lights and glamour flipped upside down. He had fallen through dark alleys where starving children cowered, slatternly women sold themselves and drunken men staggered from the pub or collapsed in the street swigging from a bottle. Those quiet unlit rooms, dark as he passed, with no bread on the table or fuel for the fire. He had returned to The Sacred Heart of his own accord, reconciled to a beating and grateful for a supper of stale bread and mouldy cheese.

He belonged out here, away from the filth and the bustle. He was thankful to have the earth under his feet and rain on his back, the sweet air in his lungs, plentiful wood for his fire and food for his belly. He was not tied irrevocably to Harrowmead, he was tied to the earth, the seasons, the life that beat in time with his heart through the trees and streams.

After the city, the nights at Glenleven were so very dark. The call of the owl, rain rattling through the leaves, the cry of a hawk and rush of waterfalls plunging into burbling highland rivers, all had been new to his unaccustomed ears. Every fresh experience was magnified and frightening, in a wondrous way that filled him with excitement and awe. His temerity passed, the lochs and glens, flora and fauna became his consolation. Real, more tangible terrors awaited him in the form of his new master. The rhythms of the estate soon became as familiar to him as his own breathing. Each season, at first so strange, became a reassuring certainty. Seasons in sequence, each one bringing its own tasks, trials and celebrations, predictable and reliable like the rise and set of the sun. These were constant in his young life when everything else had proved so inconstant and unreliable.

Delilah rushed back to the door, dripping. She shook herself, water splintering around her. He clicked his fingers and she slunk away to the back of the house to lie in the woodshed and lick herself.

The smell of bacon and egg frying on the range brought Joanna downstairs. They ate and Iain read from a pamphlet on new shotguns, which he had no chance of affording. She did not know how to talk to him, she didn't know the words to draw him out, to get to the truth beyond his intimate touch and so she suffered his silence.

"Nell is getting married the first week in December," she said when she had finished eating, holding a mug of strong milky tea.

He was distracted, his voice vague. "Good."

"You're not much interested in other people's affairs are you?"

He shook his head. "No, not much, although I think Helena's mad." He stretched his long arms above his head and yawned. "Maybe it's about time we buried the hatchet."

"Who? You and Freddy?"

"Yes, why not? I can't be bothered with it. If he's settling down to be an old married man, it's about time he started acting like one. I shall pay him a visit, I think." Yes, he had decided. "It's all so petty."

"I don't think Freddy thought breaking his nose was petty." She recalled trying not to laugh while Freddy ranted and raved, blood soaking into his shirt and Nell frantic.

A faint smile played on his lips. "I was drunk, I don't know what I was thinking to be honest. Still it's time to put it behind us."

She laughed. "You're angling for an invite to the wedding."

He pulled a face. "Not if it means going into church and mincing around at some wedding breakfast." An image flashed, Nell welcoming Freddy into their marriage bed. Bile burned somewhere in his gut.

She said, "I'd better let you get on then." She fastened up her coat, produced a scarf from her pocket and wrapped it round her head.

"I suppose you'll go to church later and pray forgiveness for your sins."

She giggled, perhaps he wasn't all that bad. "You are naughty, Iain." He could be funny. "I shall pray for your sins, not mine."

"You don't know my sins."

"I don't think I want to know."

She was satisfied then, with this shabby affair, otherwise she would have wanted to know. Women always wanted to know. She had stepped back. Lines had been drawn, there could be no more than this.

"Good. I never confess," he said. Laughing, he grabbed her hand, pulling her onto his knee and kissed her with renewed enthusiasm. He rose from his seat, lifting her up in the air onto her feet. She whooped with delight. His sudden spontaneity surprised her, she would never know where she was with this man. He waltzed her to the front door and waved her off into the rain.

Chapter Nine

On a cold November morning, two hours before the pheasant shoot was due to begin, Iain inspected the perimeter of the woodland. He checked the birds and planned the beaters' route.

Reaching the line of trees that joined North Farm land he saw Tom working a plough with two horses. The earth turned dark under the plough blade, straight runnels up and down, stripes of soil, wet and dry. Iain whistled shrilly to gain his attention. Seeing Iain, Tom pushed his cap back with one hand and straightened his aching shoulders. He hesitated before strolling down the incline towards the keeper.

"Tom," Iain greeted.

"How you doing?" He was wary, a safe few yards between them.

"Tom, there's been bad blood between us - you, Freddy and me," Iain said. "I know Freddy's getting wed in three weeks. I want to make things right, there's no need for all this. I wondered if you both would come to my place tonight, so we could talk, like grown up men, instead of kids in the schoolyard. What do you say?"

Tom stared at him and then slowly nodded. "Yeah, I suppose. Freddy's away to market. I'll tell him when I see him, shall I?"

"Aye, that'd be good. Unless I see him first, eh?"

Tom smiled, a nice looking boy, he had always been the steadying influence, the easier going of the two. "What time?" he asked.

"Six or seven. What suits?"

"We'll come at half past six," Tom said. Iain reached out his hand. Uncertainly Tom leaned forward with an outstretched arm and they shook hands firmly. He watched Iain retreat with apprehension. What would Freddy make of a truce?

* * * *

The shooting party was late. They kept the beaters waiting in the damp, chilly air. Smart in their best tweed and caps, they smoked pipes and cigarettes, exchanging humorous quips to pass the time. Spirits were high, it was a social occasion with a wage at the end of the day. Eventually word passed around like Chinese whispers, the party had arrived and the shoot could begin. The beaters sprang into action.

The pheasants, suddenly transformed into highbrow non-conformists, scattered ahead of the ragged line of beaters. The men called, whistled and sang, their staffs and walking sticks scything paths through the dying vegetation. Ahead of them, argumentative and independent, the birds thrust their necks forward, eyes fixed on a desperate escape. They were dignified until the last second when, scrabbling on clawed feet they failed to out-run their pursuers and panic and fear elevated them. The air rushed with heavy wings beating against the breeze, the painful warble clacking in their strained throats. They were almost free and away into the infinite sky. A volley of explosions, and metal and gunpowder sprayed across the short distance. Breasts peppered with shot, lead-laden, weighty and fat, they came spinning down to the damp earth.

As the dead birds were lined up on the grass Iain placated the incompetent and reassured the witless. Between shots, punctuated exclamations of, "I say," and, "young man, if you could oblige," grated on his limited forbearance.

The balding Lord from some estate in Gloucester blamed his gun for missing the unmissable - Iain provided an alternative weapon. The paunched youth with marbles in his mouth actually threw his gun, with purpose, into the long wet grass in his haste to reach the refreshments. Lady Dunlop, her mouth a red gash, repeatedly waved her gun over the party, while Iain applied all his charms to persuade her to keep it pointed forward.

Meanwhile the hip flasks, "to keep out the cold", appeared alarmingly often, reducing even the good shots to poor ones.

The day was a military manouevre; the keeper played general, the beaters were soldiers, the shooting party, renegade loose canons. The pheasants were the unsuspecting enemy, although latterly with deep suspicions. Iain's headache was not improved by the constant worry of a beater ending up on the wrong end of an enthusiastic gun, and if it lacked everything else, the party was certainly enthusiastic.

While Mr Denham's contemporaries raised a substantial part of their income from letting their homes and decanting to town for the season, Mr Denham clung to the old ways. Iain had occasion to wish he didn't.

* * * *

After several hours in the wearing company of the shooting party, Iain stopped for a swift pint at the pub before meeting up with Tom and Freddy. An evening of monotony stretched ahead, hours of cleaning and oiling guns, filling the endless cartridge cases for the following day. That one rifle discarded in the wet grass would take an hour of fiddly time consuming work; dismantling the barrel, removing moisture, oiling to prevent rust, lubricating the locks with gin and polishing the wooden stock.

The bar was quiet, the only customers were Sam Fields the Thatcher, Lionel Baker and old Mr Feeney who, in his retirement from head groom, worked in the vegetable garden at Harrowmead. Later all the beaters would be in, a tradition after a shoot, and the landlord would increase his takings threefold.

"I'm thinking of joining up," Lionel said to his three companions. "What about you, Mr Macdonald?"

"Hadn't thought about it myself," he admitted. "Perhaps I'll see how it goes. Don't think the army life would do much for me. I suppose if push comes to shove I might have to, we might all have to."

"No," Sam said, "it won't last long enough for that. There are hundreds of eager volunteers. They won't need any more. I must say I wouldn't be up for it."

"You're too old," Lionel joked. "They wouldn't have you."

"Cheeky blighter." Sam was genuinely offended. "I'll have you know I'm lithe as a tinker's lurcher and only thirty five."

Iain laughed. "What you after, Lionel? A bit of adventure, or a French girl?"

His eyes lit up. "I wouldn't say no to either."

Mr Feeney chuckled. "And there you are not married more than a few months."

Iain, recalling Nancy Brewer, Lionel's wife, could sympathise with the man. He would hate to be stuck with her for the rest of his life. He thought of Joanna, uncomplicated. He would have to put a bag over Nancy Brewer's head to make love to her.

Lionel pulled a face. "Yeah, but a French girl, can you imagine the things they could do?"

"No," Iain said, "I can't imagine anything a Frenchy could do that any of our girls couldn't manage if you treat them nice enough, not in my experience anyhow."

Lionel and Sam were deeply envious of his experience. "I can't even imagine the things they could do," Sam said gloomily, "never mind doing them."

They laughed into their pints.

"I've got to go in a minute." Iain glanced at his watch, twenty past six. He drained his glass as Freddy came through the door, stopping short. His eyes widened when he saw the keeper and the colour flared in his face. Iain slammed down his glass.

"I'll see you lot. Leave you with your Frenchy visions." Seeing Freddy, he smiled. "Evening, Freddy. I thought we were meeting at mine."

"At yours?" he said, confusion, a tight band of pain around his head.

The three men at the bar were deep in conversation. "Aye," Iain said. "Haven't you seen Tom? I asked him to tell you. I wanted you both to come to mine."

The high colour drained from Freddy's face, leaving it pasty white, and vomit pushing at the back of his tonsils. "I've been to market."

"Well you're very late back."

"What did you want us for?"

Iain shrugged, a little uncertain laugh cracking. "I thought what with you and Nell getting married and all, perhaps it was time we acted like men instead of two cockerels in a pit. So I told Tom to be at mine at half past six," he referred to his watch, "which it almost is. He's probably gone on ahead."

Freddy wavered, hands opening and closing at his sides. He was having trouble catching air in his open mouth. When he finally spoke his voice was hoarse, a loud whisper, "You told Tom to go to yours at six thirty?"

He wondered if Freddy had lost his mind. "Aye, that's what I just said."

"Oh bloody hell," he ran out of the door. Iain turned back to the bar. Sam, Lionel and Mr Feeney had their heads together laughing and had not even seen Freddy.

Iain followed Freddy into the dark. Freddy was barely visible, running up the street towards Harrowmead. Iain knew the woods better than Freddy, better than anyone. He would cut him off before he reached Keeper's House.

He whistled to Delilah and set off at speed. He darted into the woods, unlocking a gate, closing it again. He jogged, dodging trees and bushes. The path here was overgrown, hardly used, it would eventually fork onto the main route. There were shadows and obstacles, real and manufactured. He knew his way and avoided them easily enough. He heard Freddy before he saw him, running as swiftly as a man could, his breathing ragged, fearful pants of desperation, feet crashing through the undergrowth, leg muscles on fire. He had gone beyond the point where Iain could have blocked his path so he pursued him.

  When Keeper's House came into view, the pointy gable end, Freddy stopped sharp and in the darkness Iain hurtled into his back. Both men stumbled. He put a hand on Freddy's shoulder leaning forward to catch air. Freddy pulled away from him.

  They approached the house from the side. A half moon appeared, a white profile from behind tattered clouds, illuminating the main path. Iain saw something strange. About half the height of a man, like a child, it stooped upright, leaning forward at some peculiar broken angle.

  Iain and Freddy stood side by side, their rapid heartbeats slowing, fear clutching at fasted lungs. Freddy moved first, a few halting steps, then a few more. Iain was rooted to the spot, feet planted on sodden leaves. He was not sure what he was looking at and he forced his limbs to move. Freddy sank down on his knees, an unholy sound issuing from his lips.

  Iain saw the top of a dark head drooping, arms dangling uselessly. A body, kneeling, somehow kept vertical but lifeless. He closed his eyes, opened them again, the fog of his own breath clouded the clearing. As it dispersed or his eyes adjusted, he knew not which, he could see it. Hanging forward, broken, human – inhuman. How was this possible?

  He dashed to the house and unlocked the door. In the dark he scrabbled, shaking, for a lamp and matches. He carried the light outside, drawing back the velvet black curtain on a scene he would never forget. Freddy looked up imploringly his face chalk-white, eyes dilated and dark like a frightened deer. Tom was bent in the merciless metal jaws of the old mantrap from Iain's shed. It held him rigid, biting into his thighs. The blood spread in a black pool, surrounding his broken form. Freddy knelt in it, oblivious and quaking. Iain reached out a tentative hand to Tom's throat. The skin was ice cold, the pulse stilled. He clasped Tom's wrist, nothing. How could he find himself in this place again? Why was the trap here? Who had set it?

  He held up the lantern, lancing Freddy with its light. Freddy stared back, tears running down his face. Suddenly Iain knew who and he knew why. "What have you done?" he asked, a mere whisper of disbelief.

Freddy shook his head, noises ripping from his throat, uncontrolled, his face distorted with grief. Iain's mind raced. What should he do? He could not allow Tom to be found here, killed by a trap in Iain's ownership. Would Freddy admit to it or would he blame Iain? He could not risk being blamed. Who would they believe? If Iain's past were disclosed whom would they believe? Not me, he thought, not me.

He pushed Freddy with his boot. "Shut the fuck up." Permission denied, Freddy's sob cracked, half done, although tears slid unchecked down his face. "What are we going to do?" Iain asked.

Freddy shook his head. The idiot was beyond thinking. "You'll have to help me, Freddy."

Freddy managed to stand, body trembling. Iain hung the lantern on a branch. He grasped Freddy by the shoulders and shook him, gentler than he would have wished. "You've got to pull yourself together. Listen to me. Do you want to go to the gallows? Do you want to admit you did this?"

Freddy choked on tears and snot, shook his head, glancing at Tom's corpse. "Then we have to deal with this. Do you understand?" Iain said, and Freddy nodded. "We have to do it now. Do you hear?" Another nod.

Iain grabbed the lantern. Freddy whimpered, abandoned in the blackness. In the house Iain lit a second lamp, placing it in the window. He shut Delilah inside to prevent her drawing attention to them. In the unlikely event anyone should pass, he hoped they would think him at home.

Feeling strangely detached and calm he fetched old sacks from the shed and two shovels. Returning to Freddy, he said, "We have to get this thing off him. Work with me. I can't do it alone." Iain gave firm instructions, slowly easing open the trap, their hands slipping on the stickiness of gristle and sinew. An enormous metal beast, it had virtually severed Tom's legs, efficient in bleeding him dry. It took all their combined strength and dexterity to release its fatal jaws. Tom's body fell heavily between them and their eyes met over the corpse in horror and despair. With the trap safely disabled Iain spoke softly to Freddy as if he were a frightened animal that needed soothing.

"Right, we'll have to wrap him up, because of the blood trail and we don't want anything falling off him." Iain was amazed by the firmness of his own voice, when nausea was pushing for escape and shivers threatened to vibrate his teeth. They wrapped Tom like servants wrapping their king, a mummified Tom, securing the flaps so they would not loosen. Iain picked up the shovels and light.

"You've got to carry him," he said. Freddy backed away shaking his head. "You have to." He came close to Freddy's face, murder in his eyes, on his hands. "Now, listen you little shit, you tried to kill me tonight. Look what you've done. You did this, Freddy, now someone has to carry the light and shovels and someone has to carry the body. Do you understand me? So get your whining English arse into gear and pick it up."

With assistance Freddy heaved Tom onto his shoulder. The weight proved too much, his knees buckled. Iain was obliged to take half the burden and the shovels and lamp combined. He led the way through the trees. Freddy was lost, Iain had confused him, taking them off Harrowmead land up to the Common where the gorse grew thick. A seemingly endless trek – although only a couple of miles. He followed Iain dumbly. It didn't matter where they were going or what they would do when they got there, nothing mattered. The solidity of Tom on his shoulder made him insensible to his surroundings. Nothing mattered, neither the blackness of the night or the icy wet air, only that Tom was on his shoulder – dead. Freddy wanted to be dead, wanted everything to end here and now. He was swallowed whole by this predicament.

Iain searched without knowing exactly what he was looking for. He kept the lantern low, scanning the ground. Somewhere flat, clear of brush, hidden, secluded. Christ, this was impossible. Here would do, anywhere in fact. They set to, digging. Their shovels grated off the earth, the occasional clunk of stone or chalk hitting metal jarred. It began to rain, a steady pitter-patter on bent backs, cooling their sweat. It felt as if it took hours to excavate a big enough hole, arms toiling, backs aching. All the time Iain was on pins, hoping nobody would come this way on such a filthy night. As a precaution he hid the lamp under his jacket for a while and then in the hole as they dug deeper.

Freddy remained silent, his body functioning, his brain disengaged. Iain, conversely, was in a state of mental agitation. Unstoppable plotting, back tracking, whirring round and round, over and over what had happened, what would happen, what might happen. Would Freddy disclose this deed once he recovered his faculties? Would he be able to function like a normal person without arousing suspicion? Would he point the finger at Iain in some continuing revenge? He had no idea.

He jabbed Freddy in the back. They stood in a grave five feet deep, blinking rain from their eyes. Iain hauled himself out of the hole. He offered his hand as if to a friend, to pull Freddy out. Vacantly Freddy threw the spade aside, his face streaked with mud and congealed black blood. They lifted the wrapped body and without ceremony, ritual or prayers threw it into the gaping chasm. Spading lumps of sodden earth, the grave filled, eventually pushing it in with hasty hands and feet until it was full and Iain was telling Freddy to stop because he wouldn't have.

Iain stamped on the ground with solid steps, back and forth, noticing the lack of sward, and mud puddling under his boots. He palmed his knife, cut branches from the gorse and hawthorn bushes, laying them across the place and treading them flat, laying more. The rain fell heavier and heavier. It poured down Iain's back, clothes sticking like a second skin. It would never be hidden enough. He would never be satisfied. He poked Freddy between the shoulder blades to get him moving. Carrying the shovels and lamp they wearily tramped back the way they had come.

Never had Iain been so glad to see his house, the lamp a warm yellow glow in the window. He forced himself to pick up the mantrap, as weighty as death and as cold and evil. Sinew and gore clung tenaciously to the uneven jagged teeth. The flesh was like jelly between his fingers, sticky and foul, it was the only way he could remove it. With numb hands he scrubbed the trap in icy water from a barrel using a stiff boot brush while Freddy cowered by the front door, useless and petrified.

Eventually he admitted defeat. He would never be content. The gore had been washed away, but it would be there forever, he could never wash it from his mind. He grabbed the shovel, thrusting it into the soft black earth. He dug with speed. Cleaning it wasn't good enough - it had to be buried out of sight, vanishing into the earth like Tom. He shoved the dismantled trap out of sight, into the darkness, using his hands to fill in the hole, patting it flat. He knelt for a moment in the dirt, head lowered, calming his breathing and gripping fear.

He took Freddy inside. The kitchen was warm and the range still smouldered. Throwing on two logs, he poked it vigorously with an iron and sparks shot up the black gaping chimney. He closed all the curtains. Freddy was forlorn, arms hanging, expression vacuous. He shivered, dripping all over the tiled floor. Iain fetched towels, a sheet, bowl of water and soap.

"Get those clothes off," Iain ordered. Freddy stared at him stupidly. "Clothes off," he raised his voice and Freddy jumped. With trembling fingers he undid his buttons, struggling to pull off his soaking shirt, trousers dragging on his sore skin. Iain hurled a towel at him, he bent and picked it up. "Wash yourself, get all the muck off. Do a good job mind. When you're done wrap yourself in the sheet. I'll look out something for you to wear."

Iain trudged upstairs, stripped off his clothes. Pimpled with goose flesh he scanned the dark woodland from the window. The heavy rain was rinsing away the evidence, clearing their tracks. He rubbed a hand over his face and gagged at the nasty tart smell of blood mingled with earth, the earth of a grave. He took a towel and, naked, went downstairs past Freddy trying to clean his brother from his face.

At the back of the house Iain plunged his arms into the trough. The water was freezing. He rubbed at the skin on his face, neck and chest, until he could no longer bear the coldness of it. He wiped himself with the towel, the rain steady on his shoulders. Wrapping it around his hips he went inside. Freddy, spine arched over the bowl, scratched at blood that had long since gone.

"That's enough," Iain said. He dressed and hunted out something suitable for Freddy to wear.

He found Freddy perched on the edge of the chair, enveloped by the sheet. His expression had changed, the light returning to his eyes. Iain poured two measures of whisky. Freddy nursed the glass. Iain swallowed his in one and poured another.

"This is your fault," Freddy's voice croaked.

Iain's words spat from his mouth like splinters of glass, "Don't you dare. Don't you fucking dare. It was you. You set it. You broke the lock on the shed, you took the thing out and set it. I didn't, you did."

Freddy's eyes filled with tears. "It wasn't meant for Tom."

"No," Iain said, "it was meant for me. So ask yourself this, you tried to murder me tonight and yet I have helped save your unworthy little neck from the noose."

Freddy's eyes widened, absorbing this truth. "Yes," he said and gulped from the whisky glass. "Yes. Why did you do that?"

Iain reached for a cigarette, lit it, and inhaled deeply. "Because, just because," he lied. "You didn't mean to kill him. It was an accident." He sat down, a picture of calm collection, his serenity a façade. He wanted to strangle Freddy. The deed was done, tracks covered, he was furious. Iain could almost see the light dying in Freddy's eyes and feel the pressure of his hands on Freddy's throat as he squeezed the life out of him.

"We have to stay calm. We have to have a story. You must tell your parents he's gone away." Not very convincing, think, think. The war. "To the war." The story gushed from Iain's lips, unfolding lies, to cover lies. "Yes, he decided to join up and didn't want an argument about it. So he up and went. You'll have to take a few of his clothes before you tell them, make it convincing, as if he packed his stuff." Freddy nodded.

Iain turned away from him, more whisky, more, a whole bottle, two, wouldn't drown this. "It's really up to you. I can't help you now," he said. "Only you can save yourself from the drop. You have to act normal. Tomorrow is another day and you have to get on with it."

"Another day? Get on with it? Tom is dead." Leaning his head on his hand he moaned, "Jesus Christ I've murdered my own brother, Iain. God Almighty, how can I get on with it?"

Iain hunkered down in front of Freddy. "He's not dead, Freddy, he enlisted. He's somewhere training - to be sent to France. You mustn't say more, don't elaborate. You don't know anything else. If you must talk of it, come here, come to see me. Only me. You're getting wed. She must never know, do you understand? She won't marry you if you tell her, and you love her don't you? Don't ever tell her, even when you're wed. It has to be a secret. Repeat the story to yourself, until it's real, until it's true. You must." Iain knew how to make a story true, lies and truth, black and white, it was easy if there were no alternative.

Freddy stared intently into Iain's eyes, hungry for reassurance, for someone to put order back into insanity. Iain touched Freddy's hand, the hand that wanted him dead. "You can do this. Your wedding's in three weeks. You will marry and have children and be happy." Iain wasn't thinking of Nell, she didn't enter his head, not for a moment.

Freddy nodded, Iain's hard-skinned hand on his, grateful for the comfort it gave. "Now, you must dress in these. Bring them back when you can. I'll get rid of your clothes." Iain gestured to the sodden pile on the floor. "When you get home go to Tom's room, take his things, get rid of them. I don't care where. Burning them would be best. Then go straight to bed. Don't let anyone see you or hear you."

With the clothes hanging off him, and a very long oilskin to keep out the rain, Freddy left Keeper's House.

Iain shut the door on him with relief. He took his glass and the whisky bottle and collapsed in the chair.

He remembered endless nights spent in a Scottish prison waiting for the trial. Waiting for the verdict. Waiting for the inevitable death that might follow. Waking from the nightmare of the rope around his neck, the noise of the trap door swinging open, plunging down, jerking awake in the dark cell, sweating and sick with panic. How had he managed to get himself into this predicament? And with Freddy Hart?

Out there, standing in front of the body, in front of Tom, Iain had remembered with horrible golden clarity two young boys playing in the woods. And now, here they were, a corpse gone cold under the wet earth. Is this how it ended? Or was this where it truly started?

On the kitchen table empty cartridges stood testament to his ordinary life, his everyday responsibilities, guns stacked in the corner waiting to be cleaned and oiled. What was the point? He drank steadily and stared into the flames of the fire. Sleep came eventually but he did not go to bed.

Chapter Ten

Waiting was slow torture, seconds ticking on a clock, the sluggish slip of passing hours and days and weeks. Iain waited. His work did not suffer for his mental anguish. Everything was exactly the same as before. The perimeter of Harrowmead estate was neither longer nor shorter than it should be, the weather neither too hot nor too cold. He talked calmly, his tread was as even, each breath as natural and easy. But he marked time waiting, and nothing was right, everything was wrong, messed up and ugly.

When Joanna called at his door, if she found his greeting less warm or his conversation more guarded she did not mention it. Of course, they concentrated on intercourse of a different kind.

He steered clear of the pub and village. He did not want to see Freddy. He did not want to hear what convincing lies Freddy had cobbled for his parents ears. Every day Iain waited for the law to bang on his door. The days that passed did not diminish the threat, merely prolonged the agony.

Four days before Freddy's wedding Iain was in the kitchen with Cook. Nell came in, interrupting their conversation.

Her appearance affected him. He had not seen her since the Harvest Supper. She appeared to be pleased to see him at the table, a mug of tea steaming at his elbow.

"Hello, Iain," she said before turning to Cook, and her words startled him, "Tom was seen at the railway station by Mrs Yeates. So he must have enlisted right enough."

"There you go," Cook said. "I don't know why Mrs Hart was fussing, boys are like that. All looking for a bit of adventure."

He blew on his tea, face devoid of emotion or interest. It was amazing what people saw, he thought, a nerve ticking in his cheek, fighting an impulse to laugh with relief.

"It's nice to see you, Iain," Nell said. "Freddy wants you to come to the wedding. I'm so glad you've sorted your differences." She smiled at him, the sweet expression that lit her whole face. For a moment he didn't know what she was talking about and then he remembered. It was Nell marrying Freddy, not some faceless girl he didn't know. It was Nell. He was appalled.

He choked on his tea, coughed and gagged, slow to halt the reflex. "Sorry, went down the wrong way. Thanks, of course, I'll come." He could not think of a ready excuse.

He pardoned himself swiftly, taking refuge in the gunroom. In the solitude of its windowless walls with the lamplight colouring the plaster, he pressed his hands to his head to dispel the tension. Since that awful night he had found no peace, no relaxation. He was as tense as a coiled spring, every muscle ached, each sinew screamed with the weight of guilt. He could not sleep, eat or think, his hatred for Freddy, a great knot in his chest. He hated the boy, his malice, weakness and stupidity. Freddy had jeopardised the very thing Iain valued most, his freedom.

And now, Nell. How could he save her? He couldn't. Everything had to be normal, no untoward declarations or movements that might betray them. He could not beg her – don't marry Freddy. She would want to know why, women always wanted to know why. He couldn't tell her, how could he?

Seeing that frank expression in her clear blue eyes, unsullied by fear, envy or rage, he knew she deserved so much better. She wasn't getting her match with Freddy. She needed someone reliable and down to earth, an equal, a partner in love and in life. He was sick to the stomach. If only she knew. But hadn't he said it himself to the erring groom? She must never know. He wasn't saving Freddy by not telling her, he was saving himself. If he were implicated in this, it would be the end for him. No second chances, not this time.

As he left the house, standing on the driveway lighting a Woodbine, an upstairs window slid open. Joanna leaned out, her arms on the windowsill, grinning at him. "Hello," she said. "How's my boy today?"

He lifted one eyebrow. "Good." Awful – as bad as he could be.

"I might come down later – maybe." She always aped mystery. He didn't care and she didn't notice. "Did she ask you?"

"Aye, she did."

She paused waiting for him to say more, when he didn't she said, "Well? Are you going?"

He shrugged. "Looks as if I'll have to."

"It's a peace offering isn't it? So, yes, looks as if you'll have to." She laughed knowing he didn't want to go, oblivious to his real reasons. "We'll have to suffer it together."

He blew smoke into the air, narrowing his eyes. "Aye, see you after." He walked across the gravel into the woods with a heavy heart.

* * *

The night before his wedding Freddy knocked on Iain's door. Contractors were in the wood coppicing the ash and hazel. Iain expected them to call, so he was surprised to see Freddy. He invited Freddy into the kitchen and gave him a bottle of beer, because it seemed polite between two men united by circumstance. Iain sat down opposite him.

Freddy threw a bag at Iain's feet. "Your clothes."

"Thanks."

"I told them, as we agreed." Freddy was sullen, he hated this. Being beholden to Iain was like salt in the open wound left by his brother's death.

"Good." Freddy refused the cigarette Iain offered him. Iain lit his and waited for Freddy to speak.

"Why did you do it?"

"I told you before, Freddy, you did it."

"Not that. Why did you help - afterwards?"

"I don't know. I should have called the law."

"I don't think you're telling me the truth, Iain."

"You're a fine one to talk of the truth."

"I know." Freddy swigged from the bottle. "I'm sorry." He wasn't sorry. "I've thought about it. I don't think about much else. I owe you big time and I don't know why. What do you want? Tell me what you want of me. I can't live, waiting like this."

Iain saw Freddy's fear. Freddy had sewn his tissue of lies and during sleepless nights and lonely farm work he had threaded the tale with imaginary threats and terrors. Iain, the bogey man, was biding his time, waiting to call Freddy in. "You owe me, big time," Iain would say. Blackmail, of course, why else would he have done this? Dark smudges of weariness shadowed Freddy's eyes.

Iain shook his head saying, "They believed you, your parents?"

"Yeah, I did what you said. Burned his stuff, told them he'd gone. Then Mrs Yeates said she'd seen him at the station." He gave a pained laugh. "Can you imagine? Stupid bitch."

"Aye, but a helpful one, helpful to you – to us."

He could see hatred glinting in the darkness of Freddy's eyes. "So tell me the price? That's why I'm here."

"There is no price, except your silence. Never speak of it again, that is it. There is nothing between us. No friendship, no secret, no enmity either. I don't want to see you and I don't want any more trouble, we have to leave this alone, not keep on at it."

"Nell's asked you to the wedding." Freddy stared at his distorted reflection in the beer bottle.

"Aye, and I said I would come, I didn't want to offend her. She said you wanted me to come."

"She doesn't want me picking fights, keeping things going with you. I told her we'd patched things over. She said if we're friends you'd best come to the wedding or something like that. Would have been odd, my saying I didn't want you there." And he didn't want Iain there, or anywhere. "It's one day, anyway, it doesn't matter who's there. Nothing much matters any more."

"No. It's hard," he said inhaling smoke, blowing it down his nostrils.

"It wasn't only the hatchet we buried, was it?" Freddy said.

There was no answer worth giving. "There's one more thing," Iain said, "about Helena."

Freddy narrowed his eyes with suspicion. "What about her?"

"Treat her well, she deserves so much better."

His laugh was sharp, disbelieving. "Like you?"

"No."

"I've seen the way you look at her. She's not one of your tarts. Screwing her sister aren't you? Second best is she? You don't half pick them."

Iain refused to be riled by these petty remarks - the best Freddy could manage. "I'll see you Saturday, on you go."

Dismissed, Freddy left his unfinished beer on the table. The wind caught the door as he let himself out and it slammed.

Iain slipped a bottle of whisky into his pocket and wandered out into the dark night. Every seven years contractors cut the under wood at Harrowmead, an area to the north, fenced to keep out deer and livestock. The two woodsmen were brothers, Harry and Ted Barrow, with two acres each to take them through until spring. They made hurdles, roof spars for thatch, tied bundles of bean and pea sticks, brushwood faggots for kindling, ash wood for ladder poles, tools and handles. He had little need to check up on them, although he did so anyway. He was unused to having company in the woods and if a day or two passed without him visiting, they would call at Keeper's House.

He found them now outside Harry's little shelter by a crackling fire. Isaac had joined them, passing a bottle of cider amongst them. He was warmly received, invited to join them. He offered the whisky round and listened to their combined tall tales, each trying to out do the other. His black mood sank into the spirit bottle and their stories lulled him into another place, until he laughed at their jokes and joined in with their banter.

Saturday arrived and he decided he would not go to the wedding. He had not counted on Joanna flushing him out. Knocking on the door at ten in the morning, dressed in her best, she was flushed and excited, hopping around on his doorstep.

"I'm not going." Easy to say, except he meant it, sitting back in his chair drinking stewed tea, with a cigarette burning between his fingers.

"Yes, you are. You told me you were. Anyway, you have to go."

"I don't have to do anything. Why the hell would I want to go to Freddy Hart's wedding?"

"Why would you not? You've made up. You accepted the invite, you're being pigheaded and rude."

"What's it got to do with you? It's none of your business." He was not in the mood for her today. He was increasingly not in the mood for her. From the minute he opened his eyes to the weak December sunshine, the depression had descended. There were no colours today, nothing pleasurable or nice. He was all black, sour and hard, like a cough sweet in a glass jar. He was not going to humour Joanna or anyone else.

"So, what's the problem?"

"You're my problem. Bugger off. Leave me alone." He inhaled the smoke, closing his eyes, laying his head back on the chair. "You don't understand."

"No I don't and neither will Freddy or Nell."

"He'll understand. Say sorry to Helena."

"You want to show me up. Now I've nobody to escort me. How shall that look? I could have said yes to several young men I'll have you know. You're selfish, it's always about you."

"You're talking about yourself, Joanna. You can't see beyond your own wants. Nobody else exists for you."

She tapped her foot in front of him furiously. "It's as if you're two different people. The one I like and the one I hate."

He opened his eyes and regarded her coldly. "So you hate me, now get lost."

"I could have gone to the wedding with Colonel Edam's son. He keeps asking to see me, trying to spoon with me. He's going to be an officer in the cavalry, his father has a motor car."

He beckoned her closer and she moved to obey. He darted forward and pulled her roughly onto his lap by her wrist, holding her firmly so she could not escape. His face was two inches from hers. "Then he's welcome to you. Spooning with him is no threat to me. I wish you would go to him. Good luck to you both and hell mend you, lady." She tried to free herself. He released her, there was no struggle, he didn't want her.

"Do I mean nothing? Am I just someone to take to bed?"

He stood up too. "And what do I mean to you? If you've men falling at your feet and I only want you for a screw, then why don't you piss off?"

No one had ever spoken to her like that. She did not wait for further abuse, turning on her heel and banging the door on purpose as she exited. It rebounded and was left wide open letting in the freezing winter air. Delilah slunk in. He wearily closed it and returned to his chair. Delilah pushed her black domed skull under his hand and absently he ruffled the short hair under his fingers and smoothed her soft ears.

His only option was to stay away. How could he sit mute and bound watching Nell joined in marriage to Freddy Hart? To stand witness to the masquerade of a religious ceremony, followed by polite conversation and a glass of sherry at the wedding breakfast, he could not do it. His silence deceived her totally. He hadn't warned her – Freddy isn't what he seems – she was ambushed by their wordless betrayal.

Desolation stifled him, an albatross hugging his neck. He wished Joanna had not left, wished she were here to hold, someone warm and alive. He hated himself and what he was doing. Delilah pushed her wet nose into his stilled palm. He leaned forward, hands hugging her black face.

"Come on, you, time we were about, eh? Work to do." She sprang up and hopped round the room in excitement, nails ticking on the hard floor. She yipped as he stood, turning circles to catch her tail.

* * * *

"It was a lovely service, a good turn out." Cook's solid able hands stripped the skin from a yellow onion. She paused with the knife hovering over the fibrous root, her eyes misting with onion fumes and romance, gazing into the middle distance. "She looked a picture."

Iain conveyed his pie laden fork to his mouth, elbows on the table.

"Mrs Hart's sister put on some nice grub," Meg the tweeny said, trotting through to the scullery.

"She did," Cook confirmed, rubbing her eyes roughly with the back of her hand. "Nell's aunt came. Not her mother, she doesn't keep well."

He chewed silently.

"They went to a hotel in Bournemouth for two nights. A present from Mr Hart."

He could imagine the hotel room, the swagged curtains and carpeted floors, probably with a view of the sea, grey and flat as slate. He could not see the bed, although it was there in the room behind him, vast and horrible - a marriage bed.

Concentrate on the food, he told himself, breaking the piecrust with the side of his fork. He would not listen to any more, except he couldn't do anything else.

"Shame his brother didn't come back for the wedding, I don't know why he didn't wait until after to run off and join up. There's talk you know."

"What talk?" Meg returned from the scullery asking the pertinent question.

"They're saying he was in love with Nell himself, couldn't bear to see them wed and he and Freddy argued over her, so he left." Cook added the onion to the simmering pot on the black range. She lifted a cloth from the proven bread, dragged out the dough in capable fingers; it stretched glutinously as she kneaded it.

He managed to swallow the dry crust that turned to cardboard as he swallowed. "Is she coming back?" he said.

"To work? No, she's a farmer's wife now. She's done all right for herself. She doesn't need to be working in someone else's kitchen."

"Aye, but it's not really her kitchen is it?"

"Mrs Hart's right poorly, a weak heart. She needs looking after. She went to the wedding of course. She looks awful ill. She left the reception early, had to be taken home."

A sick room, Freddy's ailing mother, Nell, young and strong. How appalling. "So Helena's a nursemaid?"

She shrugged. "Hadn't thought of that. She certainly will be a help to Mrs Hart."

He nodded slowly, pushing his plate away. Nell - housekeeper, cook, maid, nurse, farmer and legal concubine, a heavy workload, no time off and no wage. She had married into slavery. It was a high price to pay for having her own kitchen. And she would work hard, her dynamic little figure getting stuck in with enthusiasm. The bloom in her cheek would die, her brow crease, her beautiful chestnut hair fade to grey. Slow, relentless work grinding her down, babies and chores sapping her youth. That remarkable smile, neglected, forgotten, put in a cupboard to collect cobwebs, lost and defunct. Sacrificed to Freddy Hart, when Iain could have taken her and hidden her so easily. He closed his eyes and breathed deeply, what an absurd idea. Why hadn't he warned her?

He abruptly scraped back his chair and Cook jumped, glaring at him.

"You all right, Iain?" she asked. He was pale as whey. He looked into her ruddy round face and, for a second, she saw the raw anguish reflected in his eyes, sorrow furrowing his features. She rested a floury hand on his sleeve. "What is it, Iain?"

He shook his head. "Life. It's life isn't it? It all rests on the flip of a coin, a fork in the road." She could see bright yellow flecks like sparks in the green of his iris. He laughed suddenly. "It's nothing, nothing. I'm fine." He picked up his shotgun. "I'll see you after." False cheer edged the phrase.

* * * *

From an upstairs window Joanna watched Iain walk down the drive, her heart twisting in her chest. She had made decisions. She would forgive his little tantrum over the wedding and all the things he had dared to say. It was not important any more and neither was he, not to her, he never had been. She had applied for a position in Bath as a ladies maid. She had a gentleman to meet and wed, a life to lead, a decent life. She couldn't live this rural idyll, especially now with Nell playing farmer's wife all loved up. Soon there would be babies crawling on Nell's knee and Joanna would not even be able to visit her.

Chapter Eleven

Light spring evenings stretched Iain's day, the hatching pheasants brought renewed purpose and routine. He fussed over them, orphaned and reliant. Any victims to hawk or frost were a personal defeat, a challenge lost. On the whole they grew and prospered, gun fodder for the autumnal shoot.

Poaching engaged his wandering thoughts, poisoned grain, a bleating girl with a bursting sack of trout, snares, and nets across the river, minor mishaps to test him. Iain caught a pair of lurchers shredding a pheasant, and shot them both in front of their thieving master. A close miss with night poachers earned him two sawn-off guns. The incidents stacked up like village gossip, each one minor in isolation but collectively, a grudge against the keeper, tiresome and wearing.

Mr Denham, eccentric and aimless, was taking his family to Essex for the summer. Miles Denham had enlisted and was at a training camp fifty miles away. Mrs Denham wanted to visit her brothers before they chased commissions abroad with the uniformed masses.

On the morning of his departure Mr Denham walked the farthest reaches of the estate with his keeper. Game, poachers, war and the cost of living, subjects touched upon and never quite concluded. Mr Denham was about to take his leave when he remembered about the horse.

"Could you take a look at Phoenix? He has been restless all night, Mr Judd can't do anything with him. Asked if you'd take a look, I know you're quite good at that sort of thing. Miles would be most upset if anything happened to him."

Iain agreed, of course, accompanying his employer towards the house.

Iain ducked inside the shady stable, ripe with horse sweat and hay. Phoenix flashed a white-rimmed eye. His breathing was stertorous and his nervous whinny pained, as he restlessly changed legs. The damp chestnut flank matched the heat of Iain's hand. As he whispered half formed comforts into the furry ear, the pink velvet muzzle twitched. He smoothed the broad neck, his tone hushed and calm. Moving the pressure of his palm along Phoenix's back, under his stomach, the coat bristled, rippling with discomfort and annoyance. Iain pressed his ear to the warm curved belly. Phoenix standing stock-still was aware but trusting. Mr Denham watched from the stable door with Mr Judd who, arms folded, chewed on a piece of straw, a methodical bovine action as if he were reverting.

Iain resumed his quiet dialogue with the animal while stroking the hair on its neck and down to the nose. "Vet been out?" he asked, loud compared with how he spoke to the horse.

Mr Judd handed him a bottle of ink black liquid, *'Pattersons Cure-All for Colic and related Stomach Conditions in Equines. Recommended by the Royal Veterinary College'*. He sniffed it suspiciously, alcohol and liquorice.

"Has he been rolling?"

"Nope," Mr Judd said. "What you thinking?"

He made a face, why did they think he would know? He shrugged. He would do his best. "I think we should try rolling him."

Mr Judd and Mr Denham nodded in agreement. Judd called Paul the stable lad who fetched Eric the head gardener. With manpower assembled they tied a rope round the branch-slim legs. Instructing Paul to pull gently, Iain and Eric helped support the horse down onto the dusty floor. Iain's gentle whisperings continued to calm and soothe. Keeping clear of the hooves they rolled Phoenix over, side, to back, to side. Iain again laid his hands on the animal's flank, then his ear. There was a reverential silence while he listened. Phoenix was at peace as he massaged the horse's stomach, rhythmic hands working, diminishing circles, up and down its flank.

"What d'you think it is?" Judd stooped down beside him.

"Might be bad colic or a twisted gut maybe. I'll sit with him a while."

The spectators dispersed, chores required attention. Iain was left alone. He could feel the horse's pain, through hands aching with heat and motion. The horse's relief became Iain's unease. This wasn't something new, he had done this before. Not often, in a strange way it repelled him, he didn't like this transference of condition, or whatever it was, this – thing – he could do. Isaac had seen him do it, had never let him forget it either. Even so, Iain hated it broadcast, he didn't have the time or inclination.

In the deepening quiet of the stable he closed down his thoughts to concentrate his mind on the horse. He could feel its distress seeping away, the tension and pain draining from muscle and ligament. He leaned back, the rough cob wall uncomfortable behind him. Working on the horse had left him too exhausted to move. Silence surrounded them for a time, air heavy with hay dust and drying sweat, the in and out swish of the horse's lungs, a shared peace, equine and human.

"I've been looking for you." Nell leaned her forearms on the half-door. Her hair, escaping from under a knitted hat, curled around her face. It was the same colour as the horse's coat with strands of gold and red running through it. Her cheeks were flushed pink with the exertion of the walk from the farm.

He had not seen her or Freddy since their marriage. She was expecting a baby in September, Joanna had told him.

It was late afternoon and he realised he had been with the horse for hours. He tugged gently at Phoenix's head collar, repeating the same quiet tones as before. In a sudden rush the horse pulled himself up onto solid legs. Calm inky black eyes thickly lashed stared, his breathing quiet and his flank cool to the touch.

"Good boy," he said. "You feeling better? You want some water?" He walked over to the half door.

"What's wrong with him?" she asked.

"Bellyache I shouldn't wonder."

"Do the grooms often call you to do their job?" she asked smiling.

"Only if the animal's really poorly, usually after the vet's been called and it's done no good." He lit a cigarette. "I don't mind. Animals are more reliable than people."

She nodded in agreement, watching the horse. "You've not had much luck with people."

"Could say that, I suppose. Maybe it's me – I don't know. On the whole, I don't like the human race," he said it with humour, but he meant it.

"That's very distrustful. It was your upbringing. You'd look at things differently if you'd had the love and support of a family. You have to trust somebody sometime. And you have no faith either, no God to call upon."

He shook his head. "Don't worry, I don't lose out. I think I've gained from it. No wasted hours kneeling in a church talking to the air." He laughed at her expression of disapproval.

"Everyone needs something, Iain, someone, even you."

"No, I don't. Anyway, you didn't come here to give me religious guidance or preach on the goodness of mankind. What can I do for you, Helena?"

She said, "I think I'm about to prove your theory correct on the reliability of man – and woman. Have you seen Joanna lately?"

He wasn't listening. Four months had passed uncounted, slipped away with the drudge of every day and he had managed to keep his mind occupied, filled with irrelevancies. Now she was here anyway, despite all that difficult distraction and mind-bending denial. He wished she wasn't here, or he wished she had come before. To put his hands on her face, feel the softness of her hair between his fingers ... Look away, don't even think of it. But he couldn't look away when there were words he wanted to say, that he couldn't even begin to think, never mind speak. She squirmed under his intense gaze and he forced himself to lower his eyes.

"Have you seen her?" she repeated.

"Who?"

"Joanna." Slight exasperation sounded in her tone.

"No, I've not seen her." He had not seen her since she had told him about Nell's baby. She had been increasingly distant after the wedding. It was as if, that day, she had seen the other side of him. He presumed she had not liked it very much. He could not change who he was, if she wanted to go cool on him, he would accept it. Their physical relationship had petered out. He wondered if her recent absence may be due to a new diversion, perhaps Colonel Edam's son had come courting after all.

"I think you should see her, Iain."

"Do you? Why is it your concern?" He opened the stable door, she stepped back. "I need to get water for the horse."

Mr Judd was grooming Mrs Denham's mare. "He's a bit better, Mr Judd. I'll come back tomorrow and see how he is. I think he could do with some water."

Mr Judd left the mare and followed Iain, walking lopsided with the slopping bucket. Nell was still waiting patiently. "Good grief," Judd said, "you're a genius. How did you manage that?" Phoenix pulled some hay out of the rack on the wall, unconcerned, chewing sedately.

"Don't know really. Good luck I suppose."

"Well, Mr Denham's gone on his way now, but I'll be sure to tell him the miracle you've worked here," he said. Nell listened, studying Iain while he was distracted. His hair had grown to his collar, spiked at the cow's lick from his worrisome hand. He needed a shave. The shadow accentuated the cleft on his chin, the curve of his upper lip. The open necked shirt, frayed at the collar, displayed the smooth column of his pale throat. The spring sun had burnished his skin and with his dark hair he resembled some exotic foreigner.

"I assure you, Mr Judd, it's no miracle. I don't do miracles." He washed his hands under the running tap in the stable yard and dried them on a piece of sacking hung from a hook. "Come on," he said to Nell since she obviously wasn't leaving.

"Mr Judd was impressed," she said.

"Doesn't take much to impress folk round here. They're all so superstitious it's untrue. They think your fortune's written in the clouds, or on the soot of the fire back."

"I thought you might go and see Joanna." She restrained him by putting her fingers on his arm. At the back of the stable block an abundance of young nettles grew very green against the warm red wall, the shadow of woodland on one side and the glum gardens on the other.

"No," he said observing her hand, "why should I?"

She withdrew it, clicking her tongue with agitation. "For goodness sake, Iain, stop being difficult. She'll be really cross with me for speaking to you as it is."

"I'm not being difficult," he said bemused. "I don't want to see her, unless you give me a good reason. How's Freddy?" As if he cared.

"He enlisted, he leaves in two days for training," she said.

"What about the farm? Who's going to run that? I didn't think anything would drag him away."

"Maybe once upon a time that was the case. Now I don't know. He doesn't seem to care much about it anymore. Before we married it was his life. Now he doesn't bother one way or the other, he can't wait to go." He obviously mystified her, she didn't understand why he wasn't the same man who had courted her.

"And are you happy?"

She was taken aback. Happy? She was barely wed. "Of course."

"Why, of course? Being married to Freddy doesn't guarantee happiness."

"He's going away. He's doing essential work on the farm, he didn't have to go, not yet anyway. What does that say about me – or about us?" she said hesitantly, then to justify it, "All the men are going."

"I thought you were a fool to marry him. You could have done better than that." The words shot out, vindictive somehow.

"What, even though you've patched things up? Is that why you didn't come to the wedding?"

"Sorry I didn't come, I'm not very good at that kind of thing," he said. "I thought…" he could not tell her what he thought.

Her eyes were fixed on him, unwavering, waiting for more. The silence stretched between them and they stared at each other. She did not look away, blush or fidget. His stomach wrenched, plummeting sickness, fear or crushing disappointment.

Suddenly she spoke, "I know," a soft penitent whisper, "I understand."

What did she know? What did she understand? The words stuck in his craw, he was quite parched, could barely swallow.

She gave a little cough to clear her throat. He had sidetracked her. "I have something important to say. Stop this. Listen. Joanna is going away today. I don't think she'll be coming back."

He widened his eyes at the revelation. "What's happened?"

"You need to go and see her. Ask her yourself, before it's too late. She won't listen to me. Her mind is quite made up."

"Made up to what? To leave? If she wants to go, what can I do?" he asked. He wanted her to leave. Now Nell had said it, he realised he longed for Joanna to go.

"There's more than that, more to it I mean." Her hand unconsciously covered her stomach, not yet swollen by the child she carried.

His eyes flickered to her hand and back to her face, understanding, pole-axed from above. "A baby."

She nodded. "You must speak to her."

"I see." A baby, Christ, he didn't see. "So why is she going away? Whose is it?"

"It's yours." How did he dare to ask? Disgust flickered in her eyes. "Please go and ask her, not me and don't tell her I told you. I have to go. I don't want her to see me. Be kind. She doesn't mean to be difficult, it's the way she is." The brief light of a sad smile shone on her face before she left him alone.

Iain retraced his steps through the stable yard to the house. He had been careful, he had always been so careful – but not that first time. That first time, the morning of the hunt, he had been sloppy like a first timer himself. Idiotic and senseless, a lust-struck fool.

He clicked his fingers and Delilah sank onto the stone steps to wait. Cook was in the kitchen drinking a cup of tea with her feet resting on a chair

"Hello Iain. Everyone's gone." She slurped her tea. "The Denhams, Nanny and Butler. The house is closing for the summer," she said. Her silly assumption irritated him. She must realise that he and Mr Denham had discussed it, he was the keeper after all, he ran the estate. Still, she continued. "The rest of us house staff go tomorrow, once all the clearing up's finished, except for Miss High-and-mighty. She's off to heaven knows where. One minute it's Bath, the next the coast. I don't think she knows herself. Buckingham Palace for all I know."

"Joanna?"

"Yes, she's packing. Taking the train tonight. I gather that's why you're here?"

He was out of the door, running up the backstairs two at a time. The hall was quiet, except for Ruby the housemaid singing as she cleaned the parlour. He took the front stairs, solely for family use, to the first floor. He did not see the harm since they were not here. The gimlet-eyed housekeeper Mrs Harris watched him from the landing.

"What are you doing, Mr Macdonald?" Her voice was cutting.

"Mrs Harris, how nice to see you looking so well."

She narrowed her eyes. "What are you doing?"

"I need to see Joanna. She's leaving and I must see her before she goes. It's quite urgent."

"Is it?" she asked.

"Have you done something different with your hair? You know you really look rather fetching."

Her mouth opened in shock, cheeks flushing puce. Her tentative hand prodded her hair. "Well, really, Mr Macdonald." A smile played at the corners of her stern mouth. "Take the servants stairs, two floors up in the attic, second door on the left and don't be long about it. It's not seemly." She inspected her reflection in the hall mirror, turning this way and that.

Joanna's bedroom door was closed. He knocked. "Come in," her reply was weary.

She went pale at the sight of him. She held a folded petticoat, pulled it up to her stomach defensively. "What the hell are you doing here?"

"Charming. I heard you were going away. I came to say goodbye."

"Who told you I was going away?"

"Cook, just now. What's this about Bath? Why are you going?" He sat on her bed as if it were his right. The ceiling sloped, closing in on two single beds and an overly large wardrobe between them. She had shared this tiny space with Nell before her marriage. No wonder she had been impressed with Keeper's House, the room was tiny. The little window had a limited view of the wood, and beyond somewhere below out of sight was the driveway.

She frowned at him as if he might dirty the bedcover. "I've had enough of it here. I told you I hate it. I've got better things planned." She put the petticoat in her suitcase. The bulge of her stomach, hidden under clothing and no doubt strapped up with corsetry, was not overly apparent, except he was looking for it.

"Tell me the truth, Joanna." He reached out an arm to pull her down beside him.

She was cross, she had not wanted this exchange. She wanted to leave unchallenged and without confrontation. "You've spoken to Nell," she said flatly.

"Were you leaving without telling me? What are you going to do?" Colour flooded her cheek. She smelt of rose water.

"Since you ask, I'm getting rid of it."

Her declaration nailed his feet to the floor, flayed the skin from his bones. He was barely alive and then she spoke and he was whole again, feet firm, voice hard. "You can't."

"I'll deal with it," she said. This was the simple, planned truth that had kept her awake for nights, fretful for days. How easy for him not to anticipate what she had eaten, drunk and wept for weeks, with the bile burning up her neck and the sickness in her fertile stomach.

"How are you getting rid of it? When is it due?"

"July. I'm arranging for an adoption of some sort." Her manner was brusque, standing up, discussion over. "Now I need to get on."

"Is it my baby?"

Her eyes flared, enraged. How typical of a man! "Of course it is. What do you think I am?"

He stood up too, bending his head to allow for the ceiling. "I don't know what you are, Joanna. You said you're giving it away. You can't give it away."

"Why not?"

Why not, he thought, tell her why not. His mind raced. "Because," he paused, "because you can't."

"I can, I will. It's none of your business. I'm not ruining my life bringing up your baby. I've got plans. I can have the baby, get rid of it, and then live my life. I won't settle for second best. I had a good job secured in Bath until I found out about this." She prodded her stomach with her thumb.

"You cold heartless witch. Do you only think of yourself? What about the baby?"

She did not flinch at his words, she would not be browbeaten after all her heart searching and tears. "What about it? It won't remember. It won't know any different."

"What if it isn't loved? What if they treat it badly? You won't know." He wanted to shake her until her teeth rattled.

"I don't care. Why think the worst? It might go to a family with money."

"Money isn't important."

"It is when you've got none."

"I don't mean that. For all the money in the world, if there is no compassion or love..." he faltered.

"What do you know about compassion and love?"

"Nothing." He sat down again deflated. "That's the point – nothing. If you give it away it will be..."

She waited for him to finish, when he didn't she said, "What will it be?"

His head leaned into his hands, fingers pale in the blackness of his hair. "It will be like me." It was a lame finish to a heartfelt concern.

Joanna's bitter-lemon laugh was scathing. "Then God help it, all the more reason not to keep it."

"You won't give it away." There was nothing about her he recognised. There was no beauty in her, there never had been. He hated her.

"I will," she said in her determined cold voice. "I will and you can't stop me. Or do you want it? Yes, is that it, do you want the baby?"

He was appalled. "You know I couldn't."

"You couldn't, but you expect me to. Who would want me with a baby? Nobody decent that's for sure. It's a mistake and I'm not paying for it for the rest of my life. Of course you don't want it," that bitter laugh again. "All too happy to make them. Not so thrilling, is it, having to bring them up?" She turned from him to hide her tears. "Please go, Iain."

"Why are you doing this to me? Why could we not talk about it?"

"Because you might have persuaded me to settle for this." She gestured with her arms, enveloping the room, Harrowmead he presumed. "I don't want to be persuaded. It's not about you." She shook her head, wiping away tears. He was hunched over, too big for the size of the room. She suddenly knelt in front of him, her hands on his knees. "I'm sorry, Iain. I'm not doing this to hurt anyone. Be honest, neither of us want this. You don't want to marry me."

He couldn't answer yes I do, of course I do. They were hollow platitudes so false he couldn't bring himself to say them. He could never marry Joanna. It would be a marriage in name, hateful and cold. His silence was so ghastly in the claustrophobic tiny space it filled the air like a bubble, growing bigger and bigger, threatening to explode and pierce their eardrums.

"Your enthusiasm is overwhelming!" her voice popped it and he flinched. "At any rate, I would not have accepted. I don't want to marry you. You're a strange man, Iain. Somewhere hidden in there is a type of charm – I think. When it comes down to it, you're happy alone, living somewhere – somewhere like this with your trees and fields. You're too self-reliant. You don't need anybody or want anybody. You're moody and depressive. If you want someone at all it would be someone who would bend to your will. I could never live like that. Look at me, it's for the best, one day you'll see." She transformed again, stern-lipped, back to business, she snapped the case shut and put on her hat and coat.

"I'll carry that," he said taking the case from her. Was he that bad a prospect? Oh, yes and worse, so much worse than she knew. He didn't want someone to bend to his will. It was a ludicrous suggestion. Closer to the truth, he didn't want anyone, he could never imagine it either. Nell was right, he was too distrustful, and Joanna's actions proved his point. Trust was a sure path to lies and deceit, love the direct route to pain and hate. It occurred to him he was no better than his own father, Bruce Sinclair, laird and martyr, no better, no worse. No consolation there.

She paused in the doorway, facing him. "Alan Stock asked me to marry him," she said.

"Alan Stock?"

She giggled, the unhappiest sound he had ever heard. "Yes, can you imagine? He's such a bumpkin and his jaw clicks when he talks."

"Did you refuse him because of the baby?"

"No, he's besotted. I don't think he would much care about the baby. If I sprouted another head he wouldn't care. I refused him because I can do better. I know I can."

He followed her down the stairs. "How are you getting to the station?" he said.

"I asked Paul to help with my case. Please go now, Iain." They arrived at the front door.

"Who knows? Does Alan know?" he asked.

"Nobody knows. Nobody must know. Only Nell, she won't tell anyone," another sharp laugh. "Oh, except she told you. Can't rely on anyone, can you?"

"What about Freddy?"

"Definitely not Freddy," she stated firmly.

He did not know how to take his leave. "Don't do it," he said.

"Goodbye," she said. His eyes bored into her, trying to understand. She could not look him in the eye and turned away awkwardly. "Goodbye," she repeated.

"I'll never forgive you for this," he muttered. At that moment he saw only her weakness, not his own, never his own. Indignant and abused.

"I don't want forgiveness. I don't need it." She stuck her nose in the air, tilting her chin in defiance. He stalked away. No looking back. It doesn't matter, none of it matters. He stormed to the back of the house, heavy footed, torn, and whistled for Delilah who scrabbled to her feet in a cloud of gravel and dirt.

Chapter Twelve

In the dying embers of the fire Iain remembered other evenings drinking under the night sky, slugging away the past, spitting on the future. Finnigan, lifting a whisky bottle to his lips, haggard face shadowed, heavy gruff laughter that chilled like ice, never reaching his eyes. On such nights they kept company with Big Dougie, Alec, Old Tam, woodsmen who worked the bow saws felling the forests for the giant sawmills. Hard men with few comforts, long hours of toil whatever the weather. Finnigan and Iain understood their lives. Although their accommodation was superior, the job could be equally tough.

He wondered if these men he used to drink with still lived or if, like Finnigan, they were cold and rotting under the earth. He used to drink more back then. A lifeline from the age of twelve when he decided to take the bottle Finnigan handed him. Initially it knocked him out and he woke up lying in his own vomit. Big Dougie was a kind man, he told Iain not to drink but Finnigan shouted him down. "Be a man, drink like a man," Finnigan said. So Iain tried to be a man. It did not matter how evil Finnigan was, or how much Iain hated him, he still tried to please the keeper, his keeper. No matter how gargantuan the effort, he never won Finnigan's approval. He did disapproval, disappointment, disgust, and by the bucket load.

He wasn't surprised to feel the weight of Finnigan's hand across his head. The boy had been hit before and harder too. The nuns were handy with the cane, lashes that left red welts across the bottom and thighs, the skin peeling back from the pressure.

Isaac brought him back to the present. "What you thinking lad? You've gone all quiet on me." They were outside the shepherd's hut, with the accompanying hiss of the fire and a lifetime of stars as shelter.

"Different times, Isaac, times past."

"You're a long way from home, son, do you miss it?"

"Scotland? Aye. No. I don't know. They weren't good days for me. They were tough times, y'know?"

"You brought up in a kids home?"

"Aye, it wasn't the home, although that was tough – sometimes – not all the time. There was a kind of ritual, you knew what to expect. It was after really, when I worked for the gamekeeper." He never spoke about Finnigan to anyone. He must be getting soft, he thought.

"Was he bad to you?"

"A bad bastard." He swigged from his beer bottle, Delilah slumped at his side and opposite him Isaac, lit by the glow of the fire. "Have you got children, Isaac?"

He smiled his stumpy gummy smile. "I did. I have."

"Tell me. Tell me about your children." The alcohol was unwinding his knotted muscles, his tied tongue.

Isaac scanned the clear night sky contemplating his answer. "Sons, a daughter, a wife. Had it all once, a lifetime ago."

"I can relate to a lifetime ago, tell me." Iain passed the whisky bottle, a chaser to their beer.

"I had a wife called Isobel. A Romany girl, hair as black as jet, curls," Isaac smiled at the sky, "a figure," he waved his hands to indicate her shape, "beautiful. And we was happy too. That was when I travelled about in me caravan. Though I was born here." The thumb he jabbed at the ground indicated right here, this very spot. This was where he came from, he had staked a claim long ago. "Started with a son, Benjamin, fine big boy. Saw him born, delivered him with these here hands." He waved his fingers in the air. "A daughter next with big black eyes. We called her Jezebel, probably is one too, like her mother. Followed by two more boys, Jacob and Luke. Had a family, can you imagine, a proper family?" He smiled at the alcohol-warmed memory, more cordial and pleasing than the reality.

"What happened, tell me?" Iain encouraged him, enthralled by the tale, the figures of his beautiful wife and handsome children dancing in the erratic flare of the fire.

Isaac threw on a log, shooting sparks, wife and children into the black night sky.

"Gone, all gone, Iain," he said. "She left me, took the children. Up and went like only a true Romany can. I was left behind, always wanted to belong, see? Didn't want to leave, didn't want to move on. And she found Lazarus, a shaman, told her he was her destiny. And destiny he was, spirited her away in the middle of the night without a by your leave. Children and all. What d'you say to that, young Scot?"

Iain studied the fire, tongues of flame licking at the branches. "Do you see the future, Isaac, are you a shaman?"

"What proper Romany shaman?" He shook his head.

"Aye, can you see what's ahead of us?" Iain was drunk, head fuzzy, his words falling easily out of his mouth.

"Sometimes I understand things, don't know. I see your gift. I see what you are capable of, but you pay me no heed, young Scot. I see you at war," Isaac said nodding.

"No," Iain said. "I've no calling to go to war. They send me feathers."

"Feathers?"

"Aye," he said, snorting through his nose at the absurdity. "Half the village, I think, enough to fill a pillow." He vastly exaggerated, but Isaac laughed. "White feathers to show me for the coward I am."

"Good for you." Isaac upended the whisky bottle to his open mouth and returned it to Iain. "You don't follow the crowd. They're sheep, all of them, falling off the cliff. You will follow, you have no choice."

Iain was intrigued. He couldn't think straight for the drink. "Do I have children, Isaac? Do you see that for me?"

"D'you want them?"

He laughed, everything suddenly amusing, even the birth of a bastard child. "No," he admitted, "but hell, do you see them?" As if by saying so it would all be different.

Isaac laughed uproariously at his insistence. Finally he admitted, "Yeah, I see them. A son first with black hair, like you, cat's eyes, like you. She tries to deny you as the father, but it is you." He raised his beer bottle and pointed an accusatory finger. "You deny him too."

Through the strength of the spirit Iain knew fear. He hated predictions, he hated himself for asking for it. Why would Joanna deny him as the father? Maybe she had another father in mind. Maybe that was why she left. But why would he deny it himself?

Isaac was still talking. "You have daughters too, young Scot," he said, "more than one, more than two." He chuckled away the fear, an infectious sound that started Iain off too. They laughed until their stomachs hurt, until their eyes streamed, until Iain could not remember what had made them laugh.

"Daughters," Isaac reminded him, shrieking hysteria, drink and gypsy magic. It was easy to believe in this spot of light in the midst of darkness and encroaching shadows, limitless space above.

Iain sobered, stopped laughing. He could not imagine having daughters, no not women. The father of women, what an extraordinary thought. He hoped in the morning he would not remember this, but he did.

Sticky eyed and with a raging thirst, his head thumped, wincing at the light easing through the curtains. He had dreamed of Tom. Sitting on the bank of the river, smoking, laughing and talking, senseless conversation beyond his recollection. The light reflected off the water on Tom's face, dancing in his brown eyes. His passive benign calm was the antithesis of Freddy. Cain and Abel.

Tom's legs wept blood. The blood dripped then poured, into the river until it ran red. He slid down the bank into the water. Iain tried to grab him. It was as if his hands were oiled and he had no strength in them and Tom was gone. Vanished, swallowed by the frothing, scarlet flow.

Iain shivered, feet jarring on the floor. He dressed, stacked fuel on the range, put the kettle on to boil. He was shaky, tired, aching, poisoned by dreams and alcohol.

He had let Joanna go and been glad to. Push it away, all of it, pile it up with the dross, locked in a place he never visited. Finnigan, Bruce Sinclair, Tom and Joanna, none of it had to exist here, now, in the moment of picking up the kettle, pouring steaming water on the black heaped leaves, tin spoon clanging against cup.

Spring had turned to summer and he heard nothing, the routine of the seasons taking hold. It was strange having no one up at the house, no game needed for the dinner table. He missed Cook, their conversations, her practical no-nonsense observations and physical presence. He would be glad when they returned in August.

He visited the pub once or twice a week to stay abreast of gossip, not for drinking. He drank heavily at home. Poachers passed on their goods at the local pub so it paid to keep eyes and ears open. A tip off was often said in passing while having a pint.

Another Sunday and the church bell tolled, a muffled pious calling, demanding attendance for prayer. Three cups of tea and two Woodbines later he set off to confront the day. A beautiful day, even in the cool shade of the trees the air was warm in the lungs. A pair of fat pigeons cooed companionably in the beech trees, the gentle rustle of the leaves a conspiratorial secret. Walking towards the river, a great stand of foxgloves grew, spires of deep pink, inset with cream and purple spots. The bees buzzed lazily in and out of the flower cups. His head thumped.

He saw a suitable branch for old Mr Baker who fashioned walking sticks, long and coiled from the embrace of the honeysuckle. The scent tickled his unappreciative nose, thick as syrup. He cut the branch, trying not to damage the twisted flower heavy vines.

He circumnavigated the wood. Nestled in bracken fronds he found a rusted poacher's snare enmeshed with well rotted pheasant, a nursery of fretful maggots. He swallowed his rising gorge, discarding the disabled snare. He found a suitable hide and rid the wood of a flock of crows. The exploding gun rattling the brain in his skull, a conker in a tin. He mended a pheasant coop at the back of the house and set off to check the young birds in his care. All the time he was grateful for the pain in his head, to remind him he was alive, to prevent all the thoughts constantly battering around, hopeless, often absurd, always better left unexamined.

The riverbank was cooler, his attention drawn by a loud splash. A pair of otters frolicked in the shallows. Busy in their play they failed to notice their armed observer. Delilah paused, beady eyed, waiting for the command that would give her leave to jump in. The smaller otter leaped onto the bank joined by the larger one. They rolled in the sedge, across the grass and back, falling into the river. Two smooth brown arcs broke the surface as they dived together. A little round head bobbed up searching for its companion. When they found each other they danced under the water.

"Iain," Nell stood behind him. He raised a finger to his lips and pointed to the playful otters. For a mad second he thought he might have wished her here with some bizarre sorcery. If wishes were horses ... but of course, here she was, merely by chance. It was natural to catch her hand and pull her close to his side, consoling. The otters gambolled along the bank, plunging into the stream, scampering out of the muddying water and whizzing down the mucky slide they had designed with their little feet and long bodies. When they left it was sudden, darting up the river, backs breaking the surface.

On the river's edge, Iain and Nell held hands, watching the clouded waters, empty of otters. They drew apart with a reluctance neither was wholly aware of.

"Aren't they lovely," she said and her delight pleased him. She clutched a sketchpad and pencil. "I've not seen an otter since I was little."

"They've got nice coats. Some folk would pay a pretty penny for those." A grim observation. She wrinkled her nose.

"The otter hunt doesn't come through here, they only hunt as far as Ebblechurch, luckily," Iain said.

She smiled. "Oh, Iain, you do see them for more than their expensive coats."

"No. I don't like all the idlers who come with the hunt, traipsing through my woods, disturbing my birds. All that forelock tugging and being polite, drives me mad."

"Heartless after all then, just don't want to toe the line." Her lighthearted tone brought a smile to his lips.

"Not a nice bone in my body." He glanced at her. "I was told you were expecting."

She blushed. "I am," she said, smoothing her dress to outline the small swelling.

"Not much there."

He saw he had insulted her. Mutiny seized her voice. "I have over three months to go yet, not everyone grows to the size of a barge you know. It doesn't mean anything." She cursed herself, too touchy by far. Freddy's departure was abandonment; he had refused home leave. She felt inadequate, her failure at married life.

"Helena, Helena," his tone was placating. "I'm kidding on, for Christ's sake."

"Well don't," she said, a tremble in her voice.

He tilted his head to see her down turned face. "What's the matter?" he said kindly. "I didn't mean to upset you. You look fine, really, you do." He would not know what to do if she cried, all those tears and how to stop them with the inadequacy of words. He tried changing the subject. "Is Freddy away then?"

She nodded, viewing the grass at her feet. "At a training camp in Suffolk. He waits every day for word about when they will leave. He thought he would enlist and be sent to France the next day. It's nothing like that. There are no uniforms and they have to train with pretend wooden rifles."

He laughed. "I expect army life's hit him hard."

"It has rather. They sleep ten or twelve to a hut, parades and marches. He complains about the food. Don't think he's very impressed. He thought it would be an adventure and it isn't."

"Aye." The thought of Freddy's deprivation was delightful. "I can imagine. He's never made do, has he? Always done what he wanted."

"Yes, he has. Too late now, the army's got him and he's going to France whether he likes it or not. He thinks everything will be better over there, more exciting, I suppose."

"Do you want a cup of tea? I'm heading back for something to eat." It was a simple invitation, no harm in it. She nodded and they walked through the dappled wood. She stopped to smell the honeysuckle and he pointed out a blackbird's nest where a harassed mother bird was trying to hatch her second brood. From a distance the unmistakable double note of the cuckoo came to them. They smiled at each other.

"Cuckoo's abroad leaving its orphans behind," she said and he laughed.

The house was cool, gloomy compared to the brightness of the day. He made tea. She wasn't hungry. He ate bread and cheese at the kitchen table.

"Can I see?" He nodded towards her sketchpad lying on the table between them.

"They're nothing much. I've not done any drawing since I got married," she said.

He leafed through the thick pages, botanical studies, minutely detailed in pencil and watercolour; paintings of overblown poppies with coal black hearts, the bursting blue stars of the cornflower and pink cabbage roses with butter yellow stamens. They were exquisite. The last sketch was the spire of foxgloves, which he had passed earlier on the way to the river.

"They're really very good." Her talent surprised him.

"I usually paint the colour in later from memory or pick them and do it at home. I haven't got time for it anymore. Today was a mad whim." She blushed. She had deliberately come to Harrowmead to seek him out, the excuse about sketching seemed so transparent to her now. Did he guess her deception?

If he knew he had the grace to change the subject. "How are you managing the farm?" He noticed there were shadows under her eyes that had not been there before. She was flat, depressed in spirit, dissatisfaction seeping from her like sap from a pine tree.

She sighed deeply, sipped the hot tea. "We'll never manage the harvest. Simple as that. Father – Mr Hart – can't do it all himself. We have Mr Feeney – can you imagine? He's ancient. Then old Mr Baker's grandsons, the youngest two, they're thirteen and fourteen, and me. We've taken on a young girl in the house to help out, Lisa George, d'you know her?"

He shook his head. "I don't recall the girl. I've spoken to her father at the pub, he's got two sons. Lisa must be the youngest. Her father went away somewhere didn't he?"

"Yes, to London I think, for work. Lisa's fifteen, some help at least. Look at me. I'm a lot of use. The child's due in September." She glanced down and blushed. "What am I to do? Father looks to me for the answers since Freddy went." She put down her tea and flapped her hand in the air. "Oh listen to me. Sorry, Iain, it'll work out won't it? All hell's breaking loose in France and I'm getting in a panic about harvesting a few crops. Who cares?"

Close to tears, the colour came and went in her cheeks. Where was the self-contained young woman he had seen on the day Joanna had left? He wondered how long she had felt this heavy burden of responsibility.

It was easy talking about the farm, harvests and painting, but somewhere, sitting in one of the other three chairs, was Joanna, listening in, the ghost of restraint. He would say her name and break the veto.

"You heard from Joanna?" Complacently said, chewing his food.

"Yes, I've had a couple of letters. She's not much of a one for writing. She says she's fat as a pig, can't wait until it's over."

"Is she still," a pause for breath to release the words, "giving it up?" He had to ask, had to know, he pushed his plate away, the food half eaten.

"Yes, she's arranged everything. The baby shall be taken by the midwife."

"Midwife? Isn't the baby going to a family?"

"I don't know the details, Iain. I've tried to talk her out of it." She leaned back in the chair. Enough. She couldn't talk to him about it, they would argue, and it would be Joanna not Nell that he was railing against. "I like it here, it's peaceful. I can never find peace up at the farm."

"No, don't suppose so." Joanna, Joanna, Joanna. She had escaped from the room where he had locked her. Push her away. "How's Mrs Hart?"

She rolled her eyes. "Hardly ever gets out of bed. Lisa is learning the dairy work, leaving me with her. It's Nell can you do this, Nell can you do that? I wouldn't mind really, Iain, if she tried she could come downstairs if only to save my legs going up and down all day. She could knit or sew, or read, but she lies there doing nothing. Nothing except complaining." She put her hands over her mouth. "Listen to me, God forgive me."

"Speaking of which shouldn't you be at church?" He had a glint in his eye, laughter in his voice.

"Yes," she said smiling at him, "I should. It's the only time I'm not missed. I'm allowed to go to church."

"Allowed? Is it North Farm Jail?"

She giggled. "I sometimes think it is. Oh heaven help me." She pulled the pin out of her straw hat and took it off. Her mussed up hair haloed her head. Her half-hearted attempt did nothing to smooth it. "Do you know," she said the laughter dying on her face, the ghost returning, "I never thought Joanna would leave. She had her big plans for Bath and all that. She was always so full of talk. I was surprised when she actually left. She has more courage than I do."

He said, "You're mistaking courage for self-interest. She thinks she'll be a lady, living in the town. She wants to marry well. She was right to leave, we don't belong together. She knew that from the start and I knew about her too. In that we were alike at least."

"Everyone needs someone. Even you and Joanna. She was in love with you once." She smiled kindly and her youth returned with her smile.

He shook his head. "She wasn't in love with me, I don't think she even liked me much. She was in love with the idea of me. She didn't really know me."

She wanted to deny it but she couldn't, anything Joanna knew about him was what Nell had told her.

"When you need peace, Helena," he said, "you're welcome to come here." Before he knew he had even thought it, he said, "I can give you a key."

"Would you do that?"

"I wouldn't have said it, would I?" He took a jar from the dresser that was littered with old receipts, bills, nails, hooks, pieces of string, lodged between mismatching pieces of china. He poked around in the jar for a second and pulled out a long rusted key. "There," he said. "Does that mean you will become a heathen and not a good practising Christian?"

She frowned at him, reached out to snatch the key in case he changed his mind. "Yes," she said, "yes, yes, yes." She tucked the key into her pocket. "Why does Freddy hate you so much?" she said.

"Still? I thought we were over all that."

"He said it was your fault Tom disappeared."

He leaned his fists on the table, the tenor of his voice changed. "What did he say?"

"Only if not for you he wouldn't have gone away."

"Who else did he say that to?"

"I don't know. Nobody, as far as I know. I asked him why he hated you and that was his reply. Why did Tom go away?"

"I know nothing about Tom, nothing, do you hear?" he snapped.

"All right, calm down. I wanted to understand, that's all. Freddy's always ready to blame someone else, perhaps it was his fault Tom went away, I don't know," she said madly trying to back track.

He turned away from her. "Aye, that'll be it." Everyone was tumbling out of the locked room today, it was laughable. Calmly, he said, "Freddy's fault, no doubt."

"You do hate him don't you?"

"Stop it, Helena. Stop talking about it."

"But you do, don't you?" she persisted. He hunched his broad shoulders, walking across to the range. He leaned on the mighty beam, resting his forehead on his arm.

"Hate him? Aye, I'm good at hate, Helena. You should stay away. It's stupid for you to come here. People talk, even when there's nothing to say. You'll survive your harvest, you'll live your life, now let me get on and live mine. You're one of them now, nothing can change that."

He did not hear her approach; her small hand on his back almost took the breath from him. He closed his eyes, his forehead pressed tight to his arm. Her fingers traced the line of his spine under his thin shirt, cool pressure through the cotton. Her hand rested at the base of his back above his belt. Her energy was a restless vibrant force through his skin. She stepped back from him, her shoes scuffing the tiles.

"It's settled. I'll see you next week," she said resolutely. He heard her leave the room and the click of the front door as she let herself out. Nothing was settled except the dust and even that insisted on dancing when the sun shone.

She had forgotten her sketchbook and later he studied her paintings at length and marvelled at them. It did not bother him that she had used the sketching as an excuse to see him, in fact, quite the reverse.

Her visit the following week was all joviality and lighthearted chatter. They could be friends. They could laugh and talk despite everything or because of it. There was no need to speak about important matters, it was enough to share time, be together. No ghosts kept them company.

"Lionel Baker left for France. Poor Nancy's terribly upset," she said.

"Is Lionel?" he asked.

"What do you mean?"

"Well she's shocking to look at." He grinned.

"Iain, that's terrible!"

"Deny it then. Tell me she's pretty and he's not gone in search of a French girl."

She gasped. "He wouldn't. You're so bad. You tease! A French girl indeed."

"You didn't hear him talking in the pub."

She covered her ears and hummed tunelessly. "I'm not listening," she sang while he laughed.

"Polly Took's baby is awful plain," she continued innocently. "Looks the same as poor down trodden Mr Took, all thin and gaunt like an old man. Now Polly Took, she's pretty."

"Aye, she is."

"Rumour has it she's seeing Noah Brown on the sly behind Mr Took's back."

He matched her scandalised expression, tutting in reproof. "Quite shocking," he said. "That's what comes of having a pretty face."

She nodded in agreement. She could not conceive taking a lover, even though her husband was safely on his way to France. I'm unimaginative, she thought, looking at Iain.

He laughed as she described how Lisa could curdle the milk with her singing and every evening she knitted and her work had more holes than a colander.

"Alan Stock married Jenny Potter last week, despite him having his clicking jaw, which you could hear quite clearly when he took his vows," she said.

"You married, Freddy," he said, "and he's got a bent nose."

"All thanks to you," she smiled sweetly.

"Joanna said Alan asked her to marry him."

"Yes, he adored her. Poor boy, he was heartbroken when she went away. She thought him common. She used to laugh at him and treated him quite cruelly. Still he has Jenny now."

Yes, Joanna would make a fool of a lad, belittling him. She was haughty and Alan could never have coped with her arrogance.

"Mr Price is selling some piglets," she said. "Perhaps I should buy some in case the harvest fails, what do you think?"

"There's definitely a future in pigs," he was being facetious, "and you, the sunny optimist, are bound to make a packet."

She took him at face value, making a mental note to advise Mr Hart. Then suddenly downhearted she said, "The army has taken our horses, all except old Willow."

"Aye, Mr Denham's have gone too."

"Even your patient, Phoenix?"

"Especially him, he's a fine gelding. The cavalry are calling out for the likes of him. Miles took him, he'll ride his own horse into battle."

"Are you not tempted to go, Iain?"

He shook his head and said, "Not yet. Maybe one day. I'll know when the time's right. Are you anxious to see me away?"

"No," she said quickly, curled up in his armchair, resting her head back on the worn weave. "No I don't want you to go. Not ever." He smiled. We're just friends, he thought, very good friends.

She visited the two Sundays following that. It might have become a habit, but it wasn't to be. The whole world was changing and they were being dragged with it whether they liked it or not.

Chapter Thirteen

Iain was up at dawn patrolling the woods. A gate swung on broken hinges. The Baker lads were hanging around the pond waiting for him. He set them to work hedging west of the river. He allowed himself twenty minutes for breakfast before heading back out to check the snares he had set.

It was a warm summer day like the day preceding it. The river ran low due to lack of rain, the earth cracked and dusty. The squares of corn grew tall and green in the meadow, interspersed with the red splash of poppies and starry blue cornflowers. Everything was in its place but a feeling of deep discontent weighed him down, a burden he could not quantify or describe. He inspected the clear blue sky to check for black clouds portending a thunderstorm. This melancholic mood had been with him for the week, since he had last seen Nell. He blotted it out with routine and work. Today he recognised it, thought perhaps to alter it somehow.

Guilt played its part in his depression. Tom walked in his dreams every night. He was never aggressive, his presence did not feel ominous, but he prodded at Iain's conscience.

He wondered how Freddy was coping with that fateful night, if enlisting had been his escape route and whether it had worked for him.

Then there was Joanna's baby. He felt an incredible affinity with the unborn child, and remorse that he was standing by letting his own life possibly be repeated. It was his passivity that sickened him, fretting and doing nothing to change it.

By lunchtime he had no cigarettes in his pocket, so he wended his way home to restock. The front door stood open an inch. His heart lifted with pleasure, only Nell had a key.

She was sitting in his chair. He did not notice the telegram, not immediately. She could not speak coherently. She sobbed, gulping air, tears running over themselves in desperate haste. Nothing tried his patience like a hysterical woman. He poured her a whisky.

"Drink that and stop snivelling. I can't understand a word your saying," he said. She did not attempt to drink it. Impatiently he pushed the glass up to her mouth, robbing her of options. She gagged and screwed up her face, pushing it away, wiping her mouth on her sleeve.

"It's – bloody – awful," she gulped air between her words.

"Aye, it's meant to be, to shut you up," he said. "Now what is it?" This was so unlike her. Drama was so Joanna. Nell was more practical, not given to hysteria. He snatched the telegram out of her hand and read it.

She gradually stopped crying, although the little involuntary gasps that shook her body continued.

His heart jarred and he understood. He understood the weighty melancholy eating away at him. He understood Nell's tears. He understood life was unfair and painful and nothing could have prepared him for it. He re-read the stilted words, then again and again, over and over as if it might change them, alter their meaning. It was from Catherine Taylor, Joanna's Aunt, a brief message, each word carefully chosen to reduce the cost and fox the postmistress. Joanna died. Please come as soon as possible.

No mention of birth or babies or anything that might give away the secret shame. He lowered his head, his chin resting on his chest. Death and shame, martyrdom and sin. And it was all his fault. It was his baby, the baby she had not wanted. And if the baby lived? A baby without a mother or a home. He remembered Bruce Sinclair, arrogant and handsome, trying to gain pity with tears of sorrow.

Iain covered his face with his hands. Joanna was gone, her dreams and lofty ambitions would be buried under the sod. He could scarcely believe someone so full of life and vitality could be snuffed out so easily and yet part of him was not surprised at all.

Nell wiped her eyes with a crumpled handkerchief. She was calmer now, practicality overtaking melodrama. Her eyes were red rimmed and swollen. "I shall have to go there, Iain."

"Aye, you will." He read the telegram again.

"I need someone to come with me."

"Do you want me to?"

She nodded meekly. "Would you?"

He fetched his cigarettes and lit one, put the telegram on the table, paced the room. "Where's the baby?"

She shrugged. "I don't know."

"Well, I should come, the way it happened. What about them at North Farm?"

"I've walked out on it all. I was in the middle of my day, all my work, left it all. Don't care if I never go back, they won't know where I am or why I've gone." She took a deep breath, picked up the whisky glass and sipped it. "Freddy's in France now, you know. Got a letter from him today."

"Aye." He could not feign interest.

"Sounds grim out there. He wouldn't want me to go on my own would he?"

"No. Don't suppose I'm his idea of a perfect travelling companion though," he said, contemplating her dainty hands holding the glass so tightly her knuckles were white.

"Doesn't matter, it's not him doing the travelling is it?"

In normal circumstances he might have laughed at her, pursing her lips doggedly, ready for an argument. "You'll have to pack some things. Where will you say you're going? It's not as if you can tell them the truth and it'll seem a wee bit odd going on holiday for a few days out of the blue."

She frowned, sipping again from the glass, now deriving some comfort in the vile heat that burned her stomach. "I don't care, Lisa's there to help, she's better than nothing. She can run around after Mother all day and fit in the dairy work like I do. I could say Aunt Cath is poorly and I'm going to look after her. Then if I wrote to them in a few days and tell them about – about Jo." Looking at him, her eyes brimmed with tears. "Not the truth of course," she muttered. She was hatless, her hair falling out of its coil, curling round her shoulders, her face pink from tears. The small curve of her stomach was visible through the thin flower sprigged summer dress. She leaned her head on her hand and closed her eyes.

He reached out and touched the crown of her head, hair soft on his calloused skin. Stooping he ran his hand down it, pressing the curls against her cheek, she lifted her face to him, eyes closed. He felt her sigh more than he heard it, passing through his cupped hand. Her cheek was hot behind the curtain of hair. He watched the movement of her pale throat as she swallowed. "I shall meet you at the station in two hours. Is that long enough?" He hurried to pull his hand away and went to the window. He did not know what had made him touch her, what had made it feel so very intimate.

Her eyes opened, colour burned in her cheeks. "Yes, long enough."

When she left him, he stared for a long time at the telegram as if willing it to alter before his eyes. A bitter, crushing rage overtook him at the waste of life - Tom, Joanna, the baby. He hit the table with a bunched fist, grazing the skin on his knuckles.

Balling the telegram he threw it across the room. It bounced off the fender to the floor.

* * * *

He waited at the station in the shade of the canopy. It was a small country station with a busy little stationmaster, Mr Pettersmith, who lived in the brick house adjacent to the line. The only shelter was the canopy with a hard wooden bench. Mr Pettersmith took great pride in his platform. It was well swept without a weed in sight and with two pots of velvet faced pansies.

Iain had intended squaring his departure with the head gardener or groom then, thinking better of it, he packed a bag, locked up and tramped across the Common with Delilah to see Isaac.

"Got to go away for a couple of days," he said, finding Isaac busy weaving a willow basket.

"Right-i-o. Bad news?"

"Aye, least said and all that." He hunkered down beside the old gypsy.

"The worst kind of news then. I'll keep me ear to the ground for trouble." Isaac grinned, hard weathered hands working the withy.

"I'd appreciate it, thanks. I've not told anyone, not at the house. Mr Denham's away. I should be back before any of that lot misses me. I only see them if they want something."

"Ain't it always the way. And what about this girl here then?" He paused in his work to scratch Delilah's ears.

"Aye, that was the other thing."

"You'll be all right with me won't you girl?" He winked. "Go on, Iain, rest easy and I'll see you later."

He put a hand on Isaac's thin shoulder. "Thanks." His voice caught with unexpected emotion. He shut Delilah in Isaac's little shack to prevent her following him.

When the afternoon train clanked into the station hissing steam there was no sign of Nell. He stood up uncertainly. "Are you for the off, sir?" Mr Pettersmith said.

"Aye, I thought…" with relief he saw her run on to the platform. Flustered, her hat was askew, hair still hanging down her back. The shadow of a smile played on his lips at the sight of her disarray.

She was relieved to see him. "Sorry, Mr Pettersmith, have you had to delay the train?"

Mr Pettersmith, who wouldn't have delayed the train for the King, raised his eyebrows at her before glancing at Iain. He would be sure to tell his wife he had seen the gamekeeper taking the train with the new Mrs Hart.

"Well, Mrs Hart," Iain said, seeing their predicament, "how nice to see you. Looks as though we'll be travelling together for a bit. Can I take your case?"

"Oh," she said and smiled, "what a pleasant surprise. Yes, thank you." What a jaunt, what a lark, what a bloody nightmare her smile said.

Iain, case in hand, went ahead leaving her to enquire after Mr Pettersmith's wife and children before alighting herself. Placated by their act, Mr Pettersmith blew smartly on his whistle as the door closed.

They took their seats and the train chugged out of the station. There were only two carriages and they sat apart, in close proximity to the motley array of passengers, young, old, smart, scruffy and odorous. In town they caught their connecting train to the coast and occupied a carriage on their own. They sat opposite each other wrapped in silence, deep in their own thoughts. They were blind to the passing summer countryside, a tapestry of green fields, trees, cows and sheep. The rhythmic thrum of the wheels on the track was a reassurance, moving forward, but to what?

Iain's last train journey had brought him the many miles south from Scotland. He was beginning to associate trains with disappointment and grief.

"I have arranged for you to go to Harrowmead. You remember John Denham, don't you? He came shooting here once," Bruce Sinclair had said.

Exile – the first word that entered Iain's head. "That's in the south of England." He had not kept the horror from his voice.

Sinclair dared to meet Iain's icy glare. "The verdict was not proven, Iain. You can't remain here as keeper. Finnigan had his acquaintances, the type to take justice into their own hands. There are those who believe you are guilty. They believe it was only lack of evidence that got you off."

"Yes," he said, knowing hate. "Only lack of evidence. Perhaps they're right."

The train carriage was too hot. Iain pushed open the window, inhaled the sharp, rushing air, dispelling the memories.

When he chanced a peek at Nell she was biting her thumb, fighting back welling tears. He quickly looked away, inadequate, unable to offer any comfort. Reaching out a hand earlier, his intention had been platonic to soothe and console. It had not felt like that at all. It had been intimate, both his caress and her reaction to it.

They walked two miles from the station to Brackenheath in the dusk. A steady mist of rain fell, dusting their clothes and hair with a myriad of minute water droplets. Climbing the steep hill to her aunt's cottage Nell stopped, a nagging ache pulled low in her stomach. She put her hand to it a couple of times.

"What is it?" he asked impatiently the second time she paused.

"Nothing, I'm tired. Come on, we're getting wet." They trudged on.

They arrived at a little row of white painted cottages. A heavy cobweb of fisherman's nets hung along the front wall, stacks of lobster pots, industrial tools of the sea. At the very end of the row was Nell's aunt's. Iain could only imagine a view beyond the cloak of dense fog. The wooden gate whined an objection as he pushed it open. A small front garden was planted with cabbages and flowers scorched brown from the sea spray, the air thick with the smell of salt and seaweed.

Aunt Cath welcomed them. A tall woman carrying extra weight round her middle, grey streaked hair scraped back in a bun, her skin smooth and lined. She hugged Iain as if he were a member of her family and held on to Nell until she managed to extricate herself. She took their coats and bags and Nell removed her damp hat.

The two women went ahead of him into the parlour. Nell's adoptive mother sat in an armchair by the window, a little broken bird of a woman, head tilted, mouth slack, dragged down at one side, greying hair plaited over her shoulder. A rug covered her knees, one hand clawed in her lap and the other tapping the arm of the chair as if to an unheard melody. With a benign smile on her lips she stared vacantly at the immaculate white net curtains hanging at the window.

Nell ran to the disabled woman, laid her head in her mother's lap sobbing as if she had saved this grief especially. She stopped tapping and absently stroked the chestnut curls that had tightened in the damp sea mist. Her expression did not alter, her gaze did not shift from the curtains. He watched them from his position by the door. The ceilings were low, he could just stand upright, except for where a beam crossed the room. Aunt Cath inspected him with great interest.

"You're Iain Macdonald aren't you?" she said.

"Aye."

"Well, I can see why she fell for you." She dabbed at her eyes with a handkerchief. Fell – like tripping over an unseen stone, he thought.

"What happened to her, what went wrong?"

Tears sprang into Aunt Cath's eyes again. "She bled. Never seen so much blood, the doctor says it happens. Nothing to be done. Baby came and all was well, then about four hours after, all this blood. Never seen anything like it, never. When the doctor came out he said it happens."

Nell raised her head from her mother's lap to listen.

"Where is she?" he asked.

"Upstairs."

"And the baby?"

"Oh, she saw the baby taken away before she died. It had all been arranged with the midwife. Once the midwife saw her all right she took the baby on."

His expression altered, Nell could see the anger in it. "Took it on, where?" His words were sharper than he intended.

Aunt Cath caught his tone. "Why? What difference does it make? He'll be cared for where he's gone. There's no mother here to have him, feed him, it's for the best."

He – him – a boy, a son. Did that make it worse? Divine justice – history repeating itself, the diminishing circles of fate. He glared at the woman with contempt. "And you'd know what's best?"

"Iain," Nell warned.

He would bite his tongue for now but his insides churned, he did not see how he could let this rest.

"I want to see her." Nell supported her weight on the chair arm to haul herself to her feet, placing her hands on her stomach.

"Oh, I can't bear it," wailed Aunt Cath sobbing into her hankie.

"Come on," he said. "I'll come with you."

They climbed the steep narrow stairs. Joanna lay on the bed. The window was open an inch, the drawn curtains stirred in the draught. A lamp by the bed effused the room with a warm light. The hair, unnaturally dark, spread across the pillow. Her face was a translucent waxen mask, lips and eyelids touched with mauve.

Nell gasped when she saw her sister, putting both hands over her mouth to quiet herself. Iain had seen death before but the sight of Joanna's lifelessness appalled him. Visions of her laughing and talking flashed through his head, touching her, kissing her, rejecting her, letting her go, feeling only relief when she had. He glanced at Nell wavering unsteadily, her pallor as anaemic as the body on the bed. He was afraid she might faint.

"Come on," he said softly, "that's enough." She did not move. He put his arm round her, his hand on her shoulder. Her slight weight leaned into him, she turned her head into his chest and then he was holding her to him with one arm. He needed a smoke and to be out of this room, away from Joanna. Everything was slipping away from him, he wasn't sure how he came to be here standing over her corpse. This was not unproven, this was guilty, guilty, guilty.

He held Nell for a time, feeling her tremble. He gave her a little shake. "Come on," he said more firmly, leading her out of the room, closing the door. She walked down the stairs in front of him.

"She needs a drink," he said to Aunt Cath, composed now, and busy. She was setting out plates of cheese and ham sandwiches, cut into civilised triangles, on the snowy white tablecloth in the kitchen.

"Oh, I don't have anything," she said.

"Is there a public house nearby?"

"Up the road on the left. Fisherman's Rest," she said.

He was glad of the excuse to escape, away from tears and the restorative order of sandwiches and tea. It was getting dark and the fresh air was a tonic.

Three old men conversed at the bar. Sitting alone in the corner was a fisherman, fresh from the sea judging by his attire. They all stopped to look at Iain. He ignored them, they could make what they would of him, he did not care, it would give them something else to talk about for five minutes. He ordered a double whisky and bought a half bottle to take out. He downed the spirit in one go, lit a cigarette and ordered another.

"You visiting?" The publican thought he would wring him for a bit of information.

"Aye," he said. "Do you own this fine establishment?"

"I do, that," the publican scratched his bald pate, eyes wandering over the dark little bar with satisfaction.

"I'm travelling the country putting together a wee directory for the Government." He knocked back his drink.

"Oh," gasped the publican, "my place going in a book. Blimey." He absently reached for Iain's glass and refilled it. "You have that one on the house, mister. I'm much obliged to you, I'm sure."

"Aye," he said, "they'll be flocking through the door, once you have the official backing."

The man, slightly sceptical, said, "Official? What way official?"

"Helps keep track of the taxes, see. Not everyone is as conscientious as you I'm sure."

"Taxes? Conshi-what?"

"Well, of course," alcohol-infused, Iain warmed to his theme, "the tax office requires lists of all public houses to ensure you're paying all your taxes. Nothing for you to worry about, not a law abiding citizen like yourself."

His eyes switched between Iain and the free glass of whisky in his hand and which the publican now wished he had withheld.

"You work for the tax office? A bleeding tax man?"

Iain winked and tapped the side of his nose. He drained his glass and made a quick exit, leaving the man in a state of alarm mentally configuring what he might owe. Iain realised it was a mean and unnecessary deception that had only served to distract him from his own guilt and sorrow for a few paltry moments.

Very little of Aunt Cath's carefully laid tea was eaten. Nell offered Joanna's mother, Iain could not think of her as Nell's, small mouthfuls of food that she ate slowly.

The yellow whisky made Nell cough. Aunt Cath sighed into her glass, pursing her lips after each taste as if it were medicine. Time for bed and the two women helped Joanna's mother upstairs. Iain was shown to the foot of the attic stairs, as steep as a ladder. The room was tiny, a claustrophobic triangle with no space to unbend his neck. The truckle bed was too short, his feet hung out at the end. He had bedded down in far worse places. He blew out the candle, escaping the day, the guilt, welcoming the dark, and fell asleep quickly.

A noise stirred him from sleep. Grey anonymity seeped through the small skylight, unfamiliar, his hand reached up into the darkness, resting on air. The rush of remembrance was heavy. Joanna, dead, laid out in the room below. Somewhere a baby slept, unwanted, alone. The creak of the wooden staircase stemmed his thoughts.

"Iain," whispered a voice. It was Nell. Sitting up he groped for matches, the sheet rucked at his waist. A phosphorescent flash briefly highlighted the room, the sharp smell irritating his throat. He lit the candle. She appeared, gingerly lifting her nightdress so as not to trip over it.

"What is it?" he hissed. She knelt beside his low bed on the dry bare floorboards, her expression softened and smudged. But she saw him clearly, crafted from candlelight, smooth skin over sculpted muscle and curving rib. Her eyes fluttered upwards and his knowing grin made the heat rush to her cheeks.

His chuckle was low and quiet. "I don't mind you looking."

She was angry because it was true and she had been powerless to stop herself and it was all so ludicrous considering the circumstances. "Don't be ridiculous." She would cover it up with her anger and he would allow her to because it was the only thing to do. She leaned forward, a hand tight to her stomach and then he realised she had not come to seduce him, if he had ever believed it in the first place.

"What's the matter?"

"I don't know. An ache, same as earlier."

"What are you telling me for?"

She was offended. "I don't know, now. It made sense a minute ago when I was on my own. Now I wish I hadn't bothered."

He rolled his eyes. "What are you thinking? Is this because of the horse? D'you think I can do something?"

She shrugged. "You did help the horse though didn't you?"

"Aye, I suppose so. You're not a horse though, are you?" He beckoned her closer. She knelt up, her small belly standing proud through her thin cotton nightdress. He put one large hand at her back, the other across the swelling. He did not dare meet her eyes that he knew watched him closely. For a brief second the idea returned that this was a ploy she had dreamed up. His hands were incredibly hot on her cool skin. As he held her the awful ache dragged through her womb again.

"That was it, wasn't it?" he said, feeling genuine pain through his hands and in the expression on her face.

She gasped as it waned. "Yes."

"What do you think it is?"

"The baby." Tears shook her voice. "It's not due for at least nine weeks, Iain. It can't be the baby can it?"

Her midriff remained in the circumference of his hands. He nodded. "It is the baby." He closed his eyes concentrating on her pain, aware of the thud of her heart, the pumping of her blood, the heat of her, the movement, though minuscule, of the foetus under his palm. His head lowered as he channelled his thoughts, energy passing through him, across her belly to his hand resting in the small of her back. Her abdomen convulsed under his touch as the pain came again. He shook his head, met her gaze coolly, distanced now, a practitioner with his patient. "It's going to come, Helena, ready or not."

"How can you be sure?"

He shook his head again. "I just know." Her eyes searched his face, a silent plea for help. "There's nothing I can do to stop it, even a doctor can't stop it. Is there any blood?" His tone was practical, unemotional.

She bit her lip tearfully. "No."

"There will be." He released her. "Come on, let's go downstairs, you can't stay up here. I'll wake your aunt. Go on to your bed, I'll get dressed, be down in a minute." She hesitated uncertainly. "Go on," he said, "I'm coming. Be careful on the stairs."

She returned to her bed and he dressed. The baby would not live, not at seven months. First Joanna, now Nell, he wished he had not come. He wished he were back at Harrowmead, alone, un-involved, detached from the outside world, from the pain and reality of life and death.

In the hall he heard her cry out. He opened her bedroom door. "What is it?"

She was half in and out of the bed, a red stain of blood blooming on her nightgown. "Oh, Christ," he muttered, running to bang on Aunt Cath's door.

Aunt Cath roused herself from her invalid sister's warm bed. "I'm coming." She pulled on a threadbare dressing gown. He stood glowering in the hall making her jump. "Oh, Mr Macdonald," then crossly, "whatever is the matter at this time of night?"

"Helena's having pains, she's bleeding."

"Pains? What d'you mean pains?" Her face blanched, registering his meaning. "Oh no, not the baby. How much can one woman take?" She pushed past him into Nell's room. Their muted whispers squeezed through the open doorway. He went down to the parlour to wait.

A few minutes later Aunt Cath came to him. "There's a big stone house down the hill. You passed it on your way up here, Rock

House written by the gate, go fetch Mrs Aitken. She does the babies round here. Not Joanna's of course. Go fetch her and quick."

Mrs Aitken followed him back up the hill, surprisingly perky and chatty considering the ungodly hour she had been dragged from her bed. Iain, unreceptive to small talk, grunted occasionally although, if pressed, he could not have repeated a single word.

He kept company with the whisky bottle and a packet of Woodbines, waiting. His idle brain turned over the problem he had attempted to sleep on, Joanna's baby. His plan for the child was hazy. There were snags, he thought, although not insurmountable surely. Aunt Cath must know where the boy had gone. He would take the child back. He could not abandon it as he had been abandoned, he knew that life so well. Any problems he may encounter he conveniently evaded in his tipsy sleep deprived mind. It all seemed fairly simple.

With the empty bottle at his elbow and on his umpteenth cigarette he listened to the muffled movements up the stairs. No voices, no weeping, the shuffle of shoes on bare boards, footsteps coming down the stairs, then back up. His eyelids drooped, the warm, fuzzy, sinking sensation that came with sleep.

A letter. A letter Iain had never seen. "Your mother sent me a letter," Bruce Sinclair said, a visitor to Iain's prison cell, a time for confessions. "She told me where to find you, asked me to care for you. And I would have, really, Iain, but my wife, she was furious, she was worried for Adam. He had to come first for her. She saw you as such a threat, you're two years older than him. Adam is the legitimate heir to Glenleven and my wife would not jeopardise that."

"Everything Finnigan said was true," Iain said, this pain of betrayal was too deep.

"What choice did I have, Iain?" His eyes had filled with tears. A crocodile, crying tears. Not Sinclair's grief, but that of his illegitimate son. A bastard.

Iain sat up, wide awake as Aunt Cath opened the parlour door.

"Well, that's Mrs Aitken away," she said.

"Already?" Three hours had passed since her arrival.

She nodded sorrowfully. "Poor little mite," she said, "a boy. Never seen such a fragile looking child, not like Joanna's." She gasped as a sob caught in her throat.

"Can I go up?"

Aunt Cath shrugged. "I don't mind. I'm beyond caring about anything." She sank into Iain's vacated chair.

He ran up the stairs, burst into the room without knocking. Nell looked up at him, eyes too big for her white face. She held the child, wrapped in a white shawl.

He leaned over the bed, pulled back the shawl with one large finger. The baby was tiny, a tracery of mauve blood vessels under jaundiced transparent skin. One hand was the size of Iain's thumbnail. The eyelids covered protruding eyes, his minute mouth gaped.

He was a delicate baby bird fallen early from its nest. There was a purposeful struggle in the gentle suck and blow of the fluttering lungs, indenting the soft skin below the ribs. A determination to survive if only for a few precious hours before it grew wings and flew free. Except it would never fly, it would die in the embrace of his mother's arms, and perhaps such desperate maternal love was better than any freedom.

"I'm so sorry," he said.

"He won't feed," she said sadly, covering the tiny body.

"No."

"He's gasping for breath. I can't bear it, Iain, I can't." She could and she would. He knew the end for this baby would be a painless release, but Nell would carry it with her – this loss, this missing part, no release for her, but imprisonment, calcifying her heart.

He pulled a chair from the corner of the room and sat by the bed, leaning his head on his hands. Dawn lightened the windowpanes. Nell drifted. Her hushed breathing occupied the air. Like the sea lapping the shore, sleep enveloped then receded, the baby still clutched in her aching arms. He watched her, waiting for daylight. Waiting for the life, not yet lived, to be extinguished.

She woke at eight to the sun squeezing through drawn curtains. His head rested on his arms, eyes closed to the encroaching day. Aware of her movement he roused himself.

She was absorbed, weeping painful silent tears, rocking the baby in her arms. "Here let me." He held out his hands. She shook her head. "Give him to me, Helena." She struggled against her instinct to hold on. Obediently she offered the baby to him, a high note of despair coming from her mouth. Iain could see by the colour of him, the stiff way he lay in his arms, he had been dead at least an hour. "Helena," he said, "I'll get your aunt, shall I?"

She could not speak, her hands covered her face, knees drawn up, shaking with agonised sobs that made no sound. He could think of nothing to say to console her. Her child was dead. He could not explain it, logically explain, give her empty expressions of condolence. There were no adequate words or actions.

"Shall I take him downstairs?" he asked.

She shook her head, no. He placed the baby in the deep drawer by the bed, put there for that purpose. He left the tiny face uncovered, he could not bear to see it masked.

He found Aunt Cath in the chair where he had left her. She woke with a start, expressing surprise at him being there, before recalling him.

"Listen, I need to speak to you," he said.

She yawned. "Sounds worrying."

"Where did the midwife take Joanna's baby?"

She hesitated. "To town."

"Where, exactly?"

She pursed her lips in the grip of indecision. "I suppose it doesn't matter, you knowing, Joanna's gone. She was adamant you shouldn't know, said she never knew what you would do next. Suppose it doesn't matter now does it?"

His smile stretched patiently, heart racing. "No, it doesn't. So tell me – please."

Chapter Fourteen

Iain had expected large and imposing - The Sacred Heart unearthed in all its nightmarish enormity; an ageless religious institution, corridors, dormitories, school halls and chapel, austere, chilling and utilitarian. Instead he found an ordinary house in a back street off the busy town roads. A high iron gate led into the front garden, dwarfed by overgrown shrubbery. The hollow sound of the brass knocker reverberated back to him. A maid answered, bobbed, invited him into a spacious hall, black and white tiled floor, sweeping staircase, gracious electric light fitting. The smell was familiar, re-heated cabbage and disinfectant.

"Have you a business card, sir?" she asked.

"No, I'm inspecting the facilities." His authority was buoyed by his ludicrous deception the night before at the pub. He had nothing to lose and everything to gain.

"I'll fetch Matron," she said bobbing her head again. "Take a seat. Won't keep you long." She stared over her shoulder flirtatiously. He did not notice. He was too wrapped up in the execution of his half formed plan.

Matron was spare and bony with an Irish accent and pavement grey hair cut short under her cap. "Good morning," she said, her handshake firm as iron. "We've had no word of an inspection."

"That's the idea. If we announce our arrival, we find things, how shall we say, spruced up before we get here."

Her smile was acidic. "Well, you will find our standards consistently high, Mr – er."

"Mr Finnigan." The first name that came to mind.

"Finnigan?" she questioned.

"Aye, Scottish born, Irish descent. County Cork, how about you?"

Her expression softened. "Ah, County Cork, home sweet home," she said. Hallelujah! "So, where did you want to start?"

This was going to be easy. "The nursery," he said.

She took him up the sweeping staircase, along a green painted corridor. Through the open doors he saw an office, an empty bedroom, a long dormitory of tidily made beds, a dank cell with bare walls and floor. They climbed another short flight of steps to a spacious airy room with six wooden cribs arranged three on each side.

"Is there nobody up here with them?" he asked.

"We have one baby with us. There's a nurse coming and checking on him, she's downstairs, she would hear if he cried. We have all night cover. Our nursery nurse is having her breakfast, she'll be up shortly."

He ran an officious finger along the mantelpiece and windowsill. He peeked out of the window, realising they were two floors up. He peered into the cribs; in the third one lay the baby. Iain knew him at once, a shock of dark hair, arms akimbo, relaxed in his sleep, fat knotted fists level with his ears. Black lashes curled on satiny, apple cheeks, a pursed pout anticipating milk. He was astonished. The perfection of the child momentarily robbed him of speech. Tied to the cot bars a printed card detailed date of birth, sex, name, mother, father. Only the date of birth and sex had been filled in, no name, no mother, no father, and in the left hand corner 'Brackenheath', the only written clue as to the baby's identity.

Matron had not noticed his discomposure and continued talking about mealtimes and schedules. He had to follow her out of the nursery, seeing the impossibility of gaining access again. Twenty tidy beds lined up in the dormitory, the kitchens and laundry passed in a blur. In the dining room numerous children aged anywhere between two and twelve ate breakfast. It wasn't The Sacred Heart, but it was an institution for the unwanted, the surplus and unloved, all the same.

"Are babies adopted as they come in?" he asked.

"Lord, no. There are so many children. It is a sad sign of the times, Mr Finnigan. Girls these days have no morals, no understanding of virtue, no respect for themselves. We even have married couples with too many to feed bringing their children here. We have successfully adopted the lucky few. Sometimes we can pass them on to other children's homes. The baby upstairs may find a family, I've nothing lined up. There's a war on. He's brand new, brought in the day before yesterday."

"It's not all the woman's fault," he said. "It takes two."

Her face was a picture of distaste, holding up a hand to silence him. "Mr Finnigan, please. Men are base creatures, they can't help themselves."

He thought it prudent to change the subject. "Do the children get fresh air?"

"Yes we have a garden. We're very strict about three hours a day outside, summer and winter."

"I shall put that in my report," he said. "Now I must be on my way. I have to travel to London."

"What a busy life an inspector has."

"I have to say, I'm very impressed by your whole set up, Matron. I'll be writing about your establishment in glowing terms."

She blushed under his gaze. "Well, thank you, Mr Finnigan."

He beat a hasty retreat, deception was easy, but he had made little headway. It was almost ten o'clock already. He discovered an alleyway between the buildings and climbed over a wall into the ample gardens of the home. The bottom of the garden was thick with rhododendron bushes, good cover. He settled himself to wait. The back of the house was not as attractive as the front, a network of drain pipes and outside plumbing adorned the walls of dirty grey render. There were bars on the outside of the windows and crows lined up along the gutter. Iain viewed them with suspicion, an omen.

He was quite starving now and desperate for a smoke, but it would give him away. Eventually the older children came out. They did not play. They followed orders shouted by a loud unattractive woman dressed in a taupe uniform. They marched on the spot, ran up and down, touched their toes, arms in the air. This went on for a good hour until he thought they would never finish. Once they had filed inside he began to have doubts that the baby would be brought out. Perhaps the matron had meant the bigger children went outside not the babies. He started formulating another plan should this one fail. It would mean entering the building undetected.

Another couple of hours passed, listening to the screams of a distraught child, shouting adults, the crashing of pans coming through the open kitchen window. A woman wheeled out a pram. She pushed it to a bench in the furthest corner of the garden. He edged closer through the bushes, from here the view of the house was limited. No sooner had the nurse settled on the bench than the maid appeared at the door.

"Iris, get yourself in here, Matron's doing her nut looking for you. You know you're not supposed to sit with them," the maid shouted.

Iris, grumbling under her breath, disappeared into the house. Iain had no time to waste. He broke cover, grabbed the sleeping child from the pram and darted back to his hiding place all in a matter of seconds. A low broken wall was easily straddled, leading into a graveyard that ran adjacent to the town park. Within seconds he was strolling under the trees through the park with the baby crooked in one arm. A surge of joy rose inside his chest, that temporary lift of the heart, a clarity painting the grass greener and the sky bluer. Everything was as fresh and new as the horizons and opportunities ahead. He wanted to laugh out loud, shout at the blazing July sun.

The worst was over, reality was yet to fog and fade his optimism.

The long quiet vigil by Nell's bed had shown him a way. His son could have a home and a mother who loved him. He would give the baby to Nell. It would be her baby, not the one who had come so early and died as the sun kissed the horizon. This strong healthy child could be brought up as Nell's and nobody need ever know. He would be sure of the child's well being with her, he would be safe in her hands. And there was nobody there to give him pause for thought, to raise a hand of dissension, to say perhaps, just perhaps, there was more to this than one woman and one baby.

He took the train from the town station and walked the two miles back to Brackenheath as he and Nell had done the evening before. This time the view from the cottage gate was breathtaking. A vast expanse of cobalt blue water gleaming in the summer sunshine stretched to the horizon. The ululation of the gulls filled the air as they wheeled and turned in the breeze.

It was only as he entered the small cottage that the pall of death covered him as surely as a veil. It was cool inside and still. In the parlour he was shocked to find a coffin had been delivered and Joanna was in it, dressed in the same gown she had worn to the Harvest Supper.

"I couldn't fasten it up at the back," Aunt Cath said.

The colour drained from his face. "Where's Helena?"

"Where you left her. You got him back, I see." She viewed the baby. There was no surprise in her voice, only a hint of derision.

"Aye," he said. She moved to let him pass.

Nell's room was sour with birth and death. She slept, hair loose, pale smooth skin young and unmarked, unaltered by the unravelling of life. The dead child still lay in the drawer by the bed. He could not bear to touch it.

He ran into Aunt Cath in the hall. "Will you take the dead child away, please?"

"Away?" she said, aghast. "Where?"

"Take him downstairs, I'll see to it after."

She sniffed huffily, pushing past him. She wrapped the child up while he watched, and carried it away. He closed the door behind her and the click roused Nell.

"Where have you been?" she asked, eyes unfocused from tears and sleep. "Aunt Cath wouldn't tell me."

"No, she didn't agree with me," he said.

"Have you fallen out?"

"No, nothing so bad. She's got the hump, she'll get over it."

"I thought you'd left. Wouldn't have blamed you if you had. What's that?" She hauled herself up the bed, leaning back on the pillows.

"He's for you." He held out his arms to her, the child an offering in his hands. The shawl fell open. The baby was awake and his arms and legs flailed.

She cried out, reaching her hands up to take him. The smile she gave Iain smoothed out the grief, shone from her eyes. She opened her mouth in amazement then kissed the hardness of the baby's cheek, breathing in the smell of him.

In giving it, his own flesh and blood, they both knew he was abandoning it all over again, absolving himself of responsibility. It was the best he could manage, the only thing, and in doing so he dared to feel selfless and heroic, and she in her turn felt the same.

Their total self-absorption brought mutual amnesia. They failed to see their major stumbling block – Freddy – the man whose wedding ring was snug on Nell's finger. If nobody gave it voice, this one problem, perhaps it did not exist. The only reality was she had a baby re-born and she felt joy and gratitude beyond expression. She would not see the risk of taking this unwanted baby. Her need was too great.

Holding the baby, her breasts ached unbearably. Iain leaned back on the door. Unabashed by his presence she unbuttoned her nightdress. The baby, smelling the milk, turned his head from side to side questing for his meal. Iain saw the full curve of her breast, swollen with milk, the pale pink thumb print of her nipple as she put it to the baby's eager mouth. He latched on and sucked hungrily, his small body relaxing, the hair so dark against the ivory skin of her chest. She traced the perfection of his shell-like ear with her finger and the velvet skin along the line of his jaw. She smiled up at Iain. He hardly dared to acknowledge his feelings as he watched her feed his child. She beckoned him to come closer and he took a few steps forward. His head told him to leave them now but his heart opposed him and he stood ambivalent halfway across the room.

"I should go," he said.

"No, no you shouldn't." Suddenly she was desperate for him to stay, patting the bedcover with her hand. "Come sit a while. Look at your beautiful son."

"Your son," he said, sitting down on the bed.

"Our son." Brave words. She knew them to be a mistake. She grasped his hand and his stomach pitched, at her words and her action. Her candid blue eyes, still red from her tears, were soft with adoration. This wasn't possible, none of this, he had to ensure she understood. The trick was not to care overly but he was frightened he did and his control was slipping further out of reach.

"Yours and Freddy's," he said tearing his eyes from hers with difficulty, looking again at the feeding baby.

"Yes, of course." She withdrew her hand. "Are you going away? To the war?"

He wasn't sure if he had told her this himself, the words were bubbling in his brain, on his tongue, waiting for the moment. "If they'll take me," he confirmed. Tears welled in her eyes. "Don't start snivelling," he warned, but not unkindly and she smiled. "I had to take him – the baby. I took him. I didn't think they'd hand him over. It'll probably be in the papers. This has to be a secret. Freddy mustn't know. He would never accept my child," he paused and she remained silent. "Joanna and her baby died, we shall bury them together. You'll never get away with him being an early baby. If you stay here a while and register his birth in say, a month, then you can go home after another month or so."

"You've been very busy thinking this through, haven't you?"

"I've got to try to get this right. Is your Aunt reliable? Will she help you?"

"Oh, yes," she said, "she would do anything if I asked it of her."

"And will you do this for me?"

"For you?" Who was she doing it for? Herself? There was nothing greater he could have given her than this. Had he offered his life, it could not have meant more. It could not supplant her dead child. This baby was sacred in his own right. Circumstances had made him so. "I will do it and for us all."

"Thank you." An insubstantial phrase. "I'm going to catch the last train this evening."

"So soon? Won't you stay for Joanna's funeral?"

"I can't, I've a lot to do."

The baby had fallen asleep feeding, she moved him up onto her shoulder, rubbing his back. "What's his name?" she asked.

"I don't know. What do you think?"

"His father should name him."

"I'm not – I won't be his father." Suddenly Freddy was a brief shadow between them. "How ironic, he'll be a Hart."

"Only in name, he'll never be a Hart, Iain," she said with certainty.

"We'll name him Joe, for her," he said, standing up.

She swallowed back the tears. "Yes, she'd have liked that."

"Would she?" His voice was bitter and his question went unanswered. He hardly knew how to leave her.

"When will I see you again?" she said.

"I don't know. It's for the best. Freddy will come home to you – and his son. You'll be a family. A child needs a family."

"Yes – Freddy – of course. Good luck then."

Later he would try to recall exactly what it was that moved him, her sad little smile, the turn of her head, the slip of her gaze away from his. He had a sudden mad need to keep her attention, grasp the very last sliver of time from the moment. All he would remember was the softness of her cheeks against his hard palms as he leaned forward. The press of her soft pliant lips on his was a confirmation, something he had known since he had first met her, melting an inner working of his heart and head that had long been frozen. The kiss was not lustful or even sexual. It was a physical pact, a contract. It did not matter what had gone before or what would come in the future, they were linked now and by more than the baby, although Iain would have cause to pretend otherwise.

He drew back first and she kept her face upturned expectantly, her expression rapt. With an uncertain smile he turned away, his heart threatening to burst from his chest, an unbearable agony he had never experienced.

When he closed the door on her, he leaned back on it, releasing a huge breath. He packed his bag and went downstairs.

"Are you going?" Aunt Cath asked.

"Aye, Helena will explain everything to you."

"What about this baby?" The dead child was tucked in at Joanna's feet.

"Leave the child in the coffin with Joanna, they'll be buried together."

"Yes, it does make sense." She was thinking of the money.

"It'll make even more sense when you talk to Helena. I have to go."

She saw him to the door. He kissed her cheek and it pinked under his lips. "Thanks," he said, "thanks for everything."

Part II

Freddy

Swift to its close ebbs our life's little day
Earth's joys grow dim, its glories pass away
Change and decay in all around I see
O thou who changest not, abide with me!

Abide with me – Henry Francis Lyte

Chapter Fifteen

The train rattled through the countryside and Nell shifted uncomfortably in her seat. She shared the stuffy carriage with two soldiers smart in khaki, and a middle-aged lady knitting. Her needles bled scarlet wool, clacking in time with the train wheels. Nell watched the passing glory of the July countryside, cows grazing, church spires, villages and towns, then back into lush green meadowland, painted hedgerows and fields of crops. Occasionally they rushed through a tunnel and she briefly stared at her reflection in the smudged glass.

She was relieved to reach Canterbury. Freddy had been transferred from France to a hospital on the outskirts of the city. She retrieved a creased scrap of paper from her handbag with the address on, to give to the driver.

The cab stopped on the tidy gravel drive and she alighted with her carpetbag. She paid the fare and walked up the sweeping steps to the front door that was propped open by a sturdy clay pot of English Marigolds, their orange faces glowing in the sunlight. The hospital was a Victorian manor temporarily converted for convalescing soldiers.

In the vestibule above the mosaic tiled floor, an impressive chandelier reflected rainbows across the plaster walls. In its day it had been a fine house, now it showed signs of neglect and decay and smelt of warmed up mashed potato and carbolic. The nurse at the reception desk smiled in preoccupied welcome.

"I've come to see Freddy Hart," Nell said.

"You're Mrs Hart," the nurse said shaking her hand. "I'm Nurse Langley. Put your bag behind the desk, you can pick it up later. Come and speak to the doctor and then you can see your husband."

The nurse led her through to a waiting room, high ceilings, ornate cornicing and a grand fireplace. The door to the doctor's office was open. "Doctor Grant, Mrs Hart has arrived," she said.

"Come in, come in." Doctor Grant was a balding man with an impressive handlebar moustache. He ushered Nell to a seat opposite his desk.

He flicked through a file. "Ah yes, you've come some distance, Mrs Hart. How was your journey?"

"Fine, thank you. How's Freddy?"

"Your husband arrived last week. He has had a slow recovery." He pushed his half-moon spectacles up the bridge of his nose. "I believe he has turned a corner. It is a serious injury, Mrs Hart, he lost a piece of his skull. The surgery they did in France is quite remarkable. They have inserted a metal plate in its place. It will be a long road to recover from this. He has had setbacks. It was necessary to operate again to relieve pressure on his brain." He paused to refer to the notes.

She looked out of the window at the gardens, sweeping lawns, an arbour and a rose bed in full bloom. It might have been a swamp for all the impression it made on her.

The doctor continued. "He suffers from headaches and, understandably, his temperament can be unstable. We're not sure if this is trauma to the brain itself or battle fatigue. Shell shock, have you heard of that?" She shook her head. The doctor smiled and said, "It is something we find is affecting our boys over in Europe. It is caused by the stress of living under the extreme bombing and shelling - a nervous affliction, a neurosis, mood swings, dreams, shaking, that kind of thing. Well, his symptoms fit with shell shock, so we are hopeful his brain has escaped damage. Don't look so worried, you will find him to be quite himself a lot of the time. And it means he won't be going back. He has received a medical discharge from the army."

Nell thought she might be suffering a nervous affliction, the return of a prodigal husband. Temperamental, cocky Freddy Hart. Once the courtship was over it was hard to say anything right. How she had tried and failed. She had almost hoped he wouldn't be himself, but someone else entirely, someone she had fooled herself into believing she had married.

"Any questions?" The doctor smiled. She had many questions and since he had the answers to none of them, she did not ask.

She cleared her throat, there was only one question she could ask. "When can he come home?"

* * * *

She followed Nurse Langley through the glass conservatory with its potted plants and easy chairs. Two men played cards at a table, one had his legs in plaster, the other had no legs at all and sat in a wheelchair. They greeted the nurse and Nell cheerily.

"On you go," the nurse said to encourage her.

Freddy, sitting on a deck chair in the sun, had his back to the house. His hair was cropped close, a livid red scar tracked across his scalp clearly visible in the dark stubble. She reached out a hand to touch it. He gazed up at her, his familiar brown eyes underlined with mauve in a pale face.

"Hello, Nell," calmly said as if life could hold no more surprises. They reached out at the same moment. It was obligatory, part of what they had imagined, relived over and over. So that is what they did and he pulled her onto his lap, his hand gentle on her face. His tears were wet, a contrast to the dry warmth of his mouth on hers. Cupping his face, she was unbearably sad. He was a stranger to her, after all, just as she remembered, and she wondered how she could possibly bridge this gap of knowledge. They would talk like they had never talked, they would connect, a husband and wife reunited. And for a moment she believed in happy ever after, because in her head she had never gone beyond this grand passionate reunion. Even now, sitting on his lap in the creaking deck chair, she could not see further than this because deep down she knew nothing had changed.

He buried his face in her neck, holding her tight. She happily submitted to his affection. She wanted a husband, to be loved and happy.

"When can I come home?" He stared at her, to absorb the detail of her face, the blue of her eyes, the colour of her hair, the smell of her. A woman, possibly any real woman would have sufficed.

"In a month, the doctor says, hopefully."

"A month? I want to come home now."

"You're not well enough yet, you have to do as you are told."

"Jack and Ginger, they're all still over there you know." He frowned at the manicured stripy lawn.

"Oh, Freddy, has it been hell? I can't imagine what you've been through."

"I don't want you to imagine it. I wish they'd sent Jack and Ginger home."

"Were they hurt too?" He nodded. "Well they must be a lot better than you. So that's good isn't it?" she said.

His eyes were black stones, hard with disbelief. "They'll send them back then won't they?" he said. "Bloody hell, you've no idea." His face softened. "Christ, sorry, let's not talk about that. I've missed you so much. How long have we got?"

"I'm staying overnight at The Golden Lion, it's down the road. I'll come back in the morning. I'll have to leave before lunch," she said.

"And how is everyone?"

She could feel the pit yawning between them. They had to discuss triviality or they would be completely lost, there was nothing else to say. She forced a smile and a jolly tone. "Oh, your mother's much the same. Stays in bed a lot, bad chest, bad feet, the usual. Poor Father is run ragged trying to keep the farm going. We have a prisoner-of-war, old Mr Feeney and Lisa who helps in the house and dairy. She's almost seventeen now and there's me. A lot of work with too few hands to do it."

"Sounds as if it's a good job I'm coming home then," he said, and grinned. "What about my boy? How's Joe?"

"He's well. A big boy, two years old next month." His birthday was next week. That was her secret.

"Can't wait to see him for real, the photographs were nice but you can't know someone through a picture can you?"

She shook her head, his enthusiasm about the boy was genuine. Of course it would be. His son, Iain's son.

"Perhaps," he nibbled at her ear lobe, his son could wait, "we can go to my room. I have my own room here."

"I don't know. It doesn't seem very respectable." Alone with a stranger.

He spoke sharply, "We're married, why the hell not?"

"Shh, someone will hear." Not a stranger, her husband.

"Come on." He pushed her out of his lap and stood up. His arm across her shoulders was heavy and possessive. She circled his waist. He was terribly thin. Through his pyjamas and dressing gown she could feel every bone of him.

They strolled back through the glass house into the sitting room. A nurse, bustling down the hallway, smiled at them.

"Showing the Missus my private accommodation," he said.

The nurse said, "You won't be missed until tea-time." She winked and hurried on down the hall.

Nell turned all shades of pink and he laughed at her. "Come on Miss Prim-and-proper."

The window in his room opened onto a small balcony. A single metal bed was pushed to the wall, a chest of drawers, a desk and chair. He opened the window, and white curtains billowed off the white walls in the breeze. He wedged the chair securely under the door handle.

"What do you think?" he asked sitting on the bed.

"It's ever so fancy for a hospital," she said. "A proper gentleman's residence."

He patted the bed beside him. Fighting her shyness, she allowed him to pull out her hatpin and remove her hat. His commanding hand pushed her back onto the bed. A firm kiss preceded his probing tongue. He lifted her skirt, wrenching at her underclothes with building urgency. His hands were rough with desperation, dreams that had carried him through France, the long-held desire for a woman he had fabricated. Not Nell, not really, but a wanton woman, who needed no wooing and knew what he wanted and how he wanted it. And suddenly Nell was that woman, pinned underneath him, dry as dust and submitting because there was nothing else for it. He closed his eyes. He didn't want to see her face, overwhelmed, uncomfortable, biting her lip as her body objected to every thrust. She was his fictional whore, soft peach skin concealing bone, bending with heat, melting with lust.

It was over quickly and he slumped weightily on top of her. The cool breeze fanned her face, his head heavy on her shoulder. She wanted him to get off her. He made no attempt to move. Tears welled in her eyes, dripping down her temples towards her hair.

"Freddy," she whispered, crushed beneath him. She gently shook his shoulder. He had fallen asleep and jerked into consciousness.

He rolled off her and she was able to get up and arrange her clothing. He was unaware of her and curled himself into a ball and fell asleep again. She took the chair from the door and sat down at the window. The view of the garden was beautiful and beyond it a wooded valley. Swallows flew low across the lawn chattering, swooping in circles and turning sharply.

He was back and it didn't feel natural. She had to admit it never had, not their wedding night or any other night of their married life together. He wasn't unkind or rough or anything dramatic. It was his inattention to her feelings, careless of her, an act well performed, lacking emotion. From the first, married life was like breathing fresh air through a sheep's fleece. She had known mediocrity and this would be the extent of her experience. Slow death, up to her neck in suffocating mud.

Her tears fell unchecked. This was her life. This was her husband come back from war. The man she had married - selfish, sociable and conceited.

She glanced at the bed where Freddy slept soundly. It was time to start again, new beginnings, she thought. Her heart was heavy with doubt. At the basin in the corner of the room she splashed her face with water, dried it on a fluffy, white towel. She surveyed her reflection in the small shaving mirror. She was still young, it would come right she told herself. Freddy was coming home, they would fall madly in love, he would adore Joe and she would be happy and complete.

He stirred in his sleep, mumbling words she could not decipher. He covered his head with his hands moaning, little animal grunts of fear.

"Freddy," she said stroking his face. "Freddy, wake up, you're dreaming."

His eyes opened wide in terror, making her start. He jumped up as if he had received an electric shock, his expression wild and unnerving. He stared at her although he did not really see her.

"Freddy." She touched his arm. "It's Nell, you were dreaming." His eyes focused and he ran a hand over his face.

"Yes," he said, "I know who you are, I know, I'm fine."

She didn't want to be here any more, she wished she hadn't come. It was ridiculous to suggest leaving already but she had to. "I had better go and find my hotel," she said. "I'll come back in the morning."

He did not attempt to disagree or reach for her. "Yeah, come back in the morning." He rocked on the edge of the bed. She leaned forward, kissed his cheek and left him.

He shakily went to the chest of drawers, opened the top drawer. At the back, beneath his neatly folded clothing, he withdrew a German pistol, a souvenir from a corpse. He stared at the dull grey metal. He checked it was loaded, silly really, it was always loaded, and yet he still checked. He was comforted to know it was there just in case. Sometimes his dreams were so real and vivid. He hid the pistol back in its place.

He had been back in the mud and stink of the trench, bayoneting a Jerry like a lunatic, stabbing and stabbing, so much blood. He turned his hands over expecting to see the red stains. Of course, he had washed the blood away and it was not a Hun he had killed but Tom. He covered his face with clean hands and sobbed, frenzied noisy sobs that shook his entire body.

Nell had been here as if in a dream, soft and kind, but he had wanted her to leave. He had taken all the comfort she had to offer, now he wanted to be alone. His head throbbed, he would ask for tablets when he went to the dining room for tea.

He thought of his friends back in France, the ones he had lost and the ones still fighting for their lives and their sanity. Jack, with his worried lined face, his hair sticking up on his head in tufts. Ginger with colouring to match his name, always singing his songs, substituting the proper words with lewd ones. He had stayed with Jack since training camp, while a lot of their mates had gone, dead or too badly injured to return. Now Freddy was one of those. He wanted to go back despite everything, the mud, corpses, shelling, food, he wanted to go back and finish the job. That would not happen now. He had accepted it. They would win it without him. He was going home to the life he had left behind.

His old life had its ghosts too. Tom, of course, dear Tom, and the terrible heavy guilt Freddy shouldered, seeping toxin into his soul. He had seen some horrific things in the war, had done some too. He had bayoneted a man in cold blood, shot a man through the head, trodden on the corpses of his own companions. But he had done worse and to his own brother in the sanity of peacetime.

And Iain Macdonald. What of him? He did not know of Iain's whereabouts. He never enquired of Nell through his letters if she knew. He hoped when he returned home the keeper would be gone. He prayed, for lately he was a praying man, that Iain would never come back. The mere thought of him brought bile into the back of his throat. His hate for Iain had not waned with time, if anything he had built upon it. His hatred rested happily alongside his guilt for Tom, they made comfortable bedfellows.

He washed his face and went down to the dining room. They served soup, and fish with boiled potatoes. He had little appetite and picked at his food, listening to the jovial conversation of Dick, the man without legs, and Stanley, who was blind.

When Freddy stood up to leave Dick said to him, "You going home, mate?"

"Yeah, soon, in about four weeks apparently."

"I'm off next week. Was that your wife?"

"Yeah," he said unenthusiastically.

"She's something worth going home for, lucky devil." Dick laughed.

"Was she a looker?" Stanley asked.

Dick laughed again. "Not much good to you, Stanley. Tell you what, we'll have to go out dancing. You can have the ugly ones and I can have the ones that tread on your toes." Their loud laughter filled the dining room.

Freddy watched them for a second. "Oh, piss off," he said under his breath as he turned away.

* * * *

Nell poured the tea into the best china cups. The perfect wife. She smiled across the white tablecloth, spread with everything their saved rations had afforded. It had to be special, Freddy's homecoming, perfect. Mr Hart stirred his tea, the spoon clinking loudly round the cup, clanging into the saucer. Lisa sniffed, discreetly rubbing her nose.

Every sound of mastication was magnified in the silence. Nell sliced the fruitcake, tidy segments cut larger because of the occasion. She realised now she had cut the ham sandwiches in dainty triangles, the way Freddy hated, like they did at the teashop in town. She wasn't even sure he liked fruitcake now she thought about it. But it didn't matter. He was concentrating very hard on ignoring her, lips pursed, hard black eyes that occasionally slipped back to look at the boy. Joe fidgeted at her elbow eating what she had set before him, one leg swinging, his foot occasionally hitting off the chair leg.

"How was the journey, Freddy?" Mr Hart said, his mouth full of porkpie.

"You already asked me that," Freddy said, "in the trap from the station."

Mr Hart sighed, silly me, the sigh said.

"You'll be glad to get home," Mrs Hart said.

He would be kind to his mother, spare her, anyway it was a sort of truth. "Yes, Mother, I'm very glad."

"Would you like some more water Joe?" Nell asked. Joe's nodding head joined his ready smile. She escaped for five minutes to refill his cup.

She stood in the little scullery exhausted by the intense awkwardness she had just left. This was awful, so much worse than she could have imagined.

Freddy knew. He knew at once, the minute he laid eyes on Joe. And how could it be otherwise? Just because she had not seen it before, not until that second when Freddy had knelt down amongst Joe's tin soldiers and he and the child had made eye contact. Right up until then, she had not seen it, had been blind. But when Freddy met her gaze, his dark unfathomable eyes were filled with shock, a question in that expression, a question she could never answer. And Joe, innocent little boy, with hair as dark as his father's and eyes as green, had looked to her for the answer too. She knew at that moment she could never get away with it. What his parents had swallowed so acceptingly, a baby was a baby after all, Freddy never would.

She filled Joe's cup, pressed it for a second to her burning forehead and closed her eyes. She returned to the tea table, smiled at each blank face, all except Joe who smiled back.

"Nell made brawn, Freddy, do have some, it's your favourite," Mrs Hart said, offering the plate.

He obliged by taking a couple of slices. "They'll be bringing in the cows," Mr Hart said, looking at his pocket watch.

"Who?" Freddy asked.

"Old Mr Feeney comes to help three times a week and we have Hans our prisoner-of-war," Mr Hart said.

Freddy swallowed, ran his tongue across his front teeth before speaking. "A Jerry?"

"Yes, we had to, there's no one left to employ, Freddy."

"There's a Jerry on North Farm?" He let out a sharp barking laugh.

"I told you about Hans when I visited the hospital. It's nothing, Freddy," Nell said. "Lots of farms have taken on prisoners. It makes sense, we'd never have managed without Hans."

He looked at her, curled his lip. "I wasn't asking you. I don't doubt Father had his reasons for taking on a Hun."

"Freddy, please." Mrs Hart dabbed at her lips with a scrunched napkin.

Freddy wouldn't apologise, not for a bloody Jerry being employed on his farm. What were they thinking? The world had gone mad. He opened his mouth to speak.

"Would you like some fruitcake, Mr Hart?"

Everyone turned to look at Lisa who leaned across the table to Freddy, the peace offering on the plate in her outstretched hand.

"More tea, Father?" Nell said quickly.

"Thank you, Nell."

Joe's foot tapped sharply off his chair and Freddy flinched. "I don't like fruitcake," he said to Lisa who blushed and put the plate down.

Nell was relieved to clear the table, and slightly premature since Mrs Hart, being a slow eater, was yet to finish. She hid in the scullery, washing dishes with extreme enthusiasm while Joe played at her feet. Lisa made a halfhearted attempt at conversation, soon giving up.

When she ran out of excuses, Nell was forced to join the family in the parlour, bright with the sinking sun. They had moved on from tea to polite schooners of sherry. Mr Hart and Freddy had lit their pipes, the smoke wove rippling banners in the air. Mr Hart was telling a story and Nell sat down almost unnoticed. Mrs Hart was getting giggly from the sherry and Freddy's tongue was loosening, an occasional breath of vaguely optimistic laughter, buoying Nell's fading hopes.

The room had never been so tidy nor indeed, the entire house. Nell had quashed her mounting pessimism before Freddy's return by scrubbing and turning out every cupboard. Her outpouring of nervous energy had cleared every cobweb, cleaned every drawer and wardrobe. She had tidied up the past, organised the future.

She was striving for a perfection she could not accomplish, plugging the hole in the dam. Freddy was home, he was really home after all this long, long time.

The tension eased with the sherry and Nell slipped back out to lend a hand to Hans and Mr Feeney. In her days in service she had never imagined herself as a farmer. Joanna would have been appalled, and yet it had become her life. The cows waited, patient in their stalls, and Mr Feeney and Hans steadily worked through them. Hans leaned away from his cow and smiled cheerfully at her, motioning with his hands, as if still milking, rolling his eyes in mock boredom. She laughed at him. She took her stool and bucket and rested her head on the warm bovine flank. She squirted the rich creamy milk on her hands for lubrication and with the alternating pressure of her fingers watched with satisfaction as the bucket steadily filled with frothing milk. When they had finished Hans departed to the camp on his bicycle and she strolled across to the house in the warmth of the evening to put Joe to bed.

She loved this part of the day, lying on Joe's bed, reading to him, tickling him, giving him hugs and kisses. Joe giggled as she played the piggy game with his toes and blew raspberries on his tummy. Freddy appeared in the doorway leaning against the doorjamb.

"Look, Joe, Daddy's come to kiss you goodnight," she said. Joe appeared doubtful.

Freddy circuited the room, picked up a toy car, set it down, kicked a ball with his foot, which bounced off the skirting board. He moved the curtain aside with one finger. Across the meadow Willow, the solitary horse, grazed.

She came and stood beside him, he searched her face, waiting. She was at a loss to know what to say. She wanted to say the right thing, except the words were unknown to her.

"Tell me about it, Nell," he said eventually.

She swallowed hard, her mouth dry. All her worst worries realised. "Tell you what, Freddy?"

He glanced past her at Joe, who turned the pages of a book with great care. "About Joe."

"I don't know what you mean."

He leaned in close to her, his breath hot on her face. "Which banana boat did he fall off?"

The steady practised lie came easily to her mouth. "Don't be so ridiculous, Freddy."

"Look at him, Nell," he hissed, "look at him."

She could not help looking at Joe kneeling innocently on his bed, black hair falling across his face. He needs a haircut, she thought irrelevantly.

"I see him, Freddy, our son. Now stop it or you'll frighten him."

His eyes switched between her and the child in confusion. He sat down on the edge of Joe's bed.

"What are you looking at, Joe?" he asked. Joe stared at him, unmoving. Freddy touched the silky blackness of the child's hair. "I'm your daddy," he said quietly, convincing himself or the child? It was then she glimpsed for the first time what she had done to Freddy by pretending Joe was his. What a terrible lie she and Iain had woven between them, a sticky enveloping web. There was no going back or confessing the truth. Freddy had a son – and it was Iain's. She pushed the thought away quickly.

Joe held the book out to him. Freddy smiled uncertainly before taking it. "Thanks, Joe," he said. He leafed through it, pointing out some of the pictures. "What's that?"

"Cat," Joe said correctly.

"And that?"

"Dog."

"You're a clever boy aren't you?" He held out his arms. Joe recoiled and his lip began to wobble. Freddy stood up, backed away.

"It's all right, Joe, it's your daddy," she said, then to Freddy, "He's a bit shy, that's all. These things take time."

"I know." He looked at her in the strangest way, dark eyes glittering in the gloom. She reached for his hand. It was limp and unresponsive in hers.

"Freddy," she said, "it will come right. You've been away a long, long time. We can be happy, when we all get to know each other again."

He stared into space, showing no emotion. "Yes," he said. "You know, I'm really very tired. Do you think anyone would mind if I went to bed?"

"No, your mother will be going to bed herself soon and your father always falls asleep in the chair by nine o'clock." She smiled and squeezed his hand.

"Thanks Nell," he said with sincerity, "you've been great."

She did not know what he was referring to, but he smiled at her and she felt better for it.

When she crept into bed later it felt odd to be sharing it with her husband. These past two years the only company she had at night was Joe when he was ill or teething. She slept fitfully, waking every time Freddy shouted out in his sleep or when his dreaming body convulsed, jolting the bed.

She had to hope that would be the end of it. Perhaps Joe was not so much like his father after all. Freddy was anxious and over-wrought, as was she. Before she fell asleep she said a quick prayer.

Chapter Sixteen

Freddy's head hurt. Sometimes the pain was slight and bearable, other days it was all he could do to stop himself banging his head off the wall. Today a steady pulsating tom-tom beat in his temple, sapped his energy and set his temper on edge. They were halfway through the harvest at North Farm. Once he had shared happy harvests with Tom. In those days he had enjoyed the hot strenuous work. The exertion numbed his body, almost eradicating the aching muscles. Now the joy of the harvest was lost to him. Everything ached, his head throbbed and his feet were sore. He was sticky with sweat, dusty from the thresher, and the day only half done.

Lisa and Nell worked in the field from necessity. There were no longer enough men in the village to recruit the gang of nine or so needed to keep the thresher going. The hot grimy work included hauling coal and water to keep the steam engine in action. Even with Derek Parsons driving the machine, the two girls, Freddy, his father, Mr Feeney and Hans the Hun, as Freddy called him, they were still short-handed.

At lunchtime Willow waited despondently at the helm of the wagon chewing hay from a nosebag. The motley task force ate lunch shaded by the oak trees, where the field bordered Harrowmead.

It was the field where the travellers had camped the evening Iain had seen them off with an ash stick. Freddy made a conscious effort not to think of it. He had only let them camp there to rile Iain. How well the plan had worked but, as usual, it had backfired, leaving Iain laughing at them. The old familiar hate flooded Freddy. His father had said Iain was fighting in France and he hoped with all his heart the bastard Scot would be killed.

Nell had packed pasties, bread and cheese for lunch and stone bottles of cool water to quench their sore throats. Freddy watched her sharing a joke with Hans. He was trying to tell her something using actions and Pidgin English. He held out his blistered palm, miming a sewing motion, pinching index finger and thumb together as if holding a needle.

She copied him. "You sew?"

"Sew." He mimicked, nodding, a smile creasing his worn tired face.

"Clothes. You're a tailor?" She clutched her apron, rubbing the cotton with her hand.

He looked at it blankly. "Nein."

"You sew," she repeated, miming as he had done.

"Ja," he agreed and laughed, she laughed too. It was ridiculous. They could not convey the smallest thing to each other.

"You sew, but don't sew." She laughed harder. Freddy scowled. His wife was joking with Fritz who had murdered almost his whole platoon. His friends fell in the mud, and his wife fed and entertained the enemy.

Hans showed her his boot, pointing out the stitching, nodding his head. "Shoes," she said. Joe danced in the wheat stubble, oblivious to the heat of the sun, picking up stray heads of yellow corn.

Hans was relieved. "Ja, shoes."

"Good," she said. "You sew shoes." She surveyed the gathering in triumph. "He's a cobbler."

"Sounds like a load of old cobblers to me," Mr Feeney said and they laughed, except Hans who was thoroughly confused.

"Great," Mr Hart said, "we have a Jerry who's a cobbler. Anyone got any shoes need fixing? We might make a bob or two, what d'you reckon, Freddy?"

He glowered at his father and chewed his pasty. "Eh, up," Mr Feeney said, "look at young Hart, he's gleaning for us." Joe brought a handful of corn to Freddy and dropped it in his lap.

"For Christ's sake, Joe." He flicked the corn off his knees in irritation.

"He's only playing, Freddy," Nell said.

"Is that what you're doing?" he asked.

"What?" she said, baffled.

"Making cows eyes at Fritz, is that what you're doing, only playing?"

She flushed, embarrassed, glancing quickly at Mr Hart, Derek Parsons and Mr Feeney who were suddenly taking great interest in their lunch. Lisa watched Freddy wide eyed. "Don't be so ridiculous. I was trying to find out what job he did at home, that's all," she said.

He raised his eyebrows. "I've bayoneted one exactly like him and gutted him for good measure, a bastard like all the rest and you sit making small talk with him."

"Freddy," Mr Hart said, "that's enough, son. She meant no harm by it. Your mother would have a fit if she heard you."

He lowered his head they all sickened him. What did they know about anything? They had not been there, thigh deep in mud, waiting for the next bullet, breathing in the stench of the decaying corpses, leaving your best mate in the middle of nowhere to rot and be picked by the birds and rats.

Nell fell quiet, stunned by his chastisement. She didn't know what Freddy thought about anything and she wondered if she ever had. He feigned sleep every night, and disinterest every day. Delusion had kept her warm in his absence and now the truth was a lonely place.

High above them the heartfelt song of the skylark filled the air. She searched the blue for a glimpse of it. "Look, Joe, look at the pretty bird." She put her arm around his small frame and pointed.

"Bird," he repeated laughing.

Freddy sneered at her with contempt. The sweet sound of the bird carried him swiftly back to the battlefield. He shuddered. The earth was hard and dry under his buttocks, but when he put his hand down his fingers sank into the sucking mud. He cried out and leaped to his feet, the group looked at him in astonishment.

"An adder bit your arse?" Derek Parsons asked.

Nell sniggered, slow to hide it behind her hand. Freddy glared at her, at all of them. He stomped away towards the woodland.

"I suppose I'd better go after him," she said.

Mr Hart stood up. "No, no, you stay here, you don't seem to be flavour of the month at the moment."

"Thanks," she retorted acidly.

Mr Hart found him by the river. He jumped when Mr Hart placed a hand on his shoulder. "Sorry, son, didn't mean to startle you. You been through some, haven't you? We understand."

"You understand nothing," he snapped, and his father saw the tears coursing down his face. "That whore and Jerry bastard."

"Shh, Freddy, don't say that, you don't mean it. You're not well yet, it'll take time. The doctor said so didn't he?"

He ducked his head as if to avoid an invisible low flying bird. "Christ, I'm a nervous wreck, my head's thumping."

"You need to rest, you've done enough for one day."

"I used to work until sun down. Will anything ever be the same again?" Freddy knew the answer.

Mr Hart shook his head sadly, his arm across his son's back. "Sometimes there are things that change us. We are what we are because of what's happened to us. It's not down to Mother and Father and where you were brought up. You move on in life and good things have a good effect, and bad things, well, you have to live with them. You need time, son, time will help it fade, get things into perspective."

"And what about Tom?"

"What about Tom? We've heard nothing."

"Well, you wouldn't have would you," Freddy said watching the running water. Mr Hart did not pick up on the remark, a throw away comment.

"He knows where we are if he needs us, he'll always be welcome back no matter what," his father said.

Freddy wiped the drying tears off his face with his sleeve. "Life's been a right bugger up until now."

"I know. Freddy, be nice to Nell. She's a good, kind girl, she's no flirt. She's not looking for trouble. Don't make something out of nothing with her. You've got a lovely wife, a strong healthy son, and the farm, it's a lot to be grateful for."

"Yeah, I know. Sometimes I can't think straight. Everything gets so muddled up here." He tapped his temple softly with his knuckles. "I see stuff, feel it, smell it, hear it, you know, as though it's really, really there. Not in dreams, everyday stuff, like just now in the field."

"What did you see?"

"It was the bird singing, then mud – only mud, wouldn't mean much to anyone else. I'm sorry, Father, I won't talk about it anymore."

"No, don't talk, it'll upset you, Freddy. Come on, you go back up to the farm, walk with Nell."

He pulled at the grass beside him, shredding a stalk with his fingers. "No I'll stay here a while yet. I'll walk up later. You go on. I want to be on my own for a bit. I'm poor company at the best of times."

"If you're sure, I'll see you later."

When his father had gone, he walked to Keeper's House, standing in the dappled shade of the wood, the gate not quite closed. The windows stared back blank and dark. The path leading to it was littered with the leaves of two winters. They had piled up at the front door.

He tried to remember where it had happened, where he had set the trap. He tried to recall what had been going through his mind to do such a thing. How would he have felt if his plan had worked? What if it had caught Iain in its fatal jaws and not poor Tom? Happy, he thought, I would feel happy, not cheated. He stirred the leaf mould with his foot to reveal the black dirt beneath. Was it here his brother's blood had seeped into the earth? He searched about him. In what direction had they taken his body? He was not sure, had never been sure even then. He had been so shocked he had followed Iain's instructions. Iain had been calm and collected, almost kind.

Why did he imagine Joe was the very spit of Iain? Why was his mind playing these cruel tricks on him? Why did he doubt Nell so much he could hardly bear to look at her? He could not touch his own wife. He would reconcile himself to her, he decided. It was like his father had told him, she had meant no harm. She had always been straightforward, honest and naïve. She had not changed or deceived him. She was simple little Nell.

Go home. Go home and make peace with her. He walked out of the trees into the sunlight at the rear of the house. It was as if Iain might at any moment appear at the back door and call to him in that damned annoying brogue, or look at him with those insolent green eyes, filling the doorway like a colossus.

A movement in the undergrowth caught his eye, he followed it back into the shade of the trees. A large black dog emerged from the brush, a menacing growl rumbled in her throat, hackles raised, squaring up to him. He stepped back startled as if the dog had been summoned by the devil from the darkest regions of hell. It was Iain's dog, he could not mistake her for another and she remembered him. She lunged forward, baring fangs as white as bleached bone against the black of her coat. Freddy backed off further, spreading his hands at his sides, unsure whether to run or stand his ground. A sharp whistle pierced the pain in his head and the dog sank onto its haunches.

"All right, young Freddy, she won't hurt you," Isaac said, catching up with his charge.

His eyes flitted disbelievingly to Isaac's brown lined face. "For Christ sake," he said, catching himself before he fell to his knees. "It frightened the bloody wits out of me."

Isaac laughed at him. "I can see that. D'you think Iain had appeared from nowhere?" He chuckled wheezily. "You're a rum one, you. It's his dog, see? Not the man himself. He's away, have you not heard?"

Freddy nodded, pulling himself together. "Yeah, course I heard, I know that."

"You've got a guilty conscience, that's your trouble," Isaac said.

"What's that supposed to mean, old man?"

"Meant nothing by it, I'm sure, I don't know everything."

He viewed Isaac suspiciously. "Best keep it that way. Do you hear from Iain?"

Isaac was highly amused. "No, I don't read. Anyway, why is he so much in your thoughts? Didn't know you cared."

"I don't."

"Didn't you run into each other out there in France?"

"Don't be ridiculous, it's not like going for a stroll round the village. There are hundreds of miles of trenches, through France to Belgium. That's the trouble round here nobody knows what the hell's going on out there, or cares."

"How's your boy?" he asked with a glint in his eye which Freddy did not much care for.

"None of your business."

"And Tom? Whereabouts in France is he?"

He clenched his fists by his sides. "Why all these questions? Why don't you mind your own. Get lost, you've no business being here, this is Harrowmead land."

"You got no business here neither, I'm doing no harm, passing the time of day asking after your brother. It was something queer, the way he," Isaac blew air through his pursed lips, spreading his hands theatrically, "vanished."

"Whatever you think you know, forget it. You stay out of my way, I'll stay out of yours." He took one threatening step forward. Delilah stood up emitting a deep rumble from her throat.

"There're more things in heaven and earth," mumbled Isaac.

"I don't care for your soothsaying bollocks and tall tales, now bugger off." He strutted away.

"You'll be left with land but no love, young man, you mark my words," Isaac called after him. It was only after he turned away Isaac realised it would be so much worse than that.

* * * *

Freddy arrived home in a foul temper. He marched up the stairs and slammed their bedroom door closed. Nell sang as she made the supper. Joe fell asleep on the soft chair in the corner of the kitchen. She smiled at him and thought of Joanna and Iain. How she missed Joanna, forever the optimist, funny and lovable. Her life was a drama, always madly in love or madly in hate, both equally absorbing and worthwhile.

In the dark intimacy of their shared attic room at Harrowmead, Joanna had spun Nell a romantic tale in the black space between their two little beds - the intriguing, Argus-eyed gamekeeper making love to the buxom maid. Joanna, whose infatuations were always fleeting, made it sound like love, his kisses, tender caresses and flaming passion. Hearing it made Nell's heart beat rapidly, her stomach flipping over, sighing with envy. After Joanna's lurid story Nell did not see Iain in quite the same way.

Iain had given her the greatest gift of all in his son. Joe had healed her, given her a reason not to fade away and die. He never failed to make her smile. She loved him no less than she could have possibly loved the son she gave birth to. From the moment Iain placed Joe in her arms, she had loved the child. And Iain had watched her with those eyes of his that saw everything. Then he sealed their secret union by kissing her. It was such a careful appeasing kiss, calm and soothing as the fluttering wings of a butterfly. She had never been kissed like that before, tenderly, as if she were something precious, bruised by the merest touch. Closing her eyes the kiss was damp on her mouth, she would never ever forget. Sometimes she would stare at herself in the mirror as if the mark of the kiss were branded there for everyone to see. No words, no promises, merely a kiss, easily given, easily taken, a secret shared, it all meant nothing.

Freddy was her husband, her future. It was all such an effort, but she had to make it right somehow.

She put the dinner in the range. The effort must start now. She made a cup of tea and climbed the stairs. Freddy lay in the middle of the bed, one arm across his eyes. At first she thought he was asleep. She placed the cup on the bedside table. When she glanced at him he had moved his arm and peered at her with dark expressionless eyes.

She smiled. "Hello, I brought you a cuppa. Is your head feeling better?"

"Yes, thanks." Sitting up, he took the cup. He watched her as she perched on the bed, swinging her legs, gazing at her feet. The silence stretched between them for a few minutes as she struggled to think of something to say.

"Sorry about earlier, I didn't mean to upset you by talking to Hans. It was nothing to be jealous of." She had not meant to apologise. She wanted to smooth things over with him, make everything right.

"I'm not jealous of a Jerry. If I thought you'd have it off with him I wouldn't still be here, or you wouldn't," he said. She winced at his vulgarity.

"Where did you go? I thought you might walk back with me. We should spend more time together," she said.

He put down the cup, half full. "To the keeper's place."

Her face was as blank as a pebble. "How's the place looking?"

"The same, but without the Jock bastard living in it." He watched her for a reaction. She gave none.

"It's easier for the villagers, they can come and go as they please, help themselves to rabbits and birds," she said.

"Do you write to him?"

She was mortified. "No! What a question. Of course I don't. Why would I?'

"Thought he might want to know about his son."

The blood drained from her face, her head went fuzzy. Finding her voice she said, "Why do you say these stupid things? I thought we'd had this discussion already."

Quicker than she could react he pinned her to the bed. One hand held her wrists together the other squeezed her cheeks hard, the pressure pushing tears into her eyes. "If you ever show me up again in front of anyone like you did today in the field, I will kill you." His hand tightened on her jaw. "You'll wish you'd never been born. Do I make myself clear?"

She tried to nod but could not move her head only making a noise of assent in her throat, tears rolling into her ears. He released her and moved across to the opposite side of the bed. She stood up quickly, holding a hand to her aching face.

She ran from the room. The distant voice of Mrs Hart called to her. Lisa was in the dairy churning butter, out of earshot, and anyway she had little patience for Mrs Hart and her ailments. Downstairs Nell scooped up the sleeping child and ran out of the house.

When Joe woke up they roamed over the Common. She tried to calm herself, to make sense of Freddy's aggression. She carried Joe through the tall bracken, forging a path. She plucked a gorse blossom from between the thorns and sniffed its sweet perfume, pressing it to Joe's nose for him to smell.

This route took her by way of Isaac's hut. He squatted in the sun, poking at his fire with a stick. Delilah ran to meet them. Her tail wagged madly in recognition, making little whinnying noises of welcome. Nell sank to her knees, putting her arms around Delilah. She pressed her cheek to the silky black coat, smelling the hot, dusty, doggy scent. Joe laughed at Delilah when she stretched her neck and licked his fingers with a long pink tongue.

"Good afternoon, Mrs Hart," Isaac called. "I seen your husband this morning."

"Did you? At Harrowmead?"

"Aye, it was. Kind of touchy ain't he? Always been temperamental that one. Bet he leads you a life."

She laughed, a weak feeble sound. Delilah pushed her nose under Nell's hand giving her no option but to scratch the domed head. "Must be nice having Delilah for a bit of company," she said.

"Sit down awhile." He indicated a wedge of log, Joe settled on her knee. Isaac nodded at him. "Looks the spit of his father that one."

She flushed. "You think?"

"That'll be the one he denies," he said.

"What do you mean, Isaac?" she asked floundering.

He flapped his hands at her. "Nothing for you to worry about. Life has its twists and turns. I see your happiness is a long way from here."

Across the valley, beyond a patchwork of pasture and crops, nestled between two vales of trees, Tump Farm was visible with its barns and straggling outbuildings. She would never be a long way from here. Sighing, she said, "I don't think I'm meant to be happy."

"We're not here to be miserable, that's for sure. We're happy when we're born."

"Until life comes upon us and weighs us down with its problems and trials. We make our choices and the gate closes behind us and that's it."

He shook his head vigorously. "There's always a way out. Maybe not the way you'd think. The gate might be closed and bolted but there's always room to squeeze through the gap in the hedge."

She laughed at his optimism. "Throw the rule book away and be happy, is that it?"

He winked. "That's exactly it." He jumped upright with excitement. "And that's exactly what you'll do."

"You're mistaking me for someone terribly brave, Isaac."

"No," he said, eyes alight, "you're mistaking yourself. When you see your chance, and there shall be one, you'll do it. By God, you'll do it." He cackled, slapping his hand on his thigh.

His enthusiasm lightened her heavy heart and she joined in with his laughter. "I can't imagine an opportunity coming my way that could change anything. But you've cheered me up."

* * * *

At dinner Mr Hart ate noisily, snorting through his nose where the dust from the thresher had blocked his sinuses. Lisa sniffed, wiping her nose on her sleeve, not daring to speak because of the strained atmosphere. Freddy glowered at his plate, tasting nothing. The clunk of cutlery on china, the jarring scrape of knife and fork filled the gaps where conversation should have been.

Nell took a tray up to Mrs Hart. She groaned at length about Nell's lack of attention while Nell gazed across the yellow cut fields. Willow, old and arthritic with a dip in his back and a snowy white muzzle, cropped the lawn at the front of the house.

She did not care about Mrs Hart's complaints, Freddy's moods or the success of the harvest. Isaac said she would escape and the thought lit a fire in her and it flickered bright and unquenchable.

* * * *

In the dairy Lisa absently turned the butter churn with an aching arm.

"Where's Nell?"

She jumped, startled from her daydream. Freddy sauntered through the door with a beer bottle in his hand. His eyes drifted lazily over her robust figure and her cheeks burned.

"She's hanging out washing in the yard, sir," she said, her hand on the butter churn coming to a standstill.

"Is she?" He walked across the dairy and placed his hand on hers. "You have to keep turning it to make butter. Did no one show you how?"

She stared at him wide eyed as he propelled her arm back into action. "Yes, sir."

"My name's Freddy not sir." He kept his hand over hers, working the churn together. "Do you like it here?" Her hand was clammy with heat, beads of perspiration broke on her upper lip. The blush in her cheek invited a kiss he wasn't free to give.

"Yes, sir." She was too embarrassed to move away and his black eyes watched her intently. She had spent over two happy years here, but things had become strained since he had come back from war. She thought him a moody, sharp-tongued man.

"You don't say much do you? I hear you talking to Nell, you're quite the gossip then," he said, imagining her compliance, the pleasure of her open mouth.

She didn't know what to say or what he wanted from her, she laughed anxiously.

"Why do you like it here?" he asked.

She tried to gather her thoughts that flew like freshly swept dust through the air. What with the prolonged silence and him looking at her in that inscrutable way she was a tangle of nerves. "Well – I – because, Nell's really kind, she never makes me do nothing she wouldn't do herself. We have a good laugh sometimes. It's as if I'm one of the family now, sir, so to speak and I'm awful fond of Joe and that." Her words petered out. He smiled as she spoke. She was alarmed by him and intrigued too. She liked his dark eyes and the promise of strength in his thick forearms.

He released her hand, stepped back a pace. "You're seventeen now."

"Yes, sir." He confused her. He knew she had celebrated her birthday two days before. Nell made a cake and gave her the day off to go to town with Meg, the tweeney from Harrowmead.

"Where's your father these days? Isn't your mother dead?" he asked.

"Yes, sir, she died of the consumption when I was ten. Father went to London for work. My brothers are in France."

"Oh, yes, France, poor bastards. I hope you write to them."

"Yes, sir, and Nell's really kind helping me make up parcels too."

"Good girl." He felt his pockets for his pipe before remembering he had left it on the kitchen table. "Have you got a bloke?"

"No."

He smiled. "A pretty thing like you?"

She shook her head mutely. All the young men were away in Europe, some even further than that, fighting in the trenches, or buried in mud. It was not a good time to be a young lass looking for a fellow.

"Do you get lonely?" He grinned at her.

"No, sir," her voice barely a whisper. He walked away laughing, leaving her alone with the butter churn. She set to work in agitation, no longer aware of the ache in her arm.

The day Freddy arrived home from hospital Lisa had decided she didn't like him. He upset the equilibrium in the house. Nothing was the same now he was back. Not mealtimes, evenings or anything in-between. Lisa was a lighthearted girl, she missed the banter at the food table, being able to put in her shillings worth. Nell who once sang as she worked in her pretty voice was quieter and smiled less. She took Joe out walking, something she had never done before.

She had to admit Nell had always been strange about Joe. Lisa refused to run after Mrs Hart but she was fond of the boy. She would have enjoyed playing with him sometimes when Nell ran errands or helped with the cows but she seldom left him. Lisa thought her excessively protective of the child. What did she know? Motherhood took some women that way. It was no skin off her nose, she had enough work to be getting on with. If she ever had a child and could afford to hire help she would gladly leave it to go shopping in town. She would have to marry well to afford a maid, and young men, rich or poor, were very thin on the ground these days.

She observed Freddy with his son and there did not seem much affection there either which was a puzzle because he was a lovable little boy, quite biddable, if a bit adventurous. Only last week Nell called her to fetch the ladder quickly. Nell had climbed it, rocking perilously, in order to rescue Joe out of the highest branches of the apple tree. Afterwards when Joe was in bed they laughed about it although at the time it had frightened them both half to death.

Lisa churned the butter and her thoughts turned from Nell and Joe back to Freddy and the enigma he represented to her.

Chapter Seventeen

Nell woke early. She liked to be out of bed before Freddy opened his eyes. She dressed in the autumnal dark, crept downstairs, stoked the range and put the big shiny kettle on to boil. This was her time. She followed her ritual of warming the teapot, spooning in the leaves, stirring the steaming brew, covering it with the knitted cosy. On these chilly dark mornings she allowed her mind free rein.

She composed another letter to Iain, written in the empty air never to be put to paper. She had lost count of the number of letters she had imagined writing to him. Sometimes she thought she was in love with him and she indulged in wild dreams in which he loved her too. She closed her eyes to remember his face, the green intensity of his eyes, the curve of his lip, the set of his chin, the cow's lick, like Joe's, that made his hair stand up from his head. She could not always recall the details of him. Today he came to her with clarity, and he laughed at her, laughed at her stupidity.

What harm was there in a daydream? A small escape from the humdrum life of farm and duty. Lately she wallowed in it, working out every detail of what might have been in a parallel life.

She worried he might die or be injured and she would not be told, only to hear in the course of time from the postmistress, Cook or Meg. It was the hardest thing to cope with.

After a cup of tea, she laid the table for breakfast. At about six Lisa came downstairs yawning, pinning up her hair as she strolled into the kitchen. She had grown into a young woman since arriving at the farm, glossy dark hair and pansy brown eyes. During the summer months she suffered with a running nose and had a habit of sniffing all year round. Nell felt maternal towards her, the elder sister, there were almost four years between them. She enjoyed her company. They gossiped and laughed as she and Joanna had once done. Of course she was not Joanna, only a poor copy of her. I have Joe, she thought, equal parts of the two people I love most.

"Morning, Nell," Lisa said, she never called her Mrs Hart, that was reserved for the senior lady upstairs in bed.

"Hello, Lisa, there's tea in the pot."

Lisa smiled and poured a cup for herself and a second one for Nell. This was the pattern of their day, starting with a shared cup of tea. The patter of feet on the stairs signalled Joe was awake. He jumped on his mother's lap and cuddled into her.

"Getting a big nippy," Lisa said.

"It is. Do you remember the harvest suppers, Lisa?"

"No, I never went to one."

"They'll have them again once the war is over, it can't last forever."

"Well, it's doing a damn good job of it."

She smiled. "It was fun. We don't have fun any more, do we? We should have a little get together this Christmas, ask some folk from the village."

"Will your Mr Hart go for that? He doesn't seem the most sociable sort."

"He used to be." She remembered the practical jokes, the humour the Hart boys were known for. "Before, when Tom was here, before the war."

"Who's Tom?"

"Freddy's brother, he ran off to join up. We've never seen him since, been over three years. I don't know the truth of it, I wonder sometimes." He would never have run away without a by your leave, not gentle mild mannered Tom who adored his mother, worshipped Freddy, whose life was family and farm.

Freddy appeared in the doorway and both women jumped. "Don't wonder," he said firmly. "Never wonder about Tom."

She shrugged, eager to make light of it. "I don't, Freddy. I was talking about having a get together at Christmas."

"You talk too much, that's the trouble with you women, nothing to do but tittle tattle."

"I've plenty to do," she said, angered by the suggestion she did not pull her weight. "You've come in halfway through a conversation. I was talking to Lisa."

He frowned, Lisa poured him a cup of tea and placed it with care on the table in front of him. He glanced at her, she did not dare to return it. Several times she had caught him watching her, his dark eyes unreadable and when she had met his gaze he had been in no rush to look away, making a game of it. She was a poor player he always won and then he grinned causing her to blush, which amused him further. She did not like the game. It made her feel foolish but the challenge was almost irresistible.

"Don't talk about Tom. It's nothing to do with you," he slurped from his teacup.

Nell sighed. Joe buried his face into her side, recognising anger in Freddy's voice. "According to you, nothing's to do with me," she said, tired of forever guarding her tongue.

"Only because hardly anything is," his tone changed to one of sarcasm.

"I'd like to know what would have happened to this place without me, when you were away. Gone to rack and ruin no doubt." Her eyes blazed with fury.

He sneered. "Saint bloody Helena."

"Saint bloody Freddy, saving the world in the trenches." A mistake, she should have known better. He pushed his chair back. It swung away from him scraping on the tiled floor, his fist crashed down on the table. Lisa almost shot out of her seat, Joe whimpered. Freddy lurched forward, grabbing Nell by the collar of her blouse.

"You bitch!" His spittle flew into her face. "You little bitch!"

Lisa put her hands on his arm. "Freddy, Mr Hart, don't – let her be – please."

He held Lisa's gaze for a moment, then released Nell. "Sorry," he said, not to Nell but to Lisa. "Sorry, Lisa, I don't know what came over me." He glanced at Nell, he was glad to see the fear in her eyes. She sickened him. He still wanted to hit her, despite his apology to Lisa. He wanted to see her blood. "I'll go help Fritz with the milking," he said, fetching his boots.

Nell found her voice, shaking though it was. "Hans, his name is Hans."

He said nothing, slamming the door on his way out. When he was gone Lisa put her arm around Nell. "Are you all right?"

"Yes, he doesn't frighten me, I'm fine," she said, her pride and dignity reduced to crumbs on the kitchen floor, sweepings for the dustpan. "His name is Hans, not Fritz."

"Yes, I know," Lisa said soothingly. "I'll make you another cuppa, and I'll do breakfast when milking's done."

Lisa had wondered at the relationship between husband and wife previously, she never heard them exchange a kind word or a kiss or caress. They only spoke of the farm, the time of the next meal or the accounts Nell kept in the big ledgers in the desk. Now Lisa saw how it really was and was horrified to feel a strange contentment.

* * * *

That afternoon, chores half done, Nell crept upstairs hoping Mrs Hart would not hear her footfall on the stairs. On her dressing table was her walnut box. It contained birth certificates, the last birthday card her mother had given to her, a poem Joanna and she had written together as children, these along with other small treasures that would mean little to anybody else. Right at the bottom, well hidden, Nell's fingers located the long rusty key. She had kept it safe all this time but never used it. The farm work was a relentless drain on her time and energy and it felt wrong somehow to go into his house when he was not there. Today, this one time, she told herself, she would go.

She took Joe to Harrowmead Wood and walked to Iain's house. Peering through the dirty windows, cupping her hands round her eyes, she could see the face of the big clock, its hands frozen, the pendulum static, his chair empty by the cold range. She recalled the first time she had come here, running her hands across the dark furniture, dreaming of the day when she would have her own house, her own kitchen. Now she knew the reality of the dream she wished she still worked as a maid at Harrowmead. She scraped the leaves away from the door with her foot. She half expected the key to refuse entry but it clicked solidly in the lock.

She opened the door, Joe on her hip. "This is your daddy's house," she said to him, feeling more daring by the second. "Daddy." Her heart ached with loneliness, Joe saw her tears and put his little arms around her trying to make things right.

The house was cold with that curious dampness empty houses have. She pushed back against the door to close it. Her feet tapped on the floor. She perused the kitchen, the silence peaceful and somehow safe. The clock, stuck at midday or midnight, appeared to be waiting for his return.

In the parlour she studied the books on the shelf, poetry and philosophy alongside novels and gun manuals. She went up the creaking staircase holding Joe's hand so he would not fall.

Everything about the man was here in the contained air, the trodden floors, thumbed books, cutlery washed of his tongue, clothing of his body. He was here, within the walls, his thoughts, his life.

Four bedrooms opened off the upper hallway, she chose the door on the right. Iain's room, there was no mistaking it. A pair of shoes was discarded on the floor as he had kicked them off, a well-worn jacket draped over the end of the bed. She picked it up, put it to her nose, only to be rewarded by the smell of the dust. The bed was unmade, the mattress bare, pillows stacked in a neat pile, one folded blanket. An envelope lay on it.

Curiosity piqued, she moved closer. To her surprise her name was written there in a curly left-slanting hand. Joe ran into the hall to chase a darting silverfish. She broke the seal. It was dated 10 October 1915, the day before she had returned to North Farm from Aunt Cath's with Joe as a new baby. Beside the date he had written the name of his regiment.

'*Helena,*' she read.

'*I don't know if you will use your key, perhaps not. If you do I leave the name of my regiment should you wish to be in touch for whatever reason. I don't expect you to be.*

I trust you and Joe keep well, that you are happy. I cannot predict what might be ahead of me but I want you to know I have always held you in very high esteem. You are a good woman and I expect we shall meet again one day. I would hope to keep such a rare individual as my friend always.

Yours truly, Iain'

She read it through twice, sinking onto the bed, shedding more tears. She wished she had come here before. Should she write? What would she say? She could tell him about his son. He probably received very little post if any since he had no family. She placed the letter on the kitchen dresser, she could not risk discovery.

She fetched Joe and carefully locked the door behind her. She arrived at the river hoping to see the otters. Apart from its tireless gurgle, there was no sound or movement of fish or animal. She watched the ceaseless flow of the water, wishing she could follow it to the vast expanse of the sea, far away from here.

The woods were empty of him and yet he was everywhere, each step she took fell in his footprint, covered by the debris of two autumns. She knew his laugh and heard it amongst the trees, in the ripple of the river. His shadow walked the well-trodden paths, shaking its head at the broken gates.

She would surely drive herself mad with this ridiculous longing. He called her his friend, a rare individual. That was not love or anything like it. It was only because things were not right with Freddy that she was being so silly, telling Joe who his daddy was. How lucky that he was too young to understand.

By late afternoon she turned for home knowing how many tasks she had neglected, hoping Lisa had thought about dinner and prepared it at the very least. Joe was tired and she gave him a piggyback across the fields. In the distance Willow, head dipped, pulled the plough. Freddy walked the furrow, hands busy with plough handle and reins. She altered her course to intercept him hoping to change this mood between them, wanting a kind word, an assurance that this was worth struggling for.

    He reined Willow to a halt, surprised to see her. Lisa had brought lunch out to him earlier, there was no reason for Nell to be here. "Whoa," he said to the horse. He put his head on one side waiting to hear what she had to say.

    She put Joe down on the dark earth, he kicked at the hard clods of soil. Nell and Freddy looked at each other and both took a step forward. His expression was hard to read, she was tearful, ready for anything he was willing to give. He put his arms out as she did and they held each other, in the middle of the field, crows cawing in the trees on the perimeter. His body was warm, firm and strong against her. She closed her eyes and leaned on him, wanting to feel safe. She rested her head on his shoulder, her hands flat on his back, feeling the heat, muscle through thin cotton. She raised her face and his lips pressed her mouth. She kissed him back desperate for his comfort and affection. She opened her eyes and they smiled at each other. It was going to be all right. Without a word exchanged he went back to his work and she lifted Joe and trudged towards the house. When she glanced back at him he raised his hand to wave.

* * * *

    By the time Freddy arrived home that evening his warmth towards her had dissipated. She had surprised him, appearing in the field in the middle of the afternoon. Something about her expression had moved him, recalling days long gone when he had desired her. Before marriage, Tom, war and injury, before suspicions and doubt had altered his feelings for her. When they had kissed it was, for that moment, as if he had come home, the comfort of familiar arms. Since then the voice in his head had reminded him of the truth, how things really were with Nell. Now, coming in the door, seeing her feeding Joe, kissing his cheek, he realised the voice spoke the truth. He watched her laughing with Lisa, talking about the weather with his father, and the impotent fury flooded him. The voice still whispered, too quiet to understand but he knew the script.

Lisa served his food and smiled kindly while Nell fussed around the child, trying to get him to repeat a nursery rhyme, pulling faces to make him laugh. There was a moment's silence while Mr Hart said grace then she resumed entertaining Joe. Sitting next to Freddy, she briefly covered his hand with her own. It was very white compared to the brown of his, he had to resist the urge to brush it off.

Lisa was surprised how lighthearted Nell was tonight, animated and young. By way of a change she made conversation and urged Mr Hart and Freddy to join in by asking questions. Freddy was bad-tempered as usual, only answering if there were no option. Nell, oblivious to it, kept up her stream of chatter.

Clearing away after supper she sang as she washed up, she hardly ever sang anymore, and she had such a pretty voice. Lisa joined in at the chorus tunelessly. Nell did not mind, it made them both laugh. Eventually Freddy shouted at them from the parlour. "Shut up, my head's thumping."

Nell giggled. "Begging your pardon, sir, I'm sure." She touched her brow, dropping a curtsy. Lisa laughed until she thought she might wet herself, begging Nell to stop. "Meaning no harm to your bonce, I'm sure, sir," she joked. In the end they laughed at nothing at all, merely because they were laughing. Freddy strode into the doorway, furious.

"I told you to shut up. It's like a flaming hen house in here, you two squawking your heads off," he bellowed. Both women looked at him briefly and burst into more peals of laughter. Freddy raged up the stairs.

By the time Nell went to bed he was feigning sleep, lying on his back. She was so aware of his uneven breathing, the masculine physicality of him, the memory of his desire that had been better than no desire at all. He had kissed her earlier in the ploughed field, and it spurred her to lay her arm across him. He flinched.

"What is it?" he hissed into the dark.

She withdrew her arm, suddenly wary of him. "Sorry, nothing. Good night."

He wondered if she could hear the voice that spoke to him so clearly. Laying in the dark its volume and persistence increased. Knowledgeable clarity, the true picture, his wife was no better than a whore. He had met a few of those in France and they only understood one thing and it was not polite conversation.

He rolled towards her and yanked her nightdress up to her waist.

And this was not desire, not even as functional as she remembered. She was meat on a slab, chilled, and his weight was forcing her legs open, hipbone hard on soft inner thigh. Her ribs were corrugating her lungs, expelling air, the sweat slick on his rigid chest where her hands pushed in a feeble struggle. His flesh was hard, painful and rasping and she was trapped within the coffin of his body, moving against her, grunting into the pillow while every muscle and sinew in her screamed silently, willing an end but unable to bring it about. On and on he ground into her, repetitive invasive blows, reducing her to nothingness, grinding her into dust, until there was nothing except the weight and the hurt and degradation.

Even when he had finished, sitting on his haunches, a form silhouetted by the window, she still couldn't breathe, still pressed into the mattress by the weight of shock, stunned by the violation, by her powerlessness in the face of brutal strength. And all the while she had been saying, "No, no, no, no," and she repeated it, dry eyed, unmoving.

His voice, low and steady, halted her mantra. "Is that how it was with your bastard Jock gamekeeper?"

His words freed her to move, she scrabbled to pull down her nightgown, rucking it between her legs. She rolled onto her side, sobbing into the pillow. He got up and dressed. She heard the door click shut behind him, his footfall on the stairs.

Tears dried, teeth chattered, a deep inner throb was indistinguishable from the bruising of her tender outer skin. She crawled out of bed, tiptoed across the landing to Joe's room. He was sleeping the deep rest and oblivion of the very young and she crept in beside his warm body. Gradually she relaxed, her shivers subsided and the burning ache eased.

He knows, she thought, he knows Joe is Iain's. But he had jumped to conclusions wilder than the truth. He believed Joe to truly be her child, hers and Iain's and at that moment she wished with all her heart he were.

Chapter Eighteen

Lisa did not mean to attract Freddy's attention. It was the small things she did naturally, serving his breakfast, topping up his teacup, bringing his boots, helping him on with his jacket. They were things Nell should have done and chose not to. Lisa, noticing the omission, did not see the harm in doing these little tasks.

His silly staring game changed, now she managed to out stare him occasionally and if she laughed he would too. They shared exchanges of commiseration when Nell indulged Joe or exasperated glances when she was stubborn over something, which had always been her way. Lisa thought nothing of this since, naturally, both she and Freddy loved Nell. She knew things were not perfect between husband and wife. Whose marriage was perfect? She sympathised with Freddy when his head hurt, and occasionally would massage his aching shoulders after a hard day's graft, but only when Nell made herself scarce.

One dark winter's night Freddy's vague interest in Lisa altered irrevocably. Mr Hart fell asleep by the kitchen range and Freddy joined Nell and Lisa in the parlour. Joe was full of cold and Nell spent the evening running up and down the stairs every time he coughed.

"She spoils him," Freddy said as her feet pattered up the stairs for the sixth time.

Lisa looked up from her knitting. "He's poorly."

He frowned. "It doesn't matter if he's poorly or not. Every whim is catered for. The child has no discipline."

"It's difficult for her, your being away so long, she only had the boy." She felt obliged to defend Nell.

"I'm back now." He sounded like a spoiled child himself. "She's a cold fish. I don't suppose you are. I reckon you'd know how to keep a man warm."

She coloured, glancing away unable to return his gaze. Nell came back in. "He hasn't got a temperature," she stated, picking up a sock to darn from the top of the pile.

He eyed her darkly. "Children have colds all the time. Why do you make such an issue over everything?"

"I don't. You make it sound as if I'm fussing. I'm not. It might be influenza, that can be dangerous, he's only little."

"He'll be a molly-coddled mummy's boy," then under his breath, "little bastard."

Lisa was shocked. "I'm going to bed," she muttered. They listened in silence to her footsteps, heavy on the stairs. He looked pleased with himself and began stuffing his pipe with tobacco.

Nell watched him, when she spoke her voice was low and contained. "You've always been a selfish man."

"Have I?" He was amused by the accusation.

"You've not changed at all. You've never made allowances for my happiness or considered what I might want. I came here as your wife and I was treated like a slave. I cook and clean, work on the farm, nurse your mother."

"What did you expect? Hearts and flowers?"

"I expected consideration, affection. Don't deny you pursued me, you weren't shy of hearts and flowers then."

"Ah, poor Nell, lamb to the slaughter," he mocked.

"No, not so meek, Freddy," she said. "I went willingly enough." She had been impressed by his humour, he was sociable, handsome and fun. The eldest son who would one day inherit the farm. It seemed naïve now. At the time she thought she could do no better.

He laughed dirtily. "Yes, I remember you being rather willing. What happened to that? Now you're a frigid bitch."

She leaned forward in the chair and her tone betrayed her loathing. "You changed, not me. After the wedding, after Tom, you weren't the same anymore."

"Don't talk about Tom."

"You left me barely three months after the wedding."

"Everyone was leaving. It was my duty to go."

"It could have waited until Joe was born. You refused home leave, you never came home when you had the chance."

"Lots of the boys didn't. You don't understand what it was like, how hard it would have been if I'd come home to go back again. It does you in." He remembered taking leave with his mates, swimming in a French lake, the heat of the sun, the willing pretty French girls, a stretch of a week, drinking, laughing and more.

"That wasn't it at all. You turned your back, you had a family here and a baby you had never seen."

"The baby." He spat into the fire, it hissed and crackled.

"You started drinking after Tom went away, you became mean. I saw it in you before we wed. I should have cancelled the wedding, I see that now."

"Is that why you had it off with the Jock?"

"I didn't."

He stood up and she was immediately at a disadvantage. "You bitch," he said.

"I hoped the baby would bring us together. When you went away I thought my life would be unbearable, instead I was liberated. Suddenly what I said mattered. Your father listened to me. I was relevant."

"You wish I'd been killed don't you?"

Tears filled her eyes. "No, Freddy, I don't."

He shook his head, she confused him, muddled his thinking. "Go to bed, get away from me," he said. She nervously edged towards the door, he made no move to touch her.

He smoked his pipe before going upstairs. He paused at the bedroom door and his eyes unwillingly followed the narrow steep staircase leading to Lisa's little room. He crept upwards, the wooden tread creaking under his foot. His hand hovered over the door handle, pausing before he pushed it open.

Lisa was undressing, he heard her breath catch as she saw him. She held her nightgown to cover her nakedness. In the shadowy candlelight her eyes glowed like lamps. They stared at each other for an interval neither daring to make the first move.

Lisa liked his looks. He always said nice things to her and watched her in a way she knew he should not but which made her feel so very special. As she watched him his gaze slid over her, the desire on his face plain. She allowed the nightgown to drop in a heap at her feet. He smiled, her body was plump and full, he put his hands on her warm skin. He was everything she wanted, except for the fact he had a wife, and that wife was Nell who had been such a good friend to her. What could she do? He was the master, he could have her thrown out and anyway if he had an appetite for her, it was no more than her hunger for him.

Downstairs in Joe's bed, Nell listened in the darkness. She did not want to listen. Lisa's bed squeaked and she recognised the timbre of Freddy's voice, the playful high note of her stifled giggle. She closed her eyes to it, the memory of being trapped underneath him, vivid. Instead of feeling betrayed she felt grateful, relief that he was not touching her. She had Joe and that was enough, she didn't need Lisa and she had never needed Freddy.

* * * *

Christmas was coming, the pig was slaughtered and they were fattening a goose for Christmas Day. Lisa, due the afternoon off, was going to town to do her Christmas shopping. Freddy came in the back door. Nell heard Lisa's high-pitched squeal, no doubt playfully warding off his amorous advances. He laughed, came through to the kitchen where she was setting lunch on the table.

The smile faded on his lips. "Where is everybody?"

"Well, that's Lisa off to town. Your father's visiting Mr Denham. Mother's upstairs, where else?" She forced herself to smile at him.

Sitting down at the table he waited for her to dish out the food. He rubbed his temples with his index fingers, closing his eyes. "Jesus, my head," he said.

She could not think of anything to say so put his food in front of him. She made a long job of clearing up while he ate in silence. Joe played outside, wrapped up warm, cracking the ice on the puddles. She watched him out of the window while she peeled potatoes, the small coat stiff across his shoulders, legs already over long with large feet. He frowned, Joanna's frown, not Iain's, picking up a shard of ice between red, cold fingers. He was such a fascinating division of his two parents, no part of him could be Nell.

"Freddy," she said suddenly, "there's something I want to say to you." He raised his eyebrows, lit his pipe and puffed at it, waiting. She cleared her throat feeling nervous. "Despite your low opinion of me, I have never had an affair with anyone. I have never slept with anyone but you. I am a faithful wife. I have never had any interest in an affair. I want to set things straight. You've been much mistaken and I needed you to know."

He contemplated her for what felt like a very long time, until eventually she met his eyes. They glinted black and dangerous. His lips parted in a sardonic smile and cocking his head to one side, almost sympathetically, slowly standing up, he said, "Dear Nell, my darling wife, you don't have to tell me you're frigid, I already know. You don't have to deny your whoring either. Look at the child." He watched Joe playing from the window. "He's certainly not mine. I imagine Iain took advantage of you, since you'd never oblige willingly, and I am sorry for that, the fact remains – no the problem remains – a boy who is a bastard and a wife who, at best, is a conniving liar."

She swallowed hard. "You have no right talking to me like that," she said rising out of her chair to gain some advantage as he stood over her.

He briefly held his head, a spasm crossing his face. "Sshh," he whispered closing his eyes. When he opened them they were blank of all expression. He nodded his head. "I know, I know," he said.

She was puzzled. "Freddy stop it."

"Stop what?"

"You're talking to yourself - again."

"I'm not," he said quickly, shaking his head as if to clear it.

"You are, you're always doing it," and then unable to hold her tongue, "it's like living with a madman. The only man who's ever taken advantage, as you phrase it, is you."

"I'm married to you," he said. "How the hell is that taking advantage? You're my wife and I can have you whenever I please, in whatever manner I please," and then to rile her, or possibly frighten her he added, "do you want me to show you?"

She backed away, refusing to alter her sharp tone. "That won't be necessary. You've got Lisa for that now. I'll keep house and work the farm, skivvy for your mother, but not that, you can ask Lisa to do that."

He laughed as if it were a big joke, sitting down in his mirth. "Lisa's a diversion, nothing to worry you. She's a slag."

"She wasn't one until you made it so. You're poisonous, Freddy Hart, I've seen your true colours, you're a cruel, nasty man."

He grimaced. "You don't understand anything, Nell, and you never have. What about your precious Jock? He's not so innocent either. What lies in his dark and secret past? What makes a man leave his home and travel hundreds of miles to escape it?"

"He's not my Jock. He's nothing to me." The truth and a lie in one. "What would I know about why he came here? Probably for work, what makes you think he has some secret?"

"Because of what he did for me." Damn, he had not meant to say that, the voice in his head cursed him for his idiocy.

"What did he do for you, Freddy? Tell me?"

He put his aching head in his hands. He had trapped himself. What had he said? He was having trouble following his own words. "Tom," he groaned, "Tom." Unbidden tears rolled down his cheeks, falling through his fingers.

She knelt at his feet, put her hands up to cover his. "Tell me, what about him?" She felt near the truth at last, she knew there was more to it than she had been told. All this time, there had been a nagging doubt about the reason for Tom's sudden disappearance. She had never imagined it involved Iain. It was so very important to her to know how it concerned him.

"Ssshh," he whispered to himself, rocking in the chair. She stroked his hair, trying to comfort him, trying to trick him. He removed his hands, the tears coursing down his face. "What about Tom?" he asked.

"Tell me what happened to him. Was it Iain's fault, what happened to Tom?" She was too close to back off.

His eyes clouded with doubt, unsure of how much he had told her. "Yes," he said slowly, "it was Iain's fault." He could see the anticipation in her face, waiting, longing for Freddy to implicate him. His voice was barely a whisper, "Iain told him to come at six thirty, I know, he told me."

"Who told you, Iain or Tom? Meet him where?" she urged.

"At his place at six thirty, and it was dark. He never stood a chance, not a chance, almost took his legs off." He looked over her head into space, momentarily unaware of her kneeling, listening.

As the silence stretched she felt compelled to speak, "Did Iain shoot him?"

He shook his head, closed his eyes, put a hand to them. "We buried him, dug a hole and covered him with the earth," he whispered, "and there was so much blood, covered in it, all over the ground. The rain was so heavy it washed it away." He focused on her, as if noticing her for the first time.

She wondered if he were still talking about Tom, or about the trenches in France. Was he getting confused? Why would he agree to bury Tom if Iain had killed him?

"How did it happen, though, Freddy? You should have fetched help."

"I know, I know, Nell, I should have. I was so frightened, so shocked." He was sweating, and fear dilated his pupils.

"Freddy, you should've told me. Why didn't you tell me?"

"We agreed, he said you must never know, that you wouldn't marry me if you knew," his voice was pleading, as if the marriage had not happened almost three years before, as if any of it mattered now.

She shook her head, unable to reconcile the idea of murder with her memory of Iain. "Poor Tom," she said, her imagination filling in the enormous gaps in his story.

"And you mustn't ever tell," he said. "Promise me, you'll never tell."

"Who would I tell? And to get you both hanged? Of course I won't." She put her arms round him, he leaned into her eager for comfort and support. He did not think she fully understood but he was relieved to have shared the burden of his guilt.

She felt nauseous. The dream she had woven around Iain's image was shattered. He was a cold-hearted, callous murderer who had left Freddy so frightened he had acted accomplice to his own brother's murder.

How foolish of her to allow such daydreams, to have drifted so far away from her real life that she condoned her husband sleeping with their maid. She saw her life sliding away, such as it was, everything she had was here. The farm and her place in it, her presence here was essential, to Mr Hart, Mrs Hart, Freddy, Joe, all of them. She clung to Freddy, felt his strong arms as he cried into her shoulder. He needed her and she had turned her back on him, on all of them, and for some silly dalliance in her head.

The door clicked behind her. Lisa had forgotten her purse and stood in the doorway, eyes wide. Tight in their embrace, they did not move. He continued to hang on to her as a drowning man to a piece of driftwood. She rocked him gently in her arms as she would Joe after a bad dream. Lisa was so shocked by them she was rooted to the spot, husband and wife reconciled, or was this how they acted when nobody was about? Was she after all only a little bit on the side, pale in comparison to the love he had for his wife? She ran up the stairs.

He pulled back from Nell, hearing Lisa's feet on the stairs. "Who was that?"

"I don't know," she said and wiped the tears from his cheeks with her hand. "We'd best keep this our secret eh?"

He nodded. "Of course, I'm good at that, I've kept it quiet this long."

"I wish you'd told me about Iain before."

"Before what? Anyway, you always knew, as well as I did he was a bad bastard."

She shook her head. "No, not really. I knew you didn't get on, that didn't make him necessarily bad."

He leaned back in the chair. "What he did to you, and leaving me to bring up his brat."

"No, Freddy, I told you he did nothing to me. Joe is yours." She desperately needed him to believe it.

He stared at her perplexed. "He can't be mine, he looks so much like him."

She stroked his hair back from his face. "No, you're muddled, he doesn't look like him. He looks like my father. He had dark hair and green eyes too."

He searched her face. "Really? Did he?"

"Yes," she lied, she could not remember either of her parents but Freddy knew no different. "The same as Joe. He can't help which side he takes after, can he?"

A ghost of a smile played on his lips. "No, course he can't, poor kid, taking after your lot."

Lisa pattered back down the stairs, her purse in her hand. "I forgot my purse," she said unnecessarily, seeing the softness on his face as he looked at Nell.

She smiled at Lisa over her shoulder. "You'd better get a move on or the shops will shut before you even get there."

Lisa left them, and Nell turned back to Freddy. "We've made a bit of a mess of things, haven't we? You and me. Can't we be nice to each other?" Even as she said it she wondered why she was giving him another chance. It was he who had abused her and crept to Lisa's room in the middle of the night. What else could she do? She couldn't leave. She had nowhere else to go. This was her life, good or bad, she had to make the best of it. He was not well, his head pained him and he was obviously damaged by his time in France and by the guilt and fear of whatever had happened to Tom.

He closed his eyes, head lolling back in the chair. "My head hurts so much," he said, "and I hear voices. Sometimes it feels as if I'm losing my mind."

"You'll have to see a doctor, Freddy, there might be something that can be done. Some help for you."

"Yes." He smiled at her, put out a hand to stroke the side of her face. "I don't always understand what I do myself. Is it too early for a drink? I could do with a drink."

* * * *

That evening Mr Hart and Freddy went to the pub. Nell hoped it would do him good to go out socially for a while. The pub hours were short because of the war, they would not be late back. Lisa kept her company, knitting socks for the soldiers. She was in a downcast mood. Nell could hazard a guess as to why. She wondered whether to talk to the girl, but what to say? To keep her dignity intact she would have to play ignorant. Perhaps it had been partially Nell's own fault he had strayed. She decided tonight she would move back into their bedroom, hoping to make things right between them.

She went to bed early, it felt strange not to have Joe beside her as she lay in the darkness and heard the men return. There were raised voices and laughing then a period of silence. Eventually she heard feet climbing the stairs, the door opening, closing. Freddy stumbled about in the darkness as his eyes adjusted. He went to the bedside table, struggled with a box of matches to light the lamp. He made a little noise of surprise when he saw her.

She did not pretend to be asleep, smiling at him uncertainly. He was tipsy, not so drunk. He laughed when he saw her smile, the noise made her heart miss a beat. He was different to how he had been only a few hours earlier when he had reached out his hand to be kind to her. It wasn't the drink that had altered him - it was more than that.

"Well, Nell," he said and laughed. "Ha! I'm a poet and didn't know it. Hells, bells, Nells, what are you doing here?"

She hesitated. "Sorry, perhaps, it was a bad idea."

"You thought to be a good little wife tonight did you?"

"Freddy, I don't know where I am with you. One minute you're being nice to me, the next you're being like this. Can't we be normal, can't we get on?" She was exasperated.

"Normal? How can things ever be normal? There's a war on you know and it's totally buggered me up." He laughed uproariously, kneeling on the bed, facing her. She had her feet on the floor at the same moment as he lunged, pinning her to the headboard by her shoulders, the force took her breath away. His face was inches from hers. "Totally buggered," he repeated.

"You're hurting me," she said calmly.

He purposely pinched her arms between his fingers enjoying the pained grimace on her face. "Does that hurt?" he asked, she nodded. He released one arm and slapped her cheek. "How about that?"

"Freddy, you're scaring me, please stop, let me go. I'll go back to my own room."

"You haven't got a room, you've been usurped by all the men in the house, oh, and Lisa. Even the little servant girl has her own room, not poor little Nell." His voice whined in a mock imitation of her.

"Then I'll go to Joe's room. Please, please let me go," she whimpered.

He leaned forward, placed his lips on her neck, his teeth on her skin sharp and cutting, she gasped, trying to pull away. She did not see his clenched fist coming. The full force hit her in the ribs throwing her across the room. She landed by the wall. Relieved to be free of his grasp she scrambled towards the door. Suddenly his hand was tight in her hair pulling her up. She cried out loudly.

"Shut up," he hissed between clenched teeth. The flat of his hand hit the side of her head, holding her firmly by the hair. She cried out again, fending him off, hitting out at his legs, landing a few blows with her fists. She captured his hand and bit down, harder than he had bitten her, the flesh firm and satisfying between her teeth. He released her hair at once, yelled, kicking her in the side with as much force as he could muster. It knocked the air out of her and her head hit the bare floorboards, winded and semi-conscious.

She did not hear him leave or climb the stairs to Lisa's eyrie. Lisa had been listening to them, the rush of angry words, the sound of hand on flesh, Nell crying out and Freddy's brief screech of pain. She was alarmed to see him, frightened he had come to hurt her now. She could not understand their relationship - it was bizarre, abnormal. She need not have feared for herself. He sank onto the bed and buried his head into her chest. She cradled him to her much as Nell had done earlier and rocked him.

"What have I done?" he said softly. He lay on the bed fully dressed and fell asleep with his head on her shoulder.

When Nell recovered herself enough to stand up, he was gone. She limped across the hallway, climbed into bed with Joe and slept. In her nightmares she belonged nowhere and had no one.

The morning dawned too soon. Her body ached from the beating, as if a horse had kicked her rather than a man. The bruises up her body were sore, she could not bear the restriction of a corset. At breakfast Freddy could not look at her. Lisa kept her head down serving out, tidying up. Nell made no attempt to help, it was as much as she could do to sit.

"What happened to you?" Mr Hart asked.

"I fell." It was as much of a convincing lie as she could manage. Joe lifted a caring hand to the cut on her cheek where the bruise had turned her face purple. She smiled at him bleakly.

When Mr Hart left with Freddy, Lisa turned to her. "You all right, Nell?"

She nodded, lifting her chin defiantly. "Yes, I'm fine. I have to go out, you'll manage won't you." A request not a question.

"Of course, you do as you must. Perhaps you should rest."

"I don't need to rest."

"I'll mind Joe for you if you want, you can get out and have some peace."

Nell raked the girl with her eyes. "That won't be necessary, Joe comes with me. He doesn't belong here, you know. He's not the same as them." Her gaze encompassed the entire house. Lisa shook her head in flummoxed agreement, while Nell fetched her coat and hat.

* * * *

She strode purposefully through Harrowmead Wood. A cold night had coated every twig with frosty rime, ice capped the ditch water, and drifts of hail edged the pathways. She opened the gate to Keeper's House, it appeared to watch her gravely. Inside she was enveloped by its safe solitude. She did not care what had happened to Tom, she could not convince herself Iain had meant to harm him. She would not lose sight of the Iain she knew. After all, how could she rely on anything Freddy said? He had proved himself to be wholly unreliable and wicked.

"Keep your coat and hat on, Joe," she said to her son. "It's cold in here and we won't be staying long." He danced around the furniture playing. At the kitchen table she took paper and pen from her bag. Her pen hovered above the page. She would not write about Freddy, not the pain and anguish of her life, she would write to Iain about Joe and Harrowmead, things he might want to hear. She would spend some of their rations, send him anything she could manage. The scratch of the nib filled the silence, a little smile pulled at her lips as she wrote.

'Dear Iain, Sorry I have not written before ...'

Part III

Trenches

We are Fred Karno's army, we're the ragtime infantry
We cannot fight, we cannot shoot, what bleeding use are we?
And when we get to Berlin we'll hear the Kaiser say,
'Hoch, hoch! Mein Gott, what a bloody rotten lot, are the ragtime infantry.'

We are Fred Karno's Army - Anon

Chapter Nineteen

Johnny 'Dusty' Miller surveyed the impenetrable darkness through the loophole, rifle poised. No moon shone and only an occasional flare illuminated the cratered battleground. He viewed the endless lengths of looped posts threaded with wire, an alien stretch of mud and the sandbags piled at the lip of the enemy trench.

He lit a cigarette. His breath mingled with the smoke, a hard frost stung his fingers inside their gloves. Despite jiggling his toes and stamping his feet regularly in boots leaden with mud, they remained numb. He couldn't wear more than two pairs of socks or his heels rubbed off the leather.

"You got any smokes?" his mate called, out of sight beyond the dogleg, in his Scottish lilt.

"Yes, thanks. Yours all gone?"

"Aye," came the disembodied reply.

"Come and get it then," he said keeping his eyes to the front. "I'm not getting a court martial for your lack of fags." A tap on his shoulder made him jump. "Bloody hell, Midge," he cried, turning a chalk white face to the tall Scotsman at his back.

The Scot laughed, taking the proffered cigarette. "You're a nervous wreck, pal, you need to take a holiday."

He laughed. "Yeah, I'm off to Torquay for a week from tomorrow, you creeping shite."

He lit a match and held it between his fingers, Iain cupped Dusty's hand to steady the shaking and inhaled. With a wink Iain returned to his post round the corner. He too was feeling the cold. Only halfway through their watch, they had another hour to go. He would call out to Dusty every five minutes to ensure he was still awake. Night duty was a tough mental drag, battling sleep, the constant urge to drift into the soft blanket of oblivion. Everyone had heard the stories; the punishment for sleeping on duty was death by firing squad. Tonight was their fourteenth in the front line, fourteen days and nights of heavy shelling. Silence had finally fallen with the darkness, and now they feared this was the familiar precursor to an imminent attack. To let down their guard could prove fatal.

The dugout and fire-step were awash with sleeping soldiers. There wouldn't be many officers alert enough tonight to be checking those on sentry duty. Iain could hear Champ, a burly ex-docker and amateur boxer from London, snoring - a powerful phlegmy rattle that usually raised numerous complaints. Not tonight, the exhaustion was too deep, the sleep too welcome.

He finished the cigarette and put on his gloves, tugged his hat down further over his ears and scratched his heavy growth of beard with his thumb. An army of lice paraded the warm folds of his body, their eggs lining the seams of his filthy uniform. He scratched with impunity, they all did, unaware of the action, second nature, like passing water, an inconvenient necessity. Despite insulating his tunic with old newspaper and the addition of a knitted waistcoat and his worn holey muffler, he shivered under his army issue great coat. He tried not to think about the steaming heat of a bath, washing with soap, the luxury of shaving and cessation of the interminable itching.

"Dusty, you still with us, pal?" he called, his breath hanging in the air. Silence. "Dusty?"

"Yeah, I'm here. I was packing my suitcase, didn't hear you," Dusty replied.

He yawned. He would have liked another fag, a cup of tea. In a week it would be Christmas. This year the villagers of Harrowford would not look to him for permission to collect firewood from Harrowmead. Isaac used to help him cut the mistletoe, the best going to the big house, the remainder to market with holly wreaths made by Jasper Potter's wife and Betsy Yeates. Harrowmead had a small plantation of pine, their smell resinous and sweet. Children gathered cones from under the fir trees. The years of needles underfoot were soft but sly, spiking the busy little hands distracted by their collecting.

He would cut the best two trees and haul them to the house by cart. One would stand in the hall, the other for the Christmas party, a distant memory with good food, booze and dancing. That's where he had met Polly Took. She observed Christmas by partying while her husband went preaching the more religious aspects of the season. He could see her now, dressed in pink, like a fallen bauble from the resplendent over-dressed tree that blazed with miniature candles. He indulged in a two minute fantasy involving Polly before his body jerked him back into reality. His eyes had been drooping, his fantasy part of a dream. He mustn't fall asleep.

"Ach, aye, Midge," Dusty called in his pseudo Caledonian.

He took a deep breath. "Ach, aye, Dusty."

Dusty had branded him with the nickname Midge. They were introduced by their company sergeant major while training at a bullring near Etaples.

"Macdonald, this is your spotter. D'you hear that Miller? You're snooping for the sniper, so you'd better make the best of it boys," the CSM had said.

"What was your mother, a bleeding midget?" The first words Dusty had uttered.

Iain had laughed. "Aye and yours was just ugly," he retorted. Dusty, grinning offered him a fag, and that was it. In time Midget had been shortened for ease to Midge.

And they had made the best of it. "You're the best bloody sniper in the regiment, Midge."

"And you're the worst bloody spotter in France, Dusty."

Iain eased the weight on to his other foot. It was glacial tonight but by way of a change he wasn't drenched to saturation with heavy rain. And no sooner had the thought come to mind than a flake of snow, like an icy arrow tip, melted on his cheek. He scanned the black sky. The stars he had observed earlier were gone. It was snowing hard when Michael and Champ relieved them, a crisp layer forming on helmets and shoulders.

"Quiet?" Champ said. His bent nose and flattened cheek bone, a souvenir from his days in the boxing ring, were temporarily lit by a flare above no-man's-land, magically shining through the snow flakes. Both men contemplated it for a second.

"Looks as if something might be blowing off in a mo'," Iain said.

"Maybe. See you in a bit."

"Aye," he said. "Tea'll be up by the time you're off."

Michael aged sixteen, officially eighteen, crossed Iain's path on his way to substitute Dusty. Iain clutched his shoulder sympathetically in passing. Michael smiled sleepily, yawning and rubbing one eye. With his falsetto voice and smooth complexion the lad was in constant demand to play the obligatory female at the popular concerts.

In the gloom of the dugout the incumbent bodies had increased owing to the snow. The fire-step had lost its appeal and had little to recommend it in the first place. On the little contrived stove, an old tin fuelled with whale oil, Iain heated enough water for a brew. Dusty removed one boot, attempting to massage some feeling into his toes.

"Christ, it's cold," he murmured. The quivering flame of the stove cast strange shadows on the woven walls, up-lighting Iain's face. "You look like a frigging pirate – Bluebeard," Dusty said and chuckled.

Supplies were exhausted. Three days without condensed milk and sugar was no joke. The tea tasted bitter, petrol edged, where the water had been transported in an old fuel can. They suffered it, hot mugs in cold hands, warmth swallowed with gratitude. A shell whistled overhead. It was instinctive to duck their heads despite the relative safety of the hole. The shell cracked into the earth, shaking the walls and floor, grains of dirt dropping out from between the sandbags that shored up the sides.

"Eh, up, here we go," Dusty said. He gave Iain a cigarette, lit them both shakily.

"We'll be back home this time tomorrow," he said inhaling smoke.

"I know you use the term home loosely."

"I'm starving, what've we got?"

Dusty eyed the rat-foxing food bag, hanging from the ceiling. "Dog biscuits, porridge for the morning – that's about it."

He groaned. "If someone doesn't relieve us in time for Christmas I'm going AWOL."

Dusty retrieved the biscuit from the bag. "Here." He handed Iain a couple of hard tack biscuits. They dipped them into the black tea, breaking the rainbow smeared surface.

"I want roast chicken," Dusty said.

"Steak and onions," he replied.

"Suet pudding and custard."

"Apple crumble and custard."

"A glass of brandy, cheese and biscuits. It's got to be cheddar mind."

"Whisky for me and I'll go for the cheese and biscuits too, none of that smelly Frenchy cheese." For them, this old game never lost its appeal.

"I'll be eating at the Ritz," Dusty said.

"I'll have mine at the Invertay Hotel, overlooking the loch."

"Yeah, that sounds good too. White napkins, silver cutlery, best lead crystal."

"Nothing but the best, a waitress to serve on the table."

"A busty one." Dusty grinned.

"And showing them off too." Iain drained the cup, finishing the last of his biscuit. "I'm starving."

"Oh shut the hell up, you. I'll pop over the top shall I and secure you a bit of Jerry sausage?"

"Ta, very much," he said. " Can I have some pomme frites with it please?"

"Since you asked so nicely, I'll be on my way." The guns crashed, British guns, then the heavy artillery joined in and the dugout vibrated. More guns, from the other side, rejoined them.

"Tell you what," Iain said, close to, above the racket, "you can finish your tea first."

"Thanks."

Tea drunk, Dusty pulled his boots back on, his circulation temporarily restored. They curled up on the wooden pallets, tucked their muddy great coats around them. The pounding guns shook the boards, a consistent, relentless medley of booming, whistling and banging reduced the chances of sleeping to a minimum.

Iain folded his arms across his empty groaning belly. He could find no comfort, the wooden boards dug into his arm, shoulder and hip, his feet were like blocks of ice. His head thrummed with lack of sleep and ceaseless shelling and he was itching, itching from the thirsty lice.

Sometimes when trying to slip into the blessed insensibility of sleep he mentally trod the woods at Harrowmead or the great forest at Glenleven. He tried this tactic now. He imagined the earth was soft and giving under his feet and he held his old familiar keeper's gun under his arm and Delilah kept him company. Deer grazed amongst the trees ahead of him pausing to observe him with dark liquid eyes. He did not raise his gun, drifting through them. He was a phantom. They did not move aside, he was no threat. He strolled to the river, Scottish water running yellow as whisky across the stones and shale. Further along the water frothed white as it tumbled, broken by large rocks, down to a pool below.

The corpse of the big man lay front down, his body on the bank, his face submerged. Blood coloured the water red, haloing his head, running away in a little rivulet. Iain watched it disperse. He did not want this vision in his dream. He would turn away, back to the forest. He began to run. His gun was gone, his dog absent. He lengthened his stride, running for his life. The big man was coming and if he caught him he was dead. His feet were sore as they hit the ground, his lungs bursting with the effort to keep going. Finnigan wanted him dead and if he wanted someone dead, generally they were. He dared not risk a glance over his shoulder. He could hear the pounding of Finnigan's feet behind him as loud as shellfire. He knew any moment he would feel the heavy weight of him at his back.

    A figure stood ahead of him in the trees. Terror clutched at his heart, it was a young man and he beckoned with his hand. Iain followed and the man turned away, running. Intermittently the figure smiled over his shoulder. "Tom," Iain called out. "Tom, wait." He could hardly speak for lack of air and his legs were becoming heavy and slow. The terror was so great he was gasping, great painful sobs. The booming of the guns filled his dream and something hit him on the arm wrenching him back to the dugout. His whole body jolted as he opened his eyes.

    "Christ, Midge, shut the hell up you noisy bastard," Dusty bawled above the din, tugging at Iain's arm. It was not his shouts that had disturbed Dusty, the artillery drowning his utterances, but he could not stand to see Iain's distressed sleep. Theirs was a brotherhood of two, many hours spent alone, out in no-man's-land or in an abandoned sap trench on sniper duty had made it so. Iain had found his niche. It set him apart and he considered that an advantage. Some men found his position unpalatable. He didn't let that bother him. He had never been popular and it had earned him a fast, if permanent, promotion to lance corporal.

    Iain closed his eyes again. He had dreamed that scenario a hundred times these last few months. The next time he opened his gritty eyes it was dawn and he swung his legs off the boards. He pushed Dusty's shoulder. It was his turn to wake with a jerk. It was stand-to in the trench and afterwards the bliss of a tot of rum from the commanding officer. In the gloom they filed out into the snow that crunched spotless and hygienic underfoot, visually pleasing but bone gnawing. Their boots left marks of drying mud in its pristine whiteness, nothing here stayed clean for long.

    The shelling ceased and apart from the whistle of the odd sniper bullet all was quiet. Corporal George Murphy cleared the snow from the brazier, lit it and made porridge with the last of the hard tack biscuits added to thicken it. Porridge at breakfast had been their only hot meal for three days and this was the last of the rations. They needed relief to arrive today or at the very least extra rations. A volunteer would be sent up the line after midday to make enquiries. Iain hoped it would be him, Dusty the same. They knew it would be neither. Escaping the front line for even a few hours was always desirable. Iain's skills at sharp shooting, so quickly discovered during musketry training in England, did not excuse him fatigues.

They had seen many comrades go west. They never listed them, didn't discuss the departed. Superstitions and compulsions, they all had their place where death drifted amongst them, waiting. While shrapnel, bullets, bombs and gas took their fair share of casualties, it was equally as likely that a stomach bug, accident or fighting out of line could finish you. Arnold Jackson had an arm and leg blown off. David Wright had been badly gassed, losing his sight. John Merit cut his finger, died of blood poisoning, Henry Axford, frostbite, James Rickman's gun exploded in his face. No it was better not to list them.

Some men remained nameless. These were the quickly dispatched, always green and clueless, unprepared, badly trained, easily panicked. More often the roll call of dead was personally painful, comrades, friends - a name to every missing face. New recruits came, young limbs in old, worn boots, in their turn sacrificed to the soil. It sickened Iain and gave him hope at the same time.

After breakfast had temporarily warmed them they cleaned their rifles, difficult work when their fingers were like frozen sausages. Dusty lost his temper over the smaller parts. Iain goaded him to try to snap him out of it.

Michael hummed softly. "Give us a song then," Iain said. "Cheer up this old bugger."

Michael obliged, singing in his silver-tones, *'Keep the Home Fires Burning ...'*

Champ, Flinty – all red hair and buckteeth, Jackie Elliott, George Murphy and Sergeant David paused in their work. Champ whistled a low warbling backing and Flinty mouthed the words silently. Michael's voice rang out, clear crystal notes carrying through the frosty air, a beautiful lament tugging at homesick hearts. When he had finished they were all silent, throats choked with tears that would remain unshed.

"Cheers, Michael," Iain spoke up. "Now we're feeling more chipper, do you know anything else like a requiem?"

He smiled sheepishly. "Sorry, any requests?"

Jackie, a bank clerk in his previous life, jauntily whistled *'Mademoiselle from Armentières'* and they all sang, *'Parlez-vous. Inky-pinky parlez-vous'* the bawdiest version they knew.

"That's better," Dusty muttered, having finally reassembled the rifle in working order. "Who's going up the line, sir?" he asked the sergeant, fluttering his long eyelashes, his irreverent sense of fun restored like his weapon.

The sergeant laughed. "Not you, Miller, you're on duty with Macdonald. How about young Michael, he looks fast on his feet."

Dusty and Iain groaned in unison. "Bring us back the bacon."

"They're tunnelling beneath us now," Sergeant David said, polishing his buttons, a practice which now it was not enforced, Iain and Dusty had abandoned.

"Great," Iain said, "any minute we could be swallowed up then."

"Makes me shiver thinking about those poor sods." Flinty searched his pockets for cigarettes.

"Aye, makes me shiver thinking any second we could be joining them."

"They've been tunnelling for weeks, it's perfectly safe down there," the sergeant said.

"Perfectly safe until they blow it to kingdom come." Dusty offered round his Woodbines. Iain was still pilfering fags from him, although his supply was also running low. Damp matches were challenging the men to keep a cigarette burning where possible in order to light the next.

"Come on, it's no good shirking," Sergeant David said. "There are sandbags to fill."

"What with? Snow?" Flinty asked taking a fag.

"The trench has been blown, up by the dogleg, needs re-building."

"Not as blown as it will be when the mine goes off," Iain muttered.

They trudged through the snow to start digging. The ground was like iron, too hard for the pointed thrust of a pickaxe.

Iain and Dusty called out commiserations, sniper duty beckoned. Iain had time to think of many things as he lay camouflaged in the mud, hiding in a hole, endless hours of waiting, while Dusty kept a tally of their hits. Dusty was proud of their high score, bragging about it when he had a drink in him. Iain wished he wouldn't, but Dusty ensured they were safe so he tried not to criticise too much. Dusty kept them moving to avoid retaliation, when Iain would be tempted to hold on, target that extra hit. Dusty always recognised a strong position with good cover, was never slack on the rules that regulated the sniper's work. He had a knack of finding an enemy officer and Iain rarely missed.

Today they fired from a sapper trench, Dusty peering with his trusty binoculars across a three hundred yard stretch.

Iain's old life was as distant here as the dreams filling his snatched hours of sleep. It was as if someone else had lived the years at Harrowmead, and before that Glenleven and The Sacred Heart. He supposed he was the same person, except now he lived his life as a soldier, a square peg firmly hammered into a round hole. The army expected a perfect fit.

The enforced fraternity of army life had not been such a struggle, regimentation had been the way of the orphanage. He tried hard to live for the moment, to concentrate on the next meal, the next rest, tried to keep his head down, he was getting through – just.

When they returned to the trench a hot meal and extra rations arrived robbing Michael of his chance to escape the line for an hour or so. This was not quite what the men had in mind. They had hoped for a troupe of fresh faces to relieve them, now they faced the assault of another night. The shelling began mid-afternoon and the relentless volley continued.

By midnight the persistent rods of rain and melting snow filled the trenches with brown, soupy, iced slush. It reached above Iain's knees and shorter men were up to their thighs. The singing and high spirits of the morning had lapsed into dismal melancholia. The dejected group had lost the spirit to communicate. They completed their watches in silence and attempted, where they could, to rest while the cacophony of metal hurtled overhead.

In the dugout Iain did not dare contemplate the idea of sleep the shelling was too fierce. The ground shook and his lousy clothes were waterlogged, impregnated with filth. There was no comfort to be found apart from raising his feet out of the liquid sludge. Around him the desperately exhausted hoped for oblivion.

This was purgatory. Where would he find the endurance and mettle required to see this through? Strange, there were days when it was all quite acceptable in a masochistic way, a shared refusal to be beaten by the circumstances, joshing with mates, small triumphs over endless adversity. But the days of pure unmitigated misery were torment. This was one of those days when the expression 'hell on earth' was wholly justified.

At dawn, with the shelling continuing unabated, relief arrived. A fresh battalion waded through the icy water wearing the same blank expressions as the men they replaced, shoulders drooping with weariness. They needed more than a few nights in a billet to recover. Sergeant David and his men cheered when they saw the new faces. They all shook hands as if something wonderful had been accomplished.

Iain followed Champ's squat, rectangular back through the trenches. It was a long four mile march to the village, boots heavy with mud and puttees caked to their legs. Rest and relaxation came closer with every miserable footstep taken.

The bathhouse was a temporarily converted pig shed, huge wine vats served as baths, an invitation of steam rose in the cold air. A motley collection of soldiers gathered at the hut, divesting their encrusted clothes in the biting open air. Doing their best to cover their dignity from gawping villagers, they dashed through the door. Shrieking and shouting wildly they jumped into the water. After a generous lathering of soap and a great deal of splashing and horseplay it was agreed they felt almost human again.

Dusty, Iain and Michael were billeted in a hayloft above the stables of a farm, while the remainder had managed to secure a Nissen hut further down the road. Clean and freshly shaven, wrapped against the cold, the three men strolled to the village café where they had arranged to meet with George, Jackie, Flinty and Champ. They ate fried potatoes and drank watery beer. Already the fifteen days in the limb numbing slurry of the front line were a lifetime away. With their circumstances so altered they trivialised their suffering. They were here in the warm, eating greasy French chips, washing them down with warm beer, laughing and joking. The moment was of the greatest consequence. Tomorrow might not exist for them. A pleasure however small had to be taken where it was found.

"I've got a concert tomorrow night and I've not learned my songs," Michael said, studying a script.

"They're lucky you're back in time. I didn't think we'd ever get away," Flinty said.

"It'll be the same old songs. I wouldn't worry about it, here let me see." Iain reached out a hand for Michael's lines.

"One day," Dusty said, "he's going to have his name up in lights." He stretched out his arm, opening and closing his hand as he said, "Starring – Michael – Rogers – voice of an angel."

The laughter was unanimous. "I know all of them." Iain returned the script.

"How's that go?" Michael pointed to the second page.

'*Where is our old CO?*', Iain sang, Dusty and Champ attempting harmony. '*Bringing up the rear. When will our relief come? Not this bloody year. All we need is bath and bed, not a bullet through the head. Think of us when we are dead, nowhere near here.'*

Michael shrugged, sticking out his bottom lip. "Never heard of it."

"You're too green, lad, that's your trouble," Champ said. "You're a good leading lady I'll give you that."

Dusty squeezed Michael's cheeks until his teeth were bared like a rabbit. "Look at that face, that complexion."

"Smooth as a baby's arse," Iain said, "and little wonder since it's never had sight of a razor."

"It has. I shave like anyone else." He was mutinous, they never tired of winding him up about his lack of facial hair.

There were general guffaws of doubt from the company. "If you squint he's not bad looking, even without the grease paint," Flinty said.

Dusty and Iain exchanged a look. "It's been a long time since he had a girl," Iain said.

"Yeah, but Michael's never had a girl," Flinty reminded them.

"Been a girl, never had a girl." Dusty laughed raising a jeer.

"We'll have to club together, take him down to Madame Goaty," Iain said. Her name was Gaultier, she reputedly had a tufty beard so Goaty had caught on.

"Yeah? Really?" Michael said.

"No, I wouldn't waste good money on you, it'd be over before you got it in, I reckon."

Michael flushed, gulping his beer. "You Scots are so tight," Dusty cried, slapping Michael on the back, causing him to choke. "Sorry, mate."

"You two been to Goaty's?" Flinty asked curiously.

Iain laughed, glancing at Dusty, seeing the opportunity to wind the boys up. "It's possible. We prefer classier establishments."

"Crikey, are you going again? Can I come?" Flinty gasped.

"We'll all go, how about that?" Dusty said. "They won't know what's hit them."

"I'm not going." Champ folded his arms in disgust. "Pick up some nasty disease to take home to the wife."

"There's more ways than one of skinning a cat." Dusty laughed. "Or in this case getting off with a Frenchy."

Champ frowned in confusion. He did not want to show his ignorance. "If you say so," he commented, "but sex is sex as far as I'm concerned and I made vows."

"Quite right," muttered Iain as he stuffed another forkful of potatoes into his mouth before saying, "Who wants another round?"

There were murmurs of agreement. He pushed his way through the crowd to the bar. He had cigarettes in his pocket, a full stomach and with three days of sleeping in a bed, albeit one made of chicken wire with a mattress of straw - things were looking brighter.

Later they returned to their lodgings. Michael recited his new songs in the lamplight. Iain, wrapped in a blanket, heated a bayonet over a candle flame and popped the lice eggs, which survived all laundering in the seams of his clean clothes. Dusty composing a letter to his girlfriend Celia, chewed his pen between bouts of inspiration. Everyone wrote letters home, except Iain. He wrote sporadic depressed ramblings in a journal. It did not make for a lighthearted read.

Iain yawned. His muscles were drained of strength. There were no thoughts in his head. Everything was sawdust, flaked, compressed and stuffed, he felt like a lifeless toy with jointed limbs. Within seconds of laying his head on the soft cotton pillow he fell into a nightmare filled sleep.

Chapter Twenty

"There's post for you, Midge." Dusty handed Iain a parcel. "Looks as if Father Christmas loves you after all." Iain made himself comfortable on the straw mattress, weighing the parcel in his hands. He had received packages a couple of times from charities that organised clothing and victuals to be sent out to soldiers.

He absently removed the string, careful not to tear the brown paper that may have future uses. He opened the box. It released a floral scent evoking strong memories. The letter was addressed to him in a neat oval script. This wasn't from a charity. This was personal. He sniffed the envelope that had travelled on top of the sweet scented soap and ripped it open. A photograph fell out from between the folds of a letter. A little boy aged two and a half stared back at him, Iain knew exactly how old he was. His dark hair sprang up from his head in a replicated cow's lick. He was a handsome strapping boy, clutching a stuffed animal. A faint smile on the child's lips was marred by the frown creasing his brow. It was the expression of a child in a dilemma, eager to please but desperate to be anywhere except posing in the photographer's studio. Iain balanced the box on his knees and laughed.

Dusty opened the first of three letters with two parcels at his feet. "Who's that, Midge?"

Iain studied the picture in disbelief, pausing before he answered. "It's Joe." He offered the picture to Dusty.

"Who's Joe?"

He laughed again. "He's my son."

Dusty, shocked, stared open mouthed. "Your what? I thought you didn't have any family?"

"Aye, so did I."

"Well, you can see he's a Macdonald, no mistaking that." He handed the photograph back. "You're a dark horse aren't you?"

Iain unfolded his letter.

'Dear Iain,

Sorry I have not written before. I thought it was about time you saw your son, you should be proud. He's growing into a fine boy and every day that passes I thank God for the gift you have given me. He is my life, making everything worthwhile.

I recently visited your house for the first time since your departure and found your letter, which touched me deeply. Now I bring Joe here if I have the time, but with my busy life at North Farm time is a rare commodity.

You would be horrified by the liberties being taken in your wood. Fences have been carted off for firewood, gates hang off their hinges and a thoroughfare has been established as a short cut to the village. Although things have certainly run to seed in your absence it is nothing you cannot fix on your return, I'm sure. I spoke to Mrs Denham last week and she tells me Mr Denham can't wait until you come back.

Delilah keeps well with Isaac, I come across them from time to time. He told me Joe looks like his father! He also said 'that's the one he denies'. What a strange thing to say, does he know something?

I need to ask you about Tom. A reassurance I suppose, about the last time you saw him. Freddy blamed you and I don't believe it. Am I right to doubt him?

Perhaps you have no wish to write, I understand if that's the case. If you choose to correspond, you could send it to me here, at Keeper's House.

I hope the parcel reaches you in time for Christmas.

God bless you and keep you safe. Your friend, Helena'

He read the letter through twice then delved into the box. She had put great thought into each item - socks, matches, cigarettes - his favourite brand - tinned fruit and fish, chocolate, toothbrush and powder, razor blades, a copy of Robinson Crusoe and the soap. His delight was immeasurable. A hand grenade without the pin might have surprised him less than Nell's gifts. He lay back on his bed, studying the photograph of the boy. This rare feeling of happiness had been absent for so long it felt new to him, its warmth made his heart swell.

Nell had certainly taken her time making contact. Although, why should she bother with him? She had a husband, home, family. He was from the past and had resigned himself to staying there, and now this - the picture, a letter with promise of more and a generous parcel. She may have tarried but she excelled herself when she put in the effort.

When Dusty finished opening his post he said, "We'll eat well for a bit between us, the others had parcels too. So come on then, tell us the news?"

Iain narrowed his eyes against the smoke as he blew it towards the slanting ceiling. He never lied to Dusty. "It's complicated. I have a son and his mother has written and sent the parcel."

"Well, all this time, you kept that quiet." He was peevish.

"Sorry, pal, I really thought it was water under the bridge. As you say, all this time and she's never sent anything before, what was I supposed to think?"

"Yeah, Midge, you're right." His tone changed. "Women! Always turning the tables on us."

Iain took the letter from the top of the box to read again. She had asked about Tom, he wondered what Freddy had been saying. What was he admitting to or denying? When he wrote back he would omit that reference. Old Isaac's mouth had been running away from him again. He remembered with clarity now the night by the fire when, loaded with drink, Isaac had foretold a son he would deny to be his. Maybe there was something in the wisdom of the old gypsy. He had also prophesied daughters for Iain, a cheering prospect, indicating he might yet survive this war.

He studied the picture of Joe, a little stranger, yet familiar, a resemblance that could not be denied. The apple hadn't fallen far from the tree, not nearly far enough.

"You going to Goaty's tonight?" Dusty asked from his bed.

"Nah, don't think so."

He tutted. "You promised to take Michael."

"I didn't promise. I said it was a waste of brass if you recall. Anyway I don't like paying for it and Champ's right about the pox."

"You don't have to go the whole hog."

"I don't have to go the whole hog, as you say, with a lass from the village and for free and all."

"I don't know how you manage it, I never get lucky. There's precious few who'll even give a kiss away for nothing."

"Confiture, mademoiselle? The taste of apple and plum affords such delights," he joked, holding up a pot of jam that had spilled onto the floor from his bag.

Dusty laughed. "Yeah, yeah and it's against regulations Lance Corporal Macdonald," he mimicked the sergeant's Welsh lilt. "Come on, keep us company. Flinty's desperate. I am above such things, I'm spoken for y'know," the last said in a pseudo-aristocratic accent.

Iain rolled onto his side, "Shut up you stupid sod, I'll think about it." He fell asleep holding the photograph of his son.

* * * *

The worse for drink, Iain and Michael staggered up the narrow dark staircase above the butcher's shop with Dusty and Flinty leading the procession. It opened up into a dimly lit sitting room, over stuffed with furniture and hot from the brightly burning fire in the grate. Madame Gaultier was knitting, soberly dressed in black. At her elbow a champagne flute was incongruously filled with red wine, a smoking cigarette in a holder clamped between her teeth.

"Bonsoir monsieur." Throwing her knitting aside, cigarette held aloft, she rose to her feet with a fixed smile of welcome. She saw Dusty. "Et Monsieur." Seeing Flinty, followed by Iain dragging Michael who was not quite drunk enough. "Mon dieu," she exclaimed, "beaucoup de messieurs, bienvenu." She spread her arms, her low cut dress revealed an ample bosom. Her hair was badly bleached. Rather than a beard, she had a thick down on her chin made all the more obvious by a layering of powder.

Two women lounged on a sofa, propping up their heads with their hands, bored. One wore a ringlet-curled wig, her white face powder and rouge were clownish. A long fitted robe covered her dress and yellow horny nails protruded from fluffy heeled slippers. The second had hennaed hair loose over her shoulders, a striking face, symmetrical with an easy smile. She sashayed across the room to Iain with her eyes alight. "Faire l'amour avec moi?" She linked her arm into his. With her high heels she was only a couple of inches shorter than him.

He laughed. "No, no." He doubted he had enough money, he had not wanted this and he attempted to disengage her arm.

"Oui, monsieur." She took a firmer hold of him.

"Don't be shy," Dusty jibed. "A big boy like you."

"I'm stony broke," he declared, holding out his hands to her. "Je suis no money, no francs." She shrugged and her hands darted into his tunic pocket. He got there first and caught her hand. He was unsteady on his feet. She put her weight against him and he put his arm round her to stop himself keeling over. He raised his eyebrows at his companions, Dusty laughing and Michael resembling a rabbit caught by the hunter's lamp.

On the far side of the room a door opened, a young girl appeared of no more than nineteen. It was her youth that was attractive rather than her face. Iain passed her as the hennaed lady invited him to follow. The small bedroom, lit by an oil lamp, was sparsely furnished with a bed and table, the faded water marked wallpaper peeling forlornly at the edges.

She swayed her hips seductively as she walked in front of him and settled herself on the bed tapping the satin cover with her hand. He stood at the side of the bed watching her, impassive. In the shadowy light she pulled up her skirts, she wore no underwear. She offered herself without embarrassment or preamble. "Ici." She beckoned to him.

"No," he said and shook his head. "Je suis no francs." Her face did not register surprise or offence at his refusal. She was used to the awkward tight-fisted British Tommy, though it slightly bored her. She reached out with scarlet tipped nails, pulling at his belt. She had his trousers down before his alcohol soaked brain registered it. She sat up on the edge of the bed. Leaning forward she took him into her mouth, one hand on his buttock drawing him towards her.

He concentrated on the crown of her head where the roots of her hair grew through dark. The whole situation was surreal. He closed his eyes, his head swimming, heat rushing to his loins, going with it, wishing he was somewhere else, glad he wasn't. Her expertise was irresistible. The motion of her rapacious mouth clamped on him made the desire throb through his body, ripples of lust, smouldering sparks of pressure mounting until he could not help putting his hands to her head.

His drunkenness did not diminish the speed with which she satisfied him. She turned away discreetly. He fastened his trousers and buckled his belt by which time she was standing, holding out her hand for payment.

"Less francs than full on jiggy," she said in her thick accent, taking the francs he had scrambled through his pockets searching for. After staring at the coins with some satisfaction, she took his arm to show him down the backstairs.

He paused at the top of the stairwell and put his arms round her, after a second she responded, wrapping her arms about his waist, her head on his shoulder. He ran his hand down her body. Her hair brushed his cheek, the unfamiliar stale smell of her was heavy with musky scent and cigarette smoke. She took his hand and pressed it against her soft breast, the nipple was hard and unfettered under the thin material. Her lips were warm on his neck, the flicker of her tongue wet on his skin. Then she hesitated as if she did not quite trust him, or possibly herself. Reluctantly he was obliged to release her. She would clean him out if he allowed it. He would have liked to lie with her, to hold her. He wanted affection far more than he wanted sex.

"Merci," he said.

"Merci beaucoup, Monsieur." She briefly touched his face.

He jogged across the road to wait for the others. Flinty was already there, grinning, knocking back a beer.

"Crikey, Midge, that was great," he said.

Iain smiled, went to the bar. He didn't think it was great, paying for love. He considered the embrace had been free and, in comparison, what preceded it felt clinical, functional and cold, despite the obvious pleasure of sexual release.

He ordered a beer, speaking to the bartender in Pidgin French trying to get whisky or something similar. Eventually he produced a bottle. "Trois," Iain said holding up three fingers. The Frenchman poured three measures into a glass. Iain drank it straight down. It was rum. "Encore? Encore, sil-vous-plait." The barman raised his eyebrows, shrugged and poured again. Iain swallowed it quickly. A deep depression blanketed him and oblivion was the best answer. He thanked the man, returned to Flinty who described in lurid detail his encounter with the bewigged prostitute. Sitting back he crossed his ankles, offered Flinty a fag, took one himself and smoked it leisurely, the effects of the rum coursing through him. Flinty whispered and giggled, blowing smoke in Iain's face. Iain was a long way off, watching the clientele.

This was a mistake. The café was full of soldiers having a good time, or pretending to, no, not pretending, urgently living before it was snatched away. And this was the right thing, the only thing to do. There was a truth to their forced enjoyment of vapid triviality.

Unbidden Helena came to mind, every detail of her, a sharp slap in his face. He rubbed his eyes and was nudged by a hand on his back.

"I'll get them in, sunshine, looks as if you need it," Dusty said, a hand resting between Iain's shoulder blades.

Michael subsided on a chair, shaking and white with a sheen of perspiration on his face. Iain glanced at him, leaned his chair back on two legs, lit another cigarette from the one he had, and drained his glass.

Dusty set three brimming glasses on the table and joined them. He lifted his glass. "A toast, gentlemen. Vive la France," he said. Flinty cheered, Michael silently picked up his glass and gulped thirstily.

"Who gives a shit?" Iain said. "I want to go home."

Dusty looked sympathetic. "Me too," he said. "Back to dear old Blighty. Best drink to that then."

"Aye, I'll drink to that." He met Dusty's eyes over the rim of their froth-edged jars.

"You got something to write home to mother now." Dusty nudged Michael.

He was horrified. "I sure as hell won't be bragging about it."

Dusty laughed. "Was it a big disappointment?"

His head sank between his shoulders, a tortoise retreating into a shell. "No, it was all right. Not all right – bad."

"Who was it?" Iain asked.

"Yvonne, the young thing," Dusty said still laughing.

"Trust me," he said, "she could never be bad. Now the old dear with the wig – that's bad."

Dusty was glad to see Iain's temper recovered. Flinty choked on his beer. "She was all right. Bit old, but the room was dark." Michael was near to tears, so they left him to drink his beer in peace.

Later, Iain and Dusty abandoned the group. They were used to two's company, the hours spent together sniping in no-man's-land made it natural to them. They ended the night in the basement of a café on the far side of the village. They played poker by candlelight with the owner, his brother and a local farmer, knocking back bottles of vinegary red wine. Iain lost the remaining francs he had been so eager to keep in his pocket, and all their cigarettes to the game. In the early hours the door was finally bolted behind them and they rolled home, arms over each other's shoulders singing rude variations of, '*If you were the only girl in the world*'.

In the morning Iain woke up with a pounding head and a mouth like the bottom of a ferret hutch. He searched everywhere he could think of for cigarettes - in his coat, Dusty's coat, trouser pockets, their packs. Eventually he caught hold of Dusty by his shirtfront. "Where are the bastard fags?" he bawled.

Dusty pushed him off groaning. "God Al-bloody-mighty, Midge, what's wrong with you? We lost them at poker."

"We did what?" He almost lost his voice. He stamped around dragging on his clothes and boots, cursing under his breath. He stumbled downstairs to the water pump in the middle of the yard and working it awkwardly with one hand, splashed it over his face gasping at its iciness. He cupped it in his palm and drank deeply, ignoring the army supplied sign reading, *'DO NOT DRINK'*. He didn't care, he was parched and it didn't taste of petrol.

He headed for the shop in the village. It was only when he had made his order and the packets lay temptingly within reach he discovered his wallet and pockets were empty. It appeared it wasn't only his fags he'd lost in the poker game.

* * * *

On the last day of respite, Iain replied to Nell's letter. He replicated Dusty's familiar pose, chewing the end of the pen, hunched over the blank paper. It was difficult to know what he could say that she might want to hear, very little if he were honest with himself. He could hardly tell her about the stench and decay of the trenches, the mind numbing shelling that left them hard of hearing and shaking, the fact he would sell his soul for a bottle of spirit and a soft mattress, or sacrifice his best mate to the next bomb if it meant saving his own miserable skin. He began uncertainly:

'Helena, I think of you when I am blowing the head off a Jerry, when I'm lying oxter deep in mud, when I'm sleeping, not sleeping, on the fire-step. I think of you...'

He scrawled the pen nib through the lines. Blots of ink dripped onto the paper, blooming into black, bleeding spots. *'I think of you, let's be honest, probably all the time. Not at first, not training, not when I arrived, everything was new and different and took every ounce of my energy. But then the small thoughts spared became longer and longer moments of time, and I don't know when it happened. I don't know when I tried to remember your face, occasionally saw you in my dreams, heard your voice and wished. A gradual thing, slowly, slowly, until there you are, at every meal, every night, every sentry duty, out in the mud of no-man's-land, through my rifle scope, under my skin. I think of you and you are here. I wish you were here. I wish I were there. '*

He stared at the scrawled out lines, balled the paper into his fist.

"Stop wasting my ink," Dusty said.

He didn't answer. He had to be sensible, he had to remember life at Harrowford never changed. North Farm would still be North Farm. War would be a horror, distanced by the black and white print of the newspaper propaganda. And he didn't feel any of these things anyway, only sometimes he was despairing, depressed, exhausted and always, always, deep in his bone marrow, lonely. Lonely for everything he didn't have even if half the time he couldn't put a name to it. So the words formed on the page, well behaved and grateful.

'Helena,

Thank you for the parcel you sent, it came when I least expected and needed it most. Joe is a fine boy, I'm glad he is everything you wished for. I can see the resemblance you spoke of, trust Isaac to see it. I recall him saying something about my having a son before Joe was born. Glad to hear about Delilah, she was always a good dog. I knew Isaac was reliable on that score.

I've not been home for over two years. I spent my home leave on the French coast looking at the English Channel, silly really. I cannot imagine this ever ending, of course it will. Hard going here, no point lying about it. I miss the woods and fields. Here shelling has destroyed the land. I have not seen a fully-grown tree for months, lots of mud and filth. I think about home, at the same time not really knowing where home is. It's like a symbol, not somewhere absolute, an idea. Mr Denham said my job would be waiting for me and when I think of peace I imagine Keeper's House at Harrowmead. Being here makes me realise what's important. We've lost so many, only my mates Dusty and Champ remain from the original crew. You can't survive this without someone to call a friend. It's taken my being here to understand there are some good people who can be relied upon and trusted. I might add that you are one of those few.

Is Freddy in France? You don't mention his whereabouts in your letter – how very diplomatic of you. I don't mind you writing about him, I am as far removed from reality here as I could ever be. Write what you wish, so long as you write. Most of the lads have families. I must admit I envied them news from home, so really you were prayers answered, if I were a praying man!

Thank you. Yours truly, Iain.'

* * * *

It was a relief to be in the reserve trenches over Christmas. Iain's pity towards those in the front line was fleeting. The previous year he had been celebrating under fire with bully beef and hard tack biscuits on Christmas Day.

This year Christmas dinner was provided in a large hut at the rear of the trenches, a substantial festive meal of roast pork with all the trimmings, and carafes of watered wine. The hut was decorated with paper chains and a spindly Christmas tree, a poor specimen. They pulled crackers and ate dinner wearing paper hats. The officers had cigars and brandy, the privates happy to make do with rum and cigarettes. When dinner was over they played cards, drank coffee and smoked, it was an enjoyable afternoon.

On Christmas night Michael had star billing at the concert party as their very own Vesta Tilley.

"He makes me right proud," Dusty said.

"He's a good lad," Iain agreed. None cheered him more than the men from his own section, their hands sore with clapping.

On Boxing Day it was as if Christmas Day had never occurred. Here they were back in the front line, rum and pork crackling a festive echo. Iain's company filled sandbags with sodden clay earth. The rain was persistent. The clay stuck to the shovels and it was necessary to use their bare hands.

Iain blinked the rain out of his eyes, fighting to keep the bag open while Dusty rammed it with blocks of mud running with water. The empty spaces they excavated filled rapidly with sludge. His back ached, fingers numb on the sacking, he could have been holding something or nothing, it felt the same. They carried the bulging bags to the bomb damaged sites. He could lift a bag on his own. After half a dozen, strength sapped, they resorted to carrying an end each, defeated by the weight.

After hours in the rain they shivered in the dugout drinking Oxo. Exhaustion sapped the spirit, robbed thought and speech. Back and arms ached and leg muscles throbbed. Later Iain would be plagued by the returning cramps that accompanied sleep. He blew on the Oxo, the savoury steam swirling into his face. Dinner was cold stew straight from the tin and bread and Tickler's jam again. It was a quiet night. The rain had subdued the fighting spirit.

Their sergeant major appeared in the doorway. Cape dripping, he showered them with raindrops as he came in. "Sorry, lads," he muttered. Glazed eyes turned to him, weariness etched on expectant faces. "I'm afraid something's going off underground and

I know you aren't on loopholes, any of you, but the others have been called off to help the RE's. So it'll be two hours at a time, any volunteers for first watch?"

A unanimous heartfelt groan rose above bowed heads. Iain turned away. He wasn't going out there. Dusty volunteered to get it over with and George followed with reluctance.

For two hours Iain allowed his mind to drift but sleep wouldn't come, everything hurt. He thought about Helena and the boy, wondered if a letter would be waiting when he got back to the billet. He envisioned her in black, mourning Freddy. How pleasing, Freddy dead, that was why she hadn't mentioned him. In the darkness of the dugout he allowed his fantasies to form unchecked, what did it matter? Nothing was real here, only death and the permanent threat of it.

He slowly uncurled himself, feeling like an old man. His feet hit the water. "Hey, Champ, come on." He prodded the big man with his knee, where he lay on the raised boards.

Champ yawned. "Was dreaming of me Missus."

"Lucky you," he said. The rain was a dark cloak, the mud knee deep, liquid and rank. He passed Dusty, neither speaking.

Champ said, "Here, Dusty, make us a cuppa if you're having one."

"Yeah, will do."

Iain adjusted his tin hat, perched for the sake of warmth atop a woollen one. A few bullets whistled over and he lowered his head, eyeing the top of the trench. Champ, a few feet away, gave him the thumbs up. He failed to respond staring out of the loophole, despondent. His gaze was drawn to the raindrops falling in the puddle at eye level. As they plopped they scattered smaller drops into the air, the effect was hypnotic. The repetition lulled him and his eyelids drooped. A sudden noise shook him back to reality. He straightened his back, distributing his weight on both legs, eyes peering into the darkness. Dusty was in the dugout cursing his lack of dry socks, followed by a stifled shriek.

"Buggers." Dusty stomped out into the mud.

"Rats," Iain said to Champ by way of explanation

"Have you made the tea yet?" Champ ventured.

"No, I haven't. Make your own bloody tea. Do I look like your bleeding batman?" Dusty fumed. Iain and Champ exchanged a look. Champ laughed, his two front teeth were missing, giving him a comical visage. Dusty glowered, sinking his sandbag clad boots into the mud as another bullet spun close to his ear.

"I'm going to get that buggering bastard Alleyman," he said. He disappeared into the dugout and returned with his rifle. Champ, seeing his chance, slipped past him to make the tea, risking the wrath of the CO.

"Dusty," Iain said, "give us a break, pal."

"Piss off," he retorted. The mud clung to him, an extra dank overcoat. He was cold, wet, hungry and beyond tired.

"Nobody's got dry socks and if they were dry, well they wouldn't be dry for long would they?" Iain attempted to lift a leg clear of the water.

Dusty jumped onto the fire-step to locate the sniper, his face a fixed grimace.

"He'll blow your head off if you're not careful. We're on duty in five hours. We'll get him, I think I know his position," Iain said. "Here have a fag, calm down."

Dusty leaned down and snatched one. He tried to light it. "My matches are wet," he snapped, seething.

Iain hid a smile and handed him a book of matches. After several abortive attempts he lit the cigarette and pocketed the matches. He climbed off the fire-step, splashing into the water and waded to the loophole to wait for Champ.

"I'm fed up with this," he said. "We're supposed to be on light work detail and sharp shooting, not bleeding lookout. They pile it on, pile it on. Christ Almighty, Midge."

"Aye, poor bloody infantry, pal."

"Well, I'm sick of it, should've joined the artillery, or cavalry, or any-sodding-thing."

"They've all got their crosses, you know that. The artillery have got guns blowing up in their faces, the cavalry are sent out to fend off shells and gas with horses. Anyway you're the best spotter I know. You could've been a miner, now there's an unenviable job. I'd rather be up here thanks very much, rain or no."

"Yeah," Dusty said, "if something is going off tonight, we could end up down there with them. At least they don't have to dodge the flying bullets and shrapnel."

"I'm not getting killed, not in this war, any road."

"Yeah, right, you're invincible, I suppose."

"Back home I know an old gypsy, a shaman, well he says he's not, but that's what he's like. He said I would have a son and I did, and he said I would have daughters, more than two, so it figures doesn't it? I haven't had them yet, so I must survive." He was pleased with his logic.

"He's just some old gyppo, Midge. It's like reading tea leaves or something."

"No, it's more than that, this guy's a wise one, really. I've never known him get anything wrong."

Dusty smiled, unconvinced. "Good for you."

"I know it sounds mad, all this is mad too. Why should things make sense to be real?"

"No, it's good, if it comforts you, it's good."

"It's not as simple as that. Love doesn't make sense but everyone insists it happens. Do you love your girl?"

Dusty shrugged. "Yeah, I suppose so. I'm glad she's there to go home to. Haven't known each other long – not even a year, I hope she'll marry me one day."

"There you go see. Keeps you going, knowing she's there. It doesn't really make sense though does it – I mean, you don't really know each other do you? How could you in such a short space of time – yet you imagine you're in love and want to marry her."

"Yeah? It's the only way I can think of to get me end away." Dusty laughed at himself. "No, I'm kidding. Celia's a great girl. I wouldn't expect you to understand, you're a cynic when it comes to love and all that."

"No, I'm not, well not as much as I used to be. It's horses for courses, pal, this place has taught me that at least."

"You mean you'll take something away from all this crap?" he said in disbelief.

"Aye, reckon I will. I won't be so quick to turn my back on someone, trust begets trust and that goes for loyalty and friendship – love too I suppose."

"Christ, you're turning into a philosopher."

"Always fancied myself one of those anyway, altered my own philosophy that's all. Reckon I've been living my life all wrong up until now. When I get out of here things will change."

"A leopard doesn't change its spots, Midge."

Champ arrived with the tea. "Sorry, no tins of milk left again," he said.

Iain put the mug to his lips. Simultaneously an almighty explosion shook them. The water at their knees vibrated and they staggered against the trench wall. Mixed in with the rain a liberal splattering of earth cascaded over the trench lip, splashing into their tea, some sinking, some floating in black dispersing grains on the top. Iain peered at Dusty with narrowed eyes. Dusty's look matched his own and they grinned and started to laugh.

Champ peered into his cup. "I knew no good would come of me stirring it with a knife," he exclaimed.

Dusty shrugged. "Might have been worse," he said, "he could've used his finger."

"Doesn't matter now," Iain said and sipped it, dirt and all. "Tastes sodding awful without milk, any road."

"Told you, there's none left," Champ said defensively, "and I wouldn't use me finger, that's disgusting."

Chapter Twenty-one

A battalion of one thousand men marched in fours passing huts and warehouses. The road, axle deep in mud, was congested with horse-drawn wagons, motorised vehicles, foot soldiers and pedestrians. The air was thick with the smell of fuel, tainted earth and horse manure. A multitude of old shells, boxes, tarpaulins, broken shafts and nameless refuse littered the verges. The hum of the traffic merged with the stamping of feet, masking the thunder of distant guns.

At the railway station the first three hundred men caught the train up the line while the remainder cooled their heels at the station, leaning on their packs, smoking, talking, waiting. Their reward was a cup of stewed tea and a bun served by two middle aged English women with ready smiles and a bottomless urn.

"I hope we get the Nissen hut this time," Dusty said, between mouthfuls of currant bun.

"Might not be any huts," Michael said. "They're comfy though."

"Glad to see the back of this place," Iain said. They all nodded in agreement with the knowledge that the next village may be different but the trenches would be detailed copies.

"They're sending us to replace those gone," Dusty said.

"Planning some big push by the sound of it," Iain said. "I overheard the corp talking to that new officer, Peterson."

"Aren't they always talking about it?"

"They asked me to stay back," Michael said, "for the shows."

"And? Why didn't you?"

"What? Leave all me mates behind? I wouldn't want that. I can sing wherever I am, don't need a stage do I?"

"Ahh, ain't he sweet." Dusty ruffled Michael's hair.

"If it kept you out of the front line, I reckon you should have stayed put, pal." Iain handed round a packet of cigarettes.

"I want to be with you lot," Michael said, taking a cigarette, as if it were natural to him, when really it made him feel as sick as a dog. He longed to be like Dusty or Corporal Murphy or Iain, taken seriously, not considered a bit of a joke.

Iain sighed shaking his head. The boy was too young to see sense. He would have jumped at the chance to stay out of it, even if it meant peeling potatoes for the duration. He was stuck in the trenches, in the mud of no-man's-land and no mistake. His ability at sharp shooting was a hindrance to promotion. If they permitted him to go through the ranks they would lose a good sniper.

He had received a letter from Helena. Freddy had been discharged on medical grounds, so much for widow's weeds. *'He's a bit moody,'* she wrote. Not much change there, he thought. The rest had been gossip, news of the boy, socks and sweets.

Dusty laughed at Michael, choking on cigarette smoke. "Leave the lad alone," Iain said.

"I am," he exclaimed. "It's not my fault he can't smoke a fag."

"He shouldn't smoke anyhow, because of his voice."

"Is that so? Could do with a bit of gruffness if you ask me." Jackie turned round to join in the conversation. "Make him a man."

"I'm not asking you," Iain said. "Smoking doesn't make you a man, no more than drinking and killing."

"Aww, Mikey, you got a fan here," Jackie said. "You could become his manager after the war."

"Aye?" Iain gave Jackie a long appraising stare and Jackie squirmed. "Maybe, I'll do that, and when I've made a mint I'll come and run you over in my Rolls Royce. How's that for a good idea?"

Jackie turned red, laughing nervously. "Right, mate, you probably will too."

"Let's not see blood before we even reach the trench, eh, boys?" Dusty said.

Iain snatched the half smoked cigarette from Michael's fingers. "You don't have to smoke to be like everyone else. You're not like everyone else, you've got a gift. You're special."

Michael blushed. "Thanks, Midge." His adoring stare was lost on Iain who smoked the remainder of the disputed fag. Dusty hid a smirk.

They boarded the second train all backpacks and rifles, armed khaki snails climbing into covered cargo trucks, leaving the remainder of the battalion to await the next one. Forty men and six horses were shoehorned into each truck. The train made very slow progress.

The train pulled out of the station at a sedate chug, iron wheels clanging on iron tracks. George Murphy slid the door open to enjoy the view and fresh air, a small freedom. They travelled through unblemished farmland, passing green fields and bare woodland, with mighty trees that Iain had dreamed about and had not seen for so long. For March it was unseasonably warm, the clouds forming a white alien landscape against the blue.

The mood was optimistic, leaving behind their planted comrades, finally moving albeit only one hundred miles up the line and to similarly dismal conditions. They had been eighteen months in the same stretch. Iain and Dusty knew every crater, trench and hiding place. A new terrain would be challenging, a good test for their map reading. Anything that brought change however subtle and possibly difficult was welcome.

Iain turned his hands over. Dry painful fissures split his fingertips. He had rubbed them with whale oil but they were no better for it. He pulled his gloves on and winked at Michael who was watching him. Over Michael's head the stitched patchwork of countryside spread out, clean air flowed through the open door. Beyond it was normality, escape. For a moment Iain imagined leaping off the wagon, hitting the dry earth with a brain shaking thump, rolling down the daisy-strewn bank strong with the green smell of grass, back to life and reality. Of course he didn't, he wouldn't. There was no escape for him. This was reality, here sitting on the hard dirty floor of a cargo truck.

Dusty leaned into him. "D'you think we'll ever come back?"

"Aye, we'll come back. If I'm coming back, I'm buggered if you're not. And I told you already, I am going home, it's fate."

"Oh, yeah, that's right, your old prophet. That's your fortune though, not mine. I got a bad feeling about this, right here." He pointed to his gut.

"That'll be too much bully beef, pal."

Dusty laughed, cuffing his arm. "Bye the bye," he lowered his voice to a whisper, "you got an admirer there in young Mikey. Reckon he swings that way, better watch yourself."

He bent his head to hide his laughter. "Christ, you're kidding, right?"

"No, straight up, can't take his eyes off you. He's been making sheep's eyes for weeks. I didn't think you'd noticed. Let him down gently won't you?"

"Gently? I'll break his jaw if he tries anything." He shook his head and began quietly laughing. "You're full of it, Dusty Miller, he doesn't swing any way. He's just a kid."

"Here," George said, "that tea's hit me bladder, do you suppose they'll stop?"

"Me too," Jackie said. "I'm trying not to think about it."

Four hours from the station the train whined to a jerking halt. The scrabble of boots scuffed up a cloud of dust. Men fell out, hurtling down the bank for a convenient bush. A handful were running up the slope as the train juddered and clanked into motion, shouting protests while scrambling on board before it gained momentum.

Darkness fell and they were shunted into a siding for the night. The horses were restless and there was nowhere to escape them, surrounded as they were by railway lines and steep embankments. The night was endless. The horses stamped and snickered, nipping with bored lips and sharp teeth at any soldier within reach, raising stifled curses. They were trapped with the combined stench of horse dung, urine and sweat.

Iain and Dusty put their kitbags back to back to afford some comfort. It was impossible to rest, let alone sleep. At dawn the wheels clanked into motion, hour after interminable hour, one hundred miles stretched to a thousand.

One of the horses fell awkwardly. There was a struggle to get it upright and its whinnying was pitiful to hear. "Let Midge have a look he's got a way with animals. He brought a dog back from the brink. Here, let him see," Dusty shouted over the crowd who had gathered.

"The dog was fitting not dying," Iain hissed in Dusty's ear. The crowd propelled him forward.

"Same thing," he muttered. He had been impressed at the time. In the lurching half-light of the moving wagon Iain reluctantly placed his hand on the horse's side, her coat quivered at his touch. The mare held her hind leg slightly askew, resting the tip of her hoof on the wooden floor. He stroked her and she was calmer, which raised a murmur of approval from the men.

Dusty crossed his arms with a knowledgeable expression. "Told you he was good."

"What do you think?" a young private asked, his face lined with worry.

"Is she your responsibility?"

"Yes, sir, she's my captain's horse."

"I think she's dislocated her hip." He spread his long fingers on her muscular rump. "Feel that." The soldier obliged.

"It's raised and she's holding her foot up. Look this leg is longer than the other. It's clean out of the socket."

The private's eyes widened, aghast. "Crikey, we won't have to shoot her will we?"

"Hopefully we can pull it back in, but not here. And she would have to rest. If it came out again, it wouldn't be so good for her. Let's be optimistic, there's no reason not to be."

They arrived at a makeshift station between the village and the trenches. The shells were plainly audible, the crump of grenades and rat-a-tat-tat of the machine guns.

It was agreed with the commanding officer to delay for an hour to treat the horse. Dusty secured morphine from an officer and in an old shed they administered it to their equine patient. With the aid of ropes they attempted to pull the leg back into the socket. It took the sheer brute strength, sweat and effort of four men on the rope to produce the satisfying click Iain was waiting for. The great ball of bone lodged back into place under his hand. He smiled at Dusty who sweated at the other end of the animal, the rope now slack in his hands.

"Bring her water. She'll need to rest for a week at least," he said to the young private who thanked him profusely.

Lieutenant Peterson drew him to one side. "That was mightily impressive, Macdonald," he said. "Where did you learn veterinary skills?"

"I didn't, I picked up a few things being around horses. Watched others who knew their stuff." He held out his hands, the tools of the trade.

"Well, it's a good talent to have. Do you work on people too?"

He thought of Helena. "I'm not really practised on people. If an animal dies it is not a legal problem. If a human does I think you find yourself on the wrong end of the law."

Peterson laughed. "That's true, Macdonald. Out here things don't always work that way do they?"

"No, sir. I'll keep it in mind."

"Very good. Now you've held us up long enough with your doctoring. We'd better be on our way. You're our top marksman aren't you?"

"Apparently."

"Who's your spotter?"

"Miller, sir, he's the best."

"Yes, so are you I've heard. What's your tally?"

"You'd have to ask Miller."

Peterson smirked. "How very modest of you, Macdonald, rumours abound, over two hundred, over three?"

"You'll have to ask Miller, modesty isn't his strong point," Iain said.

Peterson strolled away laughing. Iain viewed the lieutenant with suspicion. He was an officer waiting for the chance to prove himself and be seen doing it, which wasn't very reassuring.

They marched three miles through bombed out villages - broken fragments, crumbling walls, a chimney rising from a heap of rubble. It was all that remained of what once would have been home to a thriving community. The trees were broken stumps, like rotted broken teeth sticking out of the gummy mud. Wagons of ammunition and heavy artillery went before them, rations and supplies at the rear. They approached their destination, the grass grew green again and the trees had branches with the promise of spring in their buds.

There were Nissen huts but not enough for a quarter of the men coming up the line. The huts shouldered the road in flat mighty piles. Their platoon, separated into sections, was assigned different tasks to assist in the erection of the huts. Iain and his section worked in the nearby woodland to cut down trees for the foundations.

It was a forest of huge evergreen conifers, reminiscent of the Scottish forests so familiar to him. Wielding great jagged-toothed bow saws like the woodsmen back home they severed the giant trunks. It was hard work, adding fresh blisters to war-battered hands. But there was pleasure in it for Iain. Rising with the tangy fresh smell of the sticky resin were memories of his days with Old Tam and Dougie. He would walk in search of them occasionally in his effort to escape Finnigan. They would welcome him and stop their work for a brew. If employment in the stable at Glenleven had been his ideal, joining the woodsmen would have been second best.

Now here he was, in this foreign land, cutting trees raised on foreign soil with a wagon full of Englishmen. To be free of mud and the stink of decaying flesh was such relief. It was a normal honest day's work, although their sweating bodies stimulated the lice into frantic activity. They cut and carried all day, until their arms were rubber and their bodies ached with fatigue.

They piled brushwood and surplus branches into a giant bonfire and tired men gathered as dusk fell to bask in its heat. They drank tea from their cans, smoked and sang hymns and ballads that were sweetest to them, of home, sweethearts and mother. Their song pervaded the camp and others came out of their huts and tents to listen or join in. Beauty and sorrow mingled in the joining of their innumerable voices. Who knew when they would have the spirit to sing again?

Iain looked up at the night sky where orange sparks from the fire flew up into the infinite blackness, cooling in the night air, borne away by the wind. He wondered what Helena was doing and if she thought about him as often as he did her. He tried to imagine Joe asleep, his son, the son who would never know his father. He wished it was over and he could return to his life. He had spent so long following orders it was hard to remember the freedom of civilian life - dangerous to want it too much.

They ate well that night, good hot food from the cookhouse and after unrolling their beds in large canvas tents they slept like logs. Iain had his first dreamless sleep in months.

Ironically, they never sampled the comforts of a hut. The following day their platoon was amongst several marched an hour up the road to a small village of cottages and houses with a café, church and bombed school. They set up a temporary billet in the school, first making it water tight with a vast tarpaulin secured over its absent roof. One of the rooms still had little wooden desks stacked in the corner, piles of miniature chairs and an old blackboard which some wag had decorated with obscenities. The building held echoes of another world, a life where children learned their lessons because there was a future for them.

* * * *

The rain thrummed on Iain's bent back, one sore, cracked finger pressed against the trigger. He was vaguely aware of a rivulet of water passing down his neck, running the length of his back that, despite the cold, was damp with sweat. He knelt in thick mud, seeping through his trousers, his cramping calf muscles making it impossible to crouch on his haunches.

He pushed back his tin hat. A sharp arctic wind bit into his face. He pulled his scarf over his nose and mouth. Dusty hunkered down at his side. From their elevated position they viewed the flat open land, pitted with giant water-filled craters deep enough to swim or drown. Through the slimy mud protruded a hand or leg or other less identifiable body parts. Despite the freezing weather the stench of decay was tangible and choking. This was the first break in the shelling for forty-eight hours. Time was short, the lull temporary.

The enemy trench was only feet away and yet they were completely oblivious to Iain's riflescope trained on them. A roll of wire hovered in mid air as it was thrown into the field.

"Ready?" Dusty said. "Two, three, five, good..." Iain fired sporadically, drowning out Dusty's enthusiasm. As the last German fell they flattened themselves into the muck. Dusty was grinning, triumphant.

The lice were at work again. Iain thought one day they would send him raving mad. He had a farcical image of himself running into no-man's-land, arms waving, in an effort to be shot rather than suffer another second of this torturous itching.

Gradually they dared to lift their heads. There was frantic activity below them. In retaliation a machine gun tore through the gloom, followed by the brief flare of a match being struck.

"They haven't got a clue," Dusty said chuckling. Iain reloaded, fired twice.

"Got him!" he said. The soldier slumped over the machine gun. They could hear the raised guttural remonstrations of the enemy.

"They'll get a fix on us in a minute. We need to move," Dusty whispered.

"Aye, come on. We did all right."

"Understatement, Midge, five in one go and a machine gunner." They slid slowly down the bank away from the trench.

Within seconds of making a move a flare shot up dazzling them with a shower of red stars. Simultaneously they pressed themselves into the stinking mud. A hail of bullets accelerated past, lethal quicksilver, hitting the dirt, splattering their faces.

Dusty cursed. "Shit, shit, shit." The artillery would start up next. Time was short. They weren't safe out here. When the light died in the sky they scrambled to their feet. It was like running in a bad dream, legs weighed down by sodden mud caked uniform, boots, pack and rifles. Iain slipped and slid trying to find a purchase in the sludge, his feet making contact with things he could not see, shell cases, water bottles, haversacks, abandoned rifles, body parts, he tried not to think about it.

Corporal George Murphy and Flinty, seconded to the work party mending wire, ran ahead of them. It was easy for Dusty and Iain to fall in behind them. Returning to their trench wasn't without danger. If the sentry did not recognise them they risked being shot.

"Who goes there?" the sentry said.

Their commanding officer called out. "It's Peterson here, work party."

"Right-i-o, sir." They slid into the trench, the work party hurling rolls of wire in front of them. They sank into an untidy breathless line onto the fire-step as the first guns fired.

"I hate that," Iain said. As one they produced packets of cigarettes and fumbled with matches. Dusty was shaking too much to light anything. Iain leaned across George, lighting his and Dusty's with his steady hand.

"Cheers, mate." Dusty blew the match out quickly before Iain could light a third. Three fags from one match, roughly the time needed for a sniper to fix on a target.

"Why do they do that to us?" Flinty groaned.

" 'Cos they don't know their arse from their elbow," George said. "They should put a bit more thought into lighting flares willy-nilly. They must know there's a work party out slaving their bollocks off. Don't they think, let's keep it dark for the poor buggers so they don't get their heads blown off? But oh no, it's like bleeding Blackpool illuminations out there."

"D'you reckon they work on a points system for every casualty?" Dusty said.

"Makes you wonder don't it," George replied.

Their complaints were temporarily hushed by the arrival of Peterson with the rum bottle.

"How did you go, Dusty?" Peterson asked.

He winked. "No less than half a dozen, sir."

"Well done." Peterson paused in front of Iain, pouring him his rum ration. "The Jerries would love to get their hands on you."

Iain did not appreciate the remark it cut painfully close to the bone. His time in the trenches had made him superstitious, to speak of these things invited them. He made no answer and swallowed the tot of rum in one.

Warmed by the alcohol they trudged along the trench, back down the line. The rolls of wire and their rifles caught continuously on the sides of the narrow trench, slowing their progress. Michael and Champ were on watch.

"Nice night for a stroll," Champ said to their cries of derision.

"Bullets were thicker than lice in an armpit," Dusty quipped.

Iain laughed. "I didn't realise you were so familiar with my oxter."

Dusty crossed his fingers. "We're like that," he said.

Sleep was the usual trial. Iain was full of cold. His head and neck ached, and his nose kept running. They had taken up residence in a 'funk hole' little more than a niche in the side of the trench. They had dug out a shallow horizontal space for their legs, enough room for their bed rolls on filched duckboards.

The guns rumbled above them, the worst of it was concentrated further down the line. They might have been two moles in a hole with four feet of earth above them.

Dusty prodded him. "You got any fags?" Iain took two and lit them, placing one in Dusty's shaky hand. "Cheers. Midge?"

"Aye?"

"Tell me about your Missus."

"She's not my Missus, pal." Then quietly, almost to himself, "Sometimes I wish she was."

"What happened then?"

He turned on his side, facing Dusty. "Someone else got there first. She had a baby come early and I was with her, stayed with her through the night." Suddenly he was there - in the room, with its dimity print floral wallpaper and glazed chintz curtains, plain iron bedstead painted green, a patched quilt and the bedside clock with crawling black hands. He was there and then he wasn't, he was here, in the middle of the French earth, smoking fags, another life now as if the previous one had never been his at all. "The baby died as the sun came up."

"Where was her husband then?"

"Here, somewhere in France, over two years ago now. He's been discharged since, a head wound or something. All happy families." He grimaced into the dark.

"Nice bloke is he?"

He laughed bitterly. "No, a right bastard as it goes. I hate him and the feeling's mutual."

"Maybe it's not all roses like you think then. Do you love her?"

"Love her?" He did not know how to answer. "I kissed her once and for that moment it could have been love or something like it at any road." He could not vocalise how he felt about Helena.

Dusty propped his head on his hand. "I don't get it, mate, you kissed her? I thought you had to do more than that to produce a baby? Or have I got the birds and the bees thing all wrong?"

He laughed. "I told you it's complicated." He attempted to explain Joanna, the baby and how Iain gave him to Helena.

Dusty was quiet for a while, contemplating the story. Eventually he spoke. "It's quite simple really. It's a shame you can't be together."

"Is it?" A note of surprise in Iain's voice.

"Well, when you talk about her it sounds to me as if she means something. You've known her a damn sight longer than I've known Celia, and shared things with her too. She's raising your son. Christ, I mean, how do you think she feels about you?"

He blew smoke up to the roughly hewn dirt ceiling unable to imagine how she felt about anything. "I've no idea. If I do or did feel anything, and Jesus it's been a long time since I've even seen her, well, that's water under the bridge now. She's married and I've got to move on. The boy has a family, she loves him, I did my best for him and that's what matters to me. I've never loved a woman in my life. I don't need the complication. I'm happy as I am."

"Yeah, right," Dusty said. "No you're not. You've spent your life pushing people away. You said yourself, you've lived your life all wrong, and you'd change it too. Now you're back-paddling like an idiot."

"Then I'll have to find someone new. Love 'em and leave 'em, that's me. I can't see me settling down. I'm a loner – people have told me that a lot. Don't need more."

"You need me."

"No I don't, I can't get rid of you that's all. Shit to a blanket you are." He heard Dusty's throaty chuckle. "Perhaps when I get home I'll fetch my dog and go back to Scotland."

"Why d'you leave there in the first place?"

"That," Iain said, "is another complicated story."

"I've always lived in the city, and I thought I couldn't live in the country it's too flaming boring. How wrong can a bloke be?"

"I attract trouble. It's never been exciting I can assure you."

"Is that how you came to be such a damned good shot?"

Dusty stubbed out his cigarette on the boards. Iain listened to his breathing become shallow and steady as he fell asleep. He thought about Helena, the night he had kissed her and how it had felt very important and special at the time. He thought of Freddy with Joe sitting on his knee and Helena completing the picture. What a chump he had been. He was lying here under a muddy, French field with no one and nothing.

* * * *

"That boy is a damned good shot, Finnigan," Bruce Sinclair said.

Iain saw Finnigan scowling at the laird's back. "Aye, sir," was his reply. Iain had a feeling he would hear about this later. They were walking down Ben Leven, the autumn mist gathering in the valley. The laird had championed Iain the whole day, a fairly regular occurrence. Lord Philbert was staying at Glenleven for the weekend and Sinclair had the idea to impress him with the Scottish traditions. Iain was a good example, Sinclair said, of how beneficial it was to teach country skills at a young age.

"Look at him, only fifteen, and a better shot than most men twice that age. What do you say Finnigan?"

"Aye, sir," Finnigan admitted grudgingly. It was not in his nature to feel proud of the boy's achievement. Not this boy.

"You will be keeper here one day, Macdonald, when old Finnigan's had his day – do you hear that, Finnigan?" The laird laughed uproariously at his joke with Lord Philbert joining him. "Macdonald here was ten when we got him, couldn't shoot an elephant then – could you? Now he could take a fly off a deer's back with a bullet couldn't you?"

He smiled. "I could have a go, sir."

Finnigan strode ahead, furious. Iain fell back behind Sinclair and his friend so as not to invite further comment, but he was secretly pleased with the compliments. Finnigan never encouraged him. His accomplishments were his own. He practised shooting targets on the long summer evenings, unmindful to the biting midges, while Finnigan drank himself into oblivion.

The bracken grew high, the dogs pushing ahead of them creating a path. The evening had the chill of autumn, the air fresh and sharp.

"Put the dogs by," Finnigan ordered when the laird had left them. "I'm out to the tavern."

"Yes, sir," he replied. He whistled to the two brindle bitches, they bounded over eagerly.

He turned away and Finnigan called after him. "You'd best not get too big for your boots, sonny."

"Yes, sir," he said without pause.

Finnigan followed, gripping Iain's shoulder tightly, forcing the boy to stop and look at him. "Don't be too smart, lad, remember it's me you have to please, not your precious laird, Bruce Sinclair."

"Yes, sir." He wanted to poke Finnigan in his rheumy eyes. Iain liked the laird. He especially liked his admiration, however vague and insignificant.

Finnigan sneered. "You're a pathetic wee shite, no wonder he didn't want you."

"Want me?"

Finnigan laughed then. "Aye, want you. Why do you think you're here? The laird sent for you, from the orphanage, where he'd left you for six years, dumped baggage, lost property."

"That's not true. Any boy would have done."

"No, he asked for you by name. He paid them nuns for six years to keep you," he said. "It's true and more than that. Mighty Laird Bruce Sinclair don't favour you 'cos you're a good shot, 'cos he thinks you're clever. It's guilt what makes him puff up, guilt and getting one over on his prissy wife. She only agreed you come here so long as you kept your place. She don't want you here. She has her son and heir. She wants rid of you, same as me."

"I don't believe you. I don't believe any of it."

He pointed a meaty finger in Iain's face. "Believe it. And don't be coming on all disrespecting with me, boy."

"I wasn't, sir." The sarcastic edge gave Finnigan the excuse he wanted.

"You testing me, lad?" He cuffed Iain round the head. It caught him sharply and he stumbled. "I ain't finished with you, lad," he shouted, as Iain walked away. "I'll see you later." His voice was weighted with threat.

"No doubt," Iain said under his breath.

It was almost dark by the time Iain arrived at the keeper's bothy, a long low-level one-storey cottage, with a slated roof and small windows. He took the dogs to their kennel, fed and watered them. Once inside he lit the lamps and stoked the fire. It would only inflame Finnigan further if he found things not to his liking when he returned half cut from his drinking. Iain rested for a minute on the chair leaning forward to prod at the flames.

He wished he were not so gutless. What if everything Finnigan said were true. What if the laird were his father? That would make the laird's son, Adam, his half brother, the idea was unthinkable. So many things were unthinkable. And where was his mother? What had become of her? He couldn't ask Finnigan and he definitely couldn't ask the laird.

He decided to forget the whole thing, carry on, day to day, surviving until he could escape Finnigan once and for all. It didn't matter who his father was or wasn't, nothing would change his present circumstances. The only course of action was avoidance. He ate his supper and laid Finnigan's out on the table.

Later he climbed the hill behind the cottage, towel in hand, through the woodland to where the waterfall filled a deep pool before flowing down into the river. He undressed and plunged into the icy water. Even in summer the temperature never altered. It ran straight off the mountain and the coldness clutched him, a metal vice squeezing his chest. He submerged himself under the water. It filled his ears with chilly pressing silence. This is how it feels to be dead, he thought. He rose to the surface flinging back his head, the water droplets sparkling from his hair. He gratefully inhaled the sweet air. And this is how it feels to be alive.

When the cold proved unbearable he climbed out and rubbed his tingling skin with the rough towel, and dressed. He jogged back to the house to warm himself up and wasted no time in getting to his bed.

When he woke it was pothole dark. He was aware something had dragged him from sleep, he could not be sure what. He listened, there it was, shuffling, banging, Finnigan falling over the furniture. He strained his ears, breathing shallow, perspiration beading. Maybe twenty minutes later he heard the creak of his door opening.

"You wakened?" Finnigan growled.

Iain squeezed his eyes shut, body braced for action. Finnigan's laugh was low and guttural. Iain opened his eyes. Finnigan, silhouetted by the dim light issuing through the door, held a chain looped like a belt in one hand. He raised his arm and Iain threw himself out of bed as the chain crashed onto the mattress with metallic force. Finnigan swore, Iain scrambled under the bed and waited. In a fit of rage Finnigan beat the mattress repeatedly, hitting the wooden ends, whipping up the bedding, making a frenzied attempt at using it like a whip beneath the bed. Eventually he abandoned the task and stumbled back into the hall, the door slammed shut.

Iain hid beneath the bed for some minutes. He crawled out, grabbed his pillow and covers and took them under the bed with him. It was not worth the risk in case he decided to come back.

Chapter Twenty-two

"Come on, Macdonald, I need you to join us," Lieutenant Peterson said, sitting opposite Iain.

"If you don't mind, sir, I have no taste for it."

"Taste for it? Good God man, it's your duty. Look at you, your size and strength, you're built for it. Batter in a few Bosche skulls. You'll feel all the better for it."

"No," he insisted, "I wouldn't. I've no liking for battering skulls, Jerry or otherwise."

"You shoot them every day. Our Jerry executioner."

"It's my job," he said shortly, biting his tongue.

"Yes and this is an order, Macdonald. I think you'll find I'm right. I've got a couple of Irish lads, Duncan, heard of him? A mad swine. And Michael Rogers from your company." Peterson counted the men off on his slim fingers. He had the light of the devil in his eyes tonight and Iain didn't much like the look of it.

"Not Michael," Iain said shaking his head.

"Yes, why not?"

"He's not up to a night raid and you know it."

"Well he was very keen." He chose to ignore Iain's impertinence.

"Did you tell him who was going with you – did you mention my name?"

"He heard me talking to Duncan. He'll be fine, now get yourself sorted." His dark moustache lifted as he smiled. He strolled out of the dugout without a care in the world.

Iain groaned as Dusty appeared in the doorway. "Night raids?"

"Aye, you got it."

Dusty pulled a face. "He didn't ask me, I quite fancy duffing up a few Alleymen."

"Well I wish he had. I told him I wasn't up for it. He's a right bastard sometimes. I really can't stomach him. He wants to see blood that one. Can't wait to go over the top. One of those fanatics out of university thinking it's all some grand adventure. Out to change the world, only been here three months." He held his head in his hands. It would not be his first night raid and he knew the drill.

Dusty put his arm across Iain's back. "It'll be all right, Midge, come on. It's been a tough few weeks that's all, we've had enough, mate." Michael came in, stared at the two men. He envied their easy affection, their close partnership. Dusty didn't attempt to move as Iain took his head from his hands and met Michael's eyes.

"What the hell do you want to go on a raid for?" he said.

Michael shrugged. "I dunno, the lieutenant said it would stir them up a bit. Said you were going, me mates."

"I don't want to go. He thinks I'm some sort of killing machine – he called me an executioner."

Dusty gave him a little shake before standing up. "Stupid bastard. Executioner? What barrow of bollocks is that? Ignore such shallow shit, he's heard about you that's all, from Sergeant David probably about the raid you were on before."

He had made short shrift of a few Jerries that night. What else was he supposed to do? At close quarters it was them or him. Of course it wasn't the first time he had battered someone with an implement. It had been an easier task with his ire raised in a bar brawl or attacking poachers back at Harrowmead. The intention was always to put the fear of God into them, to keep them from returning, not murder. The trench raids were a premeditated killing spree, which he found an increasingly difficult concept. And yet he murdered the enemy every day with a quick bullet. Peterson was right. It was hypocritical to argue over how death was meted out. Either way he had orders to follow, choice had nothing to do with it.

Michael looked miserable and Dusty smiled at him. "Bit of excitement will do you good. Stuck around here too long on fatigues. You'll be fine."

Iain attempted a smile too. "Aye, sorry, Mikey, you'll do, just don't let your guard down. Follow the lieutenant, he looks up for anything tonight."

When the night was at its darkest they blacked up their faces and hands with burnt cork, Iain in a trance of dull acceptance. They armed themselves with smoke bombs and tear grenades to cover their retreat. Iain palmed a stout steel ringed truncheon.

"Wouldn't you prefer this?" Peterson held up a fist-bayonet, sharp and lethal.

Iain pulled a face to demonstrate his distaste. "No. Less blood, more damage with this." The Scotsman's intense stare unsettled Peterson and he laughed nervously, quickly looking away.

Dusty waited with Iain for the others to group. A ladder leaned against the trench wall. Iain crouched down, he had quickly discovered many trenches did not reach regulation depth and standing straight was strictly for the parade ground. For a man who had walked tall all his life in the open air of forest and glen it was a very unnatural posture.

"Good luck, see you in a couple of hours." Dusty convincingly faked good cheer. Night raids were dangerous, sometimes fatal.

Iain lit them both a cigarette and the flare of the match reflected the green and white of his eyes against his blackened skin. Dusty took it, the trembling in his hands less noticeable tonight. "Look after the boy," he whispered as Michael joined them.

They exchanged a look, mutual trust and something more, deep empathy. "Aye, course I will." He could have done without the responsibility. It was hard enough in a narrow trench with a company of Jerries on all sides.

Peterson rounded up the party of his choice. "Right, look out for trips and craters. We've got Barrowman here," slapping a squat Geordie soldier on his back, "from the RE's to see us through the wire. Ready, chaps? Quiet as you please now, do your bloodiest."

Iain climbed up behind Michael into the vast blackness of desolate bog. They advanced in Indian file, Iain following Michael following Duncan. The mud sucked hungrily at their boots, each exhaustive footstep feeling like ten. To Iain, who knew the art of silent stalking, they sounded like a battalion on the move, heavy squelching boots, tripping figures, sliding in slime, kicking unseen obstacles, rattling breathless lungs; every sound magnified in the darkness begging to give them away to the enemy.

The engineer, Barrowman, led them through a well-hidden gap in the wire before he retreated to the home trench. The wire tore and jagged as they hurried through. They manoeuvred around a series of trip wires, often triggered by the wind or rats instead of the foe they were supposed to betray. The water filled craters lay ready to swallow them in the inky blackness. Iain could make out the ghostly form of a corpse floating, distended and forgotten.

Fizzing Very lights spattered into the dark sky and the six men levelled themselves in the mud. Iain caught his hipbone on an abandoned helmet. A short scramble through the mud brought them to the lip of the enemy trench. They could hear short bursts of conversation, soldiers about their business, settling for a quiet boring night until the shelling resumed. On Peterson's command they leaped into the trench.

Peterson caught the nearest sentry with the ruthless thrust of his dagger. It reminded Iain of the stop start black and white images they watched in the picture house, an unreal quality, seeing, not seeing, feeling, not feeling. The adrenaline surged through him, the natural instinct to survive taking over. It almost felt good to be alive. He swung his weapon from side to side, striking a glancing blow to a head. The scrabble of boots on the duckboards and the dull thud of metal on flesh and bone was muffled and distanced, stealthy blades working in fatal silence.

He lost count of the blows he landed. The action of violence after days of languishing in trench and field invigorated him. Every sense was sharpened, the smell of latrines, smoke from an extinguished brazier, eyes straining in the darkness, the dormant strength in his muscles, released. He attacked without pity, it was live or die, until he saw Michael beating hell out of a German lying flat out on the boards. He watched Michael stand back with satisfaction and turn on another who was equally floored and making a vain attempt to escape. His gut twisted with a combination of shame and guilt. This violence was part of their make-up, even for boys like Michael. He jogged up the trench. One of the Irishmen stepped in front of him. "Can't see anymore. You?"

Iain shook his head. Rockets burst into the sky showering the night with red stars. Simultaneously machine guns fired then mortars and the heavy boom of the howitzers. They smiled at each other – the Jerries had the wind up. They backtracked, dispatching four more grey clad figures on the way.

"Retreat," Peterson called. Iain pushed past him searching for Michael. "Come on mate," an Irish voice said in his ear.

"Where's Michael?" he asked, the trench bathed in red light. Then he saw him, still knocking the life out of a German who had long given up the fight. He grabbed Michael who stared at him in surprise, blood peppering the blackness of his face.

"Come on, we're off." He grasped the boy's arm firmly. "Good job done."

The duckboards vibrated with the weight of German boots heading towards them. They threw tear grenades and were up and over the parapet with the noise of guns shattering overhead. They ran, casting smoke bombs behind them in a wide arc to cover their route. There was no easy way back. They cut the wire, as thick as Iain's index finger and viciously barbed, with monstrous cutters. They worked speedily, thankful for a dry mild night. Cutting complete, they fought their way through. The barbs caught painfully, ripped through their khaki into the skin, snagging and snatching as they went, their bodies prostrate in the slimy mud.

The German guns blazed, an explosive retaliation. Peterson and his party hurled themselves over the top of their trench with words of reassurance to the stunned sentry. The British guns were answering now and what had been a quiet night turned into a blaze of massed artillery. Communications were working well tonight.

Peterson, lying in the mud on his back, laughed hysterically. "Christ, lads, that was good. Never saw us coming did they?" He reached up a hand and Duncan hauled him to his feet. They were some distance from where they had started. Iain beckoned to Michael, who was all excited smiles, to follow him. Peterson caught Iain's arm. "You can't say that didn't make you feel alive again, if only for a bit?"

He nodded, looked down at the hand restraining him. "Aye it did but don't you reckon, sir, it's a sad day when the only thing makes us feel alive is when we're knocking the shit out of someone?"

"Not someone, Macdonald, the Hun, the bloody Hun." He was alight with his murderous accomplishment. "Here let's get some rum."

"Goodnight, sir." Iain freed his arm. "Come on, Mikey." He hunched his shoulders, trudging through the mud.

"What about the rum, Midge?" Michael said behind him.

"Bollocks to the rum, I can't abide that man." He had never been known to say no to the rum ration. Michael was amazed.

"We did all right though, didn't we, Midge?"

"Aye, we did well, you did well. And I know these things have to be done, but somehow it gets harder. I think maybe I should have had the rum before not after." Back in that German trench, vigour and strength had coursed through his veins. It had evaporated now, replaced by an exhausted deflation. What use was a tot of rum anyway when he could quite happily have polished off a bottle?

In the dugout he listened to Michael relate the tale of the raid with great excitement. In his half-broken voice he embellished the gory details and his part in it. Iain did not contradict him. He thought the boy deserved to glorify himself for a while. Iain dampened a rag with water from his bottle and rubbed at his blackened face. He would look grey until they got back to the bathhouse. Dusty leaned on the sandbags picking at his nails, singularly unimpressed. When Michael had told his story and repeated parts of it several times in different ways, Sergeant David appeared.

"Where have you been, Midge?" he asked.

"Night raid."

"On whose authority?"

"Peterson, sir. I argued my case, much good it did."

"Damn, where is he?" Sergeant David exclaimed.

"Problem, sir?" Dusty asked.

The sergeant leaned forward, lowered his voice. "You're my best shooter, Midge, and he risks you on a night raid. It won't happen again. I'll be speaking to the captain. Give him enough rope that one. He's getting quite out of hand. If he corners you again, I want to know about it, understand?" Iain nodded. The sergeant marched out into the night.

"No more raids for you then," Dusty said.

"Can't ever get this stuff off," he moaned. His efforts to clean up were increasingly ineffectual. "I want to go home."

"Must be due home leave soon, surely."

"Probably, but home leave? Where would I go?"

"Go back to England, you need to go back. You've still got your house haven't you?"

"Aye, my job's waiting, the house is still there." For a second he imagined Helena, pale amongst the darkness of the heavy furniture, her small hand composing a letter to him. He would walk in on her, sitting at the large kitchen table. She would glance up and smile, the one that lit her up so radiantly. Then what? Would they stand awkwardly discussing the weather? Would he crush her in his arms, vowing never to let go? How absurd, he thought. "No," he said decisively. "I wouldn't bother going back, not until I'm through here." A dark shadow caught his eye moving at the back of the dugout. "Here, Dusty, watch this." He reached into his pocket for his catapult. He pulled a stone from the earth wall, aimed and fired with neat precision killing the rat outright.

Dusty cheered, picked the creature up by its tail. "Look at the size of that."

Champ whistled between his teeth. "Ruddy hell, I've seen smaller cats."

Iain grinned, cheered by his marksmanship. He tucked the catapult back in his pocket. It had dispatched many a trench rat this last couple of years.

"When we get back to the village we'll get very drunk, how about that?" Dusty said.

"Sounds good. No playing poker this time and losing all our fags and wages."

"No fair enough. Wonder if there's a Goaty's round here."

"I'll give that a miss too," he said. "I'd prefer to try my luck with a village girl thanks."

Michael was alarmed by the idea of trying his luck with anyone. "You'll find the right girl, Mikey, then it'll be like a duck to water, you'll see. Didn't it quite happen with Yvonne?"

He shook his head, blushing at the memory. She hadn't managed to arouse him at all and much later at the billet he had cried into his pillow like a girl. He was mortified at the idea that any of the lads might get to hear how he had disgraced himself.

The cacophony of gunfire diminished and Iain sighed, lying on his back. They had abandoned their funk hole when the latrines had overflowed a few days previously. Dusty went outside to sit on the fire-step. He was on duty shortly anyway. He faced two hours of struggling to watch the enemy through a periscope of angled mirrors.

The following day they marched three hours back to their billet. The little school had been hit by a stray bomb and was a mere crater in the ground. Sergeant David and Lieutenant Peterson had to hunt down alternative accommodation. They spent their first night in an orchard under canvas before securing a small cowshed for the majority of the men.

Sergeant David was Welsh with a singsong lilt to his voice. He had a large moustache and smoked a pipe of fragrant tobacco sent from home. He had a wife and two children and was a devout chapel man. When they arrived at the shed he winked at Iain and took him to one side.

"How d'you fancy a proper bed, Midge?" he asked.

"Too right, sir."

"Pick one other and I'll show you how the other half live."

"Oi, Dusty," he called. Dusty was miserable at the thought of spending a night in a cowshed. Scowling he wandered over, kicking the dirty straw under his feet.

"Go on, tell me you've secured us a place at the Grosvenor Hotel," he said despondently.

"You underestimate my Celtic charm, Dusty. I'm no mere Sassenach. Come with me." He led Dusty out of the shed across the farmyard to where the sergeant was talking to the farmer, a wiry man with wild fair hair.

"Come on," Sergeant David said as they approached. The farmer's wife showed them up the rickety winding stairs by the light of an oil lamp. The room nestled under the eaves with four proper beds, sprung mattresses and clean cotton sheets.

Dusty laughed, bouncing gently on the edge of the bed. "Crikey, this is something else."

The farmer's wife disturbed their laughter, bringing them a tray of hot cocoa, and buns warm from the oven, dripping with yellow butter. Corporal George followed her, claiming the fourth bed. For one night they slept like proper people. Iain's exhaustion ran so deep that a week of a soft bed would not have gone amiss but one night was better than nothing. His last thought before falling asleep was of the others bunking down in a cowshed. It was only a brief thought before oblivion swallowed him.

They awoke to the sound of the farmer's four children playing and laughing downstairs. A childish voice sang a French song. It struck Iain as bizarre, lying in bed tracing the cracks in the sloped ceiling, being part of this domestic household with its everyday normality when a few miles away a war raged.

The four men washed and joined the family for breakfast. Dusty met Iain's eyes in amazement as the farmer's wife served eggs, sausages, a type of black pudding, fresh bread, croissants with apples and cheese. Four children under the age of six sat in a line at the table, three boys like Russian dolls each a head taller than the last. The youngest child was strapped in a high chair, a dark eyed chubby toddler with black hair tied in a ribbon. She laughed heartily every time Dusty or Iain pulled a face at her and, once they caught on to it, they did so repeatedly.

"Er – nom – er – de fille?" Iain turned to George. "Is that how you ask what the baby's name is?"

He shook his head and the sergeant shrugged. Madame smiled. "Violette," she said and continued with a stream of French they could not understand.

When she paused for breath Iain pointed at the baby girl. "Violette?"

"Oui, Violette." She nodded vigorously.

He struggled for the words. "Très jolie." He smiled pointing at Violette.

"Merci, Monsieur," the wife said.

His poor grasp of the French language frustrated him. He had never spent enough time with the locals to pick up much. They left the sergeant to struggle with thanking the farmer for breakfast and the comfort of their beds, while they packed their kit, to return to reality.

Stationed in the reserve trenches, they marched to the front line each day, working the daylight hours and returning to relative safety at night. Iain and Dusty were excused night watch to free up their time for sniper duty but comforts were few and fatigues, exhausting and repetitive.

Early summer stretched their working day as the evenings became lighter. Iain and Dusty found a good position where Michael, Champ and the corporal were digging a stretch of trench and dugout. Further along the trench the rest of their platoon laid duckboards and stacked sandbags. The hot sun burned the back of their necks. High above them in the clear blue a skylark sang with oblivious joy in its heart.

Dusty kept watch while Iain waited for a careless head to peer over the parapet. A robin landed on the barrel of his gun. It stared at him with beady black eyes, its red breast vivid in the sunlight. He wondered why it had strayed here so far from hedge or garden. If he could fly, he thought, if only he could fly. He nudged Dusty and the movement frightened the bird and it fluttered away.

Mid-afternoon the artillery started, shells hurtling overhead unnervingly close. They abandoned their position to help finish the digging having only added one to the tally

"Are we to keep going?" Dusty asked the sergeant.

"Yes, we'll need this trench in a few days," Sergeant David replied.

"We going over?" Iain said.

"You know how it is. They never say too much, but it wouldn't surprise me."

They made good progress on the dugout, while Michael and Champ hauled the earth away for filling sandbags. The Royal Engineers advised them on shoring up but the infantry did the donkeywork. They stopped for a break, smoking cigarettes and drinking a welcome brew, thick with sweet condensed milk. The guns shook the ground.

"I've had enough of this," Dusty said. "The light's going and we're out in no-man's-land shooting in three hours."

"Aye, they're determined to get it finished." Iain disappeared into the dugout. Dusty stooped at the doorway. An explosion impacted directly above them. It blew Dusty out of the dugout into the trench wall. He heard the roof collapse as dry earth, forced out of the aperture, hit him like iron hail.

Inside, masses of black earth rained onto Iain, a sudden intense weight pressing him into the floor. With his hands pinned by his face he dug like a mole with his fingers to enlarge the small breathing space. His brain had not caught up with the events that trapped him and he was calmly thinking through his options. He quickly concluded he had none. Trying not to retch he spat the earth out of his mouth, snorted down his nose to clear his nostrils. He couldn't move his legs and he could hear the muffled boom of shells overhead as the earth shook, shifting unsteadily. His breath was coming in increasingly painful sharp gasps. He was not sure if he were injured or merely being crushed.

Without warning the earth caved into his small air space and it filled his mouth and nostrils again. This time there was no escape. With all his considerable strength, every muscle tensed, he pushed to move his body. Nothing happened, only paralysis, entombed by solid darkness. He panicked, a blind terrible horror grabbed his heart, flooded his mouth with vomit, wrenching his stomach. He gagged against the dense soil. He screamed, soundless, meaningless. He screamed and screamed until the blackness that filled his mouth filled his mind.

Dusty dug frantically. Initially he used the shovel, before resorting to his bare hands, fingers numb and bleeding. Lumps of clay were mixed with finer black stuff that ran through the fingers. He did not know where Michael and George were. He had no time to think or fetch help. He had seen Iain disappear. He could roughly pinpoint his location and he had seconds to find him if there were to be any chance at all. His heart pounded with fear, desperation spurring him on.

He couldn't believe his luck when he reached his head first. Grabbing a handful of hair he pulled Iain's face free. He gained a purchase on his tunic and hauled with all the strength he could muster. He dug a space at Iain's shoulders, scrabbling in the dirt. Michael appeared at his elbow.

"Help me, get hold of him. Let's pull him," Dusty ordered. Their combined strength moved Iain barely an inch. It gave them the extra gumption to try again. Another jolt, the earth shifted, they used their entrenching tools to open the space. They grimaced with the effort, burning muscles, fighting the agony of exhaustion. With a final effort they freed him, careering into the trench with Iain a limp dead weight between them. They propped him up. Dusty poured the contents of his water bottle over Iain's face, blanked by soil. He rubbed the earth from Iain's nose, mouth and eyes with his fingers.

"Midge, Midge," he shouted above the din. He beat Iain on the back with his fist followed by his chest. Holding Iain's head, he slapped his wet cheek. Michael knelt beside them mute with shock.

Iain opened his eyes. The smoke from the guns tumbled around them, grey against the sky. He coughed and gagged, sitting up he grabbed Dusty's arm. His limbs went into spasm. The sudden freedom of movement felt exhilarating.

"You're all right, mate, you're all right," Dusty said and there must have been a lull in the battle because Iain heard him. He scrabbled away from them, hands spread in the mud, and retched until he was sick. Slumping back in the sludgy trench floor they clasped each other tight. They were alive.

Iain grappled to pull his wits together, to quell the terror, and when they separated he even raised a smile.

"You hurt?" Dusty said. There was a kind of hysteria as they realised they were all fine. "Where are Champ and George?"

It was only then they noticed Michael, splattered with blood and gore, his eyes filled with tears. "Champ went for help, but Corporal Murphy, he's gone," he said. "I don't know where."

Chapter Twenty-three

Iain had never visited London before. It was the busiest, dirtiest place he had ever seen. Everything built on top of the other, a jumble of humanity, not with the wide, spatial feel of Glasgow. There was more of everything, motor vehicles, carriages, trams and people. Dusty's family lived in a brick built terraced house. The washing hung across the street and reminded Iain of the back street stone tenements in Glasgow.

When they were rostered for home leave in the same week, Dusty had been quite insistent Iain should accompany him to London. His arguments had been persuasive and Iain eventually agreed. He wrote to Nell from France to tell her he was on home leave in the capital. Dusty snatched the letter and scribbled his parents' address on the back.

"She might want to post you something." And he laughed as Iain protested.

Dusty's family were the salt of the earth, his mother and father welcoming Iain like a prodigal son. Dusty had two sisters, Pearl and Mabel. They both worked in the ammunition factories. Mabel was engaged to a sailor. Pearl was generously attentive towards Iain.

The house had three bedrooms. They were happy to share. It had been a long time since Iain had slept alone and having Dusty in the bed opposite was second nature. It was unbelievable luxury to sleep in a proper bed with clean sheets, fresh towels, a geyser with hot water and a proper flushing lavatory in the yard. On the first evening they stayed in and Dusty regaled the family with his favourite stories. The two boys were treated to the best of everything. They did it with such pleasure it was impossible to refuse although Iain knew it cost each of them some sacrifice.

The second night they planned to go out on the town. "We'll go dancing," Pearl said with a twinkle in her eye for Iain.

"You're not coming," Dusty said. "Cramping our style." She was mutinous but Mrs Miller agreed with her son. They walked round the corner to the local Crown & Anchor with the intention of moving on later.

"Real English beer," Dusty said, sipping from his frothing glass.

"Real Scottish whisky." Iain raised his chaser. They didn't get any further that night, staggering home drunk, singing at the top of their voices, '*It's the wrong way to tickle Mary*'.

"I can't believe you stayed in the Crown all evening," Mabel said.

Iain sitting at the breakfast table cupped his head in his hands. "Och, my head."

Dusty smiled cheerfully and then winced. "We meant to move on, but the door kept moving."

"Dick had a lock-in I suppose," Mrs Miller said, disapproving, putting a plate of sausages and bacon on the table.

"Aye," Iain said, "feels as if my head's had a lock-in."

"Serves you right," Pearl said in disappointment.

"Leave them alone," Dusty's father said from behind his newspaper. "What opportunity do they get over yonder? Let them enjoy it while they can."

A loud rat-a-tat on the doorknocker caused Iain and Dusty to jump, they caught each other's eye and laughed. "Go get it, Pearl. Do I have to do everything?" Mrs Miller said.

"I'm off anyway, see you later, Mother, Father, boys." She pulled on her hat, pouting at her reflection in the mirror.

Voices mumbling in the hall preceded Pearl's reappearance. "A telegram for you, Iain."

"Thanks."

She hovered, suddenly in no great rush. The whole family looked at him. Mr Miller lowered his paper. Iain read it, glanced at the expectant faces. Privacy wasn't an issue to them. "Er – it's from a friend, coming on the train tomorrow for the day."

The family exchanged glances, widening eyes and raising eyebrows, and Dusty sniggered. "He's being cagey – it's a girl I'll bet."

Pearl sniffed sulkily, the front door slammed behind her as she departed.

"Come on, eat up, or it'll be cold," Mrs Miller scolded.

He couldn't face food. He chewed on a piece of toast while Dusty did his best with a bacon sandwich.

"Is it a girl?" Mabel asked quietly. She had eyes like her brother, fringed with long eyelashes. Her skin was jaundiced and the front of her hair a strange shade of yellow. Dusty said it was due to the TNT she handled in the munitions factory. Mabel said it was a small and temporary sacrifice compared to that which the soldiers made every day over in France.

Iain nodded. "Aye, but she's a friend."

"Come on," Dusty said after breakfast, "we're going into town."

They roamed the streets of central London, the noise and bustle amazed Iain. By noon, appetite restored, they lunched at a restaurant.

"So who's the lady friend then?" Dusty raised his hand as Iain was about to speak. "No, no let me guess. Would it be Helena by any chance?"

He smiled. "You knew she'd come. Don't act surprised, that's why you insisted on sending your address isn't it?"

"Well, let's say I hoped she would. It's difficult to second guess when you've never met the lady in question."

"Why? What are you hoping for?"

"Nothing, Midge. Is she bringing the boy?"

"Aye."

"I think it will – I don't know – do you good. You'll meet your son. Make you see there's some reason as to why we're going through this. There's so much more. It'll be something to take back with you won't it?"

"Aye, you're right, I haven't been able to see the point in doing anything lately I must admit."

Dusty leaned across the table, speaking gently, "I know that, I'm not blind. You've been as down as I've ever seen you. That's why we're here. And tomorrow you'll see your son and it's time I saw my girl."

"Am I going to get the chance to meet her?"

"Yes, she's coming over later, you'll meet her then."

They went into the city that night with Dusty's fiancée Celia, and Pearl who had recovered from the disappointment of the morning and was hell-bent on making the most of Iain's company. They dined in a swanky restaurant where Dusty had once known the chef, before he joined up and got killed on the Somme. Then on to an exclusive club where he was friendly with the manager, whose two sons were in the Navy, and the doorman, an old school friend who had been invalided out of the army.

Drinks at the bar flowed freely, because 'the barman's cousin is like my brother' he assured Iain. He was one of those people who knew everybody and they all revered him. Iain was quietly impressed by his friend's popularity. The two men were certainly poles apart, Iain held sway by clout and authority, Dusty by being his affable blasé self.

With champagne, a first for Iain, in front of them and a band and dance floor it wasn't long before Pearl found herself where she wanted to be, in Iain's arms. "You're a very good dancer," she purred into his ear.

"Thank you, so are you."

"I suppose it's your girlfriend coming on the train tomorrow," she said.

She wasn't as attractive as Mabel but he noticed she made the most of herself. Her full lips were smudged with rouge, a turned up nose, eyes of marbled blue and an inviting smell of cheap scent emanating.

The bubbles in the champagne jostled in his head. "No, it's not," he said squeezing her warm hand. She's the mother of my son, he thought and smiled to himself.

She could not meet his eyes without blushing awkwardly. "Oh, well, perhaps you're on the look out for a girl then?"

He did not want to offend her, but he could not help his reply. "No, not really." The colour rose in her cheeks, her teeth pulled in her lip as she stared straight ahead at his shoulder. "Sorry," he said. "You don't know what it's like out there. Sometimes it's hard to believe it'll ever be over and if I'm going to live to see the end of it. I wouldn't promise anything to anyone, you see?" Her eyes flickered up to meet his and then away again.

"Course," she said, "I understand. It's just that if you did – you know ..."

"Aye, I know and thank you." He lifted her hand to his lips and kissed it in an attempt to make amends. He had only one girl on his mind and it wasn't this one.

He was glad when the dance ended and he escorted Pearl to their table where Dusty was deep in conversation with Celia. As tall as Dusty, and fair with an appealing smiley face, Celia was outspoken, forthright and humorous with a strong cockney accent. She was one of the new modern women with short hair and smoking cigarettes. Her warmth and open affection towards Dusty was refreshing. Iain liked her at once and could understand why Dusty was enamoured with her. The pair of them fitted, one complimenting the other, a partnership like a dovetail joint and as strong and long lasting.

"You getting off with my sister?" Dusty said quietly when Iain re-took his seat.

He filled their glasses, drank and said, "Well, she's lovely, but you know me and women. Nothing is for keeps and I wouldn't do that to your sister."

Dusty laughed. "If she got you on her own she'd have a good go at making it for keeps, I can tell you. I've not seen her so lovelorn since she was chucked by the boy next door."

Iain smiled at Pearl who laughed too long and loud, eager to touch him with lingering caresses that once he might have reacted to. She was knocking back champagne. He tried to imagine Helena getting drunk on champagne and couldn't quite manage it. He felt a tug of excitement inside his chest at the thought of seeing her. She was already with him and nobody could distract him with flirtations. She was coming, here, not somewhere familiar but London. How could he possibly think about anything else?

They caught a cab home, laughing when Dusty told him they didn't have to pay. "That's my Uncle Bert," he said and grinned. Pearl leaned her head against Iain's shoulder on the way home. In the dark interior of the cab her hand stroked his thigh. Champagne did not have quite the same effect on him, staring soberly out of the window. Even at night the city was wide-awake. He helped Pearl to the house, leaving Dusty and Celia to make an amorous goodnight. Mrs Miller had helpfully waited up and relieved him of her rather tipsy daughter.

He woke early the next morning. His sense of trepidation had deepened. He was meeting Helena and it shouldn't feel as important as it did. Washed and dressed he ran downstairs. Dusty's snores followed him.

The girls had left for work and Mrs Miller, on her hands and knees, cleaned the grate. "You off, love?" she asked.

"Aye, I'll eat out today, don't worry about supper. Tell Dusty I'll see him after. I'm meeting my friend at Waterloo."

"Oh, yes," she smiled knowingly, "that's right. Have a good time last night?"

"Aye, grand, thanks," he said.

"Hope Pearl behaved herself, she can get a bit rowdy. I told Dusty to watch her."

"No, no, she had a good time. She was fine, really."

She got up off her knees and approached him. She was small and round like a mother hen. She straightened his collar, brushed invisible specks from his shoulders with the flat of her hand.

"You boys look right handsome all togged up. Reckon your friend will be very impressed. She seen you in uniform?"

He knew she was fishing for information. He smiled at her transparency. "No." He kissed her cheek. "See you after, Mrs Miller, and thanks."

He stopped at a café, ordered a cup of tea and smoked a cigarette. Life carried on as normal here, as it should he supposed. He traced the patterns of the tape stuck on the large glass windows, a precaution against bombing. The café was filling up with shift workers. Groups of women from the factories arrived for breakfast. Before the war, he thought, you'd have never seen that. The war was changing the world and everyone with it.

After a second cup of tea he headed towards the city centre. He had no stomach for food. He was apprehensive. He didn't feel as if he were this person walking down a city street dressed in khaki, he was somebody else entirely living a parallel life. The sun broke through the clouds and it was warm. The rumble of traffic assailed him and he had to make a conscious effort not to flinch at the noise although it grated on his raw nerves.

Waterloo was busy, groups of soldiers milled around, women, children and men in civvies. He asked a guard which platform he needed for the train from the west. He was half an hour early. He bought a newspaper from a stand, waited on a bench on the platform. He read the news of the war. Strange to see it here when normally he was in it. They never had the opportunity to read about it - any war news came in letters from home. So much of what was written was propaganda, half-truths, exaggerations and omissions. Perhaps nobody would believe the truth, censorship made it more palatable.

The train chugged into the station roughly on time, hissing steam, doors opening, people pouring out onto the station. He had a good view over the top of everybody's head but Helena was so small he wondered if he would see her. And then he did, standing at the train door, stepping out, reaching back, bending down to the child out of sight. He pushed forward through the thinning crowd.

He stopped in front of her. Her dark blue coat was unbuttoned, a raffia summer hat pinned into place. In an attempt to tame the curl in her chestnut hair she had plaited it into tight coils, rebellious whorls had formed along her hairline. Her cheeks glowed pink and she smiled. The sight of her filled him. He had no choice except to pull her into his arms. He was not sure what she expected but his reaction was irresistible and her arm circled his waist pulling him closer still. She looked up, her head against his chest and they laughed. If he had followed his gut instinct he would have bent his head and kissed her laughing mouth. He stopped himself, remembering her position, knowing his. They drew away simultaneously and she crouched down beside Joe.

"Look," she said, "this is your daddy." His green eyes grew larger in a pale face as he frowned suspiciously at Iain.

Iain hunkered down like Nell. "Hello, Joe," he said, incredulous that this was the baby he had held almost three years before. He recognised himself reflected in the boy's face.

Joe glanced between them. "Hello," he said quietly, to please his mother.

Iain reached out and held Joe's small hand, soft-skinned and firm, giving it a little shake. The boy smiled, tugging his hand away.

They stood up and Nell shrugged her shoulders. "So," she said, "here I am."

"Aye, here you are." He ran his finger down the side of her face, watching the pink of her cheek deepen.

She cleared her throat, embarrassed. "Don't you look smart," she said struggling to control the emotion in her voice.

"Come on then." He offered Joe his hand. He stared at it warily, shook his head with vigour. Iain laughed not in the least offended. "Well, if the wee lad won't take my hand, perhaps the lady." He swapped sides and offered her his arm. She took it without hesitation, beaming at him.

"Joe will be hungry. Are you hungry, Joe?" she asked. The boy nodded.

They left the station. Iain felt elated, as if he were part of something. They strolled among strangers who would look at them and mistake them for family; the idea pleased him. He hailed a cab. He had no idea where to take them or how to get back to Dusty's house from where they were.

A horse drawn cab stopped. They climbed in and Iain asked the driver to take them somewhere nice for breakfast. He probably took the longest route but Iain didn't care.

"How did you get away?" he asked.

She laughed. "I caught a train."

"Really? I'd never have guessed. Won't he want to know where you've been?"

"He'd probably love to ask me but he won't and I won't tell him."

Joe fidgeted between them, leaning forward trying to see the horse and all the sights en route.

"Interesting arrangement," he said raising his eyebrows.

"I can't believe I'm here," looking into his eyes.

"No, neither can I."

"You look – different – I don't know – you're uniform, I suppose. Your hair, cut so short." It was as if her eyes could not get enough of him.

"You took your time writing," he said.

"I didn't go to your house, didn't realise you might want me to write, that I might want to write, and then when I did..." she trailed off. "Look, Joe, the river. That's the Thames."

Iain strained to see it too. "How is Freddy?" There he had said the name.

She shrugged. "He's always been a one, Iain, selfish. Now – well – now he's that much worse. He was injured by a piece of shrapnel in his head. They hoped his brain was all right, but it isn't. He thinks the world is against him and he hears voices. He's a very, very difficult man."

"He's always been difficult," he muttered.

"It's different," she paused trying to find the words, "not good."

"No more babies? I thought you might have another by now," he said trying to ascertain her relationship with Freddy.

She met his eyes, her look was challenging. "I don't sleep with him," she said simply. "I sleep in with Joe."

He felt compelled to turn away. "Oh, I see." He could not say why this pleased him, it was exactly what he wanted to hear.

"Probably not. Nobody seems to see. It's a different matter when you have to live with it."

"And the boy? Is it wise telling him who his father is, like you did back there?"

Her tone was biting. "I don't care, Iain, I don't care. You are his father. And rather you than him."

"Well," he said lightly, "thanks very much."

"Let's not speak anymore about him, I don't want to. Let's pretend, for the day..." she stopped and her eyes filled with tears. He saw them but couldn't acknowledge them. "Just for the day pretend this is how it is, you, me and Joe, please."

He nodded, dipping his head to see Tower Bridge. "Of course, whatever you say." He reached out his hand. She pulled off her glove before taking it. Their hands met across Joe's lap, he was oblivious to the gesture. Her hand in his was small and work worn. He wanted to know what she was thinking but did not dare ask.

"Boat." Joe pointed and they were both relieved to be able to smile and repeat the word.

They breakfasted at a riverside teashop, basking in the sun on the veranda overlooking the brown river. "Have you been to London before?" he asked

"No, never," she replied. "It's so busy, so many people."

"Aye, that's what I thought."

He took Joe to the edge of the river and pointed out the boats and barges. From a distance Nell watched as he picked up the boy. Seeing them together gave her an immense tight feeling in her chest that made it hard to breathe. Joe was filled with wonder at being so high in his father's arms, a world of horizons and vistas.

They took a boat down the Thames and laughed when they compared it to the river that flowed through Harrowmead, recalling the day they watched the otters playing.

"No otters would live here," she said wrinkling her nose. "No fish either if they had any sense."

He stared at her, holding on to her hat in the breeze, an arm protective around Joe as he leaned on the barge rail, speaking into his ear on occasion. She was so familiar, such easy company, that was why she felt like balm on his weary spirit, he assured himself. It wasn't love he felt only the comfort of somebody who knew him, who had shared a part of his life before the hell of war. Her presence soothed, making him feel whole and at peace. He felt the need to justify his feelings, if only to himself.

They left the river behind them and he carried Joe on his shoulders. They found an area of vast open parkland and crossed it, stopping to rest in the shade of a willow tree. Joe, with renewed vigour, raced around, arms outstretched like an aeroplane.

"How is it out there?" she asked.

"Perhaps we should add that to our not to be discussed list," he joked.

"I read about it in the papers and I've heard terrible things. They're all true I suppose?"

"Lately it's been the far side of hell and I don't know what I'm doing there or why. I have to go back, I have to do it, there's no turning away. I don't want to turn away, I want to see it done, finished, but there's no denying it's hard."

"What do you do? You're in the infantry aren't you?"

"Aye." He could not tell her he was a sniper, he could not imagine her reaction. "Just another soldier."

"Is your friend Dusty a lance corporal too?"

"Aye and we're stuck there too, they won't give me promotion. It takes me away from my section into training and a command post."

"Training for what?"

He grimaced. "Scouting, rifles, that sort of thing."

"And at the end of it?"

"If I'm really honest, I don't know. I suppose I'll come home. That's all we ever talk about when we're there – coming home."

She turned to him, frank intensity burning in her clear blue eyes. "Home, Iain? Where's home for you?"

He had expected the question. He tugged at a blade of grass between his feet. "I don't know, Helena, that's the truth." He dared to look into the blueness of her eyes. "Really, I don't know. What do you want me to say?"

She put a hand up as if to shade her face. "I don't want you to say anything, I was asking your plans." Her voice was high and emotional.

"When you're out there it's hard to make plans. I suppose Harrowmead is what's waiting for me. Somehow I want more than policing a piece of woodland, don't know what. I've had my fill of violence." His expression was despairing. "I need peace." A monologue ran through his head of what he would like to say, how he really felt, knowing by saying it he had nothing to lose but fear or circumstance held him back.

"Peace," she repeated quite unable to lower her eyes. A hand fluttered to her throat. "I - ," she could speak the truth no more than he. She made a poor show of concealing her agitation by pulling off her coat. The short sleeves of her summer dress revealed small dark bruises on her arms.

"How did you do that?" he asked.

"Clumsiness, working with the cows, it's easy done," she said. There was something guilty in her words, in the turn of her head. He caught hold of her arm, stroked the soft underside of it with his finger. She caught her breath as if it were almost more than she could bear.

"Tell me, it's not what I think," he said, studying her.

She swallowed hard. "It's not what you think."

"Why did you come here? Why are you telling Joe who I am?" His face was close to her. He could see the fine down on her cheek, the pulse at the dip of her throat.

Pulling away, she hugged her knees to her chest, voice less than a whisper. "It's what I want. I'm sick of denying what I want," then passionately, "I don't know when I'll see you again, I thought perhaps I never would. I had to come. Nothing would have kept me away least of all fear of the truth."

He watched Joe picking the daisies, stuffing them into his pockets.

"Has it brought trouble to you, having Joe? He is very…" he paused, looking at the child again, "like me."

She shook her head. "No," she said vehemently, "he's the best thing that ever happened. I love him, he's my life – my life, Iain."

He stood up. Her certainty and passion were overwhelming. "Hey, Joe." He crouched down to the boy. Joe smiled and Iain walked his fingers up Joe's belly. He laughed, ran away and Iain chased him. He darted one way and then the other, Iain making a show of catching him, twirling him round. He laughed, a fat delicious chuckle and Iain launched him into the air for a second, catching him safely in large hands. When Iain looked up he saw the tears that Nell quickly wiped away.

They strolled to the pond where a little girl and boy sailed their toy boat on the water. "There is something I want to ask you," she said.

"Go on then," he replied, watching Joe at the water's edge.

"It's about Tom."

"Oh, yes, Tom, of course."

She caught hold of his sleeve, drawing his attention to her. "Did you kill Tom?"

He wanted to laugh but didn't. "Did Freddy say that?"

"Not exactly – he was confused – he gets muddled, he hears voices, sometimes it's hard to make sense of him."

"Great," he said with sarcasm, "he will happily see us both hanged then."

There was fear in her eyes. "You did kill him."

He turned to her. "No, I didn't, I swear it – I didn't."

"You helped hide the body though," she probed.

He shook his head, perplexed. "It's not what you think. Tom was all right. I never had a gripe with Tom, he never deserved – look, Helena, you're going to have to take my word for it – I didn't kill him. I did something far worse." He paused while she searched his face, waiting. "I let you marry Freddy Hart – and that was unforgivable."

"You couldn't have stopped it."

"If I'd told you the truth I could have."

"Tell me the truth now."

"Let's leave it, add it to our list, eh?" He smiled wanly.

A flock of ducks swam over to them expecting free bread. Iain held out his hand and they pecked at his fingers while Joe hid behind him, his hands very small on Iain's wide shoulders, peeking nervously.

"I remember the first time I saw you in the woods. You frightened me to death," she said.

He laughed. "You said I didn't at the time."

"Well, you did. You had your gun and that look on your face."

"What look?"

She blushed. "A look. I don't know. I thought you might tell Cook I'd been idling my time away picking flowers."

They circled the lake, trying to keep in the shade of the trees, glad of a slight cooling of the air that blew off the water. Joe stopped every so often to pick up a stick or stone to throw into the lake.

"You've not changed any," he said.

"My life has."

"So has mine." He stopped to wait for Joe who ran back to pick up a swan feather. "Listen," he said and reached for her hand.

"What?"

"No cuckoos."

They laughed, acutely aware of walking hand in hand. Joe skip ahead of them holding the large white feather aloft. "Joe's a cuckoo," he said.

"No he's not," she said. "That would make him unwanted."

"He was. Joanna didn't want him."

"She didn't know him," she said quietly. Then to lighten the mood she said, "Anyway, that would make me a reed warbler and aren't they plain and brown?"

"You're neither. You're more of a robin really."

She narrowed her eyes at him and he burst out laughing. "A robin," she said flatly.

His voice was warm with laughter. "I like them. They're cheery and companionable, friendly. They're gutsy too. I had one land on my rifle not so long ago, out in that hellhole. Quite often a robin used to follow me at Harrowmead, I'm sure it was always the same one."

"Or one very much like it," she said laughing too.

"It is quite tricky telling them apart," he conceded.

"Well, this particular robin is hungry."

He gave her hand a little squeeze. "Then we'd better eat. I don't know where we are." He surveyed the area. "Which way did we come?"

They ate lunch in a hotel off Piccadilly and afterwards they sat in the lounge side by side on a soft floral couch drinking pale tea from fine china and Joe fell asleep.

Nell covered him with her coat, unpinned her hat. She watched Iain remove his tunic, light a cigarette, a slight tremour in his hand. He inhaled and blew the smoke towards the ceiling. He smiled when he saw her observing him. "Helena," he said slowly drawing out each syllable

She echoed his smile, boldly returned his gaze in that self-composed way of hers without blushing or coquetry. "I was worried about our meeting," she said. "So much has happened, time has past. Now I'm glad. I'm glad I came."

"Me too. Thank you for the letters and parcels. They mean a lot to me, much more than I can say."

"It's part of my routine now, I go to your house, write a letter, check for post."

"What would happen if he found out?"

She made a face. "I suppose he'd kick up merry hell and I don't care."

"You keep saying that – really, don't you care?"

"No, I don't. If not for Joe there would be nothing and you gave me Joe. I owe you a vast debt. The least I can do is send a few letters – anyway I look forward to hearing from you. I hope it's over soon, so you can return home," a pause, "to whatever life you choose."

He pulled on the cigarette. "I choose daily baths, no lice and no mud, a soft bed and ..." Instead of finishing the sentence he peeked sideways, cocking one eyebrow, teasing her.

She giggled and quickly finished his sentence for him. "And peace."

"Do you think," he glanced around the foyer, "it would be out of order if I put my arm round you?"

She sidled towards him allowing his arm to encompass her. "No," she said, "I think it would be most in order."

Nobody cared or even noticed as he rested his hand on her arm where she could see the pale half moons of his cuticles, the flat dark hairs on his wrist, a new watch counting the seconds to when he would leave her. He pressed his cheek against her hair that was coming loose in longer curled tendrils. She smelt of the soap she had sent in her Christmas package and felt so small in the crook of his arm, the gentle warmth of her filtering through the thin cotton of her dress. He had images flit across his mind which he immediately tried to dispel, trying not to think of her leaning back her head so he could kiss the pinkness of her curved lips.

She took his other hand in hers, feeling it tremble. She examined the healing splits in his fingers, lowered her head and gently kissed each one. He was fascinated by the pout of her cool dry lips kissing the tip of each cracked digit and in that moment he knew desire for her. He wanted to book a room and take her there, hang the consequences and doubts, but the boy was here, and there would be consequences. She released his hand and leaned her head on his shoulder, snuggling into him like a child and he was rendered mute and ineffective.

She knew it was forward to reach for his hand, do what she did. She wanted to be kind, to show how deeply he affected her. "Dear boy," she wanted to say, though he was older by a half dozen years, "dear, dear boy." She hoped her action said what she could not, because she had no adequate words for him. She sighed, touching the buttons on his shirt, tracing the roundness of one with her finger. Safe subjects, she thought, talk about home. "I'll tell you all the gossip shall I, from Harrowford?" He nodded dumbly as she continued. "Miles went to Turkey and is missing. Noah is in Belgium, I think. Polly Took, remember her? She and her husband moved to Kent."

Her voice was soothing, his craving for her dissipated as he pushed it away from him. Once more they were on safe ground, away from the shifting sands of emotions and feelings. He listened to the minutiae of village life, putting in asides of his own from time to time and they laughed at their shared memories of villagers and events. Then Joe woke up crying and they had to leave, back out into the bustle and turbulence of a hot London day.

An ice cream cheered Joe considerably and they caught a cab back to Waterloo to catch the six o'clock train. It was on the platform when they arrived with only two minutes to spare before it pulled out of the station.

"Crikey," she laughed breathlessly, "cut it a bit fine, didn't we?"

"No other way to cut it," he said. He carried Joe in one arm and settled them in an empty carriage.

"When do you go back?" she asked.

"Three days."

"I'll write."

"Me too."

"I'll tell Isaac I saw you, he can keep a secret, can't he?"

"Wouldn't be too sure about that, still, if you don't care."

She laughed. "I don't."

Suddenly there was no time left and the guard blew the whistle. Iain knelt beside Joe. "Goodbye, son, be a good lad for your mam." He kissed the silken cheek and the boy smiled.

Nell swayed towards him and he put his arms out to catch her. "Bye, Helena." For a brief moment they held each other tight.

"Quick, the train's moving," she said. The carriage lurched forward.

"Helena." An urgent plea.

"What?" Their eyes locked, his hands tight on her shoulders. "What is it, Iain?"

He smiled, shook his head. "Goodbye."

He left her without turning back. He stepped off the train, running along the platform, searching for her carriage. He saw her through the window but the train had picked up speed, her small hand pressed on the glass, spectral from the pressure. He waved and the train puffed away, watching until it was out of sight. His spirit sank. She was gone, back to her husband, to her life. He had only borrowed her for the day and giving her back was the most difficult thing he had ever had to do.

He roamed the busy streets aimlessly, sitting for a time on a busy thoroughfare, elbows resting on his knees, smoking. Walking again, he found himself pushing against the heavy oak door of a church. The smell of furniture polish and rank flowers, the pressing stillness, the chill of the air compared to the heat outside, familiar but hateful to him. The rows of wooden pews spread out either side of him as he approached the altar. An effigy of Christ spread-eagled on his cross stared down at him sadly. Iain sank to his knees on the red carpeted steps, tears coursed down his face. He was lost and alone. He clasped his hands between his knees, head lowered trying to gain control. Opening his eyes the carpet swam with blood, enveloping him, he put out a hand feeling its sticky wetness, daring to look at his palm to see it.

A small cough behind him jolted him from his vision. He jumped to his feet, rotating quickly to see a priest in his black cassock standing at a polite distance, a slightly fearful expression on his kind worn face.

The priest put out a placatory hand. "Are you all right, son?"

Iain stepped back warily. "Aye, Father, thank you." Despite his agitation it was deeply ingrained in him to show the priest respect.

The priest approached him slowly, putting out his hands, taking Iain's arm. He allowed himself to be led to the front pew.

"Won't you sit down?"

He followed the priest's example, kept his head bowed, studying the floor.

"Are you on leave?" the priest asked. Iain nodded. "Do you want to talk about it?" He shook his head. "You're not alone. All you brave young men out there fighting the devil every day. God is with you."

"We don't fight the devil," he said, "we fight men." He met the priest's eyes. "Men like ourselves, Father. Flesh and blood and we spear them with bayonet and riddle them with lead. Not the devil, not God – there is no God in those fields."

"I'm sure it must feel that way sometimes," he admitted. "Have you no faith?"

"Not even in myself."

"I don't know you but I have a feeling you judge yourself harshly. He takes care of you faith or no. He's out there in those French fields. I have been there. I was there for six months last year. I know what you're going through."

He smiled. "It's not my fighting ability I've lost faith in, Father, it's myself, I feel…" He could not explain how he felt. His mind was befuddled.

"Is this about a woman?"

"It's more than that, I don't want to be afraid any more."

"What of?"

"Things I have done, the way I have lived my life – and I don't mean the war – although that's one more burden to carry with me."

"We've all done things we shouldn't, said things, the past can't be changed. But if you can change the future – now that's really something."

He stood up and the priest followed him. "Can someone change?"

"I believe they can, more than that, I see something in you and I think you will. Wanting to make it so is half the battle."

"I don't want to be alone." He stared at the priest imploringly.

He placed an inadequate creased hand on Iain's. Iain observed it coolly for a moment before turning back down the aisle.

"You're a long way from home," the priest called after him. "When all this is over your way shall be clearer."

He pushed open the heavy door. The hot air was like a solid wall, the clamour and smell of the city pushed back on him. He found the nearest pub and ordered a double whisky. When all this is over, he thought, nothing will have changed.

Chapter Twenty-four

Michael squinted at the sun, rubbing his eyes briefly before concentrating down the telescopic sight. He didn't know how Iain and Dusty endured hours of this waiting. He had listened to their lighthearted banter, laughed at their jokes, enjoyed being with them, being included. Now after several dragging hours the relentless sun was level with his eyes, bringing a slow end to a long duty. He marvelled at their patience. His pelvis ached against the dry cracking mud. He could easily imagine their endless discomfort on a cold wet day.

Dusty sang quietly, binoculars fixed to his eyes. "I want a fag, I want a fag, ee-ii-a-di-oh, I want a fag," he paused. "Eh, up, movement down the line."

Iain barely shifted, easing the weight slightly off one elbow, not relaxing his aim for a second. "Good for your health this," he jibed.

"Chocolate break, five minutes."

The monotony of waiting freed Iain's mind to mull over his leave. He had pondered Nell's visit this last month, reviewed each word, building up their time together like bricks in a wall only to knock it down again with excuses. Her letters were distant in comparison to the warm humorous reality of her.

Somehow he staggered back to Dusty's house from the pub that night quite drunk. He couldn't bring himself to talk about his day with her, and Dusty didn't press him. The following night they went to the West End to see a show. Pearl held his hand and back in the little hall of the terraced house she had caught him off guard and kissed him. He had kissed her back and the last two days she had been starry eyed with adoration. Now she was sending letters too.

"You've never been so popular," Dusty joked.

"Aye, me and Pearl, you know, there's nothing to it," he said.

Dusty laughed. "I know, don't worry, she'll get over you. Once this is finished and everyone goes home, she won't know what she saw in you," he reassured. Iain would never go for Pearl even without the wraith of Nell in his head.

The two men had watched Britain dwindle from the stern of the ship, swallowed by the rising sea mist, the cold dark water churning below them. The thought, unspoken, "When will we return?" Dusty had made some joke about how long it would take to swim back to shore if they jumped off now. They had remained side by side, resolute.

Dusty's voice brought him back to the field. "Don't shoot, Michael. Ready yourself, Midge. Do you see the buggers?" It had been the sergeant's idea to bring Michael out with them. His shooting practice had been increasingly impressive but Dusty was afraid he might have lost his nerve and did not want to risk missing their target when they had waited so long.

"Aye, ready," he said. Dusty continued scanning the trench line for reprisals. Iain let off a single shot hitting his quarry in the head. The artillery pounded further away, down the line. The Germans were popping up like rabbits and he fired randomly.

"Yesss," Dusty hissed, punching the air he lowered his field glasses and rolled over onto his back.

"Give me the glasses," Iain said, peering through them. "Let's give the lad a chance."

"How many did you get?" Michael said blinking rapidly down his rifle.

"Never mind, concentrate," he said returning Dusty's binoculars and peering down the riflescope.

He saw a head bob as did Dusty. When Michael's gun went off it stunned him and he jumped. They laughed at him. "Don't look so shocked, you pulled the trigger, mate," Dusty said.

Michael flushed, grinning. "I know. Did I get him?"

"Aye." Iain had not moved. He squeezed the trigger. "And another, Dusty."

The earth scattered under their noses. They scrabbled backwards. "Shit," Dusty squealed, "they got a mark on us."

"Aye, no wonder." Low to the ground, they ran to the next crater. Iain and Dusty shared a smoke before heading back to the trench.

* * * *

The field stank of putrefying flesh and chloride of lime. Iain tugged the scarf higher over his nose. Sweat trickled down his brow and dripped into his eyes. While they dug one mass grave the priest said prayers over another. Wheeling in the sky above them, crows cawed like portends of doom, the sound was mournful, their presence fitting. Michael and Dusty wrapped the dead bodies, stacking them at the edge of the pit. Champ's shoulder muscles rippled as he wielded the shovel, the sun catching his naked back.

Away to the west the guns boomed. Both sides were giving their best and they were burying the resulting casualties from the last week, there were hundreds of them. The smell was noxious. They had tried to work in their gas masks but the heat and hindrance on their vision defeated them.

They were in a 'rest' camp behind the lines. Hundreds of tents, cookhouse and huts were set in a field of mud that, despite the heat, had not dried up due to the nightly rainfall. These camps were not so much a rest as a change. At least at the end of a hard day they could clean up, eat a proper hot meal and sleep in a warm dry bed unlike those in the trenches.

The impact of spade on earth jarred Iain's body. Repeatedly he wielded a pickaxe, swapping tools to shovel the loose soil.

He dragged himself out of the hole and stood beside Dusty. His voice was muffled through his scarf. "How many more d'you reckon?"

Dusty glanced behind them. "Too bloody many."

Taking an end each, they lifted a corpse down to Champ and Michael who waited, ready. The bodies were heavy and cumbersome. Some were rotten, fingers sinking into the cloth, emanating a gut-churning stench; others were fresher, stiff with rigor mortis. Fat greedy flies buzzed in black hordes, blowing the dead with eggs. Seeing them packed into the grave, faceless massed carcasses, was sickening. Worse still was knowing a great number would have been left behind in that desolate lonely stretch to putrefy and be picked at by rats and crows, food for the writhing maggots.

They spread shovelfuls of lime and covered them with the dark forgiving earth.

"Our Father who art in heaven." The priest's monotone spoke to them all. "Hallowed be thy name." Iain didn't look up from piling in the soil, putting his fellow soldiers to rest for eternity. All this praying to God felt overdue to him when they already found themselves, too late, in hell.

They resumed digging and a few joined together to sing, *'The Lord is My Shepherd'*. The tune swelled until the distant guns were a lesser rumble. Some of the men stopped work to sing. Iain toiled on, the place was a charnel house and he had no voice for hymns.

They marched back to camp in the dusk. Swallows chattered and bats dipped in the early evening light, hunting for insects. Champ whistled merrily despite the general low mood. They carried their rifles, shovels, picks and gas masks. Their route took them through a bombarded village close to the front line where the guns were louder. Ahead of them prone horses lay in the road and lifeless soldiers scattered the dirt, staring sightlessly at the sky.

Sergeant David brought his men to a halt. They dropped their tools and took up their rifles.

"Easy, men," the sergeant said. "Let's see what's happened here."

Slowly they edged towards the scene. The first dead soldier Iain saw had drawn his knees up to his body, hands at his throat. The next held a similar posture, and the next, their skin shades of green and mauve. There were over thirty men and not one of them alive. The obvious cause was gas and yet only two of them had made a futile attempt to pull on their gas masks. He counted eighteen dead horses still harnessed. Flies had settled and flew up in swarms as they passed. It was a dreadful bloodless massacre, rendering each man speechless and momentarily inactive, lacking direction.

Sergeant David harried them into action, his voice stern, to mask his emotions. "Right, lads, nothing we can do right now. I'll report it – someone else's problem – we've had enough for today."

Following his instructions they formed pairs and picked their way hesitantly through the corpses. They marched sedately in fours, silent apart from the tramping of their boots on the dusty road.

The images stayed with them all. They ate dinner from their mess tins in the company of Jackie, Flinty, Champ and Michael. There was none of the usual joking and chatter; the day had taken the hope from them, leaving them despondent. They were hardy and young and after a meal and rest the old optimism resurfaced.

Flinty offered his cigarettes round. "They're vile." Dusty winced as he inhaled.

"Got them off Fritz, last week on a raid."

"Christ, no wonder they've lasted you a week," Iain said and grimaced.

"Trying to off load them onto us," Champ said.

He shrugged, rubbing at his red hair with one hand. "Sorry fellows. Can't waste them, can we?"

Michael hadn't attempted to smoke since Iain had stopped him. He was whittling a piece of wood with his pocketknife. "Cheer us up, give us a song," Jackie said to him.

Champ whistled a tune. Michael took it up, singing clear and high. After a verse or two they all joined in the chorus, tapping a beat with their feet on the earth floor. Jackie lit the primus stove and made coffee and they smoked roll-ups from Champ's tobacco that were much more to their taste.

"I've got cake from me mother," Flinty said and he cut it into large slices, improving the mood further.

"She's put a generous amount of something in this," Iain said appreciatively.

He winked. "That's my mum. She and Dad run a pub in Hampshire. When this is over you'll all have to come and visit."

There were murmurs of agreement, heads nodded, one of many plans they had made for when the show was over.

"Next time," Dusty said, "perhaps she can hide a small bottle of something inside?"

They laughed, the day momentarily buried in their subconscious, the horrors giving way to the mundane that kept their world turning. Rain started drumming off the canvas tent and they all rolled their eyes heavenward groaning. Iain's thoughts drifted back to the men lying beside their horses on the road as it turned to mud.

* * * *

Iain presumed the work party was out to fix wire. He was wrong. It was very much intact and that had been the problem. Unmarked by the shelling and bombs their own men had been sent over the top into a wall of wire to be shot to pieces on its barbs. The bodies hung in the dark, khaki-clad ghosts, hovering mid-air, bent and forlorn, heads loose on broken bodies, limbs twisted. More bodies carpeted the ground, difficult to pass between them without treading on a hand or leg or foot. Occasionally, disconcertingly, a 'corpse' would cry out, not dead but barely living. Stretcher-bearers rushed to clear them while Iain's section disentangled them from the murderous wire. Sometimes they cut it, aware a work party would follow to do repairs, but it was quicker to slash the uniforms, leaving tattered flags of khaki fluttering in the breeze. Beyond the wire, the German stretcher-bearers worked at an equally speedy rate. Easy pickings for a sharp shooter, except a rare truce had been agreed upon to allow both sides to retrieve their men. The guns had fallen silent. A strange humming disturbed the air, the united moans of the injured.

Iain was numb to the ripping barbs on his skin as he manhandled the bodies from the fence. He worked with Michael, while Dusty and Flinty toiled further down the line. Champ was on leave for a week in Blighty with his family. Sergeant David and the new Corporal Williams worked tirelessly beside the men sickened, as they all were, by the task in hand.

This was the first lull in a battle that had pounded continuously for days. Unspoken was the knowledge that their time was coming. One regiment gone, another in to replace it. Death was hungry, breathing hotly down their nervous necks.

They would never get all these boys, living or dead, back to the trench before firing resumed no matter how frantically they worked. Some of these bodies had hung here for days. Iain dreaded one of them, still clinging to life, reaching out a ghoulish hand. When it did, an observer would have noted his lack of reaction. There was so little left that could startle him no matter how obscene. An ageless uniformed figure, skin paper thin over the fine bones of his face, his shallow breathing barely raised his chest. Iain lifted him, a smashed doll, and held him. He beckoned Michael to fetch a stretcher-bearer and knelt amongst the dead rocking the man until the stretcher arrived. The soldier's eyes fluttered closed as he was carried away. Iain would never know who he was or what became of him. He returned to the fence and continued the grisly task.

Wire was abhorrent to Iain. He had never used it for fencing in his work. It couldn't be sat on, birds couldn't nest in it or animals shelter. Lazy farmers and keepers wrapped it round trees like a noose, damaging and killing them. How ironic, he thought, that he should spend his entire life around it now – and not ordinary stuff but with razors that cut or barbs that tore through the flesh.

A light drizzle began to fall, covering everything with a fine mist of water. They worked for hours but when a flare went up indicating commencement of firing they were only halfway through. They retreated, leaving the fallen where they lay.

Back in the trench Iain listened to the howitzers howling over, followed by their abysmal crash. The rattle of artillery joined the thumping shells vibrating the air, a building cacophony until speech was rendered impractical. He lit a Woodbine, his hands shaking more than Dusty's, who was on the fire-step next to him. The sergeant gave the signal and they filed through the narrow trench, Iain with his head bowed as low as possible. They could not hear their feet on the duckboards and their rifles caught repetitively on the narrow trench walls.

They left the trenches behind and with the gunfire still loud in their ears they began the long march to their village billet. Every week they had been moved further and further along the line, never staying at a camp or billet longer than a week, often less. They had no opportunity to become familiar with the lie of the land, sniping was far more of a hit and miss affair than it had been in the past.

They marched at ease, strolling companionably, smoking and talking. The rising sun lightened the sky and with the battlefield further away it was possible to make out the strains of the dawn chorus. The fields were yellow with swaying corn, a furze of red poppies growing amongst it, splashed with blue cornflowers on the periphery. The men might have thought themselves back home if not for the roll of the guns.

They camped in tents and huts. Every day the camp became larger with more troops arriving. Something big was on the way and they all knew it, although not quite when or what. It was said the Germans were less than forty miles away from Paris. Information at the Front was always sketchy.

Every day Iain expected it to be the one where they would find themselves out in the open against the enemy. The days passed with monotonous work parties, fatigues, parades and inspections. The hot weather brought more rats and flies into camp. Fat brown rats scampered through the tents, over their boots and inspected the men fearlessly at close quarters.

"One more parade and I'll do my nut," Dusty cried, aiming a tin of bully beef at a rat.

Iain took off his shirt, sticking to him with the heat. "Christ, when will this end? I thought we'd get away tonight into town or something."

"No leave until further notice, that's what it said on the board."

"It's not fair," said Michael sitting on the edge of his camp bed. "I'm due leave."

"Overdue a couple of nights off myself," Iain said, throwing a packet of cigarettes to Dusty. "Here, I'll get it." He leaned back on his bed, screwed up his eyes against the smoke issuing from his fag and aimed his catapult at the rat, now perched happily beside the tin of beef. "Ready, aim, FIRE." They said the last word in unison. The rat hit the canvas with a whack and was motionless. They cheered. "Throw it out, Mikey boy. Fancy a game of cards, Midge?"

Michael, uncomplaining, picked it up by its scaly tail and threw it out the tent door. Flinty stuck his head in the tent flap. "We don't want your frigging rats out here."

"Well you don't want it in here when you're sleeping either, do you?" Michael said.

"Tea up," Champ called from outside.

"Mikey, bring ours in," Dusty said. They were forever taking advantage of the young boy's good nature and willingness to please. "It's like having our own little batman," Dusty said when he had gone for the tea.

"D'you reckon it'll be soon, Dusty? I think I'm going to lose my mind. I want to get gloriously drunk, I mean, really, really drunk."

He laughed, shuffling a pack of greasy cards. "Nice cold beer with a whisky chaser." Michael brought in the tea. Dusty took the mug and peered glumly at its dark orange hue.

"Cheers," Iain said. "Got anything to go with it? It's a bit wet." Michael fetched the last of the biscuits in a battered old rat-proof tin. The hollow sound of the gas alarm filled the camp. "Christ Al-bloody-mighty," Iain ranted. "Can't even drink a cuppa." He pulled on his shirt, reached for his gas mask. "It'll be another buggering drill."

Soldiers appeared from their tents, trudging towards the parade ground, unidentifiable in their gas masks, all protruding eyeholes and snake-tongue air tubes. Again, it was a practice run. By the time they returned to their tent the rats had finished the biscuits in the tin that, in the rush, had been left open, and their tea was cold.

Jackie arrived to stem the tirade of abuse against the British Army and their safety drills with a stack of mail. Iain had a letter from Nell and Pearl, raising ribald comments from Dusty. He opened Pearl's letter first.

She wrote as she spoke, her factory mates figured predominantly, the music hall they had visited, how she couldn't afford a new hat and she signed off with all her love as if they were promised to each other.

He unfolded Nell's letter, sniffed it for any vestige of her scent. Her rounded tidy script filled two pages.

'Dear Iain,

My mother died four days ago and I am writing this from Aunt Cath's. The funeral was today. They buried her next to Joanna. Feeling rather low, wondering how you are feeling. Joe is with me. He thinks it is a holiday and for him I suppose it is. I took him to the beach this afternoon, such a hot day. We built sandcastles and paddled in the sea, it was quite warm. He's caught the sun across his face and looks more like his father than ever. He's here as I write, fast asleep, the sea air has worn him out.

  I looked across the sea today knowing you are on the other side. We hear conflicting reports about how things are going over there. The Germans have made such advances. I worry about you so. They would let me know if something happened, wouldn't they?

  I was glad to leave North Farm behind, though I would have wished it to be under different circumstances, of course. Lisa has taken over most of the household duties. I prefer to work the dairy and help with milking. I'm a first rate milker now!

  I really don't think anyone would miss me if I left for good. They manage quite well, all except for Mrs Hart. Lisa refuses to wait on her as I do, which is probably a good thing. When I'm away she is forced to help herself and get out of bed.

  Saw Mr Denham in town who spoke of you kindly. Also saw Isaac. Delilah is well. I chose not to tell him of our meeting as you said and yet he asked me how you were! Miles Denham is home on leave, alive and well. He was posted missing after being captured in Turkey and kept as prisoner of war, so Mrs Denham is mightily relieved. One of Jasper Potter's boys was killed in action, Jack, I think. I don't know them very well.

  Wish I could think of something cheery to write and my wit evades me. Hoping to write about happy things next time.

  Take care. God Bless. Your friend, Helena'

He read it several times. He wondered about Lisa George and her role in the Hart household. Nell made it sound as if Lisa had usurped her and that she had stepped aside happily too. He folded the letter, closed his eyes to the canvas. Dusty, Michael, Flinty, all his little group were sharing news from home, joking and laughing. He lived with these men, ate, drank, slept with them, it might even be his lot to die with them and while he was here they were all he had. Sometimes it was enough. But at that moment, only for a moment, he felt a long, long way from home and very alone.

Chapter Twenty-five

They crouched in the assembly trench. Too narrow to lie in or sit straight, too short to stand, they used their entrenching tools to dig hollows deep enough to hunker down. Smoking was forbidden but they smoked anyway. Iain's calf muscles were cramping, Dusty complained of numb feet and pins and needles. Michael quivered, a complete bag of nerves. Champ and Flinty were quiet, Jackie next to them.

The barrage started not long after they entered the trench. In the deep darkness of the moonless night the sky was awash with the glare of flares. A dull thud heralded the start of British guns firing followed by the crash of field guns, then heavier artillery further behind those. Like percussion in an orchestra, one cancelled out the next until the noise was colossal, impossible to think or talk. The shower of dirt and dust falling on their heads ensured they kept down, the Germans were replying. A watery grey light filled the sky and a heavy mist rose from the field, mingled with thick poisonous gas from the firing, producing an impenetrable fog.

The soldiers in the front trench went over first. It was impossible to see their progress. The full force of the British Artillery had knocked out the enemy guns and the firing was now much further away. Sergeant David referred to his watch repeatedly, Lieutenant Peterson beside him and their sergeant major. Iain's watch had stopped, time literally stood still. At that moment, ground shaking with the bombardment of shells, head and back aching, eyes stinging from the gas, it was believable.

Lieutenant Peterson indicated there was one minute to go, mouthing the words with the aid of sign language. Dusty gripped Iain's arm, placed his thumb and forefinger together in a little O. Iain stuck two fingers in the air and they both laughed mutely.

Their rifles pointed up in the trench, all bayonets skywards. If anyone had jumped in on top of them they would have been impaled. Michael fidgeted at Iain's elbow, struggling to write on an old fag packet. Iain leaned forward to see Champ kissing a crucifix that he kept in his pocket. Flinty held the pose of prayer, head bowed, but he too was fidgety and jumpy. Jackie, trying to make light of it, caught Iain's eye and ran his finger across his throat, poking out his tongue. Iain saw Michael's eyes streamed with tears.

He prodded him with his elbow. Michael managed a shaky smile. Iain realised the tears were from the gas and that his eyes were smarting too.

The ladder was directly in front of him. He didn't want to be first over. He didn't want to go over at all. They stood up, heads down, although the German shells were more distant now. Lieutenant Peterson pushed in front of Iain to go before him, he stepped back willingly. The order came to move out, he followed the lieutenant over the lip of the trench. Tanks had gone ahead of them, invisible in the mist, efficiently flattening the wire. They met no gunfire from the first German line. The weight of the tank had collapsed the trench and was full of enemy corpses, crushed as easily as flowers in a field.

They threw grenades into dugouts, moving on as one, towards the ridge. The ground was hard going, uneven and hilly. Overhead the air buzzed with the drone of aeroplane engines, little biplanes by the score, like a swarm of dragonflies.

They climbed higher and the mist became less dense making it possible to see further ahead. They arrived at a lightly wooded area, walking through the trees, guns at the ready, held across their chests. Iain couldn't believe they had progressed this far without losing a single man. The artillery and tanks had done their job well.

Further up the ridge whined the flight of bullets. The enemy had seen them. Taking cover they threw grenades; earth and debris flew into the air. Iain sank down on his knees with Dusty, Michael and Flinty close to. They moved onward. The lieutenant gave the command to throw more grenades. They marched on, firing as they went.

The loud rat-a-tat-tat of the machine gun at very close quarters caught them off guard. Sergeant David went down, Champ and more. Iain flung himself onto the damp ground, the smell of wet earth and gun smoke dilating his nostrils. He threw two grenades, fired his rifle in the general direction of the machine gun. Peterson stood up, marched forward, an impervious demi-God with his pistol to protect him, his men followed.

Iain jumped into a German trench with immense relief. Roughly ten enemy soldiers raised their arms aloft. "Kamerad, kamerad," they shouted.

The gunner hung, sunken eyed, gaping mouthed, over his machine gun. Iain grinned at Peterson who whooped with joy. Killing was in the lieutenant's blood and he was enjoying every minute. They rounded up the prisoners and sent them down the hill under guard.

Peterson ordered the gunners to set up their own machine gun. Rounds were fired and more grenades thrown. The company was divided. Iain was amongst those sent ahead with Dusty and Michael. The ear-splitting roar of the shelling was closer - the enemy had a position on them.

"Here we bloody go," someone shouted.

Iain was out of the trench and the shell hit. The British company scattered, running for their lives, the dead and injured thrown onto the breaking earth. He scrambled forward. He could not see his commanding officer or any of the men. He headed back the way he had come, falling into the next trench. Losing his grip on his rifle, it hit the duckboards. He stared up at the faces of enemy soldiers, at least twenty. He knew surrender would mean nothing to them. They could as easily run him through with their bayonets or shoot him. They laughed at some shared joke. Slowly he reached for his gun, which had fallen directly in front of him and then the unthinkable happened.

Multiple palms raised in pale unison. "Kamerad," one said stepping towards him. He grabbed his rifle, drew back the bolt and pointed it at them; their surrender was ridiculous, some sort of miracle. He laughed at the lunacy of it. Peterson arrived and British soldiers filled the trench behind him and there was Dusty and Michael.

"I thought you were a goner," Peterson said.

"Jesus," Iain said, "I thought you were."

Dusty squeezed his shoulder. "They got Champ and Sergeant David," he said. It would take hours for the stretcher-bearers to get to them if they were still alive, if they got there at all.

"And Flinty?" he asked. Dusty shrugged he didn't know. They had to move on. They had lost their cover, the fog had dissipated and a weak sun shone through. Their orders were to take the ridge and secure all enemy positions.

They were in small clusters now, spreading across the hillside, Iain, Dusty and Michael together, part of a larger group. They traversed the hill at speed, unable to ascertain enemy positions.

By late morning progress was halted by sniper fire. A grenade was thrown. It tore through the party, pieces of body were flung with the dirt. A rush of air swept over Iain and he was thrown to the ground. He searched wildly for Dusty, keeping his head low. He located him quickly, crawling on his stomach towards Iain. Iain threw a couple of grenades in retaliation, not entirely sure of his aim. Dusty pointed frantically. Michael was sprawled on his back nearby. They made slow progress towards him. He was crying, mouthing words neither could discern.

The injuries to his lower abdomen and legs were a mess of blood and gore. Together they pulled him towards a crest of land that would provide adequate cover. He screamed when they dragged him, his eyes rolling back.

Safer in their hideout Iain held Michael's head while Dusty ripped out his field dressing. Michael's eyes flickered open and he stared straight up at Iain.

"It's all right, son, we're going home," he said, the brief lull allowing him to be heard.

"Midge, oh, flaming hell, Midge," Michael cried. Dusty looked at Iain.

"Christ," Iain said, "we've nothing to give him." Only the commanding officers carried morphine. Michael's tears rolled down the side of his face, his skin a pasty green hue. Dusty had no chance of attempting first aid on a wound of this scale and he regarded Iain hopelessly.

"Finish me, Midge," Michael sobbed, his whole body shaking in Iain's hands. He cradled the boy's head trying to be of comfort. Short of shooting him they had no relief to offer.

"What are we going to do?" Dusty said.

"We need morphine and a stretcher."

"One of us stays here and the other can fetch a medic."

"I'll go back," Iain said, clutching the boy to his chest.

"What if they won't come?" Dusty asked.

"I'll make them, or I'll bring morphine."

"You stay with him," Dusty said over Michael's pitiful sobbing. "I'll go." They stared at each other. Their orders were to leave the injured where they fell, but they couldn't leave him. "I'll look for the lieutenant, he can't be far. He'll have morphine."

Iain looked into the boy's wildly staring eyes, the terror dilating his pupils, the blue iris barely visible.

"Do something, Midge, for Christ sake," Dusty said as a bullet whistled past his raised head. It would be suicide to make a move now.

"Can you see who's firing at us?"

"No, give me your scope."

Iain scrabbled in his webbing with one hand, threw his scope to Dusty who fixed it to his rifle. Michael writhed, his head pressed hard on Iain's chest. "Midge," he croaked.

"What is it, son?"

He whimpered pitifully, eyes wide. "Shoot me, Midge."

"No, you'll be all right. Hang on, Michael, we're getting out of here."

He wept, stifling a scream of pain. "Christ, no."

Dusty fired repeatedly over the ridge. "They've got us taped to a bleeding inch," he called back to Iain.

"Dusty, what about Michael, we've got to do something."

He briefly glimpsed over his shoulder. "Then do something."

"Michael, I'll see you in Blighty, pal," Iain said quietly.

"Mother," Michael's voice a broken plea, "Mother?"

"Your mam's here, Michael, close your eyes." Iain placed his large hand across the narrow sweat drenched brow. He felt the boy's pain and fear. He concentrated and the heat of his hand intensified. To Iain there seemed to be a shimmering field where skin touched skin and Michael's eyes closed, the pain rolling away in waves.

An incredible heat swelled in Michael's head, a piercing whiteness, an enveloping warmth and blissful release. His mother's arms embraced him tenderly pressing him against her gently, stroking his hair, singing, her beautiful voice filling his ears. The agony flowed away and with it the light was fading too. He felt himself borne away by the heat and comfort of the great arms and hands holding him.

A powerful explosion erupted over their heads. Dusty ducked and Iain shielded Michael with his body. A cascade of earth and lumps of mud showered them. The shelling started again, closer still.

After a second Dusty peered over the ridge. "How's he doing?" he called preparing to make his move.

Michael was silent. His hands relaxed their grip on the glutinous mass of his stomach, eyes almost closed. Dusty knelt down beside them. He put his fingers on Michael's throat, then to his wrist, brought his ear to the open mouth listening. Iain looked at Dusty and shook his head. He rocked the boy gently.

"He's dead, Iain. It's for the best, the lad was too far gone," Dusty said. Iain nodded, thinking his head might explode, the pain of grief in his chest threatening to overwhelm him. He had seen this before, but Michael was a kid, barely sixteen. His beautiful voice would sing no more.

While Iain held Michael, Dusty went through the boy's tunic. He found his pay book, a postcard, a stub of pencil, an old fag packet with the first verse of a poem or song. *'Time is up, Mother dear, the angels call my name...'* Iain looked away, he could not bring himself to read more. Michael had been at his side writing it seconds before the whistle to go over. Dusty stuffed it all in his pockets to send back to Michael's mother. Michael's head lolled heavily against Iain.

"We'd better leave his identity disc, they'll come back for him later. We want him to have a proper grave," Dusty said, grasping Iain's arm. "We have to leave him."

He shook his head, in sorrow, not refusal. He would have to place Michael's head on the dirt. It was almost more than he could bear. If nobody came back for him he would be left here to rot. He carefully laid the body down, Dusty pulled at him to hurry up. He bent and kissed Michael's forehead, the sweat there already drying in the breeze and cold as ice. He wiped away the tears that slid down his face. When he turned to Dusty his face was grim and composed.

"Put the scope away," Dusty said. Iain obediently tucked it back into the webbing. It meant certain death to be caught by the enemy with a scope on a rifle.

They were leaving behind one of their own. It lay heavy on both men. They scrabbled to their feet without daring to look back at him.

Once in the open they pulled their rifles from their shoulders ready to fire. Bullets careened past them. They stumbled and slipped over the uneven ground, dodging craters made by the grenades and bombs. They found an abandoned enemy gun position and rested in the trench, catching their breath, drinking in choking gulps from their emptying water bottles.

They joined with the next wave of soldiers coming up the hill. Tagging onto the end they fired, claiming the next enemy stronghold, taking prisoners by the hundred. When the land flattened they marched through the dead, firing, sheltering, lobbing grenades.

Darkness fell quickly and they holed up for the night. A small piece of land stretched between them and the enemy. German machine guns fired at regular intervals to ensure there was no complacency. The relative safety of their position did not last, some time after midnight shelling restarted and scored a direct hit. Iain and Dusty searched desperately for cover. Shrapnel rattled around them as they tripped from one tree stump to the next, tumbling through craters and unexpected holes. The darkness half blinded them but when Dusty went down, Iain noticed. He managed to clamber to his feet and lurched forward a few steps and then collapsed again. Iain grabbed him, hardly noticing the dead weight. He hauled him into a large shell hole. A burning kick seared Iain's right shoulder before he ducked down beside his injured friend.

Dusty was laughing. "They got me," he shouted with indignant outrage - how bloody dare they!

"Where?"

"In my flaming leg. Bastards."

Iain tried to discover the extent of the damage in the dark. Blood spurted onto his hand, warm and sticky, through Dusty's trouser leg.

"Fuck," he muttered. The bleeding was heavy, gushing from the thigh. Dusty would die if he could not stop this. He ripped at the field dressing in his tunic, two rolls of bandage and a precious phial of iodine. He tore at the khaki material and feeling his way he found a single entry hole. Dusty was oblivious to the liberally applied iodine. He bound Dusty's leg at the groin to quell the bleeding, wrapping the remaining bandage as tightly as he could manage over the wound. Blood seeped through the dressing although it had stemmed the flow.

"Pain?" he asked.

Dusty shook his head, something akin to mild toothache, deep but sufferable. He trembled violently.

They had little choice except to sit it out. He put his water bottle to Dusty's lips, he drank thirstily, careful not to waste it. Iain took the small amount that was left.

"Chocolate." He broke up the small bar he had in his pocket, pushed some into Dusty's mouth.

Crouching beside his inert form a strangled fear came over Iain. They were not getting out of this. Three years away from everything he valued, living in this hellhole and why? For it all to end tonight in this crater in the middle of a French hillside? He wished he had baled out months ago, gone AWOL. He might have been shot for cowardice but at least he could have had a few decent months of life first, instead of this.

He imagined Nell receiving a telegram, would it alter her life one iota? Would she not continue her life regardless? Would it make any difference to anyone?

'Say hello to Mother, Tell her that I love her. Tell her not to wait for me 'cos I'm not coming home,' so went the song in his head. Michael often sang it and everyone would jeer at him for being melancholy and tell him to shut up. They would not ridicule and laugh at him again.

Dusty could not walk, he would die if he began to bleed again. Iain could not leave him here to die. His friend who had dug him out of a certain death with his bare hands, who had taken him into his family, who shared every parcel, every dream, whose laughter had saved him so many times, the best friend he had ever had.

After midnight came the rain. The guns and bombs fell silent and the persistent drumming of the water drops replaced them. Both men fell in and out of an uneasy sleep. Iain guessed it to be about two in the morning when he made the decision to move on. He shivered, teeth chattering. His shoulder throbbed, blood seeping through his tunic. Dusty lay soaked through beside him, he had not moved for hours. Iain touched his hand, he felt dead already, dead like Michael lying cold in his solitary open grave.

"Dusty." He gave him a small push.

"What is it, Midge?" His voice was hoarse.

"We've got to go."

"Can't do it, mate."

"Got to, this is it, we're going to die. Nobody's coming for us, it's been hours. Got to get back, if we don't bleed to death, we'll freeze. We can't let it end for us, pal, we've got to fight for us now. Michael's gone – we're not going the same way. Hey, I've not had my daughters yet."

"Might be best if you go on, Midge. Come back with reinforcements. Go get me a stretcher."

He shook his head. "Don't be soft, it'll be like carrying my wee son."

"Cheeky sod," muttered Dusty. "Hope you know which way you're going."

He slung both rifles over one shoulder and dragged Dusty awkwardly onto the other, staggering to his feet.

When he hit the valley floor the craters were deeper and filling with water. The infantry and tanks had churned up the earth and the rain was swiftly turning it to mud. It sucked at his feet and he had to take care not to trip over the half buried bodies. An arm flung up here, a boot stuck out there, a slimy head crowning through the dirt.

One face in the mud he recognized. Flinty ogled him with filmy eyes, mouth gaping open catching the rain. He stepped back in horror. It was a journey through a landscape that resembled the far side of hell.

The swirling mist and remnants of smoke produced phantoms before his eyes like lost souls wandering the night searching for escape, while at his feet lay their redundant bodies. He shut down his mind and concentrated, one foot in front of the other. The weariness of his body was enveloping, Dusty's weight increasing with each step, heavier and heavier. Isaac told him he would live. Isaac had foretold it. There would be daughters. Isaac had seen it all.

Chapter Twenty-six

The nurse laid her cool hand on Iain's burning forehead. The infection in his shoulder wound ransacked his body. In his dreams he whimpered and called out.

Her shadow fell across Dusty and he opened his eyes, it was past midnight. "How's he doing?"

She shook her head. "He's poorly. His temperature is very high."

"He won't die will he?" he whispered.

"No, no," she replied, too brightly, too quickly, adding, "we're doing all we can for him."

Discomforted he pressed his head back on the pillow and closed his eyes. Tomorrow he was leaving for Blighty to convalesce. He had a touch of pneumonia and they wanted to get him out. He would have preferred to wait until Iain was conscious, but Iain couldn't be moved until the infection was under control. A couple of days ago he had been quite lucid drinking tea and dictating a letter to Helena.

Dusty could not comprehend how Iain had managed to get them both back to the Dressing Station, but he had. Muddied and bloody, he imagined how they must have looked. They had made it and if Iain died now it would be a total injustice, one to add to all the others.

He listened to Iain talking in his sleep. He called out for Helena. Dusty thought he heard him crying, when he strained to look, there were no tears. At one point Iain opened his eyes, turning his head on the pillow. "Where's Michael?" he asked hoarsely. Before Dusty could even form a reply he fell back into unconsciousness and was muttering again.

He considered writing to Helena, except somehow it seemed unlucky. It was the type of thing you did if someone died. Besides which, what could he say? Your brave friend is beside me dying? He is here, calling out your name? Dreaming of the dead? Failing, fading away. He could not bear the futility of it all. Life and death were cheap currency in this foreign, war torn land.

He called the nurse and asked for a sleeping tablet. If only he could sleep and escape it all. He could not stand listening to

Iain's wanderings any more. He wondered if he were going mad. By rights he should be half mad or completely. They all should.

* * * *

The fever burned through Iain's brain. The past came back to reclaim him, times lived and unchangeable. This was Finnigan at his most dangerous, calm and drowning in whisky.

"Your mother," quietly spoken, "was a silly bitch."

"You don't know anything about my mother," Iain retorted. He wondered if he imagined the tears that filled Finnigan's eyes as he swigged from the bottle, throat bobbing as he swallowed.

"I know more than you think. You're the flyblow of some waster and you know whose. But she – she was mine." He leaned back in the chair. Iain needn't have even been there, listening, it was pure chance he was, and Finnigan kept talking.

"Silly wee lass from the village. Comely enough, tall, built like a young lad really, something about her though, a tinker's girl. I wasn't the only one looking. And if I'd offered her the earth she wouldn't have been looking at me. Oh no, though she come calling when she found herself in trouble. Too late by far, Mr High-and-mighty was welcome to her, but he didn't want her then did he? He'd have been disinherited if he hadn't married that stuck-up troll what he wed."

Finnigan looked up then and realised Iain was entranced, staring wide eyed at him and he laughed. "Aye," Finnigan nodded, smirking, "that's right, you ruined her life, you and your father, ruined her, ruined me too. There was nobody else for me. Should be pleased with yourself all in all."

"If that's true – all that…" Iain had no reason to doubt it, not really, "then how could I help it? It wasn't my doing, it was – was her and him. Not me."

"I won't rest easy until your dead. You've known that awhile," Finnigan said it easily, a threat he had repeated intermittently and apparently without reason for years.

"All your swagger and shit, well I have news for you, I'm not scared any more. There's nothing you can do to me now."

They both stood up. Iain was eighteen and a head taller than the gamekeeper. Finnigan squared up to him. "I can kill you – how about that?"

Iain backed off. He had the muscle, but lacked the confidence. "You'd be hanged for me? I doubt it. That's a lot of hate."

"Nobody would find you," he said. "Nobody would care to look. You're nothing. Think you're someone 'cos you're the laird's bastard? Swanning round preening like a peacock. Time to wring the peacock's neck. I'll deliver what's left of you to your Da."

Iain rushed at him, pinned him against the dresser, the crockery rocking perilously.

Finnigan fixed him with his liverish eyes, his spittle hitting Iain's cheek. "And how did she earn a living, saddled wi' you to feed? She dragged her arse round Glasgow while she tupped for a penny. And then when she'd had enough she wrote to your Da to look after you before walking into the Clyde and drowning herself. He didn't want you either."

"You liar."

"No, no I'm not. Think about it – if you're able."

And it all made sense and it was more than he could stand, especially from Finnigan. He brought up his fist, landing a punch on Finnigan's jaw. Finnigan fell back, knocking two cups and a plate crashing to the floor, dropping the bottle of whisky that spilled its contents across the boards. He lumbered to his feet and with a roar he had Iain by the shirt, an arm tight on his windpipe. He kicked Finnigan on the shin.

In a second Iain had his opponent on the floor. They rolled across the open space, hitting the chair legs at the kitchen table. Iain struck blows to Finnigan's body, receiving punches of equal strength. He put the palm of his hand under Finnigan's chin pushing his head back. Finnigan rammed his shoulder into Iain's side sending him across the room. Finnigan scrambled to his feet.

Iain, raised on all fours, gasped for breath, the blood trickling down his nose, metallic in his mouth. Finnigan's boots scraped the floor, lurching over him. Iain glanced up through his black hair. In the gleam of the lamplight he caught the dull flash of a long knife blade in Finnigan's hand. He slowly stood up, his eyes never leaving the Irishman's leering face.

"Should have drowned you in the river like a kitten in a sack the first day Sinclair lumbered me with you. What does the laird know? Never had no sons of your own, he says, so I brings you one from the poor house to train up, need some young blood he says. And look what I got? His bastard, brought here out of guilt."

Iain let him ramble as he wavered on unsteady, drunken legs. Finnigan snorted on his laughter. "And here you are, a millstone round my neck." He swung the knife in the air. "Now it's over, all over. I'm gonna get you Macdonald, cut your hide, slit your gizzard. Always toadying up to Sinclair, makes you feel special do it? You're nothing to him, just some diversion. He's got his son and heir. You're the charity case, made him feel good about himself for a bit. Done the right thing. Except he didn't, did he? 'Cos you're the eldest, you're the heir, born to a whore. Look at Adam Sinclair and weep, Macdonald, 'cos he got what should have been yours." He stepped forward, knife flailing.

Iain had heard enough home truths. He was leaving and this time it would be forever. The Irishman lunged at him from behind. He wrenched Iain's head back with a handful of hair, the knife a whisper away from the skin of his throat. "One move," Finnigan rasped, "one move and you're in the sod where you belong. Even if your Da don't thank me his prissy wife will."

Iain's breath came in shallow gasps. Finnigan had pushed his whole life into place. Finnigan's hate, the laird's interest, really only self-interest, his wife's complete disregard and his mother floating in the Clyde when he had always imagined her living the high life without the bother of him. He wouldn't apologise for who he was, he had endured years of ceaseless bullying and it stopped tonight. With all his force he brought his elbow back into Finnigan's stomach. The knife glanced off his throat, nicking the skin, as Finnigan, winded, keeled onto the floor.

Iain fell out of the door into the night. He was a strong young man and yet as he ran he felt none of his power. Once again he was the young boy who had travelled to Glenleven frightened and alone, unaware of who he was or where he was going.

* * * *

Iain opened his eyes. A nurse leaned over him. He was confused. He thought he was back at Glenleven. She smiled and encircled his wrist with firm, cool fingers to check his pulse. "Hello, Mr Macdonald. How are you feeling?" she said.

"I – I don't know. Why am I here?"

"You have a bullet wound to your shoulder, remember? You brought in your friend Johnny Miller."

"Johnny? Who?" He could not recall knowing anyone called Johnny.

She gave a little laugh. "Dusty, I mean."

He remembered, Dusty had been bleeding and he had carried him. "Yes, yes I remember." Then he realised, "I'm in France." He was miles away from Glenleven that had been a different time.

Another little laugh. "Yes, you're in a hospital in France," she confirmed.

He smiled in relief, of course, all that with Finnigan and the police had been a long time ago now. Thank God and yet it had all been so clear, as if it had happened yesterday. He closed his eyes, he was safe, everything was fine.

His eyes snapped open. "Where's Dusty?" He leaned forward to see who was in the next bed.

The nurse, with a reassuring hand on his left shoulder, pushed him back. "He was right beside you until two days ago. He'll be home by now, back in England."

"He's gone home?" he said.

"Well, to a hospital in Britain anyway."

"That's great. Christ, have I been here long?"

"You were drinking tea and writing a letter eight days ago, don't you remember? We thought you were on the mend, then you got poorly with an infection." He shook his head. He remembered nothing after walking through the mire with Dusty on his back. The nurse continued, "You've been here ten days but you've a way to go yet. You never know you might get home too. Would you like that?"

"What to another hospital? Will Dusty go home? Will he see his family?"

"I think he was going to Kent to convalesce. At least his family can visit him there. You're a bit further away from home than that aren't you? If you went back you'd probably end up in a hospital in England too, not Scotland. Why aren't you in a Scottish regiment?"

"Och, I was living in England before the war. I didn't much care about which regiment I was in. I joined the one who would take me," he replied.

"Well, let's see how you go. Now, are you hungry? Perhaps some soup, I'll see what I can get you," she said lowering her voice. "The matron's a bit of a tyrant about eating between meals. I think you've lost enough weight. I'll be back shortly." She strode away, her slim hips swinging. He tried to change position and his shoulder burned in protest.

Closing his eyes he remembered Michael begging for relief, how he had failed to give him it. Champ was gone, Sergeant David, two wives without a husband, between them six children without a father. The image of Flinty's decapitated head planted in the filth surfaced. He had been with them on the ridge. How great had been the explosion that had flung his head back to the flatness of the field? He wondered if Jackie Elliot were still alive and Peterson. Had Michael's body been picked up and buried? Was he in some mass unmarked grave? He felt Dusty's absence keenly. If only he were here. Who could he talk to now?

The nurse returned, the pressure of her weight dipping the mattress as she sat down. He opened his eyes. "Right," she said in a business like tone, "let's see what we can get down you." She held the spoon to his mouth. Obediently he drank the clear runny broth. It was tasteless and salty, sliding down easily. She smiled at him encouragingly offering another spoonful. He guessed her to be in her mid-thirties. She wore no wedding ring, a crescent of dark hair visible at the front of a long nurse's cap. Her hazel eyes were kind as she ladled the broth down him like a child being spoon-fed, with occasional pauses to wipe his mouth with a napkin.

"I think you'll be on the mend in no time now. The doctor will be pleased to know you've eaten. You'll be able to get up in a couple of days. That'll be nice." She kept up her one-sided monologue in a cheerful, upper crust accent.

Somewhere on the ward someone groaned loudly. The nurse was deaf to it, happily perched on the bed as if she had all the time in the world.

"Who's making that noise?" he asked eventually.

"A poor boy, terribly burned. Those flamethrowers have given us some bad cases."

"Can't you do anything for him?"

"He's quite dopey with morphine." She peered down the ward. "Don't worry, there's someone with him, he's not alone. Come on can you take some more?" She waved the spoon in the air. He shook his head. She was aggrieved as if it were a personal slight.

"D'you know if Jackie Elliot is in the hospital?" he asked.

"There's no one of that name on this ward, I could enquire if he's in the hospital. Is he a good friend of yours?"

"No, not particularly, he's the only one that might be left. I always found him a wee bit annoying. I know the others – the others are gone," he said, trying to block out the noise of the boy moaning.

"I'll try and find out. You're Lieutenant Peterson has been in to see you. You weren't too good then. I'm sure he'll be back – he should know about you're annoying friend," she said laughing.

"Might have known the lieutenant would still be with us – I expect he saw Fritz off single handed."

"We're doing well, I know that much, but I think it took more than the effort of your lieutenant to pull it off." She said off with an 'r' in it.

"How long have you been here?"

She rolled her eyes. "Oh," she looked up to the ceiling trying to recall, "six – no – seven months. Went home for three months. Before that I was posted to Belgium for almost a year, and before that a year back in a British Hospital, 1915 in France…"

"Aye, I see, been through it then," he said.

She gave a little titter. "It's been a while. How long have you been in it?"

"Since 1915. Do you reckon my fighting days are over?" he asked.

She wrinkled up her nose prettily. "I don't really think so. If it were up to me I'd send you back to Blighty – but I'm afraid it's not."

"No," he was disappointed, "shame that. What's your name?"

"Julia Holmes – Nurse Holmes to you," she said efficiently.

"Well, Nurse Holmes, thank you for the soup. I'll do my utmost to get better so I can go back and do my bit." He was trying to joke but there was a harsh edge to his tone.

She took his hand and squeezed it, her eyes unexpectedly filling with tears. "You've done your bit." She rose briskly, sniffing and said, "Now try to sleep."

* * * *

Two days later Iain trailed up the ward, clutching a shaving kit in his hand. His right arm was strapped in a sling and his shoulder ached abysmally, but he was still here, he would mend. In the bathroom mirror, a shaky thin bearded stranger stared back with large luminous eyes. Dusty had called him Blackbeard and he smiled at himself, seeing the resemblance. It was the first time in a while he could not feel lice crawling on him.

Shaving proved a difficult, slow job, with the razor trembling dangerously in his left hand. He prided himself on his steady hand, while teasing Dusty, but not now. It was an uncontrollable palsy through his limbs. He cut himself twice and was relieved to put the razor down. He lit a cigarette, his first since crouching in the assembly trench a fortnight before. The smoke made him lightheaded.

He climbed into bed exhausted with the effort. He put his head on the pillow and attempted to quell the shaking which had inexplicably spread to his whole body. The double doors flung open for the arrival of a new batch of patients, groaning and bleeding. The ward erupted into chaos. One doctor arrived for over twenty injured men. The first aid and painkillers administered at the dressing station had long since worn off. The nurses wheeled the occupied beds up the ward to make room for more.

When he could no longer bear the sight of the blood and helpless gestures of the dying and pained, he rolled onto his side and closed his eyes. His ears could not so easily block out the sounds of their shouts and screams. The tears fell hot on his cheek as they squeezed out of tightly shut eyelids and his body continued to shake.

A vision replayed in his mind, a night almost three years before when the Jerries had come across no-man's-land in a vain attempt to take their trench. The British had fired until their rifles had been too hot to hold and the bodies of the Germans had piled up in heaps. At Iain's side had been Dusty and Champ, David Wright, Arnold Jackson, John Merit, Henry Axford, Sergeant Evans and Captain Simmons, a favourite with the men, who later had been blown to pieces and scattered to the four winds. They had slaughtered the enemy that night until the sight of their muddied corpses sickened them. Their victory had been hollow, the Germans hadn't stood a chance. They had stumbled into their fire as if oblivious to it. The few that had broken through ended their lives speared on British bayonets.

Iain tasted blood in his mouth, the smattering of dampness on his face as Andrew Long was blown to pieces in front of him. He wiped it off his face with his sleeve, grasped his gun, loaded, fired, loaded, fired. They had seen what no man should see. Felt the rush of death, been lifted by the power of murder, rejoiced in the sight of human blood, shaken hands with the limb that stuck out of the trench wall, trodden with careless feet across the corpses of enemy and ally. After all everyone was the same once they were dead. Then later, in the safety of an estimanet or billet, they laughed and joked, making light of it all, bravado and bluster saving them from themselves.

The dead made no fuss, but the injured screamed and the shells shattered, shaking the very depths of the earth where they crouched like the rats that swam around them, terrified but set for the battle to come. Prepared for, if never accepting, the fact that they might be next to sink into the mud, to mingle with the bones that already rested there.

Iain trembled, his teeth chattering, tears dried on his face, willing his visions to disappear, until he fell in to a deep unconscious sleep as dark and lonely as the grave.

* * * *

Iain awoke to find Lieutenant Peterson by his bed. Peterson smiled and offered him a cigarette.

He took it with tremulous fingers, leaned forward for Peterson to light it. "How are you feeling?" the officer asked.

"Not too bad, really. They told me Dusty went home. Do you know how he's doing?"

"Oh, yes, inflammation of the lungs. His wound is healing well. He'll be fine. Don't worry about him. You saved his life. I think there'll be a commendation in it for you."

He grimaced. "Well, there shouldn't be. Perhaps he saved mine. If I hadn't been so determined to get him out, I might not have made it either. I wouldn't have left him not even if he'd been dead, not Dusty." There was a brief silence and he struggled to get the words out. "We had to leave Michael, you know."

"Yes, I know. He was picked up. He'll be in a proper marked grave."

Iain was relieved. "Good, I couldn't stop thinking about the crows picking at him."

"Well, don't think about it any more. The roll call was pretty depressing I can tell you."

"Aye, Champ and the sergeant and Flinty. Flinty's head…" he stopped, his shaking hand lifted the cigarette to his mouth.

Peterson lowered his dark head, smoothed his moustache with his fingers. "Yes, all of them. I wrote to Champ's wife and Sergeant David's. They were fine men, good soldiers. I sent a letter to Michael's mother and Flinty's too."

Iain could not speak. He puffed determinedly on the cigarette. He wished the lieutenant hadn't come, seeing him laid low and vulnerable. Any visitor would be more welcome than the lieutenant. Peterson took the fag end from Iain's fingers and stubbed it out.

Peterson said, "They tell me you'll be back with us in no time."

"Is that supposed to comfort me? I can't wait." He hauled himself up the bed awkwardly with his one good arm.

Peterson laughed. "Sorry, my bedside manner needs working on. You did really well, Macdonald. I wanted you to know that."

"Is Jackie all right?"

"Jackie?" His face was blank for a second. "Elliot?"

"Aye, I wasn't sure about him. Didn't know if he made it."

"Yes, fine, he's fine. A group of new recruits came this morning. He's been attached to them for now, a mentor."

"Lucky them," he said wryly.

"We're running out of old hands, we need you back. Perhaps you'll get some home leave out of this, when you're better."

Back with Dusty, Iain thought, the idea was appealing. "That would be good."

"They're shipping you out tomorrow, not Blighty I'm afraid, some hospital in the French countryside to convalesce. Better than here." Peterson looked askance at the bleeding, groaning patients. "Less dying going on."

* * * *

As Peterson anticipated, the following day Iain travelled by ambulance through the lush late summer countryside towards the coast, away from the front line, war and death. He shared the ride with a corporal who had lost a leg and a private with a shell wound to his back. They arrived at a large château after noon, a pale pink building as if many rainstorms had washed out the colour, with open shutters and a porch over the weathered front door. The rambling gardens were neglected, overrun with wild flowers and seeding grass.

The orderlies were German prisoners and volunteers, two British, the remainder French and Belgian. The hospital accepted whatever help was available to them.

Because Iain was mobile an orderly took him up the grand sweeping staircase, which once might have been for family use only, along a narrow corridor to a small bedroom. A maid's room, Iain thought, possibly even a kitchen maid and a housemaid. He pushed open the shutters to view the garden and beyond, the equally neglected vineyard stretching across the hill.

His room had an air of gentle dignified decay. Cracks road-mapped the pale plastered walls, a plain jug and bowl rimmed with blue stood on the washstand. Clean towels hung over a wooden rail. He touched the crisp starched white linen on the metal bed that squeaked under his weight. There was peace here, soothing and calm. He laid his head on the plump white pillow that smelled of lavender. From the bed he could see out of the window across the valley and the beauty of the place filled him with deep sorrow. His tears were heavy in his throat.

Depression was not unknown to him, and yet he had rarely felt such deep, dark loneliness. He was humbled by his experiences, by his own survival. He was an irrelevant statistic compared to those who had gone. Nobody here knew him, understood him, cared for him. So many men had been lost who had wives and children, parents, siblings. He lived and yet his survival altered nobody's life, left no impact on anything. He closed his eyes for a second and sleep took him immediately.

A few days later he rested on the veranda. A chess set, in disarray from a previous game, littered the table in front of him. A French soldier, his leg in a plaster cast, wheeled himself over. He was a similar age to Iain. He spoke at length and Iain shrugged his shoulders. "Je ne comprend pas. I don't understand."

The Frenchman rearranged the pieces on the chessboard and indicated for Iain to play. He had never played the game, but the Frenchman was determined and showed him the basic moves. Their conversation was stilted, a mixture of Pidgin English and French, resorting to mime, hand gestures, eventually turning to laughter and jokes they had no hope of sharing.

Lying in his room later, watching the sky darken and listening to the far distant boom of guns, he thought about Helena. A worried letter from her had been re-directed from the hospital at the front. He thought he should end his correspondence with her. She had a husband, a farm, a child, a life, and what she chose to do with it was her concern. He had messed about with other people's lives long enough and where had it got him? He knew it was time to let her go but, for all his good intentions, he found he couldn't do it. She was an essential lifeline and to lose touch would be to cut himself adrift from his only anchor. Part of him hoped his being alive affected her in some way, because her presence in his life had become so necessary to him.

He lit the lamp by his bed, took off his sling and started a letter to Dusty. His shoulder pained him as he wrote. He kept it short and wrote a few lines to Nell too, tore them up, wrote them again. Nothing he could write was acceptable. He didn't even know what he was trying to say. His head ached, his shoulder throbbed and he wanted nothing more than to go home.

When he woke the next morning he gazed out of his small window, the sun split the sky and the swallows were preparing to fly south, clustering together discussing their route. He received a letter from Dusty saying he was recovering well and thought he would be returning to the front within two months.

Iain bounded down the stairs in a buoyant mood. He collided with one of the nurses and she dropped her neatly folded clean sheets. He helped pick them up, apologising, laughing. He replaced the last sheet and the nurse rebuked him softly in Belgian.

His French chess-playing friend was writing a letter in the day room. It would be to his chic mademoiselle in Paris whose photograph he had proudly shown off.

Iain wandered into the sunshine, to the back of the château. Without thinking he strolled across the gardens, through tall sweet scented fronds of aniseed fennel, timothy grass brushing his calves and self seeded orange poppies that lived and died all in a day. He climbed the hill to the vineyard.

It wasn't over, nothing was finished. He might return to the war and he might die, but he would be remembered. Joe was his son. His blood ran through Joe's veins. Nell would never forget and one day she would tell his son. If it all ended tomorrow there would always be Joe.

He meandered slowly between the vines, the grapes hung heavily, rotting in places attracting wasps and bees that hummed drunkenly round the fruit. He kicked up the dry dust, little brown clouds at his feet coating his shoes. He lay down in the heat of the sun, warm dry earth, solid and dependable underneath him. He closed his eyes, bathing in the blissful sensation of being alive. Dust and sun and acres of blue sky, alive, alive, alive.

Chapter Twenty-seven

Iain was back where he started. The mud was as thick, just as cold, wetting and brown; the reek of rotten meat and sewage just as strong and sickening. The boards he lay on at night with a number of complete strangers in the darkness of the dugout were as cold and uncomfortable. The lice invading his body were equally excruciating, itchy and dementing. The shelling continued undiminished often all night and all day. Shelling was like rain, he decided, it passed. He told himself he could get used to anything in time. But shelling was nothing like rain and he would never get used to any of this.

He was reunited with Jackie Elliot who received him with delight. "My God," Jackie said, "you're looking fit. If that's what being hit by a bullet does for you, I can't wait."

Three weeks at the château had bolstered him, given him the courage to face all this again. It was like a mirage now. All too briefly it had reminded him there was joy to be found in what had increasingly appeared to be a useless ghastly existence. While there was no sense in the death of his friends, in the suffering of Michael or the poor burned boy at the hospital, he had pushed away the guilt of the survivor. He lived and he would not be sorry for it or question it. Now he was back and he wondered how long he would remain. Perhaps there was no future for him beyond the wire and the trench and the guns.

He traversed no-man's-land alone, refusing a spotter to replace Dusty. The solitude suited him, gave him time to think. Without a spotter as witness there was no longer a tally, any kills went unverified. The death of a German was its own reward, Iain thought blackly. He could not think of them being flesh and blood like him or he would not have been able to do it. He had to concentrate on what the enemy had done to his friends, think of them as beyond human. His aim was not so sure now he had the shakes and many escaped his bullet.

Since leaving the château he thought a great deal about Helena, in fact, he thought of little else. He went over every moment they had spent together. There was no great passion there, he decided, although there was some deep abiding affection between them, something that would last so much longer than the lust he had

had with Joanna. He reconciled himself to the idea that, although he might have a special bond with her, she was married and it was something he must accept.

Now sitting on the fire-step he clutched his Lee Enfield rifle to his chest, a roll-up smoking between his fingers, puttees caked with mud, shaking as the shells flew over, the air solid with screaming metal. The British guns answered the German's ferociously and he braced himself against the vibrations that shook the earth.

Jackie appeared at the dugout door, the water at his feet rippling with the pulsation of the ground. Tea was served, thick, and sweet as toffee. Dryden, a loud Yorkshireman, opened tins of Maconochie's stew for their supper, no hot meal today.

The shelling petered out along with the daylight until only the occasional sharp aim of sniper fire came tearing over the trench. Jackie and his new best mate Jessop played sevens in the corner of the dugout with a damp set of cards. Dryden tracked lice eggs in the seams of his dirty shirt with only his tunic on. Plenty of new faces shared the trench, Danny Mason, John Bracken, Diddy Dimchurch.

Iain sloshed through the water, aimed his scoped rifle at a loophole waiting for a careless head to appear over the parapet. He missed Dusty desperately now he was back in the front line. Dusty thought he would be returning once he had been passed as fit by the medical board. Iain hoped he would, knowing how selfish that was but unable to help himself. The hours passed, punctuated only by the occasional bullet fired from his rifle. He was bone tired and aching after two hours, with one hit, unrecorded. He waded back to the dugout despondently.

He was removing the scope when Lieutenant Peterson appeared in the gloom of the doorway, bending over to gain entry. He eyed the company, saw Iain and, sitting beside him, said, "How's it going Macdonald? Hard to come back here I bet." Iain thought he appeared older, the excitement and animation that marked him apart from other officers had abandoned him.

"Aye, it is, especially without the old faces, that's the tough part."

Peterson bit at his bottom lip regretfully. "Yes, it's hard to believe they're gone. That was an awful night," then quietly, almost to himself, "so many awful, awful nights."

Iain still didn't trust the man. "You after something?" he asked.

Peterson's laugh was forced. "You always were a quick one – never took anyone at face value – good for you – best way to be." Iain said nothing, he didn't know if Peterson were being serious. Eventually the lieutenant spoke again, "Yes, I did come to speak to you about something. Come with me, back to my dugout."

He reluctantly followed Peterson into the rain, the water sluiced around their ankles. They pushed past the gas curtain into the officers' dugout. There were three truckle beds, two chairs, pictures curled on the damp walls in a laughable attempt to make it homely. Peterson poured two glasses of whisky and handed one to Iain.

"There is a village to the east of here," Peterson said. "Haven't quite managed to capture it back from the Bosche. I have orders to take a group of men. Sharp shooters, with a bit of experience, take them by surprise and regain it, or stir them up anyhow. There is only one gun placement. We need to secure it. So what do you say?"

He sighed taking a slug of whisky. "How many of us?"

"At least forty I'd say. You deserve a bit of recognition for the way you got Dusty out, Macdonald. You've been overlooked but you've not gone unnoticed by the captain, higher than that even. If you agree to be my second in this you're promoted at once and you'll be on the first ship home to Blighty for training. No more front line either if you didn't want it. You'd be passing on your skills. You wouldn't turn that down would you? The men look up to you. You're a natural, some men demand respect, some are like you and are respected regardless. I envy you that. You're a good soldier, Macdonald. A man like you could get a commission."

Iain glanced at him, offered one of his cigarettes. He struck a match, the flame briefly illuminated their faces. "I'm not interested in a commission. I don't want to be responsible for the lives of these men - any men." That was true, but to be out of the front line was beyond tempting. "I want to keep my head down and get away with it still attached to my shoulders."

Peterson puffed a smoke ring into the air, it hovered for a second before dissipating. "They'll die or live under someone else's leadership. With or without you these things happen. I didn't take you as a man so easily afraid."

It was Iain's turn to laugh. He knew Peterson was trying to rile him, force his hand. "Ach, well, sorry to disappoint you, sir." Peterson's batman, Private Johnson, hovered in the doorway. Peterson ignored him.

"There's talk of a treaty, an armistice. I think we'll all be on our way home soon. If not, this will guarantee you survive what's left of the fighting. This might be your last chance at glory, man."

He glared at Peterson in disgust. "There is no fucking glory in war." He had been riled, although not in the way Peterson had expected. "If you don't see that after all this time, then I feel sorry for you. Where is the glory for the poor bastards lying out there with lungs full of mud, for Michael with his insides laid out on his tunic, for the poor lads burned by the flame throwers? Don't speak to me of glory – Christ." He pitched forward leaning his chin on his hand, annoyed for preaching to the lieutenant who knew full well the horrors.

Peterson shrugged, totally unconcerned for Iain's impropriety. "So will you be my second in command on this mission or not?" he said, his tone bright.

Iain stared at the dirt wall, tracing the channels of earth, intermittently spattered with stones. "Aye." He was defeated, and had been for a long time.

"Good man, you'll be going home soon." Peterson patted him on the back, satisfied. "Fetch your stuff." He clicked his fingers at Johnson who still hung about the doorway. "Johnson, be a good chap and help Macdonald. You can kip in here, Lance Corporal. You're on your way up. It's a sight more comfortable."

Iain's eyes passed over the muddy hole, his gaze coming to rest on the bed. It was a damp dismal place, nonetheless a better hole than the one he had left.

* * * *

Iain dreamed. Sprinting, feet beating off the soft peaty ground, dodging the trees. He wanted to get as far from Finnigan as possible, far away from Glenleven, the laird, everything. He thought his heart might burst from his chest. He stopped, leaned over, hands on knees trying to catch his breath and the thoughts wheeling in his head. He knew Finnigan wasn't far behind him. He ran again, arms rocking in time to the rhythm of his legs, forcing him on, jumping over fallen trees, tearing through the bramble that ripped at his legs, flattening the bracken.

He stopped sharply at the boggy river edge, crouching down. The river fell over the rocks, burbling across the shale. He searched the length of it as far as he could see, memories tumbling through him like the water along the banks.

Inert, mesmerised by the swirl and eddy of the river every one of Finnigan's beatings, punishments, tirades and belittlements flooded his consciousness. He would leave and never come back. He could be his own man and escape the tyranny of Finnigan and the condescension of Bruce Sinclair, have his own place, a decent life, where nobody knew him and he could hold his head up without shame.

He was so engrossed in the vision of his new life he did not hear Finnigan approach. Suddenly aware of the presence of another, he twisted round, rising to his feet. Finnigan still held the knife, knees bent, legs apart, weaving the blade in patterns in front of his face.

"Come to me, boy."

"Piss off, Finnigan, leave me alone."

"Frightened?"

"Of you? An old drunk? I'll never be frightened of you again. You're a warped old bastard."

A crack of laughter preceded his words. "A bastard? That's rich, coming from you. My Da was Tommy Finnigan, me Ma was Milly – I knew them, not like you, with your whoring mother who couldn't get rid of you quick enough."

"I'm not responsible for how I came to be. Let's call it a day, Finnigan, you've had your fun for tonight," he said.

"And me having to put up with you all these years, a cocky little brat of a boy, a millstone round me neck." He threw the knife in the air and caught it again by the handle as if to prove his sobriety and dexterity. Smiling he said, "Time for the millstone to sink."

"I'm not so little any more. It'll be harder than that, so why don't you forget it, go home and finish your wee dram and I'll be on my way."

"I don't think so."

It was hard to say who made the first move. They fell on each other like two dogs in a pit and the knife flashed in Iain's face, too close for comfort. They rolled over and over on the bank, first Iain getting the upper hand, then Finnigan. Iain landed a punch and Finnigan lunged with the blade. Iain caught his arm. The fight was on for his life. Murder shone in Finnigan's eyes. He would not stop until Iain was dead, it was what he had wanted for years and he meant to accomplish it this night.

Iain and Finnigan, face to face, a battle of strength and wills as the blade came closer and closer to Iain's nose. Just when he thought himself lost, he brought his knee up into Finnigan's groin and he fell. Iain grabbed at the knife and they plunged into the water, scrambling in the icy river to gain a foothold. Iain attacked while he had the advantage and they disappeared underwater.

Finnigan had lost his knife by the time he surfaced. Bellowing, he pulled Iain under, held him by the throat, his head submerged. Iain spluttered and choked, icy water pressed into his ears, up his nose. He pushed his feet against the soft shale riverbed and knocked Finnigan over. He punched the older man in the side of the head, positioned his knee on his neck, thrusting him into the water.

Iain stumbled towards the shore, dragged himself out of the river coughing and spluttering. Finnigan was behind him and Iain delivered a final exhausted uppercut to his jaw. Finnigan keeled back into the shallows, emitting a mighty groan as the water splashed out around his form.

Iain watched the rise and fall of Finnigan's chest, breathing raggedly, semi-conscious and he knew he had to make a decision. He could walk away, let it lie or he could end it now as Finnigan had intended. At that second, he knew hate. It was senseless, blind, deaf and mute. It consumed him like flames. He hauled the large man by his sodden clothes and roughly rolled him onto his front. Now face down in the shallows, Iain pushed Finnigan's head into the gravelled bottom with his foot.

He stumbled out of the water and waited on the bank. Blood trickled in a rivulet from Finnigan's head, carried away by the flow of the river. Iain watched, hands hanging by his sides, unmoving. His terror melted away, any measure of emotion drained from him, he was numb, uninvolved.

Finnigan was drowning, unconscious breaths dragged icy water into his lungs. Iain watched. He waited to feel something, anything - sorrow, pain, elation. He felt nothing. Still he waited, a mere spectator, without the power to act.

In his dreams he pulled Finnigan from the brink of drowning one hundred times, pressed the water out of his soaked lungs until he choked and retched. But that's not what happened. Iain turned away from the river, away from the big man, and he did not look back.

* * * *

Under cover of darkness the posse Peterson had gathered made their way up to the village. It had sustained heavy bombing for days with the aim of weakening their defences for the surprise attack. Few buildings remained intact. The hillside location gave the Germans the advantage and the British were eager to gain control of the gun placement which had a good view across the British held valley.

Fifty men moved as one up the hillside, blacked up faces, loaded with grenade and bandoliers of ammunition. Iain's trepidation had evaporated and he was feeling invincible, life or death suddenly was such a small matter. It was not a depression influencing his mood, quite the opposite. He was gripped by a ludicrous optimism, fate had dealt its hand and he had to make the best of it. Their orders were to ascertain the lay of the land and not to act rashly. If they considered the German position too strong they would retreat, if an opportunity presented itself, they would act.

When Peterson discussed his orders with Iain, he recognised the lieutenant had no intention of backing out. Peterson saw it as a personal challenge. They were taking the gun placement come what may.

It was a chill night and the rain fell steadily. They saw this as a good sign, sentries were always less observant in bad weather, it was human nature.

Peterson and Iain stayed together at the head of the group. They skirted the village. The church steeple loomed tall above the lower floors of a house, probably with a good cellar. The rest of the village had been reduced to piles of rubble. The earth, pitted and cratered, filled with rainwater.

Moving low to the ground Peterson ordered his men to wait while he and Iain investigated further. They approached the centre of the village, now hard to recognise as such. Peterson whispered, "What d'you reckon?"

Iain put a finger to his lips. The sound of German voices raised in song drifted on the wind. "Church." He pointed towards the steeple. Two sentries looked across the valley, sheltered by the rubble of the wall. Iain slung his rifle over his shoulder, removed a knife from his webbing. Peterson swapped his pistol for a short blade. They glanced at each other, a small nod passed between them. They attacked the sentries from behind, the sharp metal doing its work swiftly and without sound. Edging along the piles of rubble, they past a standing wall, heading towards the church. Another pair of sentries met an equally swift end.

Iain pointed to the highest ground behind the church, the gun placement. A group of men were below the steeple, out of sight. He could hear them singing and talking.

"I'll go back." Peterson's voice was less than a whisper. "You stay." Iain nodded, gave him the thumbs up. Back tight against the steeple, he watched Peterson disappear into the dark. Glancing to his right he saw unburied German corpses piled up, twisted and grotesque, stacked like logs and as lifeless. Below him, in the church vault, they ate supper singing their patriotic songs while the bodies of their comrades awaited burial. It wasn't only the British who had grown so unsentimental about their dead.

He cleaned the knife blade on his tunic before replacing it in the webbing. His hands were sticky with blood, he wiped it off as best he could against the wetness of his rain-soaked leg. He grasped his rifle, happier with it in his hands. The shadows of Peterson and the men moved up behind the piles of bricks and mortar.

Iain heard the sharp sound of the German soldier's boots as they trotted up the steps from the crypt, their backs to him. They turned round simultaneously, astonishment etching their faces into caricatures. He lunged forward with his bayonet, skewering one, the second soldier ran, impaled on another British bayonet.

They jogged up hill, the time for silence was over. "Fire, fire," Peterson commanded. They fired with their men grouped either side of them, releasing a staccato barrage at the gun placement. All at once the air was alive with ricocheting bullets. With nowhere to run other than forward, Iain kept going, head down, releasing round after round, reloading. The German soldiers scattered, stunned, they had been unaware of the threat of attack. Judging by their appearance, he wondered if they had given up caring. They were all bearded with tattered, filthy uniforms. They collapsed under the gunfire and he registered no surprise when the men at either side of him fell too. He continued to run doggedly and the German voices of surrender carried through the air from all sides.

"Kamerad, kamerad," they called, arms raised, stepping forward out of the shadow of the night, worn tired faces glad to be caught, desperate for it to be over.

At the cost of six of their own, they had killed about fifty men and captured roughly the same, marching them down the hill under guard.

He and Peterson went down the crypt steps. Lamps burned brightly and a fire crackled in a makeshift grate, the smoke spiralling through the ceiling to the roofless altar. Peterson uncorked a bottle of brandy, sniffed it and took a swig. "Hey, Macdonald, here, good French stuff, this'll warm you up."

Iain drank deeply from the bottle, the liquid searing a path to his stomach, drinking some more. Peterson watched him approvingly. Iain laughed. "That was –"

"Damn good, don't you think?" Peterson interrupted. "Glad you came now?"

He took another gulp, handed it back. "Aye, sir, we're going to win."

"Too right, sir, we're going to win," Peterson rejoined, and from nowhere an explosion of unimaginable volume shook the hill. The muffled roar sluiced through Iain's brain, shaking him to the floor where he sprawled, quaking. It rumbled through the crypt and everything moved around them, shifting walls and floor and ceiling. A moment of deathly silence stilled the air. Sudden chaos, rushing and crashing, blocks of stone, rubble and rock, the mighty collapse of the steeple caving in above them.

Iain covered his head. The oxygen was sucked from his lungs. His eyes and nose filled with dust and debris. He remained conscious but didn't move for a long time.

* * * *

Gingerly he wriggled his legs. It surprised him that he could do so freely. He opened his eyes, sore and gritty, his vision blurred. Peterson was gone, rubble and dust. He glimpsed the floor above him. It was intact. To his left a vast open space gaped and the rain pattered down on remnants of fallen steeple.

"Lieutenant." His voice echoed back to him eerily. He shouted louder, "Peterson, Peterson." He rose shakily, thick dust clogging his airways. He scrambled up the rubble on all fours, out into the open. Taking great gulps of wet air he saw the gun placement had gone, the side of the hill had been blown away. He limped towards the crater. There was nothing left, none of their men, no gun, nothing.

They had surrendered too easily, he realised. They had put up a fight long enough to booby trap the gun placement. Peterson had not checked and neither had he. He sank to his knees, forty men gone. Fifty Jerries saved and forty of their own gone - all for Peterson's foolish escapade and to bolster his egotistical mania. How futile, how foolish. Their orders were to suss the area out, not march in with all guns blazing, heroes of the hour. Peterson had been determined to have what he termed as his moment of glory, and this was all they had achieved, death and destruction. He laughed, Peterson had his glory now and Iain raised his face up to the black sky. The rain wetted his dust-coated skin and he laughed at himself, at Peterson, at the whole ridiculous war. He knelt there until dawn lit the sky, when a British platoon arrived to take command.

* * * *

Four days later Iain drank coffee in the village café. He refused all offers of company and was seated alone at a table while the noise and cheer rang around him. The bell above the door jangled as it opened, Iain did not look up. Dusty took the seat opposite him and offered a Woodbine from his packet.

"How goes it?" he said, as if he had never been away.

Iain took the cigarette, lit it. "You know, Dusty." Words could not express how it went. He grinned at his friend, a lump rising in his throat.

"They're saying it's over," Dusty said. "Imagine my luck, getting back in time for the party."

"Aye? They're saying it. They've been saying it for a while now and the bullets are still flying and we're still dropping in the mud aren't we?"

"Some bloke out there in the street on his horse, riding up and down shouting like a lunatic about it." He turned to the merry revellers playing poker, drinking their spiked coffee at the table behind him. "Hey, you lot," he shouted. There was a lull as they turned their attention on him. "They're saying it's over, finished."

"Who says?" – "You're joking, right?" – "More bloody nonsense." – "Bugger off."

He jerked his head towards the door. "Come out, Midge, come see." Iain pulled himself to his feet. Sure enough, there was a lot of shouting going on, lorries and wagons stopping in the street. The usual business appeared to have halted.

Dusty lay an arm across Iain's shoulders, Iain did likewise and, side by side, they grinned at each other like fools. "We'll get really, really pissed what d'you say?" Dusty said.

"Aye." He smiled at his friend close to. "It's good to see you, pal, really. Are you legally wed yet?"

He shook his head. "I couldn't, not without my best man. Besides, I'm not that easy."

Iain was sceptical. "That's not what I heard."

"You must have been nice to somebody. It came to my ears you're off to receive a commission or training post or some bollocks."

"Aye, just my luck. About to get the batman and everything – you'd have had to call me sir. Don't think I'll bother with it all now, I might go home instead."

They stared at each other, unable to stop smiling. "You'd have been a right pain in the ass – your head's swelling just thinking about it. Come on," Dusty said and laughed, "let's get that drink."

Part IV

Peace

*And here's a hand my trusty friend, And put your hand in mine.
We'll take a right good willie-waught, For auld lang syne.*

*And surely you'll lift up your glass, For surely I'll lift mine,
And we'll drink a cup of kindness yet, For auld lang syne.*

Auld Lang Syne – Robert Burns

Chapter Twenty-eight

It was fitting that Dusty accompanied Iain on the last boat trip home. They had had three months to digest the good news – peace at last. In the first week of March, they performed their final duty with the army and marched their last parade. It was the end, but also a beginning when they could scrape together what was left of their fragmented lives and look to the future.

They reported to the dispersal station, received their ration books, twenty-eight days pay, and claimed their cheap civvie suits. Dusty got an additional pound for his army greatcoat. Iain decided his might see more service yet.

Civilians once more, on a wet afternoon, they arrived at Charing Cross. They abandoned the dismal grey streets and took refuge in the familiar bar of the Crown and Anchor. The barman sent his boy haring down the street to fetch Dusty's mother and before teatime his whole family had arrived. Iain was unquestionably included in their raucous celebrations. In the warmly lit smoky bar they held an impromptu party with more customers than the publican had seen for six months.

Celia joined them straight from work and threw herself squealing at Dusty. They laughed at her enthusiasm, unperturbed by the gathered company, kissing him so hard he fell off his stool.

"Let's drink a toast," Mr Miller said. "To our boys and peace." Everyone cheered loudly, clinking glasses, a momentary lull as everyone took a gulp.

"Another toast," Dusty said, and the room fell silent in his pause. "To all the lads who never saw peace and won't be coming home." A hush fell over them. A few tears were shed. Then he added, "Right, enough of that, get the drinks in." They managed a little cheer as everyone recovered and rushed to the bar.

Pearl hung attentively at Iain's elbow, but he was on a mission to get drunk. She soon forgot about trying to win his attention and knocked back the gin, gaining the interest of another man fresh from France who had gate crashed the party.

After a lengthy lock-in, the party broke up at midnight and they stumbled back to Dusty's parents' house. Iain had one arm round Dusty who encircled Celia, and his other held up Mrs Miller who wept joy and gin.

Iain woke the next morning draped over the sofa in the front room, one leg hanging over the end and an arm dangling numbly to the floor. He sat up slowly, his back aching. Mr Miller was slumped in the chair asleep. The young ex-soldier who had made amorous advances to Pearl the previous evening snored quietly in the other chair.

Mrs Miller bustled noisily in the kitchen, banging the teapot and humming tunelessly in an effort to wake everybody and be rid of any extra unwanted houseguests.

Iain dragged himself to the bathroom and washed his face. In the hall he stumbled into Celia, sleepy and dressed in her petticoat coming out of the room Iain and Dusty had shared while on leave.

She smiled drowsily when she saw him. "Morning, lovely," she said and strolled down the stairs to use the privy, yawning.

He stuck his head round the door. Dusty was stretched out on his stomach snoring.

"Eh, up, Dusty, rise and shine, you're a free man. It's a new day." Then approaching the bed, close up to his ear he said rather loudly, "TIME TO FIND A JOB, PAL."

Dusty jumped up, bleary eyed, swearing. "Jesus Christ, I wish you wouldn't do that you Scottish git."

He leaned against the doorframe and pulled out a cigarette, offered one to Dusty. "You have a good night?"

He took the cigarette, waited for Iain to light it, then laughed, remembering. "Oh, yeah, right, Celia's here isn't she?"

"I'd say she is, aye." He laughed. "Looks as if you'll have to get wed now."

"Wasn't up to much last night, I can tell you," he said. "Where's she gone? I'm well up for it this morning." A wide cheeky grin stretched his face.

"She's done a runner, probably knew what was coming. Come on, your mam's making tea, she'll be shouting on us in a mo'."

After evicting Pearl's new friend Mrs Miller provided breakfast for her family and guests.

"I'd better be on my way today," Iain said. Pearl was too hung over to protest. The rest of the family chorused their disapproval.

"What's the rush?" Dusty said. "We've not spent all our severance pay yet."

"I know, pal. I've got an employer waiting, haven't I?"

"Yeah, and what else?" Dusty goaded.

"You know fine there's nothing else." Iain knew what he meant.

Later, when they were alone, Dusty broached the topic again. "What are you going to do about your son and Helena?"

"What can I do? She's married and we are friends despite what your dirty mind makes of it."

Dusty grinned. "I don't make anything of it, but when you talk about her – well…"

"Well, what? What about when I talk about her? You make me sound as if I'm a mooning idiot."

"No, not that bad. Still, plenty more fish in the sea, eh?"

He rolled his eyes. "I'm not interested in fish – and before you say anything, I'll do all right on my own – I need to get my life back in order don't I."

"Yeah, me too, I've got a wedding to arrange, a house to find and I suppose a job wouldn't go amiss either," Dusty said.

"Well, if there's a job to be had, you're in the right place and let's face it you know everyone. You're related to most of them. Come on I've got to get my stuff together."

* * * *

After an uneventful train journey Iain arrived at Mr Pettersmith's station. The sprite little man himself came hurrying out to greet him.

"Well, Mr Macdonald, welcome home, back to Harrowmead is it?"

"Aye. It's good to be here." An uninviting arctic wind whistled across the platform. It was as tidy as ever, minus the carefully planted pots he remembered from his journey with Nell. The station sign creaked, swinging in the wind, a lonely sound.

"So many lost, so many not coming back, such a pity. Mr Yeates two eldest boys gone, one of the Potter boys too. I could make a list." Mr Pettersmith shuffled alongside him giving a running commentary of his views on the war.

Iain didn't listen. He didn't want anyone's views and he didn't want to hear a roll call of the dead. Instead he absorbed the familiar, suddenly so vivid because of his absence from them.

He bid the stationmaster good day while the man was still talking and strolled up the road. Cawing rooks arranged their untidy twiggy nests high in the elms against a silken grey sky. Watching them, an image of Michael came to him bleeding and begging for mercy. He closed his mind to it. Go away, he thought. He felt strangely emotional listening to their sad call. They had been oblivious to the passing years and the death and violence they had wrought.

He walked on, his bag over his shoulder, cutting through the trees onto Harrowmead land. The gate that once would have barred his way, hung open swinging loosely in the wind. This path was worn, obviously now a well-trodden thoroughfare for the villagers. His return would hit them hard, no doubt reminding them of old resentments. Perhaps he would be more lenient, he certainly felt less passion for his old job. War was a great leveller, what might have riled him once now was less significant.

He arrived at the edge of the Common, his eyes briefly scanned the trees to the rise where the gorse grew and Tom's body mouldered. At the river he followed the banks for a stretch, its gentle gurgle calming his ragged nerves. The wind was icy and snow blew in the air. He thought how cold it would be today in the trenches and lifted the collar of his army greatcoat over his ears.

The gate to Keeper's House was closed, with a gentle push it swung open on quiet hinges. The path was clear of debris and the door opened smoothly. The interior had the chilly dampness of a house long empty. Everything was the same, what did he expect? So much had happened to him, almost four years gone and here time had stopped.

The first thing he noticed was the clock, silent and still. He automatically reached for the key and wound it, setting the time with his index finger. He opened the clock case and pushed the pendulum into motion, its companionable ticking a whisper of returning life.

The range was empty and cold, the oven door half open. If Helena came here there was no sign of her. His footfall resonated in the enclosed stairwell, echoing up through the rooms. His bed was as he had left it, a bare mattress, one blanket folded on the end, the pillows piled up. She had been here, of course, because she had found his letter and written to him.

He went to the window with the familiar perspective across the bare canopy of branches and twigs. He placed his bag on the bed, emptied out his clothes, letters, his journal which Dusty called Iain's 'pissed off prose'.

Back downstairs he went to the woodshed, carried in fuel and lit the range. Once it was well stoked he reached for his coat and headed out into the cold to see Isaac and Delilah.

* * * *

Across the valley Nell pulled her aching feet out of her boots; her chilblains pained her. Lisa read to Joe at the kitchen table. To an outsider, unaware of the strange undercurrents that eddied within the house, the scene would have been one of happy family accord. The relationship between the two women was no longer the easy, friendly one it had been. Lisa spent her time ingratiating herself, through guilt and shame. Nell treated her with civil courtesy and nothing more. She didn't want Freddy but could not quite forgive their blatant affair in front of her nose, and it didn't prevent his occasional unprovoked abuse. Secretly she wondered if Lisa could not have tried to influence him. She had witnessed his small sadisms countless times. She was certainly aware he had hit Nell, forever mindful to spare her face.

Lisa was in love with Freddy. A small part of her worried that if Nell did not receive the brunt of his anger, then she might. She could not fathom their marriage. Occasionally they were almost fond of each other. Mostly their interaction was frightening to watch. So Nell and Lisa viewed each other with a certain suspicion, both wishing something to change but not quite sure how to manage it.

Nell held her hands out to the fire in an attempt to restore circulation, listening to Lisa's monotonous voice failing to breathe life into the story of Hansel and Gretel. Staring into the flames she thought of Iain. When he wrote to tell her of his injury she hoped his war would be over and was devastated to hear he was going back into it all. She had not heard from him now for three weeks. His last letter told her he was to be demobilised within the month, so she had not written in the hope he was on his way home.

"Do you want a cup of tea, you look frozen?" Lisa said.

Her civility grated on Nell, she nodded, not taking her eyes from the flames. Joe climbed onto her lap, cuddled into her. She held his small body, rubbing his back absently with one hand. Freddy and his father were due back for their dinner at any time and Lisa laid the table for them.

Before Christmas Freddy spent three weeks at the psychiatric hospital in town as a voluntary patient. His headaches became so bad and the voices in his head so persistent that Nell was increasingly fearful. She told Mr Hart to call the doctor and seeing the threat Freddy posed, he agreed. Since the various therapies and stronger medication Freddy had been calmer and she had enjoyed a couple of months without the constant threat of his aggression.

"Come on, Joe, I have to go check on Grandma," she said wearily. "I'll get the tea when I come down."

Lisa smiled sweetly. "Right-i-o, Nell." She persisted in her refusal to wait on old Mrs Hart whose health had deteriorated so rapidly this winter.

Nell climbed the stairs, Joe at her heels, holding a tray set with the invalid's dinner.

"Hello, Mother," Nell said. "I've got your dinner here. Let's sort you out first." She plumped up Mrs Hart's pillows, hauled her bodily up the bed and smoothed the covers before putting the tray down. "I'll empty the pan." She took the bedpan to the outside privy, her feet rubbing in her boots. Back upstairs she encouraged Mrs Hart to eat. Lately her appetite had been poor. Nell talked about the village and any gossip she had heard.

"You're a good girl, Nell." Her cough rattled. "Nobody else bothers with me. And that Freddy, I know he doesn't treat you well." This was not the first time Nell had heard this.

"Don't worry yourself, Mother. Everything is fine with me and Freddy." An often repeated lie, said without thought.

"Where's Joe?"

"He's in his room. Joe," she called. The little boy peered round the door. "Come and see Grandma." He raced in and dived on the bed enthusiastically and Mrs Hart laughed which started her coughing again. A brief hug and he slithered off the bed, bored with the affection, and hopped out of the room on one leg.

"He's a fine boy, so handsome. I remember when Tom and Freddy were that age, seems only yesterday, always being naughty. Joe is such a good boy," Mrs Hart said.

It was true, Nell thought, his adventurous spirit had vanished. He had become a nervous, insecure child, which was hardly surprising, being raised in this household. Freddy made the boy jumpy with his loud voice and abrupt manner, he had no time for him. Although he had never accused her since, she knew he still viewed Joe as the result of an affair with Iain. The very idea was laughable.

She looked out of the window at the stark wintry landscape, the snow dancing against the glass. Freddy had loosed the old horse for the evening, laying a blanket across its back, and was striding across the home paddock. From here he appeared to be the same young man who had wooed her, when she thought he loved her, before reality destroyed the dream. She wondered how different he might have been if he had not been injured during the war or if it were a coincidence and this was his true disturbed personality. He glanced up and saw her at the window, he didn't smile or raise his hand, his scowl deepened and she turned away from him. She no longer cared how he saw her or how he felt. She told herself she didn't hate him although she could find no other word to describe the black emotion he evoked in her.

Darkness was falling and she lit the lamp. "Freddy's coming for his meal, I'd best go down," she said, eager to escape the sour smell of the room and Mrs Hart's enquiring gaze, her breath wheezing in failing lungs. Descending the stairs, she heard Lisa laughing with Freddy. If she went into the kitchen now she would probably catch them in an embrace or him planting a kiss on her neck. She perched on the stairs, suspended in limbo, waiting. But for what? She could not say. Everyone's life went on around her, despite her almost. She could hear Joe playing, Mrs Hart coughing, the bang of the door and Mr Hart's feet stamping on the mat as he came in and the low intimate voices of Freddy and his lover, the maid. She felt so absurdly sorry for herself that an involuntary hiccup of laughter escaped her.

I am a fool, this is my house, she thought. She thumped down the remaining stairs to warn them of her approach and took her place at the table, as Mr Hart was about to say prayers. Freddy glanced at her. She smiled brilliantly at him and refused to bend her head for grace.

* * * *

Freddy glowered at his reflection, meeting his own dark gaze. Standing back, sucking in his breath, he studied himself side on. His mirrored self scowled back. He admitted his reflection resembled him, but he did not feel much like Freddy Hart.

He had received electric therapy, injections, tablets and the doctor had talked, encouraged him to talk. He had big gaps in his memory, empty spaces before the hospital and during his treatment there. When he first arrived home from the psychiatric hospital for Christmas he was at peace, blank, like a piece of paper ready to be written on, a second chance. He was devoid of worries, hopes, dreams or imaginings and best of all no voices. He was gloriously numb filled with interminable, uninterrupted peace.

During this quiet content, he felt positive and able to plan for the future. Occasionally that old black anger passed like a cloud across the sun. He recognised it, dark and vile, powerless to resist. When he was well he had some control over this. As time passed he began slipping back.

Gradually snatches of the past returned, small worries filtered through the drug-induced bliss, prodding at him, thoughts creeping unasked into his mind.

His nights became dream filled once more. His body grew accustomed to the strong drugs and occasionally he forgot to take them despite Nell putting them out for him on the dresser. The worries became pressing, the thoughts louder until they spoke to him. Sometimes the voices whispered, more often they shouted and all the noise in the world could not drown them out.

Before France he never suffered from headaches. Now a day barely passed when he did not have pain in his head. It varied, sometimes mild, occasionally agonising, making it impossible to get out of bed. The shades of pain in between gave him vertigo, spinning his world and inducing vomit.

This morning when he woke up he heard the voices again, returning like a lost friend. They spoke to him of Nell, the child and his need to punish them. He had no proof, beyond the adamant ravings in his own head, and it rankled. He wanted her confession. He disciplined her on occasion and yet she said nothing. And now, even when he was lucid and the voices were silenced, he still could not bring himself to make amends with her. He was sure, at some point, he had told her about Tom. He would catch her looking at him and he could not fathom her thoughts, but he imagined she thought the worst of him. Lisa, on the other hand, was such an ineffectual little thing, a simple soul who knew how to please a man. Nell was always so sour and cross, Lisa so welcoming and kind.

He laughed at his reflection. Mad as a hatter, he thought. Murdered his own brother, beats his wife, sleeps with his maid. How did his life become such a mess?

* * * *

In the kitchen Nell helped Joe put on his shoes. She glanced up at Freddy as he came in, her expression blank. He went through the scullery to the back door. Lisa rummaged in a cupboard for potatoes. He slapped her rump sharply and she hit her head. She cried out and emerged muttering crossly. When she saw Freddy she smiled, her cheeks reddening. He pulled on his boots and trudged into the rapidly melting snow.

It was late morning and he headed for Harrowmead Wood. He was hoping to see Mr Denham whose cattle had been tramping his fields again. This farming proposition was new for Mr Denham and, in the absence of a keeper or farm manager, he did not have a clue about fencing. He wanted to breed cattle and produce a prize specimen for showing. As usual with the wealthy, Freddy thought, it was all about appearances.

He would make an effort to keep his temper with Mr Denham, no point in making an enemy. It was increasingly difficult to control his anger. In days gone by he had been such a sociable person, now he preferred being alone, thereby guaranteeing there was no one to shout at or offend.

The motion of his feet made his brain throb miserably. Confounded war, he thought, no men to work and a permanent headache. They had even lost Hans the Hun, who had been repatriated home to Germany. Nell had been unreasonably upset about his going; Freddy only missed his muscle power.

The wood was touched by magic this morning. Every branch and twig sparkled with melting ice. The morning sun kissed the branches, shining through the water droplets, dazzling as diamonds. Freddy took little notice of such adornments as he tramped irritably along the path. A noise attracted his attention and Delilah scampered through the undergrowth, stopping short of his heels.

In one swift movement Iain cocked his gun and took aim. "Oh, aye," he said and laughed, "well if it isn't my old pal Mr Hart."

Freddy scowled at him. "Macdonald," he said, "fancy – you're back are you? Whole and unharmed it seems."

He lowered the gun spread his arms as if to demonstrate his well being. "Looks as if I am. Where are you off to with such great purpose this morning?"

"I'm after Denham." He had no intention of explaining himself.

"Me too."

Freddy eyed the gun. Damn Iain, he always had the advantage.

"We can walk up together, won't that be nice." He uncocked the gun, gesturing for Freddy to walk ahead of him. Because of the narrowness of the path Freddy had little option except to oblige and walked stiffly in the lead.

"When did you get back?" he asked turning his head slightly to keep Delilah in view.

"Four days ago. Things have gone adrift without me. Won't be long and everything will be back to how it was."

"What? Harassing the locals and bullying the poor?"

"Aye, something like that."

They continued in silence until they reached the drive, Freddy growing increasingly agitated, Iain relaxing into his old sang-froid.

"You back for good?" Freddy asked.

"Aye."

"You'll be in charge of fences then."

"Aye, that's right, what of it?"

"Your cattle are riding rough-shod all over my pasture that's what and if they're not out by tonight I'll shoot the damn lot. I'm going to see Denham to tell him the same thing – no point in telling the monkey." Freddy pulled an acidic smile.

"The cattle will be fenced in by tonight. Speak to Mr Denham, as you wish. By the way," he said, "just now, you were trespassing. I'll let it go this time, but I don't want to see you on my patch again."

"As usual, getting above your station. I'll walk through the woods when I please, I have permission from the man himself remember?"

"Well, it's at your own risk, because when it comes to this estate, I am the man himself, Freddy. Mr Denham plays at it, he knows it and I know it and so do you."

Freddy's fury was palpable, he stuttered with a threat forming on his lips. Iain spoke first, "Don't say something you'll regret."

"I've nothing more to say, and not for fear of your fist. I'm going to see Denham, and I won't be sneaking in the back, I'm not his frigging flunky."

"Do you know something, Freddy?"

"What?"

"I've really missed you."

Freddy turned sharply on his heel and disappeared to the front of the house. Iain watched him and whistled for Delilah who had decided to see Freddy off. She bounded back, paws sliding on the frosty path, leaping from side to side as if it were a game. He rolled a cigarette and smoked it. This job was like slipping on an old coat. For all his good intentions he couldn't help himself. He laughed and went in the back door to see Cook for a cup of tea.

Chapter Twenty-nine

Nell couldn't believe her ears. She calmly pushed the food around her plate while her heart pounded and face flushed. "I can't stomach the bare-arsed cheek of the man," Freddy said to his father.

"And have the cattle been moved now?" Mr Hart asked.

"Yes."

"Well, no need to get in a state then is there? He said he'd move them by the end of the day and he has."

"Barely," Freddy mumbled. "I've come straight from the river pasture now and he was still rounding them up."

"Did you help?"

Freddy was amazed. "No, why the hell should I? Anyway he had Paul and the new lad Ben with him, they were managing."

"Don't forget," Mr Hart said reasonably, "he had to fix the fences before he put the cattle back in."

"I don't care if he had to go to Timbuktu before he got them in – I'm only saying," his voice increased in volume, "he took his bloody time getting them in."

"Freddy, if you're going to start all this again with Iain Macdonald..." He left the threat hanging in the air.

"I'm not starting anything, Father. You make it sound as if it's all my fault. He virtually marched me up to the house at gunpoint."

Nell hid a smile behind her napkin. At the sound of Freddy's raised voice Joe shrank back in his chair. She reached out a reassuring hand to him under the table.

"I've never met the keeper, not properly," Lisa said. "I've seen him at a distance, heard about him. When I was little we never went near Harrowmead Wood, 'cos of him. We was too scared."

Freddy scowled at her as if she were quite mad. "Scared? Don't be ridiculous. He thinks he's better than everybody else, throwing his weight around. He'd have loved the war, all that killing."

Nell flashed him a look. "Killing, Freddy?" she could not resist saying. "What do you know of killing?" It was possible she would pay for that remark later.

His eyes held pure venom as he looked at her, then turning back to his father he said, "Denham's no better – virtually laughed in my face."

Nell hurried Joe through his dinner, cleared the plates immediately everyone had finished. She served pudding before Lisa had the chance. Only Lisa noticed her alacrity but could not think of the reason.

Nell left her to clear away, got Joe ready for bed, told him a story as she did every night. It took amazing control to remain calm and not give herself away, though her heart hammered and her stomach flipped with excitement. She tucked Joe in and sat in the parlour as she often did, picking up a sock from the pile to darn. She held it in her idle hands waiting. At half past eight Freddy and his father went to the pub and Lisa joined her, a regular routine.

"Lisa," she said, "I have to go out. Will you listen for Joe and Mrs Hart please?"

Lisa was astounded, Nell never usually went anywhere without Joe. "Yes, you know I will. Is everything all right?"

"Quite fine, thank you, I'll be back before Freddy, there's no need to mention I've been out," she paused, staring at Lisa, "is there?"

She shook her head. "No, Nell, if you say so, of course."

"I do say so. It would only cause trouble and we don't need trouble do we," she stated. Lisa nodded, her big brown eyes earnest in their agreement. For all her faults Nell knew Lisa would never willingly bring Freddy's wrath down on her.

She tidied her hair in the hall mirror, pulled on a knitted hat and winter coat. Wincing, she pushed her swollen feet into her work boots. She took Mr Hart's electric torch and slipped into the frosty night. She found her way was well lit by a full moon and the frost shimmered off the road, rendering the torch surplus. She was unsure of the woodland paths but decided to risk it. She didn't want anyone to notice her. The silence amongst the trees was unnerving, the crunch of her footsteps in the frost sounded very loud to her. She saw shadows lurking behind every trunk, darkness distorted into menacing forms. She concentrated on keeping to the path in an effort to control her imagination.

When she thought herself hopelessly lost, turning full circle trying to get her bearings, she caught a whiff of wood-smoke from a chimney. Glimmering through the trees was the light of a lamp. She made haste towards it, running, her breath escaping in feathery plumes of mist.

Her relief at arriving at the gate of Keeper's House was immense. She knocked on the door, a little too enthusiastically. After a brief pause Iain opened it. She was all white and pink from the cold and exertion, her face lit up with one of her brilliant smiles. He laughed at the sight of her, beckoned her in with a quick movement of his head. He scanned the empty woodland as she passed him. In the warm kitchen she pulled off her gloves and scarf, unbuttoning her coat. He smiled at her, she thought he looked older, tired.

"I heard you were back," she explained, stuffing her pockets with gloves and scarf. She shrugged off the coat, folding it tidily over the chair. He looked at her with an amused expression on his face, folding his arms as she continued speaking. "I couldn't believe it when Freddy started talking about you out of the blue. I mean obviously, I knew you would be home sometime, but it's been so long and I hadn't heard…" she stopped aware suddenly of her excited prattling and his contained calm.

"I was going to call in for tea," he wrinkled up his nose, "then I thought better of it."

She laughed. "Yes, I know, it's not very easy with Freddy."

"Come on, sit down, it's freezing outside." He pulled the chair closer to the fire and took a seat opposite her, leaning forward his elbows on his knees.

"He was furious," she said and giggled. "He said you frog marched him up to the house with a gun at his back."

He rolled his eyes. "Ach, he does exaggerate. I had the gun, it wasn't cocked, and I certainly didn't have it pointed at him."

"And he said you'd left the cattle to graze his land for the whole day before rounding them up."

"I can't fix fences within an hour, not even for his royal highness. He's an ungrateful swine. I worked that fence all day to get those blessed cows off his precious pasture. What damage can they do when the ground is hard as iron anyway?"

"It's not important about the pasture – he cares nothing for that – it's because it's you," she said with glee.

"You look cold, I'll get you a drink." He poured two measures and handed her a glass. Fumbling with a packet of tobacco and papers, he rolled a cigarette with shaky fingers and lit it.

She sniffed the drink warily, took a sip, making a strangled noise in her throat. "Christ, that's horrid," she spluttered.

He narrowed his eyes through the smoke and laughed. "Good stuff that."

"It's vile." She took another tentative sip, pulling a face.

"Drink it, you managed it before." His smile faded, remembering the last time he had given her whisky, after Joanna had died.

Nell nodded, took another gulp as she recalled it too. It was fire in her throat and the effect was immediate and relaxing. She stepped on the heel of her boots to pull them off and tucked her legs under her. "You're like a hedgehog," he said.

She was amused. "I thought I was like a robin, now it's a hedgehog. How do you figure that one out?"

"The way you curl yourself up."

"Not because I'm prickly then."

"Aye, you can be that too, when you choose."

"Not if you ply me with booze, I'm not feeling at all prickly at the moment."

"No, I can see that. How's Joe?" He sipped from his glass.

"He's fine, I put him to bed before I came out, he won't wake up until morning. I expect Lisa thought me mad, coming out in the dark on a night like this, especially leaving Joe." She paused. "I don't usually leave him."

"Really?"

"It sounds silly, I can't really trust any of them. He feels safe with me."

"Why wouldn't he feel safe, Helena?" he asked.

She had backed herself into a corner. "Oh, well, Freddy, he's so temperamental and Joe doesn't cope with it very well."

"Do you?"

She gave a nervous titter. "I have no choice. I can manage him, I live with it."

"And Lisa? Where does she figure in all this?"

"Lisa?" She flushed and took another mouthful of whisky. She couldn't tell him. The shame of it, admitting to it. She closed her eyes, tears rising. She swiftly swallowed them back with the alcohol in an effort to control herself and cleared her throat. "It's quite simple, Iain." She dared to look at him. His eyes were fixed on her hypnotically, as if he could read her mind. She lost her train of thought unsure of what she had been about to say.

He blinked, inhaled the smoke from his cigarette, blowing it up into the air above his head. "Oh, Helena," he said and sighed, "if only it were simple."

The whisky fuzzed her head. She noticed he trembled, throwing the cigarette stub into the fire. She leaned forward and taking his hand in hers, studied his fingertips. "Look," she said, glancing up, their faces close together, "your fingers are quite healed."

He smiled, the flickering flame of the fire shining in the green and yellow of his irises. "Aye, now I have splinters from the fence." He opened his palm where two long black shards of wood burrowed under the hard skin.

"So you have. Fetch a needle and I'll get them out," she said. He searched the dresser, found a needle amongst a pot of fishing hooks, returned to his seat, offering his hand. She poked the needle in and he pulled away sharply. "Oh, for goodness sake," she scolded, "keep still and it won't hurt."

"Aye, right." He allowed her to have another go, studied her face as she concentrated. He had dreamed about her, conjured her image on long dark nights in the dugout. Now she was here, now she had come to him, he could have watched her all night. With one cool hand she flattened his palm on her knee while attempting to liberate the sliver of wood. She impaled the splinter on the end of the needle raising it to eye level with a look of triumph on her face.

"Want me to get the other one out too?"

He chuckled low in his throat. "Aye, go on then." He waited patiently until she had finished, studying the wave of her hair as it grew from her scalp. He could smell the warm floral scent of her.

When she had eviscerated the area and removed the last fragment she attached the needle to her collar, a habit she had when sewing, and stretched her toes towards the fire. "This is my favourite place," she said, "and now it's even better, a fire, a drink," she made a face as she took a sip, "and you." Smiling now as if she had said something very brave. She winced as she flexed her toes in the heat.

"What's wrong?"

"Chilblains," she said.

"Sit back, put your feet here." He indicated his lap. She put her feet on his knees and he enveloped one foot in each hand. The action was intimate, inappropriate, but the pain in them eased immediately. He emanated an intense heat, it felt blissful through her stockings and she sighed.

"Lisa and Freddy are lovers aren't they?" he said.

She was caught off-guard by his forthright manner. She blushed, ashamed to hear it said out loud, of her acceptance of it. "Yes," she said meekly.

"And yet you don't leave or throw her out?"

"No." She wanted to explain it as much to herself as to him. "I don't throw her out because, if he's with her..." how could she put it in terms she could speak of, "he leaves me alone. It makes it easy for them. I want it to be easy for them – I don't want him. And," she closed her eyes, making it less painful to say, "I don't leave because I have nowhere else to go and I have Joe and it's the only place for me. It's not much," her eyes flickered open, "it's all I have." She gave a little self-depreciating shrug. "It's probably hard for you to understand, it's a woman's lot. I have no means of making my own way, not at the moment. Maybe one day."

"I understand, perfectly. I'm sorry for it, but I understand it. What does Lisa see in him?" He gently rubbed her sore toes, a barely perceptible movement which made her flesh goose pimple.

"I don't know – master of the house. He's quite nice to her."

"Is he very good in bed?"

She clasped a hand over her mouth to quell her laughter, deep and throaty, the colour flaring again in her cheeks. She withdrew her feet. He laughed at her embarrassment, shaking his head as he poured another drink. He tried to refill hers but she put a hand over the top of the glass. "No," she squealed, trying to recover herself. "I've not finished that and I feel quite drunk already."

"I'll see you home, no bother." He parted her fingers with one of his and poured a little between the gap. She giggled now and couldn't stop, the laughter rising like thistledown. It was contagious and Iain laughed with her. While she tried to control herself he said, "I didn't ask to embarrass you, I'm genuinely interested as to how a guy like Freddy could hold on to anyone. He's obviously failed miserably with you, I wondered what Lisa found so appealing."

Still giggling she said, "I couldn't say, really. Not what you said, I don't think. Although you have to see I'm not well experienced on that score," and then giggling helplessly again, "I can only hope I have better in the future."

"Perhaps you have had enough," he replied snickering into his drink.

"No," she said, "that's what I'm saying," she widened her eyes candidly, "I've not had enough," a pause, "experience."

"I meant you've had enough to drink, Missus." They both convulsed with laughter and did not stop until their stomachs hurt. Iain rolled and lit another cigarette. "I suppose you'll want to start smoking next."

"I don't know, I might. I've not tried it before," she said reaching forward eagerly. She felt like a bold daring version of herself.

He offered her the cigarette, she took it, placed it to her lips. She took the smoke momentarily into her mouth before quickly blowing it out again, she widened her eyes with dissatisfaction. "Is that it?"

He chuckled again. "Not quite, you're supposed to breathe it in."

She tried again and something in her action, the intake of breath, the coughing that followed, eyes watering, reminded him of Michael. He suddenly saw the boy with such clarity in the chair opposite him, choking as he tried to inhale the foul smoke, trying to smile at Iain through blue eyes running with tears. Without warning he snatched the cigarette away quite fiercely. She jumped, defensive, shrinking back into the chair. They stared at each other soberly, the humour of a few moments before quite gone.

He saw her fear, the knee-jerk reaction he had prompted in her. Michael was gone from his vision. He knelt in front of her chair.

"Sorry," he said, throwing the cigarette behind him into the flames. "Sorry, I thought – I frightened you – you don't like it, you shouldn't smoke."

She relaxed a little, the fearful expression melting. "Don't worry, you startled me."

He caught her hand. "You startle too easy. I never meant to frighten you – I'd never frighten you." He clasped her hand to his mouth, kissed the soft palm. It felt like she dreamed it might. She wanted more but was powerless to assist him and watched in awe as he pressed her hand to the side of his face, rough to her skin. He briefly closed his eyes as if, perhaps, he had dreamed of it too. Then he stood up briskly, turned away, his voice quiet, "Come on, I'd better walk you back, it's late."

She nodded wordlessly, pushed her feet into her boots. He helped her on with her coat, buttoning it up. He wrapped her scarf around her neck, tucked it in, as if dressing a child and, like a child, she allowed him to do it. He smiled when he pulled her hat over her eyes and she was forced to readjust it. He whistled to Delilah, who rose stiff-limbed from her place in front of the fire and followed them out into the crisp night air where snow was once again blowing around.

Nell tucked her arm through his and she lit the way with her torch, the moon long since obscured by snow cloud. Their silence was companionable. The air was filled with the gentle sounds of the night, the trees rustling in the icy breeze, the fall and crunch of twigs, the dull beat of their feet on the frozen leaf mould, Delilah padding patiently behind them. It was beautiful in the wood at night, a different, secret place, now she was with Iain.

He chaperoned her to the home paddock. She glanced nervously at the farmhouse, a light shone dimly in the parlour where Lisa waited. She hoped Freddy hadn't returned early from the pub. Iain noted her apprehension. They both went to speak at the same time, laughing quietly. "You can take the torch," she offered. "It's so dark."

"I know my way blindfold," he said. "Go on then or they will be back."

She smiled at his perception. "I'm really glad you're home." She stepped backwards, away from him.

"You'll come again," he confirmed in case there were any doubt.

He could not see her expression in the dark, but her voice was warm, happy he had said it. "Yes," she said, "of course." She turned and ran into the house, quietly let herself in and dragged off her winter garments.

Without pausing to see Lisa she raced up the stairs, crept into Joe's room. She lit the candle by the bed, held it high to view the child asleep on his side, black eyelashes shadowing his cheek, the perfect small arc of his nostrils and bow of his lips.

Her heart fluttered with excitement, like a young maid who had walked out with her beau for the first time. As she undressed her finger caught on the needle she had placed in her collar. She removed it and purposely snagged her fingertip on the same sharp shiny point that had pushed into his skin. She placed it safely in her walnut box.

Despite the alcohol, she heard Freddy come home, listening numbly to his and Lisa's fumbling in the room above. Her feet did not hurt and she succumbed to a sweet dreamless sleep.

Chapter Thirty

Iain absently plucked an elm leaf from the tree as he passed. One side was smooth and hairless, the other rough as sandpaper between his fingers. Mr Denham had been talking and waited for a response. Iain smiled at him affably and hoping it was the right answer said, "Aye." Mr Denham was pleased.

Only that morning Iain had returned from an overnight trip to London for Dusty and Celia's wedding. He performed his duty as best man, safeguarding the rings and giving a speech at the wedding breakfast that had everybody laughing and crying. It was a happy day, sunshine and spring flowers, family and friends. It lifted Iain's spirits. But he and Dusty only managed to have one conversation and it was dwelling on his mind.

In the bustle of last minute arrangements and panic, they had finally been left alone to dress in their wedding attire. Iain noticed Dusty's melancholic expression as he struggled with his tie.

"I must say you're not exactly the picture of the happy groom," he said, tying his shoelaces.

Dusty abandoned his tie and tried to flatten his hair, grimacing at his reflection in the mirror. "Yeah, I know. It's all been mad, I've not had a chance to speak to you, Midge."

He straightened up. "Why? Is there something wrong?"

"Everything, nothing." His hair remained stuck up as he sat on the bed next to Iain. "I suppose I thought the worst was over, and it is, course it is. You know, we came home, and to what? There are no jobs and it isn't any good now, knowing people. For a start, so many are dead. Almost all my mates, kids I knew from school, they're all gone or injured. It's a different world. I dunno." He leaned his head on his hands. "Miserable sod, aren't I?"

"No," Iain said. "If that's how it is, I'm not surprised you're fed up. At Harrowmead it's as if everything's stopped. It's bad in a different way. I've been to a different planet, while everyone else has stayed at home, that's a fact. Nothing is the same, yet everything, incredibly, is exactly like before. Everything except the memorial they're building into the churchyard wall, naming every poor sod who went west."

Dusty bit his lip. "I wanted to rent a place down the road, nothing much. I can't even do that. We'll have to shack up here with Mum and Dad for a while."

"Couldn't you have waited to get married?"

Dusty shook his head, cheeks pinking. "Celia's expecting."

He laughed. "Congratulations, no surprise there, randy devil." He cuffed Dusty's arm playfully. "And there's no work at all?"

"Christ knows how many men chase after each job. There's work going on the Underground. I've applied, but God, I don't want to be stuck down there, never seeing the light of day. I don't even know if I want to be in London any more. Mum says I'm a moody bugger. Dad doesn't understand, not about the war and that. I feel as if it's all messed up."

Iain nodded, stared at his linked hands ineffectively. "I didn't realise. I thought everything would go back to how it was before." Their mutual silence said more than words, a deep understanding of the dilemma, the difficulty of returning to a civilian life, a changed society.

"Nothing's ever going to be as it was before," Dusty said.

"No, I see that now. What about Celia?"

"She's a good girl, she understands how I feel. She wants us to be together, wants all this marriage lark, more than anything." He contemplated his future for a minute. "Celia's the only good thing I've got really. Listen to me, I'll be using this to hang myself next," he indicated his tie, laughing. "It's not so bad, it'll work itself out."

"If there's something I could do…" Iain started, but his words rang hollow, there was nothing he could offer. The moment was over. Dusty's mother arrived, all brisk efficiency sweeping through the room, fastening Dusty's tie, holding Iain's jacket. They were pushed out of the door for the short walk to the church.

There was no opportunity to speak again and now Iain's thoughts were with Dusty, far away from Mr Denham praising his hard work.

Iain had brought the place back into order these last three months. Fences had been mended and gates hung back on their hinges. The game stock was not quite what it once was but it would be soon.

Mr Denham noticed a change in his keeper. He was not so quick to anger, more serene somehow, the dangerous fire that burned below the surface had been extinguished. Although far from slacking in his duties, he was not quite as zealous as previously. Mr Denham was not sure if it were a new found maturity or the effect of war. Iain's speech with his employer was less blunt and, although never one for idle chat, he was even quieter.

As he spoke, and Mr Denham liked nothing better than the sound of his own voice, it crossed his mind Iain was simply humouring him by being so quietly agreeable, although he shrugged the thought off.

"We shall have our first shoot in November. I know the head of game isn't quite up to par but I expect we'll manage a couple this year. Very exciting," Mr Denham said, "not had a shoot these last four years…"

Iain wondered what Nell was doing. From here he could see through the gap in the trees, the start of North Farm land. Now the days were longer she called at the house with Joe most evenings. They would walk through the woods, take Joe fishing, or simply sit in the house, or at the back enjoying the last rays of the sun.

He feared Joe might betray them with his innocent tongue. He didn't fear it for himself but for Nell. He knew it could cause a repeat of the violent behaviour she had only hinted at before Freddy's spell in hospital. If he ever hurt her again Iain didn't know what he would do. It was more than he could think of that someone, a man, might raise his hand to her.

He dragged his attention back to Mr Denham who had left the subject of the shoot. "So Miles shall go to university now he has returned, resume where he left off."

Ah, yes, Iain thought, university, where the sons of the rich learned how to be well read and idle.

Still Mr Denham rattled on, his elongated vowels resonating in the summer air. "And the new motor car is being delivered next week, you must come up to the house and see what you think. Did you drive in the army? Had a go in Colonel Edam's motor yesterday, perfectly splendid way to travel, splendid." It was a sunny day and they had trekked the perimeter of the estate, Delilah limping between them. She was ten years old, her muzzle peppered grey. She managed well, although a life outdoors had left her with rheumatism that slowed her down.

In one of Mr Denham's pauses for breath Iain said, "I'm going to The Tump later. Mr Price has some pups. Delilah's got some time left yet, she's not as quick as she was."

"Good idea. I didn't know he had pups, what are they?"

"A retriever breed, ideal for the work."

"Wouldn't mind one of those myself," Denham said, his well-fed face flushed with heat.

Iain immediately wished he hadn't mentioned it, he hoped Nell and the boy would accompany him. His consternation was hard to ignore and Denham, eyeing him nervously, was quick to clarify. "Perhaps, if there's a suitable dog you could secure it for me and I can go tomorrow and look it over. What do you say?"

"Aye," he said, "it's a dog you're after not a bitch?"

"Yes, they work better."

Iain disagreed but held his tongue and smiled cordially. If there were a decent dog to be had he would find it. Finally Mr Denham took his leave. Iain reclined under a beech tree and lit a cigarette, laying his gun beside him, Delilah watchful on her haunches.

Once he would never have relaxed during a working day. It was such a warm afternoon, he had to take a minute to appreciate the beauty of looking up between the tracery of leaves, from palest to darkest green depending on the depth of the canopy. A blackbird sang somewhere close by. He closed his eyes to it, aware that lurking in the back of his head was the old nightmare of mud merging with blood and the stench of his dying comrades.

Sometimes, in the tranquility of these trees, he could hear the spatter of the machine gun and feel the ground shake as the shells hit the earth. When he managed to leave it behind, return to reality, he would be shaking, a tremour in his hands that could last the rest of the day. His nightmares often woke him. He would brew tea in the early hours of the morning before the sun had lightened the sky.

He refused to let these dreams and hallucinations rule his life, he had a blind faith that they would get better in time. He took happiness where he could find it. He had promised himself he would make an effort to sever connections with Nell. Despite his best intentions the opposite had occurred. Joe was their common ground but conversation came easily. They laughed at the same things. Their familiarity was comfortable and irresistible. He had never dared to hope he might build a relationship with his son and yet he had. Together, Nell and Joe made him feel content.

Cigarette finished, he got to his feet and strolled the length of the river. He had intended going into town today. He had new parts to collect for two rifles and various other sundries for the gunroom. Nothing was quite so pressing anymore; he would go tomorrow or the next day. He wasn't much interested in Mr

Denham's new car, everything was heading that way, but he didn't like it. They were horrendously expensive. He wondered if Sinclair had resorted to a motorcar, money had never been a problem at Glenleven.

He met Nell with Joe in the early evening on the way to Harrowmead as he knew he would. Her face lit up and Joe hurried to meet him. He swung the boy into the air and he squealed. "You'll make him sick," she warned. "Where are you going anyway?"

"To The Tump. I thought Joe might like to see some puppies." Bending down to the child he said, "Would you like that, Joe, come with me and see some pups?"

"Yes, yes." Joe hopped from foot to foot with excitement.

Walking along the road could invite comment. She could claim coincidence in travelling the same route. She hardly cared if she got away with it.

She was disappointed when Mrs Price dragged her unwillingly into the farmhouse for a cup of tea. She could hardly refuse although she would rather have viewed the puppies.

Joe happily gave his hand to Iain and they went into the brick built cowshed. A doe eyed Jersey cow regarded them from her stall, lazily chewing her cud. In the neighbouring stall a regal yellow retriever bitch fed her brood of seven puppies, two black as coal and five as yellow as their mother. Iain led Joe into the stall and hunkered down beside Mr Price.

"What do you think, Iain, fine pups, eh?" Mr Price said enthusiastically.

"Aye," he said. Delilah cowered miserably across the barn with large forlorn eyes. The pups stopped feeding and yipped and jumped around their visitors. "Look Joe, clap them nice, they're wee babies." Joe stroked a golden pup with one finger, smiling in delight. The puppy rolled over exposing her baby pink tummy, soft as silk. Iain picked up a black one, a dog when he checked, put it down.

"There's a black bitch here if that's what you're after." Mr Price handed him the pup. She peered at him, gleaming black eyes set in a matching coat with a wet shiny nose, a body fat as butter, bowed frog's legs set with oversized paws. She was soft in his hands, trying to bite his large fingers with teeth as sharp as pins.

"Aye, she'll do me. What do you think, Joe?" The child placed one hand on his father's shoulder the other touching the pup's domed skull. She cast her head back, licking his finger with a flicker of bright pink.

"She's a lovely puppy," Joe said earnestly.

"Then we'll have her. When will she be ready, a couple of weeks?"

"Yes, that should do it. Come up in a fortnight, or I can bring her down if I'm going your way," Mr Price said. "Now come in the house for a drink before you go."

"Mr Denham was after a dog," Iain remembered, pointing at a large yellow pup. "That looks a good one, is that a dog?"

"Prize of the litter, yes, you always had a good eye. I was keeping that one myself."

He shrugged. "Fair enough."

"No, I'll let Denham have him, reckon one of the others will do me. Come on then."

They left the puppies bouncing around their tired mother. Nell was sitting at the kitchen table. Her expression spoke volumes. She was annoyed at being railroaded into the kitchen, a fellow farmer's wife. She wanted to see the puppies too. She amused him, sitting as she was, like a petulant child being forced to attend an arithmetic lesson. She managed a weak smile for him while Mrs Price regaled her with a story about a batch of chicks she had bought which had turned out to be cockerels every one. Mr Price opened two bottles of beer, poured them into cloudy glasses. They discussed Mr Denham's prize cattle which he was entering in the County Show next month.

"You can't go wrong when you've the money to buy them in like Denham does," Mr Price said. "We breed ours pure. It takes years to build up a good herd that way, it's the proper way to do it."

"Not that I could have known myself how they would turn out," Mrs Price said, smoothing her apron over her knees. "They were quite small, but I reckon the wifey was in the know. I couldn't believe it when they all started crowing."

Joe, dwarfed by the high backed chair, swung his legs, eating a slab of Mrs Price's seed cake. The kitchen smelt of yeast from the batch of loaves cooling on the counter. Cheese cloths hung over a line from the ceiling drying beside bunches of herbs. The dresser shone with blue and white stoneware in pristine, newly washed order. The kitchen table was still damp from its recent scrubbing and a cat jostled for space on the windowsill beside two pots of scarlet flowering geraniums.

"You see," Mr Price said, "when I started out I didn't have a bull, I used to go across the valley to Connor's place. Do you know it?" Iain nodded.

"I'm a great believer in bantams myself." Mrs Price topped up Nell's teacup. Unobserved Nell glanced across at Iain who happened to be doing the same thing. When their eyes met the irresistible fizz of laughter filled her throat and Iain, seeing her smirk, quickly put up a hand to cover his grin.

"There's a lot to be said for not having a bull, of course," Mr Price said. Iain drank from his glass, not daring to look in her direction again.

In a lull in Mr Price's monologue Iain heard Mrs Price, "And fancy, you both turning up here at the same time. It's lovely to see you, dear. You should come over more often, you and Freddy, of course. Did you come for something particular?"

In a clear voice she replied, "No, Mrs Price, I came with Iain, so Joe could see the puppies."

Iain refrained from choking on his beer but barely. Mrs Price smiled, glanced at her husband and then between Iain and Nell. "Oh, well, that's nice," she said weakly. It was obvious she was desperate to ask about Freddy's view on this. The bad blood between the two men was common knowledge. The question hung unasked in the air.

Nell opened her mouth to speak. Iain had the feeling she was about to fill in the blanks for Mrs Price and quickly stepped in. "I'd best be off." He took the final mouthful from his glass. "Did you want me to walk you back to North Farm, Mrs Hart?" The name for her sounded strange in his mouth.

He could see her amusement, her devil-may-care attitude amazed him sometimes. "Thank you, Mr Macdonald, that would be most kind. Thank you for the tea, Mrs Price. Say thank you Joe." Joe smiled and thanked her in a small voice.

The sky was streaked silver and pink as they strolled down the lane, Nell carrying Joe on her hip. Delilah slinked behind them, sniffing every bush and blade of grass. "Sometimes," Iain said, "I wonder what's going to come out of your mouth."

Her eyebrows shot up. "What's that supposed to mean?"

"Back there, you were about to say something about Freddy weren't you?"

She burst into giggles. "Well, between them both, honestly. They're lovely people, but I could almost hear Mrs Price's brain working overtime figuring out how we came to make arrangements to go and see puppies."

"You could have made it easy on yourself and said we happened to arrive at the same time, that's what she presumed anyway."

"Oh, I know, it's silly, I can't help myself sometimes."

"Here, Joe, I'll carry you. I think you're getting worse, you'll say something you might regret one day."

She knitted her eyebrows together stubbornly. "I don't care."

"How did I know you were going to say that?" He lifted Joe onto his shoulders where he leaned his hands comfortably on the top of Iain's head.

Relieved of his weight Nell walked with a lighter step, breathing in the warm scented air. The hedgerows were a riot of white campion and spires of puce foxgloves.

"Don't scold me," she said. "I'm always getting told off for something. I fully expect Freddy to find me out eventually, so it really doesn't matter. Anyway he doesn't socialise much, he's unlikely to hear of it."

"He goes to the pub, that's enough. Hot bed of gossip and nonsense."

"Don't worry. I'm sure you never used to worry as much."

"Maybe I had nothing to worry about."

"And now?"

He held on to Joe's feet. "And now," he said firmly, "you worry me."

She smiled, content with the idea that she worried him in whatever fashion.

* * * *

Two weeks later Iain collected the puppy. He named her Destiny. Delilah was offended by the young intruder. Sitting at the back door in the dying light, the puppy tried to bite her tail, until she snapped at the pup in irritation. Nell did not come down to visit, so he bathed in the outhouse where, since his return from France, he had rigged a pipe that fed hot water from the range into a tin bath with a soakaway into the ground. Tonight the range had gone out and the bath was cool but the evening was warm and nothing compared with feeling clean.

When the lamplight began to attract insects, he shut the two dogs in their kennel and retired to the house with a book, drink and a packet of cigarettes.

At almost ten o'clock, as his eyes began to ache with tiredness, he put his book down. A small knock sounded on the door, so quiet that at first he wasn't sure he had heard it. When he checked, he discovered Nell on the doorstep. He invited her in by standing aside. He could tell she was agitated immediately. She wore a cardigan over a blue print summer dress, curls escaped down her back where it was loosely tied. She looked very similar to the first time he had ever seen her picking primroses in the wood. The memory made him smile.

"Do you want a drink?"

She shrugged. "I'll get a taste for it eventually I suppose."

"What's got your dander up?"

"Nothing – nothing that matters anyway. Throwing his weight around, lord of the manor. He actually barred my way – can you imagine?" she raised her voice.

"Did he touch you?"

"Did he hell. I'd have gone for him if he had, and he knew it," she said.

He was relieved. "Here drink that, calm down." He had never heard her rant before.

"Calm down? Upstairs playing with the maid and lecturing me."

"He heard about going to Tump Farm didn't he?"

She gave a shrill guffaw like a trapped vole. "No, not that. Mrs Dobbs at the post office told him I had spoken to you in the street last week."

He frowned. "Did you?"

"Probably, I see you every day, how can I remember if we ran into each other? Yes, I saw you in the village not long since – I'm hardly going to ignore you – we're friends."

"Did you tell him that?"

She tipped her head back and swallowed the whisky in one. She shuddered and ran the back of her hand across her mouth. "Yes I did."

He admired her fortitude. She could be quite formidable even if she didn't have the strength and muscle to back it up. "What did he say?"

"He threatened to kill me."

Iain could well picture the scene. "When did this happen?"

"Before supper. It was my first opportunity to get away, and I had to get out, Iain, or I would have gone mad." She sat down. "I'm sorry I shouldn't drag you into all this. It only makes trouble. He has no idea I've left the house. I said I was going to bed. I only had to wait until he'd gone upstairs with his little trollop." She laughed when she met his slightly stunned gaze. "It's not funny, I know, it's all so ludicrous sometimes."

He smiled. "I know." He stifled a yawn.

"I'm keeping you up, I should have waited until tomorrow." She stood up again to button her cardigan.

He watched her, captivated by the colour of her skin, the curl of hair against cheek. He wanted to touch her, feel her diminutive form in his arms, more than anything he didn't want her to go. He was not sure what her response would be. He did not think she would reject him, the feelings he harboured for her were about so much more than sex. If he crossed the boundary it was a commitment, something which in the past had repelled him and which now, with her, was irresistible.

"Helena." He placed his hand on her shoulder. "You don't have to go, not just now."

"Well, I'd better, it's late, like I said I should have waited." As she spoke something in her expression, in her eyes, invited him.

He moved closer, bending his head as she tilted her chin, meeting him halfway. Their kiss was soft, tentative and unsure. She drew back, keeping her eyes fixed on his, they shared a smile, a pause, a revelation. On tiptoe, she reached up and kissed him with a vehemence that sent a surge of heat through him, rushing through veins that could barely contain it.

Without breaking their kiss he undid buttons, hooks and eyes. She was desperate, her stomach twisted, excitement pushing up from inside until it gasped from her mouth. His hand skimmed her breast and he manoeuvred her against the kitchen table, a chair falling aside. He lifted her skirt and undid his trousers. They were consumed by this. She did not care for the impropriety of him having her in his kitchen, on the table. She wanted him. She offered herself, rushed him in her eagerness. She cried out from the sheer pleasure of it. He had not expected her to be like this, he thought she might be reserved, nervous or uncertain. She was none of these things, she wanted him as a man wanted a woman, hungry and hot, thoughtless of subtlety and finesse. Her desire was magnificent to him.

At the last second he pulled out of her, wet heat spilling down her leg. He held her to him, cradling her head, standing between her thighs.

"Come with me," he said. She nodded. She would have followed him to the edge of the world. Holding her hand he took the lamp and climbed the stairs.

She waited uncertainly in the middle of the bedroom while he pulled the curtains. He held her and when she lifted her face he kissed her lips. His hands wandered over her hair and he untied the ribbon which contained it. It was springy and soft under his fingers, the chestnut and gold strands gleamed in the lamplight. She closed her eyes to his soft mouth brushing her face. They only needed to shrug off their open clothing, leaving the garments on the floor anyhow.

She was self-conscious now and folded her arms across her bare breasts. She wanted to cast her eyes away from his nakedness when he faced her. She thought him beautiful, so tall and straight, long perfect limbs and slim muscular body. Heat rushed to her face. Forcing herself to abandon her modesty, she dropped her arms to her sides.

"Lie down," he said. His voice sounded different to her.

He leaned over her. She touched the scarred cleft below his clavicle bone, a healed memory of war and rested her mouth there for a moment.

Carefully his lips grazed hers, softly parting with his tongue and the heat of her mouth became part of his. She stretched back on the bed, his touch like warm oil on her skin, unhurried and soothing. The cool path of his lips followed the trail of his touch down her body.

Competent, tender fingers explored and her heart quickened, a pleasurable tightness squeezing her womb. Firm and intense or gentle and soft, he knew, until she was desperate for all of him. There was nothing beyond the heat of sensation, the thrill of hands and mouth on skin.

He captured her, every nerve ending, every fibre, body pooling, bones melting under his fingertips. He looked into her eyes and saw her soul and she would never need more, because she had reached beyond desire. He made her complete. She was without body, or weight, beyond time or earthly restriction, thistledown exploding into infinity. And she would die from it and gladly, except only life could bring this exquisite agony of delight.

And then she was back, earth bound, in his bed, rocking together and he was deep inside where she longed to feel him. They barely moved, bound in intimacy, an unspoken promise realised. She cried out and he quieted her with his mouth, his breath, rapid and shallow on her lips. Bodies pressed together basking in delicious ecstasy, diminishing circles of heat and heaven, high on their mutual gratification.

She wrapped her legs tighter around him. "Don't pull away," she said.

"There'll be a baby," he said.

Her arms circled his neck pushing up against him until he groaned. "Good," and she meant it.

He rolled onto his back taking her with him. She relaxed, the reality of a long held wish freed her. In the circle of his skin she closed her eyes and slept. He felt her breathing become shallow, her body loosening in sleep, warm and damp against him. One hand settled in the dip of her back, the other entwined with hers. He did not sleep. He was overwhelmed, astonished. He loved her, he recognised it, that elusive emotion. She was everything and without her it all meant nothing. His future was hers.

He was wrong about there being no great passion between them. This was a passion he had not dared to consider. She was the reason he had survived the war. She was the mother of his son and would be the mother of his daughters. He knew it with such certainty it was like a vision, as clear as his hallucinations of war, but heaven sent and blissful.

She stirred and something like dread clutched at him. He didn't want her to leave, to return to Freddy's house. She peered up at him, her eyes very blue and wide.

"I have to go," she whispered and pressed her lips to his chest, salty and smelling of soap and tobacco.

"Not yet."

She moved off him into the crook of his arm. They kissed, long and hard. "It's late," she said and giggled when she felt his arousal.

"I know. I want you to stay with me."

She laughed. "I can't, you know that."

"We must find a way. You're not staying with him." It was no good discussing it now and he knew that. He sat up, irritated by his powerless position. She could see the outline of his ribs under the clear skin, his spine, a long curved track, where she placed her hand. "I'll walk you home," he said.

"Don't be cross."

"I'm not."

She put her nose to his cheek, breathing in the scent of him. "You are. I'm married – you like married women. I'm not the first."

He met her eyes sharply, without humour. "You are the first."

"Married woman?"

"No, not that. You're the first woman I've ever wanted. I mean really wanted, forever. Married, divorced, widowed, single I don't care. You're the first." He did not take his eyes from hers.

"Oh," she said inadequately.

He laughed then turning from her. "You'll think me foolish." He had spilled his heart, he felt foolish.

She angled her head awkwardly to kiss his mouth and her eyes were wet with tears. "No," she whispered, "no." He kissed her back, long and deep, questing for more. She pulled away from him, her hands cupping his face. "I love you, Iain. If you're a fool then it's for keeping me waiting for you for so long, when I've been dreaming of it since," she paused, "well, for a long time. I can barely remember when it began for me."

He laughed again, this time with pleasure, and pressed her back onto the bed. "I'll take you home, in a minute, I promise."

Chapter Thirty-one

The sheep had come down from the Common into Freddy's pasture again. He was furious and the only person he could blame was himself. It wasn't as if they had done much damage. Part of him knew he was being irrational, but his lack of control had been increasing. At the pub two nights ago he punched Jasper Potter and he couldn't remember why. When the constable arrived yesterday to question him and warned charges might well be brought, he invented some lame excuse. Well let them charge him, he thought, do their damnedest. He didn't pressed charges when Iain punched him on the nose, he hadn't thought of it. In retrospect, he wished he had.

He took off his shirt, the sun hot on his bare skin, a whisper of a breeze blowing over him. He grasped his billhook and set to work, hedging to prevent any more sheep getting through. It would be easier to erect a wire fence. His father insisted the pasture had always been properly hedged and it was cheaper anyhow. Cheaper monetarily, Freddy thought, but expensive as hell time-wise. He had taken aspirin for his head and the ache had eased considerably, so after twenty minutes or so the task at hand became, he had to admit, almost pleasurable. There was satisfaction in the skill of laying a hedge.

But where was Nell? The little voice in his head speculated. She had been increasingly absent these last weeks. Rumours had reached him that she had been seen in the gamekeeper's company. That would be about right, said the voice, what with the boy being his. He wondered if Nell had some ludicrous notion of giving it a go with Macdonald. Well she wouldn't if he had anything to do with it. Anyway, she was a cold fish, incapable of a normal relationship. Still he would speak to her tonight, put her straight on a few things. She had been quite outspoken and disrespectful of late, not to mention neglecting her duties at the farm.

He paused in his work, wiped the sweat from his brow with his arm. A hare crossed the field, unaware of the man's presence. His father had bought a new rifle. Later, he thought, he would come down here and get a few rabbits or a hare. That would stop his father nagging about the expense of everything. He employed one of Lionel Baker's sons to ease the load since Mr Hart was getting too old and slow.

He saw Lisa skipping along the edge of the field with his lunch. Even she had become an increasing irritation, more demanding, everyone wanted a piece of him.

She smiled as she approached, dark hair blowing off her face. He noticed her blouse and skirt did nothing for her figure. "Hello," she said. "How's it going?"

He glowered at her. "I'm laying a hedge, Lisa, it goes as it always does." Her simplicity could be annoying. He took his lunch, leaning on the bank in the shade of a young ash tree. She stayed with him while he ate, she usually did. She picked a daisy, plucking off the petals one by one. Some might have thought her charming. Freddy couldn't see it. Perversely, he wished Nell had brought his lunch. Of course, she hadn't done that for a long time. In the hope of riling Lisa he said, "Where's Nell?"

Her colour rose, keeping her eyes averted guiltily. "In the dairy I should think."

"You think? Don't you know?"

"Yes, I'm sure she's in the dairy."

"Really? You're not much of a liar. Off with her fancy man is she?"

She flushed, startled. "W– what fancy man?"

"You know perfectly well. I suppose you have some sort of arrangement between you do you? You cover for her, keep things smoothed over." He pursed his lips, dark eyes narrowed.

"No," she said, "not at all. Really, Freddy, she's at home, there is no fancy man – well, not as far as I know."

"We shall see won't we and if I find you've been lying to me I won't be very happy."

Her smile was nervous but she wasn't too worried by his threat, he had never hurt her before. "I wouldn't lie to you," she said easily.

He finished his lunch in silence and despite trying to humour him, she took her leave with Freddy ignoring her.

Lisa was perspiring after her brisk walk across the fields. She searched the cool, damp dairy, the barns and sheds and finally the house, even daring a peek into Mrs Hart's room. The old lady was quite alone and sleeping. She wondered where Nell was. She too had heard rumours about Nell and the keeper. To Lisa he was an elusive figure. She had never seen him close enough to know his features, except that he was tall and dark, with a reputation for fighting and drinking. She could not imagine Nell going for the likes of him besides, Nell very rarely went out without Joe. Surely if she were having an affair she would not take the boy. Although, on reflection, there had been a handful of evenings when she had slipped away for an hour or two.

By the time she laid the table Nell and Joe arrived home. Nell was flushed, her hair in tight curls as if it had received a wetting, holding a canvas bag in one hand, she hummed to herself. "You sound happy," Lisa commented.

She laughed. "I am, Lisa, I really, really am." She picked up Joe and danced across the kitchen with him before running up the stairs to change their clothes. She had spent a blissful afternoon with Iain.

He took them to where the river pooled. He had brought her here once before to tickle trout. "Do you remember?" she said.

He laughed. "Yes, I remember." He locked the gate behind them. "Nobody ever comes here."

"What are you doing?" Her turn to laugh.

"Undressing. Joe, do you want to swim?"

Joe was not waiting for an invitation, his shorts were already at his ankles, tripping him over. They stripped to their underwear and swam in its delicious coolness. Joe was a poor swimmer and in one afternoon, under Iain's guidance, he improved considerably.

Later while Joe played in the shallows, building a dam with stones, they frolicked in the depths. Joe was oblivious to their snatched kisses and groping hands under the cover of the water.

Nell tipped out their damp underclothes onto the bedroom floor. She re-dressed Joe, tickling his tummy, playing little piggies with his toes. She had strolled home wearing only her summer dress, totally indecent, her underwear wet in the canvas bag. She had never felt so free and alive and loved. Now properly attired, she turned to the mirror, brushing the curls of her hair, turning them to a wild frizz. She closed her eyes, remembering him pressing his lips to a ringlet of hair that he held between his fingers. She had laughed at him and he had kissed her, until she had pushed him away breathlessly, afraid that Joe would see.

She sank onto her bed, hairbrush clasped to her. She thought of the water running off his sculpted chest, the definition of the muscles across his back, down his long arms, the warmth of his damp skin on her mouth. She hugged herself. She had never known this was possible. She had wanted it for so long, wanted him, but had never understood quite how profound their union might be. She blushed when she thought of herself so brazen in her mad want for him, the delight he took in pleasing her, her ready acceptance of it, always eager.

When she woke up it was getting dark. She glanced across at Joe who had fallen asleep too. It was hardly surprising, he had had a busy afternoon and they had eaten at Keeper's House before coming home. She was suddenly aware something had woken her and someone hid in the gloom by the door.

"Where did you go this afternoon?" Freddy asked.

"Nowhere," she said, wondering if Lisa had betrayed her. "I had work to do."

"Tell me where you went. I know Lisa is lying. You hardly do any work nowadays. You're always taking Joe off on little jaunts to goodness knows where." His voice was even and quiet although she detected a menacing undertone.

"Oh, yes, I went for a walk with Joe this afternoon."

"Did you visit Iain?"

The lie caught in her throat. "No."

"Liar."

She wondered if he had followed her, attack felt like an appropriate response. "Did you sleep with Lisa last night?" she asked.

He was beside the bed in an instant, close to. "Well, I didn't sleep with you," he replied.

She could smell the sour whiff of beer on his breath and turned her face aside. "Too right," she said and withdrew further up the bed away from him. He followed her, sitting now on the edge of the mattress.

He gave a low laugh. "If I find out you're seeing him you'll wish you'd never been born."

"Stop it, Freddy." Her tone was fearless, but a chill sent a shiver down her spine. "Go downstairs and we'll talk."

She was amazed when he left the room immediately. She tidied herself in the mirror, hurried into the hall, quietly closing the door behind her. Freddy was waiting and pushed her across to his bedroom with force. She fell painfully to her knees as he closed the door behind him, barring her way. Standing over her he unbuckled his belt.

"Leave me alone," she said. He laughed and, with a jerk of his hand, freed the belt from his waist. He wrapped it once round his hand ensuring a good grip, leaving the buckle end dangling. As

Nell lunged for the door he brought the belt down across her back, the metal buckle bit painfully. With his free hand he dragged her onto the bed. She attempted to fend him off with her hands and feet as he hit her mercilessly. The buckle cut into her skin, all she could do was pull herself up into a ball, hands over her face and head and wait for him to finish. He lashed at her repeatedly, breathing laboriously with the effort. The whirl of leather smacked the air, the buckle soft against flesh, hard as it struck the bedstead when his target was missed.

His anger spent, he leisurely re-buckled his belt and strolled out, leaving the door ajar. She lay on her side for some time, eyes shut, arms over her head, a slight whimpering coming from her throat. The thought of him returning spurred her to move, painful though it was. She stumbled across the hall to Joe's room.

* * * *

Mr Denham's new car caused quite a stir. Deep red and sparkling chrome, its shiny headlamps staring like bulbous amphibious eyes. It sped merrily along the lanes, horn beeping. Mr Denham, wishing to share in his new toy, invited anyone and everyone to have a ride. Iain was one of the first to be proudly shown the leather interior and fathomless mystery of the internal combustion engine.

Despite his new purchase Mr Denham was a nervous driver and encouraged Iain to try. His repeated refusal was ignored until he eventually buckled to the pressure. He knew the theory of driving. The only practical experience he had gained was driving an army lorry across a French field under Dusty's enthusiastic instruction. In Mr Denham's opinion, sitting in a vehicle with an engine was qualification enough.

So Iain nervously drove Mr Denham, his daughter Sophia, Mr Price, his wife and Betsy Yeates through the village. Once he had mastered the clutch and controlled his initial qualms he warmed to the experience. The engine roared satisfyingly as Mr Denham urged him to put his foot down. They certainly turned a few heads, although after some careful experimenting with the accelerator, Iain realised, it wasn't much faster than a horse at full gallop.

It was late on in the evening by the time he took his leave. He found the mechanics of the engine impossible to grasp and spent more time under the bonnet with Paul, the groom, than behind the wheel.

Walking away from the house he wondered why he hadn't seen Nell for three days now. The previous night he had been certain she would turn up. He jogged back home in his haste, eager to see if she were waiting for him, disappointed to find she wasn't. He ate supper. Later he smoked at the back door watching the bats, waiting. An hour later still he decided to walk up to North Farm. With a bit of luck Freddy might be at the pub. He missed her. He could not wait indefinitely. It was painful.

The temperature had dropped since that afternoon. He strolled purposefully across the North Farm fields towards the house. He hovered in the shelter of the bank by the home paddock and watched and waited for a while. He could see no sign of Freddy or his father. Irritated now by his own indecision he marched up to the door and knocked. After an interval the door opened and a dark eyed girl appeared. He knew the George family, recognized the girl to be one of them at once. She stared open-mouthed at the visitor, her cheeks turning red.

Before he could speak he heard Nell. "Who is it Lisa?"

She turned her head. "I think it's for you, Nell," she said in a stage whisper, backing away as Nell appeared at the door. Nell was visibly shaken to see him.

"What are you doing here?" she hissed.

He leaned against the doorjamb as if he had all day to ponder the question. "You weren't coming down to see me," he stated simply.

She glanced over her shoulder to see where Lisa was. "No, I have my reasons. I'll see you next week."

"I don't think so," he said. "I want to see you tonight."

"Iain!" She was exasperated, keen to see him gone. "I can't see you tonight."

"Is Joe sleeping?"

"Of course he is."

"Is Freddy out?"

"Yes."

"Then come with me now."

Her expression hardened. "No, go away." He thwarted her attempt to slam the door shut by placing his foot in the way. She glared at it in irritation. "Iain," she scolded.

"No," his tone was harsh. "Something's wrong and I want you to come with me, just for an hour." He glanced at his watch. "It's almost nine o clock. You'll be back by ten. I won't go unless you agree."

"How can I? Lisa will know exactly where I've gone."

"She'll cover for you – what choice has she got?"

She could see he had no intention of backing down. She disappeared for a minute and he heard her voice, Lisa's response. She appeared smiling, as if there were no obstacle to their seeing each other, pushing her arms into her cardigan.

"Come on then," she said, walking briskly ahead of him. He followed her. When they were out of sight of the house he caught up, took hold of her hand. She wove her fingers through his. The gesture was confusing. He thought she had gone cold on him. They continued in silence. He noted a depression of her spirit, she was different tonight. Perhaps her feelings for him hadn't changed but he knew something had.

They arrived at Keeper's House and he ushered her in. "So what's wrong?" he asked moving the lamp to the kitchen table where she had seated herself – a physical barrier to keep him away.

She smiled warmly. "Nothing, I'm sorry, I've been so busy."

He was doubtful. "Really?"

"Yes, really." She reached across the table and took his hand. He leaned forward to kiss her. Stirred by the heat of her mouth, he pulled her up, holding her tight, enjoying the sensation of her body pressed to him. He was desperate for her. He undid two buttons at the throat of her blouse. She withdrew from him sharply making him start. "I have to go," she said.

He snatched her wrist as she turned. "No," he said, his tone hard. "What's the matter?"

She tried to get away from him, turning her wrist painfully in his tight grip. "Let me go." Her voice was loud and shrill, almost a scream and tears filled her eyes. He released her and she covered her face with her hands, tears creeping through her fingers. He did his best to comfort her, rocking her in his arms. He stroked her hair with one hand in an attempt to soothe her. Her dismay frightened him. He had only seen her cry twice, over her baby and Joanna's death.

She knew she could not hide from him, could not avoid him or lie.

When she was quieter she said, "Come with me." She carried the lamp up the stairs ahead of him, to his bedroom. She indicated for him to sit on the bed and he waited. She paused in front of him, her eyes dry now but filled with anger and determination. She shrugged off the cardigan, undid the buttons which she had objected to him undoing. She wore no corset and the camisole did little to hide the dark bruises and scabbing blackness of cuts across her chest and back. She lifted the material, they ran up one side, across her diaphragm.

He sprang to his feet. "I'm going to kill him." His face was murderous, fury like poison in his belly, twisting with jealousy and hate. It was bad enough that she was Freddy's wife, but that he had done this, dared to hurt her like this.

She shook her head. "No," she said, "you're not. Where would we be if you did that? I knew what you'd say, knew what you'd want to do."

"It can't happen again."

"It can – I'm his wife – he can do what he pleases," she said and her head drooped, a wilted flower.

He put a finger under her chin, raised her face to him and wiped away her flowing tears with his fingertips. He attended each bruise and cut with his lips, pushing the straps off her shoulders.

"No," he said at length, "you're no longer his, you're mine." He kissed the cleft above her lip. "You shall come here and live with me." He held her tight, safe and treasured, she relaxed, calmed by his touch. "You're mine," he repeated, gazing into her eyes, his lips on hers again, hot with his craving. "We belong together." His hands were in her hair, fingers trailing down her back. "I won't let him do this," he murmured into the crook of her neck and she undid the buttons of his shirt. "You're mine," he repeated. His resolve was absolute and she nodded dumbly. They belonged together.

* * * *

It sounded obvious when he said it and she had been safe in the circle of his arms. It was easy with his kisses hot on her skin, strong hands soothing her, hypnotising her into a false optimism. Now, alone in her room at North Farm, the case packed on her bed, it was impossible. It could not be done, she reasoned. It was socially unacceptable. The whole village would erupt with gossip about them. Freddy would go mad and try to kill Iain or her or both. It wasn't reasonable to expect her to go through with it. They might live in a modern age, but life in Harrowford had been the same for hundreds of years and they weren't broad-minded enough to accept them. A man or woman could commit adultery, but they didn't actually leave their spouse to move in with their lover. It wasn't done.

Her courage had failed. It was late afternoon and Iain was coming here at six. What could she do? How could she stop it? He reassured her endlessly and she was desperate to believe him. Now she was filled with doubt – not for her love of Iain – but for the life they would lead, the threat Freddy posed. She feared he didn't fully appreciate Freddy's vengeful nature. She wasn't completely confident about Iain's intention towards Freddy either. She felt herself to be in the eye of a storm, some sort of catalyst, the outcome of which she couldn't even begin to ascertain.

The house was quiet around her. If she were going, she thought, the time was now, not later. She could visualise Iain coming, making a scene, Freddy's dramatics, Joe's tears. She wrote a letter to Freddy, straightforward and honest. *'I cannot live like this any more. I have a chance to be happy so I am leaving you.'* She hardly dared think of what his reaction to it might be. At least, she told herself, she would not be there to see it.

She was only able to take what she could carry. When the dust settled she intended fetching the rest, even so, without help, she was fairly weighed down. She put her two suitcases in the hall. Despite the sunshine outside she pulled on her coat to save carrying it.

Lisa was busy rolling pastry for steak and kidney pie, something Nell had taught her. "Blimey," Lisa said when she saw her, "you won't need a coat on if you're going out."

"I've a lot to carry. Joe, come on, you can help me with something, we're going now," she said. He scrambled to pick up his tin soldiers from under the table, dropping them into the carpetbag which she opened for him.

Lisa eyed her suspiciously. "What's going on?"

"I'm leaving, Lisa, you can have him and welcome."

Her brown eyes widened, mortified. "Leaving? You can't leave, where will you go?" Lisa's expression altered as the truth dawned on her. "Oh good grief, you're going to Harrowmead, to the keeper."

"Yes, I am. I've left a note, nothing to worry about." Her voice trembled.

"Blimey, Nell, you know how it's going to be. He'll go mad, he hates the keeper, he told me. What will happen?"

She was forced to agree. "I don't know, Lisa, but if I stay – well, you know how it is." She didn't want to explain about Iain, not to Lisa who slept with her husband. She said to Joe, "You must be clever and carry the carpetbag. I can't hold your hand, I have to take the cases." She picked them up and Joe obediently followed at her heel with his large bag. "Goodbye, Lisa, I'm sure I'll see you soon." Lisa was speechless, scarlet cheeked and gaping.

Out in the sunshine her responsibilities fell away from her. She hadn't even said goodbye to Mrs Hart, who now would suffer neglect and loneliness. What option was there? Martyr herself to the Hart family for the rest of her life? She couldn't do it. She would have sprinted down the lane if not for her luggage. Freddy was at market today so she knew she wouldn't see him if she took the easiest route through the village.

Keeper's House was locked, so she used her key to gain entry. "Are we going to live here now?" Joe asked.

"Yes, we are. Come upstairs and we will put your things in your new room."

She had chosen the smallest bedroom for him, with a white fireplace and a view of the fields at the back of the house, it would catch the afternoon sun. It was plainly decorated in faded pale grey stripes, the single bed of painted white wood was curved head and foot like a little sleigh. The floors, like those in the rest of the house, were wide polished boards. It was all quite familiar to Joe from their many visits and she left him unpacking his carpetbag. It was full of all that was valuable to a little boy of four, tin soldiers, books and the leather horse sewn by Hans the cobbler.

She went along the hall, her feet ticking on the floor, into Iain's bedroom. The large iron bed was unmade, as he had fallen out of it that morning. Riding boots stood to attention against the wall, there was a large double fronted wardrobe and a dressing table with a mirror reflecting the bed behind her.

Up here she was part of the woodland, a view into the world of branches and leaves. A jay regarded her quizzically before flying away. Everything was so different now he was back. A shirt hung over the chair, gun parts and string next to a hairbrush and a small pair of silver nail scissors. Books were piled on the floor and chair seat, pamphlets on shooting and a variety of country pursuits, mirroring the collection in the parlour and kitchen. By the bed a brass candleholder held a half burned candle and beside it were discarded wax stubs he hadn't quite managed to throw away.

Iain saw her cases as he came in the door. He climbed the stairs two at a time, bursting into the bedroom. She spread her hands out at her sides, as if to say, yes, I'm here. All her fears and doubts drained away, as she knew they would once he was with her.

It was done, she was here and all they had to do was ride out the storm.

* * * *

The urgent banging on the door came before six. Nell envisioned Freddy's actions, home from market, reading the letter and straight back out. His anger would be at its peak. Iain plainly saw the terror in her eyes.

"Take Joe upstairs," he said firmly. She obediently took Joe's hand, led him to his room.

Freddy's rage and disbelief were barely contained behind a pale slipping mask. "Macdonald." His words were strangled. "Is Nell here?"

Iain's concerns vanished. Freddy was a weak character. It would take little to send him on his way. "Aye, she is and this is where she stays."

He was trying to see over Iain's large frame which adequately blocked the view. "I have to see her," he said.

"No."

His eyes flashed with frustration. "Iain, I have to. She can't live here, with you. She's my wife, mine."

"You don't own her. She's not a slave to be owned. She can divorce you and then it won't be a problem will it? Any road she stays here with me and she shall remain unmolested and safe. I don't want to hear that you've been anywhere near her. I don't want you to come to the house again, stay away and we can all live our lives." He spoke calmly, aware of Nell listening somewhere out of sight.

"No, it doesn't work like that. I won't allow it."

Iain laughed. "You have no threat to frighten me, Freddy, you know that. So much has happened between us, I know you too well. Remember, I saved your worthless skin once."

"This time it's different. I make no threats I shall not carry through."

"Make no threats at all and we'd all be content."

"Please," he implored Iain. "Let me speak to her, for a minute."

Iain felt Nell's hand on his back. He stepped aside and stood squarely behind her, watching Freddy distrustfully. Freddy's expression altered when he saw her. He smiled, the darkness in his eyes struggling to take control.

"Nell, you can't stay here," he urged. "I forgive you. Come home now. I've been wrong too, I know that and I'm sorry. Things will be different from now on. I'm your husband, you must do as I say."

She shook her head, took a slight movement backwards into Iain who remained firm. "I'm never coming back. We don't love each other, do we? You can manage without me, you have Lisa."

"Lisa?" he said as if he could not believe his ears. "She's a foolish girl. Don't turn it around because you've rekindled your affair with him. All happy families is it? The two of you with your son. What of that Iain? All this time I'm cuckolded, raising your child as my own."

"I thank you for it, I'm sure," he said.

Freddy's mask of containment slipped away, his face a black contorted vision. "You bastard."

Iain pushed Nell behind him into the hall as Freddy charged at him. He easily rebuffed the challenge sending Freddy flying out of the doorway, thudding onto the soft earth at the front of the house. Iain whistled shrilly and Delilah and a young big pawed pup with gambolling, uncontrolled limbs appeared. Delilah, even in her dotage, could be impressively fearsome, her teeth bared, growling ominously in her throat.

"I've no time for you now, Freddy," Iain said. "Go on before I set the dog on you. We'll talk when you're calmer. You really need to get a hold of yourself, man."

He shut the door, leaving Freddy backing away from the two dogs. Delilah took a small step forward for each of Freddy's steps back, until he was able to close the gate to bar the animal's way, forgetting she could have easily jumped over it.

Nell, shaky and agitated, paced the floor. "What shall I do? Oh, Iain, what's going to happen? I shouldn't have come, I knew this was impossible."

He gripped her shoulders. "Stop it, Helena, this is what he wants. He's full of hot air, always has been. You knew he wouldn't roll over. Don't fall at the first fence, he'll calm down. It would have been strange if he hadn't come shouting the odds, wouldn't it?"

She had to agree. "Yes, I know, but I shall be frightened to go out, jumping at shadows."

"Freddy's done some stupid things in his effort to take petty vengeance but I think he's learned his lesson from Tom."

Tom, what had happened to Tom? At that moment Joe bounded down the stairs, there was supper to prepare and eat, the moment to ask had passed. Iain showed her his contrived bathroom, running a hot bath, which she shared with Joe while he split wood in the back yard.

Once Joe was tucked in bed they sat companionably in front of the fire in the parlour. Her worries and doubts gnawed at her. Iain tried his best but he knew he failed to comfort her. This would be their first night together and the spectre of Freddy hung in the air an intangible future threat, which would inevitably have to be confronted.

The rumble of thunder rolled round the valley, the sky lighting up with electric, large drops of rain wetting the dry earth, purging the air with its unique ozone. It was an apt end to a difficult day.

They went up to bed, it all felt so strange to her. She lay in the large bed where she would spend the whole night, watching Iain undress, the sheet pulled up to her chin. She was unused to sharing her life with someone so intimately.

She climbed out of bed. "Where are you going?" he asked.

"To check on Joe." She tiptoed across the hall, kneeling by Joe's bed, his breathing was rhythmic and shallow in sleep. She stroked his hair back from his forehead, kissed his firm smooth cheek.

"He's still there then," Iain said when she returned.

She flushed. "Sorry, it's silly, I'm afraid Freddy might do something stupid."

"How long has he known about Joe?"

"He always knew – but – he got it all wrong. He thinks he's our son – yours and mine. I never could tell him the truth in case he threw Joe out. As long as I denied everything he always had doubt. He assumed we'd had an affair."

Iain released the clasp in her hair. "And now we do." He smiled, lowered his head to kiss her open lips. He carried her to the bed and with ravenous mouths and hungry fingers they made love until the first light of dawn touched the sky. They finally slept tucked into each other like a pair of spoons, her back against his chest, his arm under her neck, hand cupping her bare shoulder.

* * * *

When he opened his eyes he saw her chestnut hair fan the pillow beside him. He was not in a dream, this was real, last night had been real. He felt totally at peace with the world, everything was perfect. He put his hand under the covers, down her small warm body. She shivered and turned over curling into him.

"Don't," he said, meaning, "do". He kissed her dry unresponsive mouth. Feeling his arousal Nell opened herself to him with an urgent immediacy. His lips brushed her neck and he raised himself on his elbows and studied her face as he moved in her. She returned his gaze unabashed.

Outside the woodland dripped with rainwater. The river raced faster and deeper from the deluge, the wood shone cleanly. The redolent, rich smell of the earth filtered through the trees as the sun peered cautiously from behind the clouds, its heat evaporating the sparkling drops. Rooks cawed high in the elms, the reverberating knock of the woodpecker's beak against wood. It was a shiny new day full of promise and summer.

Across the valley Freddy woke up, he had no thoughts, only a blank, black enveloping vileness. His heart beat time with the thump in his head. He was not alone, the voices filled the room, chanting tonelessly, keeping him company. From the back of a drawer he withdrew the German pistol. His fingers traced the cold metal. Visions of blood danced in front of his eyes. He was on a journey. It would lead him to oblivion but he was powerless to resist the pull to join in the dance.

Chapter Thirty-two

September started cool and misty. The Hubbleford Hounds were reinstated. The few pups born during the war now came together to create a pack ready for the hunt reforming. Iain's woods ran with pheasant and wild partridge; there would be more game than Mr Denham anticipated.

He had paid for Phoenix to be shipped back from France, and he was the only thoroughbred in the stable. They supplemented the shortfall with horses bought from local markets. Iain drove Nell and Joe in Mr Denham's motorcar to a horse fair in the next county. He bought a fine mare with a slightly temperamental disposition, which he was confident could be cured with kind, firm handling.

Mr Denham heard a half thoroughbred stallion was up for auction at Dunford Market, some twelve miles away. Iain and Mr Judd were to accompany him, their opinions being paramount. The horse was an expensive investment and he was keen not to be ripped off.

At Keeper's House Nell settled into her new life. Six weeks passed and Freddy did not disturb them. With the passing of each week, she became quietly more confident that all would be well. Iain noticed her relax, singing at her tasks, laughing more easily, she was less jumpy and nervous.

A similar change came over Joe. He shed his cloak of quiet caution. He was no longer anxious but talkative and confident. He loved this tall softly spoken man who his mother said he was to call Daddy and who never raised his voice, or banged the table with his fist, or hit his mummy, or threatened him with horrible things. Joe liked sitting on his knee, warm and safe, listening to that strange, lilting voice reading to him, or playing games on his fingers.

His new daddy sang odd little songs he'd never heard before, made up rhymes with his name in them. He was a giant amongst the treetops, high on his daddy's shoulders, pointing out the nests, birds, little animals and secret hiding places, that Joe would never have seen on his own. They would sit on the riverbank, quietly companionable, waiting for the fish to bite at their hooks, and his father made such a fuss of him if he caught anything. Joe was happy and his mother was happy, there was love and laughter, security and peace.

The morning of the Dunford Market Nell and Joe accompanied Iain to the house to see Cook. If their living arrangements were common knowledge they had not been commented on directly, much to Nell's intense relief, although she had noticed people cross the road to avoid her who might once have bid her good day. Iain had no problem with being the topic of gossip. He had Nell exactly where he wanted her and there was nothing anyone could say that would dampen his high spirits.

* * * *

Freddy walked the perimeter of his field holding his father's new rifle over his arm. A hare nestled in a furrow of the field the same colour as the earth. Raising the gun to his shoulder, a noise suddenly distracted him. He scrutinized the shadow of Harrowmead wood, lowering the rifle. He heard voices and they weren't in his head. He knew who it was. He knew her laughter.

He climbed over the fence into the woodland, his feet sinking into the leaf mould. The leaves were a hundred shades of gold and brown, gently pattering onto the ground. He headed along the track at speed. The sharp crack of a branch startled him. He saw a little boy crouched at the edge of the path picking up acorns. Joe was shocked to see Freddy, his startling green eyes filled with tears. Freddy placed a finger to his lips and narrowed his eyes in threat. Joe froze in fear.

Freddy scanned the woodland. He skulked past Joe, moving carefully from tree to tree. He heard a titter of her laughter, the low intimate voices of lovers. He saw them, his chest tightened, an intermittent pain throbbing in his left temple.

Iain held her tightly against him. She giggled when he kissed her. Freddy was rooted to the spot. He could not tear his eyes away. There was such fervour between them. They melted into each other. Her hand, white on his black hair, drew him as close as she could. His large hand emphasising her trim waist was possessive. He was so tall, in an old army coat. Powerful and commanding, Freddy thought. The kiss finished, they stared into each other's eyes with intimate intensity. Nobody else existed, only the two of them - bewitched.

The sight of them together aroused Freddy. He wanted to be Iain. For a moment he imagined how it would feel to be the keeper, the one who dominated her, possessing her, ruling her.

Those large hands on her white throat could so easily break her dainty neck.

He understood now, how they related to each other, how Iain had demanded her, how she had been powerless to refuse him. But then, as he finally made sense of it, Iain put his hand up to her face, confusing Freddy completely. In a tender, feminine gesture Iain tucked a stray curl behind her ear. He caught hold of her hand quite gently, kissed her fingertips and a look passed between them of understanding and mutual trust. They both laughed, seemingly at nothing. Freddy felt sick. They sickened him, he loathed them and he loathed himself. "Joe," Iain called still smiling at Nell, "come on." Joe warily edged past Freddy and ran after them.

* * * *

Iain drank a cup of tea in the kitchen with Cook and Nell while he waited for Mr Denham. He was impatient to be off, it was already eight o'clock. As usual Mr Denham knew nothing of punctuality. Mr Judd appeared in the doorway equally agitated, "Isn't he ready yet?" he said, his hat perched jauntily on his baldhead, a bright yellow neckerchief tucked into his collar.

Iain paced up and down, muttering. "Good grief," Cook complained, "you're like a lion in a cage, go knock up Mrs Harris to give him a shove – or get someone else to."

"Here." Judd retrieved a letter from his pocket. "This arrived for you." Iain's post came to the big house, usually Paul was sent down to Keeper's House later to deliver it.

Iain took it absently, reading the ornate script on the front before pushing it into his jacket pocket. Mr Denham arrived buttoning his tight waistcoat. "Ready for the off, chaps?" he said brightly as if he were bang on time.

Judd and Iain suddenly transformed into the picture of calm. Nell and Cook smiled at each other. Mr Denham followed Judd out of the back door.

"Right," Iain said, ruffling Joe's hair. The boy grinned at him. "See you after, Joe. You're not going anywhere are you?" he addressed Nell. He didn't mean to sound possessive. He was suspicious of Freddy's prolonged absence and this morning he woke with a strange feeling in the pit of his stomach that made him uneasy.

"No," she said, aware of Cook's rapt attention. He hovered for a second, torn between bidding her a formal farewell in front of Cook, or kissing her as he wished.

"I'd better be going, I've lots to do, come on Joe," she said, taking a bag of cooking apples Cook had given her, more than a kind gesture Nell thought.

They stood together on the steps at the back door. "I'll be back by three," he said.

"Don't worry, I'll be fine."

"I know." He embraced her.

"You know she's watching through the window." She smiled as they parted.

He laughed. "Aye, give her something to talk about won't it." He winked and strolled towards the stable yard, tall and straight. Sometimes he held himself like the Lord of the Manor, she thought.

The car sped up the drive, the horn beeping dully, the wheels crunching and spitting up gravel. Iain was driving. For someone suspicious of the motorcar revolution, he was adapting admirably. She waved and Mr Judd waved back through the small rear window.

They walked home with Delilah and the growing pup Destiny. She constantly tried to entice Delilah into a game of chase, throwing herself in front of the older dog, head down between her splayed front legs, bottom in the air, tail wagging. Delilah was having none of it sidestepping with agility and occasionally snapping if the puppy were too enthusiastic.

Nell was slowly trying to gather up Iain's work implements and gadgets which littered the house, insisting he control his obsession with coils, springs and bits of string. He could not be persuaded, all she could do was pick them up and assign them to a drawer or receptacle.

Her job in the kitchen at Harrowmead had hardened her to dealing with game and she skinned two rabbits efficiently, jointing them, adding vegetables, stock and herbs to the pot. She found her flour bag empty and no sugar. "Come on, Joe, we'll go to the shop."

The village shop was busy and she had to queue for her flour and sugar and a twist of pear drops for Joe. She noticed the sudden intense quiet that came over Mrs Scup's customers the minute she walked through the door. There was an awkward clearing of throats and a couple of women looked her up and down. Colonel Edam's daughter whispered to her companion behind her hand. It was one of those places where it was hard to hide, this reception was only to be expected. Nell lowered her eyes, feeling her cheeks burn. She would not be cowed by them. If she turned away now she would never be able to shop here again. She gave her order in a haughty voice and Mrs Scup had the grace to answer politely, although her smile was strained.

Outside, Nell steadied herself against the postbox to regain her composure. A little cough drew her attention, while Joe, looking over his shoulder, tugged on her skirt.

Lisa was pale and drawn, biting her bottom lip. Her eyes flitted nervously around them. "Hello, Lisa," said Nell, relieved to see a familiar face. "How are things?"

"I called on you at the gamekeeper's place."

She smiled. "I suppose I wasn't in."

Lisa returned the smile faintly. "Well, you're here now, so that's good. Freddy asked if you could go up this afternoon to collect some of your stuff. There's not much. He really wanted to see Joe."

"Joe? Why would he want to see Joe?"

"He is the boy's father," Lisa said patiently.

"Oh, yes, I see. I'm not sure."

"Why? It'll be all right. I must admit he was upset for a while. He seems a lot better now. He's been quite – good lately," she said. "He seems to have accepted – things."

"Really? Well, I suppose it wouldn't hurt. Will you be there and Mr Hart? I can't stop long."

"You won't have to. Come over after lunch."

"Two o'clock then," she agreed, thinking how cross Iain would be with the arrangement. Some of her most precious belongings had remained at the farm, her walnut box for one, and it would be better to go with Iain out of the way.

Leaving Lisa, she went home to finish dinner, putting it in the slow oven at the bottom of the range. She made apple pie, singing into the pastry crumbs as they ran through her fingers.

She pushed away the discomfort of her experience in the village. She wanted her love for Iain to be acceptable. She would not apologise for it and yet neither could she imagine it ever being tolerated here. She had once been a respected member of the community, now she could not even face attending church. She knew making this choice would have consequences and she was determined to deal with them. It helped that she liked the quiet domesticity of her new life. At North Farm the multiple calls for her time and attention had been wearing, all drudgery and daydreams.

She prayed that in time memories would fade, resentments heal and gossip run its course. Meanwhile she must keep to herself and avoid confrontation. If time were not the answer the only alternative was to move away and that did not seem to be an option at all.

Her eyes felt heavy, tiredness too overwhelming to ignore. It would not hurt to put her feet up for a minute in the parlour. Curling up on the couch with Joe in her arms they fell asleep.

She woke with a start, it was almost two o'clock. Joe stretched and yawned. She stared at her pale, tousled reflection in the mirror, pulling her skirt tight over her flat stomach she peered sideways at herself and smiled. Her secret was safe, growing, nestled deep inside, hers and Iain's. She would tell him later. She had been uncertain at first. Now she had missed two months and that wasn't normal for her.

She wrote a note for Iain although she hoped to be back long before he returned. Locking the door behind them, she held Joe's hand and set off along the woodland path towards North Farm.

* * * *

Bidding on the horse went well and Mr Judd secured him at a good price. Its temperament was equable, it was physically strong and well cared for. Mr Denham was thrilled with his new purchase and the approval of his two reliable servants.

Judd left earlier than Iain and the squire, riding the stallion, a fine black with a dappling of dark grey on its haunches. Iain had half an hour to fill while Mr Denham finished some business. He wandered to the beer tent and bought a pint then, tired of the noise and bustle, he inspected the last few lots not yet sold. The gypsies were selling little Shetland ponies, white with brown patches on their backs. One tried to nip him through the fence with stained square teeth and he laughed at its audacity.

He lit a cigarette, leaned back on an upturned beer barrel, remembering the letter in his pocket. He ripped it open. He scanned the formal heading on the heavy, watermarked paper. It was from a lawyer in Scotland.

'We regret to inform you of the death of your father, Bruce John Sinclair, Laird of Glenleven, Glenleven Hall in the County of Stirling. Could you please attend our office at the earliest opportunity for the reading of the Last Will and Testament. I enclose a letter from your late father at his request...'

He opened the second letter, from Sinclair to Iain, dated a week before his death.

It read: *'I understand, from my doctor, I have a short time left to me. I lost my son, Adam, in 1916 in France. My wife and I divorced the following year. She met some poor devil with a purse heavier than mine and left for America. You are now my sole heir. You will receive the bulk of my Estate and I am in no doubt you deserve it. They say the meek shall inherit the earth and in your case the unassuming has. I know you survived your war. Mr Denham was always kind enough to keep me informed of your progress. I am sad my part in your life has been played at such a distance. I have always had a deep affection for you, always wanted the best for you. It is fitting my eldest son should become the new laird. Should you choose to live here and raise a family it would make me deeply happy. If you choose to sell, then I understand and do so with my blessing. I will always be your undeserving, inadequate, Father, Bruce Sinclair'*

Iain contemplated the news for some time. Sole heir to Glenleven. It was unbelievable, quite ironic. Bruce Sinclair, the man who left him in an orphanage for six years before placing him in the hands of Finnigan, abuse layered by abuse. But Iain knew he was also the man who paid vast sums of money to secure the best lawyers possible when Iain was accused of murder. He had Bruce Sinclair to thank for his freedom and his life. He had not been a man of pure bluster, he cared, deep down. Somewhere he had a conscience. If Iain would never know the truth of his mother then at least he had known his father and, despite everything, he had liked the essence of the man.

He thought of Joanna, her ambition and dreams, and Nell who wished only to be happy and secure. This offered security that he had never even dreamed was possible. It probably wasn't all he was set to inherit either. Sinclair had a few bob. He laughed then, loudly so heads turned to look at him, but he didn't notice. He slipped the letters inside his jacket. The tide of life was turning and nothing would ever be the same. The amazing idea of being Laird of Glenleven set him laughing again.

He went in search of Mr Denham, found him eventually, looking for Iain.

"Come on," Iain said. "I'll buy you a drink before we go. I've got some news I want to share with you."

Mr Denham beamed at him affably, pleased with what the day had brought him. "Good show, Macdonald, could do with a snifter of something."

He led Mr Denham to the beer tent and pushed his way to the bar.

* * * *

Before Iain found her note, he knew something wasn't right. Not merely the absence of her, it was that strange sensation he had woken up to. He had dismissed it as a remnant of a dream and all day it rubbed like a hair shirt on his conscience. As the day wore on he had a strong desire to get back to Harrowmead, and it wasn't to do with sharing his news about Glenleven. When he found her note a ghastly feeling of déjà vu came to him. He read it and a horrible sickness gripped his stomach. Freddy had asked her to the farm to collect some of her stuff. A vision of Tom hanging in the jaws of the mantrap came into his head. It was a ploy to get her to the farm. Freddy had some vengeful plan in his head, he hardly dared think what.

He didn't stop to grab his gun or lock the door and it swung open behind him. Delilah and Destiny raced at his heels as he sped through the trees, legs catching in the undergrowth, jumping over bramble and ditch. He scissored over the fence that separated Harrowmead and the farm. He traversed the field where the gypsies had camped all that time ago, feet hitting the stubble where the corn had been cut, sinking into the soft earth, slowing his pace. His heart hammered in his chest, breath thundering in his lungs. He didn't slow or dare to pause.

He hit the front door of the farmhouse with a loud wallop, careering through it as it gave under his weight. His feet scrabbled on the tiles and he gripped the kitchen doorframe to steady himself. Nell, sitting at the table, glanced over her shoulder, eyes very blue and wide. Freddy had his back to the fireplace, the dull shine of a pistol in one hand his finger poised on the trigger. Iain froze, his eyes fixed on Freddy who stared back at him, a slow smirk spreading across his face.

"So he's here, your knight in shining armour, Nell," Freddy said with glee.

She turned back to Freddy a look of grim determination painted on her face. Iain found his voice as his breathing became less ragged. "What are you doing?" he asked.

"I'm holding a gun and threatening your tart with it." Freddy aimed the gun directly at her.

"Where did you get that?" he asked.

"A souvenir from Fritz. I brought it back to kill you with." His eyes glinted with obsession.

"Why don't you put it down and we can talk it through?" Iain raised a hand to placate him, his movements slow and predictable.

"You want to talk? Yes, all right, let's talk about the truth shall we? After all these years."

"What truth?"

"The truth about Tom - and you - and Nell - and everything."

"Put the gun down. Let Helena go, this is about you and me, it always has been."

"I like it better this way. Nell needs to hear the truth too. Now let's start with Tom."

"I can't enlighten you about Tom, can I?"

"Why did you help to bury Tom? Why didn't you go to the police?" Freddy asked.

She looked between the two men, held her breath. Iain took a slow step into the room. "I had too much to lose, Freddy, it's as simple as that."

"What have you done? What are you hiding?"

Iain glanced at Nell who stared at him, waiting for the truth that Freddy spoke so easily of. "I've done nothing I haven't paid dearly for, unlike you, who appears to get away with murder, quite literally." He watched Freddy carefully.

"Come on then, I'm sure Nell can't wait to hear your confession." He really thought he had Iain nicely.

Iain smiled at his folly. "Many years ago I was charged with murdering a man." The words sounded even worse spoken out loud.

Nell turned pale. Freddy said, "Who?"

"The gamekeeper, Finnigan. Back home in Scotland, I was the gamekeeper's lad. Finnigan drowned and I was accused of his murder."

"And did you?" he asked.

"I was put on trial, the verdict was not proven. In Scotland it's an alternative to guilty or not guilty."

"What does it mean?" she asked in a choked voice.

"It means he's a cold blooded murderer."

"It means," Iain stared at her unblinking, "they thought I had murdered him, but they couldn't prove it." She nodded her head slowly. He turned back to Freddy. "So you see when you set a mantrap for me, a trap locked in my shed, set in my woods, and that trap caught your brother instead and killed him," he spelt it out for Nell's benefit so there should be no misunderstanding, "it didn't look too good for me did it? I had an unproven verdict for murder behind me, and a dead man lying at my front door. What was I supposed to do? I couldn't trust you to confess, I couldn't control what you might say or accuse me of."

Freddy laughed manically. "Christ, yes, of course. What a pickle. If only I had gone to the police after all."

"If you'd done that it wouldn't only have been my neck in the noose, Freddy, and you know it. I liked Tom, I was sorry for what you did."

His eyes filled with tears, he said, "I am sorry for what I did." He wiped his eyes with the back of his hand. "And what about you two – what about the boy?"

"Can't we stop this now?" She stood up facing the gun.

"Sit down," Freddy said, with a sharp movement of the barrel.

She sat. "I've told you before there was never anything between Iain and me, never. I was always a faithful wife."

"And yet, by some miracle the boy is his. Don't deny it, you only have to look at the child."

Iain's eyes searched the room trying and failing to locate Joe.

She looked despairingly at Freddy. "Yes, Iain is Joe's father," she said. Iain saw the confusion in Freddy's face as she continued. "Our baby died, Freddy, our baby died. He was born too early and Joanna's baby lived." Tears welled in her eyes. "I wanted a baby so badly and Joanna's baby needed me so much." She stopped, putting her hand across her eyes, tears falling. She was appalled by her own weakness, unable to get her story out without breaking down. Her hand subconsciously covered her stomach and Iain noticed the protective gesture.

"Good God, there's a revelation. I've been quite an idiot haven't I? Joanna? Is that why she made such a swift getaway? And she died, didn't she. Christ, she died having your baby." He glared at Iain. "Sometimes I talked myself into believing you, Nell. I really did believe sometimes. I thought it was part of this," he tapped his temple, "this confusion, but it was true. You made me think he was mine – denied it and denied it – all this time. I bet you've been having a good laugh at my expense." Clearly the disclosure had stunned him.

"Hardly," Iain said. "I didn't do it to antagonise you, nor did Helena. Joe needed a mother, Helena needed a child. It was simple – at the time. It didn't seem to hurt anyone. How can you be so petty? You've been in a war where hundreds of our boys were lost. We're talking about the life of one son, a decent life instead of one spent in a children's home. Anyway, Joe's not your responsibility any more, I'm glad to take him on."

"Yes, and my wife too, it seems. Is there nothing you don't destroy?" Freddy said.

"I didn't mean to take your wife. I didn't plan it. I should have told her the truth about Tom before you married her. I've been dishonest, to her and to myself. I have always cared about her even if I didn't know it, but she chose you, above me, above anyone. She chose you. She wouldn't have turned to me if you'd made her happy. You wouldn't be in this mess. You beat her, Freddy, I wouldn't abuse a dog like that."

Freddy winced, dejected, a child caught out in a naughty act. "It's all been destroyed, Iain. Surely you see that." His demeanour changed, he stared at the gun in his hands.

"It hasn't," Iain said. "You need to move on. You've survived Tom's death. You survived your own death. You almost died. You've survived – the war is over, don't let it end in more destruction. Live the life you have left."

Iain took a few steps closer and held out his shaking hands for the gun. He saw the sheen of tears in Freddy's eyes. "I can't let it go," Freddy whispered. "I've tried. I murdered Tom. I didn't mean to, but I did and I can't live with it."

"You're going to have to try harder," he implored. "There are things I've done which I have to live with."

Freddy swung the gun back up, aiming it squarely at Iain. "Yes, you have."

"And we all did things in the war which we have to try to forget," he said.

Freddy nodded, the gun was heavy in his hand, recalling the thrust of the bayonet, the scream of the enemy, young like Tom as handsome and strong. "I can't forget," he said. "I wish I'd died out there, I wish I'd never come home. The biggest part of me died long ago."

"Don't do any more damage. Give me the gun." Iain was so close now he could have reached forward and touched the grey metal.

Freddy thrust it forward into Iain's face and he stepped back. Nell was at his shoulder, the steady grip of her hands clasping his arm, warm and reassuring. As soon as Iain withdrew, Freddy pointed the pistol under his own chin, one finger tight on the trigger.

Iain shrieked, "No." Behind him Nell tightened her grip on his arm. Freddy paused, the tears he had held back rolled down his contorted face, the tip of the gun pressed flat against his skin.

"It's over now, Iain."

"Please, Freddy." He reached out his hands, begging. "Please don't, Freddy, please don't." Iain's face was wet with tears, the terror grinding in his chest, his hands trembling, out of his control and still he begged. "No, Freddy, please, don't, please…" He was still pleading as Freddy squeezed the trigger. The room shook with the reverberating crash of the explosion. Freddy was thrown against the fireplace. Blood and brain splattered up the wall and across the ceiling. With a resounding thump he slid to the floor, leaving a trail of blood that continued to ooze. His head lolled back, unseeing black eyes stared up at the pattern of red above him.

Iain fell to his knees. Nell stood behind him transfixed. After a moment she sank down beside him, put her arms around him. He was racked with raw, burning sobs.

"Iain, stop. Iain, Iain," she said his name over and over, rocking him, trying to calm him, averting her eyes from the gore across the room. Slowly his sobbing subsided. He shuddered uncontrollably, stared uncomprehending at Freddy's body. She crouched in front of him, blocking his view of the corpse.

"Iain, listen." Her voice was calm with forced composure. "You must listen to me, this is important." His eyes focused on her with difficulty. "Good," she said. "Listen, Lisa took Joe to the pond by the Common. Go there and fetch him home. Go straight back to Keeper's House, don't speak to anyone, don't tell anyone. You mustn't say you were here. It'll be simpler if you weren't here. There will be no questions then. Nobody knows you came, so fetch Joe and go home and when the police have been I shall come to you. Do you understand?"

"I - can't – leave – you – here - with – this," he said haltingly.

"Yes, you can. I don't want any questions about us, or Tom and you, anything that happened in Scotland, it's all so complicated. Please do as I say, please."

He understood. He could see, despite his anguish, it made sense. "Why did he do it?" he said.

"I don't know. Because he lost his mind, Iain. Now go and do as I say." Somehow she helped him to his feet and shoved him out the door. "Keep your head, Iain," she called after him.

He tripped over the Common, the two dogs trailing at his feet. To anyone observing him he appeared to be quite himself, perhaps a bit hunched over, his head flicking every so often as if from a bothersome fly. He smoked one cigarette after another trying to control his shaking hands. He could hear the sound of shellfire and he had to stop himself visibly flinching.

He found them by the pond. Lisa smiled nervously when she saw him. "Hello, sir," she said. "Nell's up at the farm."

"Oh is she?" he said, his voice controlled but cracking. "I'll take Joe home if that's all right with you. I expect you've got work to do, you can head back."

She was keen to return and check on Freddy and Nell. She was frightened Freddy might want Nell back and that would not help her position at all. She bobbed a curtsy to him as if he were the squire.

He watched her scurry over the Common towards the farm. He closed his eyes. Cool drops of light rain fell on his face. Images of Michael flashed through his brain, the terror in his young eyes, of Freddy falling back against the fireplace, his lifeless body sprawled across the kitchen floor. Joe pushed his small hand into Iain's. He glanced down at the boy's trusting face.

"Hello, Joe." He picked him up and held him tight in his arms, smelling the warm salty scent of the living hard flesh of his body. He cried quietly into the boy's neck. Joe was unperturbed, used to tears and stretched his arms, as far as he was able, around Iain's broad shoulders. "Come on, son," he said and carried him home across the Common, through the woods.

* * * *

Nell returned home hours later. Iain had long since put Joe to bed. Darkness had fallen and he waited until he saw the small light of her electric torch shining through the trees. He ran out to meet her, threw his arms around her and hung on as if his life depended on it.

    That night he lay awake watching the trembling tracery of shadows reflected from the branches outside. Nell slept soundly encircled in his arms, exhausted from the day. The local constable had interviewed her, wheezy from his bicycle ride, his pencil that he licked repetitively snapping against the notepad. He spoke to Mrs Hart only briefly. She had been woken from a deep sleep by the gunshot. Mr Hart had arrived along with Lisa shortly after Iain had left. The constable had been kind, assuring them that a verdict of suicide would undoubtedly be reached. Only last week a young man had killed himself, injured in the war like Freddy.

    Iain went over and over their conversation in his head and everything that followed. The bloody image played repeatedly like a silent film at the picture house except in gory, coloured detail. In the early hours he drifted in and out of sleep. Even then he found himself in the grip of horrible, vivid nightmares that jerked him back to consciousness.

Chapter Thirty-three

Iain opened his eyes to the rays of weak, early morning sunshine forcing their way through the curtains. While Nell slept he watched her composed face, the fall and rise of her chest, her fingers curled on the pillow. He studied every detail of her, the arch of the eyebrows, the neat triangular nostrils and symmetrical peaks of her lips. Soundlessly he rose from the warmth of the bed and dressed. He crept across to Joe's room. His son slept deeply, hair very dark on the pillow, relaxed and soft in his repose.

Outside he released the dogs from their kennel. They bounced round him enthusiastically. Without his gun he walked with his hands in his jacket pockets through the woodland. The trees arched above him, a magnificent natural cathedral. In the silence he could hear the gentle sound of leaf hitting leaf as the stray ones fell to the ground, the steady rhythm of his own breath and the soft tread of his boots in the damp earth. Now their initial excitement was spent, the dogs trailed him sedately.

He wasn't mourning Freddy but the loss had shaken something deep within him, awakened the powerful sense of all that had been lost. Freddy's blood had brought back, with sickening clarity, the smell of death; it clung inside his nostrils, turning his stomach. He lit a cigarette to quell the stench. The smoke trickled comfortably down the back of his throat, filling his lungs. Damn Freddy and Tom, Michael, Champ, George, the whole bloody lot of them. They were gone and he lived. He wouldn't be sorry about it.

He strode across the Common purposefully heading for Isaac's hut. Isaac fed a small fire with wood. He didn't look surprised to see his visitor.

"Cup of tea?" Isaac asked.

He crouched down on a damp, mossy log. "Please," he replied, taking out his Woodbines offering them to the gypsy before he took one himself.

"I heard about Freddy." Isaac hung a can of water over the fire.

Iain stared at the sulky flames. The wind eddied through them blowing smoke and grey ash towards him. "Aye, bad news travels fast."

"It's how it was meant to be, son. Ain't nothing you could've done. He should have died out there in France, that one." Isaac disappeared into his hut returning with a bag of tea and sugar and two chipped tin mugs.

"That's what he said." The end of his cigarette glowed angrily as he pulled on it.

"Maybe afore that even."

"What do you mean?"

Isaac nodded sagely. "You know, Iain. Since Tom, he ain't ever been the same. It was all over for him then."

"Really? Do you think so?" He shook his head sadly. "How do you know about Tom?"

Isaac laughed. "Don't get much by me up here."

"Stupid of me, of course. You saw us didn't you?"

"Maybe I did, it doesn't matter any more. There was no saving Tom and there was no saving his brother either. Don't ever think any different. Some people are hell bent on destruction. Freddy wouldn't have rested until he'd done his worst. It was the only way."

"What, him dying? I can't see it as the only way, Isaac. I've seen too many die and not by choice either. He made the choice. He turned a gun on himself. If I'd done more, perhaps, just perhaps…" he drifted off.

"No, Iain, there was nothing. Fate, it was fate. I seen it all, up here." He tapped his temple with a grubby finger.

"How could you see it all?" Iain said sharply. "That's stupid, you know I don't hold with all that."

Isaac laughed at his annoyance. "You know it ain't. You believe it when it suits you, like everyone else. And it's true, I saw it for Tom and I saw it for Freddy, a long, long time ago. Not everything makes sense, some things happen that way."

Isaac's dirty, brown hands poured the hot water onto the tealeaves. He stirred in several spoons of sugar and gave a mug to Iain.

"You know when you shoot a rabbit," Isaac said, "a clean shot right through the head, sometimes it keeps running."

"Aye, round and round like a demented thing as if death is the last thing on its mind," he agreed.

"It has more energy, more power than it ever had, legs racing, goes nuts, then suddenly," Isaac clicked his fingers and Iain's two dogs raised their heads expectantly, "it's stone dead."

"Aye."

"Well that was Freddy, that rabbit. Frantically running round trying to make sense of his life, knowing it was all over for him, then dropping dead in his tracks exactly like that rabbit."

He sighed. "I don't know, Isaac, I just don't know anymore." He cupped the mug, stubbed out the cigarette butt in the dirt. "Maybe you're right. If you see it all, what about me?"

He shook his head, meeting Iain's eyes. "Well, you're no rabbit, that's for certain. You don't need your fortune read, boy, you got it all at your feet. You know what to do and you know where you're going and who you're going with."

Iain sipped at the strong, black brew. "Aye." He smiled then. "I suppose you're right." He thought of Helena, warm in his bed.

"You're going home," Isaac said simply.

* * * *

Iain sat by the range. The desire for work had abandoned him. His thoughts strayed to Glenleven and to the future which beckoned and suddenly was rather foreboding. During the long, weary years in France he dreamed of finding love, peace and fulfillment. That was behind him and the reality of his dream stretched ahead like a shimmering prohibitive mirage.

He had been given a chance with Helena but he was beset by worries, things outside of his control. He had never been one to dwell on or ponder the future. Had he changed so very much? Every good thing was shadowed by a greater bad. Dusty had found love, but not success and security. The hopes he had shared with Iain in the mud of the trenches had proved beyond him. Gaining Helena had been at the cost of Freddy's life. Would Glenleven be the realisation of his dreams or a return to a childhood nightmare? He had left Scotland, been exiled; branded a murderer and a bastard. Could he return and become laird? Could those who found him so unacceptable then, suddenly tolerate him as their laird? So many shadows, so many ghosts.

He went to the desk in the parlour. In the pressing silence he put pen to paper and wrote to Dusty. Iain had been offered his birthright, his mind bubbled with plans he had no idea how to implement. He couldn't balance a ledger, or write a business plan. His expertise lay in the management of forests, streams and earth, not paperwork. He had no preconceived notion of what he would write. The words tumbled onto the page. If Dusty and Celia would

come with them, give this new life a chance, even for a while…
Dusty had business acumen, he would be invaluable to Iain and at the same time he could help the friend who had saved his life, pulled him through those hard, endless days.

He read the letter through, smiling at his wording, a mixture of pleading and stuffy business proposal. He could imagine Dusty's face when he read it, probably raising one eyebrow in disbelief. He sealed the envelope and wrote the address on the front. He wandered into the kitchen, propping the envelope on the dresser and returned to his chair by the range. Maybe Isaac was right, perhaps everything was mapped out, nothing left to chance, a greater force playing with their pitiful lives.

He wondered what would happen now at North Farm, Tom long gone, Freddy too. Why did his heart ache so for the loss of Freddy's life? It appeared the pain the man had suffered was so futile. After everything he had endured, and to end it all by his own hand, so young, so alone. Iain knew he must cast away this desolation. It wasn't his. He had nothing to feel depressed about, it was someone else's misery.

"Are you going to mope all day?" Nell, still wearing her nightdress, stretched like a cat, stifling a yawn.

He sighed, the novelty of her presence was fresh. He wanted to touch her. "No. Yes. I don't know."

She watched him for a moment, her expression sad. "I'm shocked by what Freddy did too. It was horrible, I've never seen anything so horrible." She gave a little involuntary shudder. "I can't say I haven't wished him to be dead though – over and over."

"So have I," he admitted. "Right up until when he turned that gun on himself – and then – then I would have done anything – anything at all to save him."

She stroked flat the blackness of his hair, put her face against it. He smelled of wood-smoke. "Too much death," she said. "It's over now. It has to be over." She had already managed to put it aside, her relief outweighing trauma. He didn't know if he could do that, if he could ever recover. Joe paddled down the stairs out of the back door in some make-believe world of his own.

"He was so bad to you, Helena, and I hated him for it and for Tom, and yet I feel so very, very …" he could not express the void inside him.

"He was damaged, Iain," she said. "There was no saving him – not from himself."

He reached for her with shaky hands and pulled her onto his lap, holding her tight placing his head on her shoulder. They were quiet for some time, taking comfort from being close. He was determined to keep the past where it belonged. He could not let anything ruin what he held so firmly in his grasp. He would take a chance with Glenleven if she would take it with him. It was all a leap of faith, he thought, a faith he had spent his life denying. Perhaps nothing was impossible. If he were not afraid, if he could trust and believe, knock down the walls he had spent his whole life building, to allow her in.

He raised his face to kiss her. She tasted sweet in his mouth.

"I'll make you some breakfast," he said.

"No, I'll make it. I'm not hungry."

He put one hand across her stomach. "Yes, but the bairn might be hungry."

"Oh," she cried, "you know. How do you know?"

"I know everything." He laughed at her disappointment, pushing a curl out of her eyes. He loved her so much it felt like an ache inside him. "Would you marry a penniless keeper, Helena?"

She giggled then. "Yes."

He smiled at her coy laughter. "Would you marry a Scottish laird with a castle to call his own and three times more acreage than the squire of Harrowmead?"

She raised her eyebrows, rolled her eyes theatrically up to the ceiling as if it were a very big decision. "No," she said finally. "I'd rather marry you than some laird with a castle."

"So you'll marry me then?"

She laughed. "You're mad. I'm carrying your baby, a brother for Joe."

"No, not a brother, you're having a girl."

"You know everything do you?"

"We shall have at least three of them," he paused. "Will things be easier for us now? Can we look forward to spring?"

She smiled. "We will survive our winter. Spring will come and we will listen for the cuckoo."

"Ah, yes, the cuckoo, with its lonely life."

"Loneliness isn't for us," she said pressing her cheek to his. "Summer brings the swallows too. Flocks of them, families, flying together."

He wondered where they would find themselves when the swallows came, but he remained silent. He wondered if there were anything he could have done differently, any point in time when he could have altered destiny. But he couldn't see it. At that moment it was hidden to him.

* * * *

Outside, down in the dip among the beeches where the badgers' sett nestled between the roots, two little boys played a game - bows and arrows made of brittle branches cut many years before. The air smelt of warm earth and falling autumn leaves. A secret innocence echoed through the trees, the call of brothers long gone - the residue of what once had been and only then when no one was looking.

Printed in the United Kingdom by
Lightning Source UK Ltd., Milton Keynes
140146UK00001BA/190/P